A
SNOW COUNTRY
Christmas

LINDA LAEL MILLER

A
SNOW COUNTRY
Christmas

ISBN-13: 978-0-373-78931-3

A Snow Country Christmas

Copyright © 2017 by Hometown Girl Makes Good, Inc.

This edition published by arrangement with Harlequin Books S.A.

For questions and comments about the quality of this book, please contact us
at CustomerService@Harlequin.com.

www.HQNBooks.com

Printed in U.S.A.

A
SNOW COUNTRY
Christmas

December 23rd

The young lady sat with her chin on fist, the firelight shining off her dark hair. She was reflective but not pensive, content in her solitude on this cold evening. A log in the old stone fireplace snapped and crackled and there was the smell of pine in the air. Her father's old dog lay asleep at her feet, gently snoring; the sound comforting. Two days to Christmas and she'd spend it alone for the first time.

From the opening paragraph of The Aspen Trail
Matthew Brighton, 1965

1

RAINE McCALL FIRST frowned at the screen and then stared at the clock.

Her computer was right. Two in the morning? No way.

Oh, she'd be the first to admit that when she was working she lost track of time, but she was always there to put her daughter on the school bus and make sure Daisy had done her homework and had a healthy breakfast.

She'd always suffered from what she called WSS. Whimsical Sleep Schedule.

Awake at all hours, losing track of time if the muse was in the mood, and she'd been guilty of falling asleep in the chair at her desk. Daisy had told her more than once, with a maturity beyond her years, she thought she worked too hard, but then Raine didn't really think of it as work. Spinning dream images into reality was a unique joy and she felt sorry for every person in the world that had a job they disliked.

She wasn't the only one awake, either. Taking a break, she checked her email and was startled. Mick Branson? *The* Mick Branson had sent her a message? Hotshot Hollywood executive, way too focused, and no sense of humor—though come to think of it, he did smile now and then. He was good-looking, but she couldn't get beyond the sophisticated polish. She was a Wyoming girl through and through and thousand dollar suits weren't her preference. Give her a hat, jeans, and some worn boots.

Of course she'd met the man quite a few times at the ranch because he was the driving force behind the documentaries that Slater Carson, her ex-boyfriend and the father of her child, made, but getting an email from him was a definite first. Sent five minutes ago? She was too intrigued not to open it.

I'm going to be in Mustang Creek for the holidays. Can we have a business meeting? Maybe over dinner?

That *was* interesting, but currently she was up to her ears in deadlines trying to produce artwork for the labels for Mountain Vineyards wines. Her graphic design business had really taken off, and she wasn't sure she could handle another project.

From what she knew of Mick Branson, it wouldn't be a small one, either.

She typed back. When did you have in mind?

Tomorrow night? If you don't already have plans, that is.

On Christmas Eve?

Well, Daisy did usually spend that evening with her father's family and Raine spent it alone with a nice glass of wine and a movie. They always invited her, but she went the next day instead for the big dinner celebration and skipped the night before in favor of solitude. It was never that they made her feel like an outsider; quite the opposite, but Slater needed some time with his daughter to make memories without Raine always in the background. So while she appreciated the invitation, she'd always declined. It had been difficult when Daisy was little to spend such a magical evening away from her, but he was entitled. He was a wonderful father.

She typed: On the 24th of December, I assure you no place is open in Mustang Creek. This isn't California. You'd have to come to my place and I usually just eat a hamburger and drink wine.

He wrote back: That sounds fine. I like burgers and I

enjoy wine. Let me bring the beverages. Please excuse me if I'm inviting myself.

She couldn't decide if he had, or if she'd done it. She really did need to get more sleep now and then. She typed: Mountain Vineyards for the wine.

You got it.

Have a safe flight.

Thank you, but I'm already here. See you tomorrow. Don't mention to anyone, especially Slater, that I'm in town please.

Raine sat back and let out a breath. She hadn't ever anticipated spending an evening with someone like Mick Branson, much less Christmas Eve.

Luckily, she thought, she'd thoroughly cleaned the house the day before when she realized that sound she abstractly heard in the background was the vacuum. Daisy was *voluntarily* doing a chore she usually argued over? Raine decided then and there—once she recovered from her shock—that maybe she had been spending too much time in her office. Sure enough, the house needed dusting, the kitchen floor had crumbs on it and the laundry room was in dire need of a workout.

Not that someone like Mr. Hollywood Executive

Mick Branson, who probably lived in a mansion in Beverly Hills, would be impressed with her small and eclectic house anyway, no matter how tidy. Wait until he got a look at her Christmas tree. There was no theme to the ornaments; if something caught her eye, she bought and it put it up. There were owls, glittery reindeer, a glass shrimp with wings wearing a boa, all right alongside her grandmother's collection of English traditional antique glass orbs in brilliant colors. Those heirlooms were hung up high thanks to Mr. Bojangles, her enormous Maine coon cat. He was somewhat of a reclusive character, but he became positively playful when the Christmas tree went up. Walking past it usually meant an unexpected guerilla attack on your ankles because he considered it his covert hiding place every December. Therefore the ornaments on the bottom were soft stuffed squirrels and bunnies with a few fake pine cones he could bat around. Add in Daisy's giant dog, Samson, who accidentally knocked an ornament off every time he walked by, and her tree had no hope.

"Definitely not a designer tree, unless a deranged leprechaun arranged it" was how Daisy described it.

Raine loved it.

It was exactly her style. There was nothing wrong with being quirky. She went and switched off the lights and headed off to bed, wondering how she'd gotten roped into this situation.

Hollywood Hotshot Mick Branson eating hamburgers at her house on Christmas Eve?

Slater Carson was going to laugh himself into a fit.

The plane had touched down on a snowy runway and Mick had said a small prayer of thanks for an experienced pilot and maybe some luck of the season as the snow continued to pile up. It had been a bumpy ride and he wasn't at all a nervous flyer, but coming over the mountains he'd had a moment or two.

He'd been everywhere. Asia, Africa, South America, Australia, Europe…he lived in Los Angeles, but he liked Wyoming. It felt like being on vacation and he could really, really use a vacation.

It wouldn't be a hardship to see Raine McCall again, either.

The thought surprised him because she was *so* not his type. Frothy skirts, and as far as he could tell she thought makeup was optional, or maybe forgot it altogether, and if she owned a pair of heels he'd be surprised. Her artistic temperament was the antithesis of his rigidly corporate lifestyle, but he somehow found it intriguing. She was naturally beautiful without trying. Maybe that was it. There was no artifice to Raine—what you saw was what you got. Not to mention he had a feeling she could care less how much money he made. Material things, he guessed, to her, were little more than a necessity now and then.

Anyway, he had planned this trip with a dual purpose.

He wanted to surprise Slater, who was not just a colleague but a friend, with the television premier of the documentary of *Wild West...Still Wild*—and he wanted to see Raine. Two separate goals but also intertwined, since Slater and Raine had a past and shared a daughter. Slater was now happily married to someone else, but through a few very casual questions, Mick knew Raine wasn't seeing anyone.

This might get complicated and he hated complications. Business deals were a dance back and forth but he kept his personal life as simple as possible.

Raine was far from simple. Her art was exemplary and over the top, and the vivid mermaid label she'd created for the Carson winery's sparkling wine had resulted in more bottles sold in one day upon release than were sold of all their other wines combined, and they had been doing quite well before. Somehow he doubted Raine even registered the triumph.

But he wasn't interested in her for her talent—well, he was impressed, but that wasn't first and foremost in his mind. Maybe opposites did attract, though if you'd told him that before he'd met her through the Carson family, he'd have laughed it off.

He wasn't laughing now. It wasn't that he didn't have a good reason to be in Wyoming at the moment anyway, but he was essentially there because of a certain woman he couldn't seem to get off his mind.

Grace Carson met him in the dining room of the Bliss River Resort and Spa, her eyes sparkling, and gave him a welcoming hug. Slater really did have good taste in women because his wife was a stunning redhead with a confident air. She also apparently had a good memory, because almost immediately a waiter came over with coffee and a rack of rye toast, which was his favorite.

She joined him, pouring coffee for them both. "Do you have any idea how hard it is to not tell Slater about Christmas Day?"

"I've actually struggled with it myself, so maybe I do." He admired the view of the snow-capped mountains out the huge windows as he sipped his coffee and thought about all the strings he'd pulled. Considerable was the answer. He looked back at Grace, which was also a plea-sure. "The time slot was the hardest part. But everyone is pretty much home, and hopefully by then Christmas dinner will be over and there will be a worldwide desire to watch something other than the old classics."

She added cream to her coffee. "I think it's a brilliant

idea. You do realize you just usurped my gift to him, which was a new saddle. He'll probably kiss *you* under the mistletoe instead of me."

Mick chuckled. "I doubt it, but if it happens, let's not catch that on film." Not knowing remote cameras were taking footage, Slater's younger brother Drake had gotten caught in a romantic moment with his now wife, Luce, and was none too happy about it being used in the film, but had grudgingly signed the release.

"Maybe Raine will kiss you instead." Grace took a sip from her silver-rimmed cup, a knowing look in her eyes.

He'd never understood how women had magical powers when it came to sensing a possible romance. Men just blundered on, unaware, and females were like wolves sniffing the air. He was a man who played angles, so he admitted noncommittally, "I can't imagine any man minding that. How is the resort business these days?"

She caught on to that just as easily. "Subject changed. I can take a hint. It's going well. Ski season is in full swing. We're packed. The spa is booked out two months. The owner is pleased and it keeps me busy and, well, I'm expecting again. Luce is also in baby mode. We're just waiting for the same kind of announcement from Mace and Kelly. Then all the cousins can grow up together."

Mick pictured a bunch of toddlers running wild around the sprawling Carson ranch. To his surprise, the image was immensely appealing. He hadn't had much exposure to babies; his only brother was childless by choice even though he'd been married a long time. He and his wife tended to spend the winter in France or at their house in the Caribbean, and as an investment banker, Ran could work from anywhere, so their attitude reflected their sophisticated lifestyle.

Prior to his business association with Slater, he hadn't thought about it much, but Mick had to acknowledge that his upbringing had left a hole in his life. Warm family gatherings had just never happened. His parents traveled widely when his father was alive and now it was tradition to meet his mother at the country club for Christmas dinner.

Elegant, but not exactly cozy. He'd been to celebrations at the Carson ranch before and they were usually quite the boisterous experience. He said, "Congratulations. Slater is a lucky man all the way around."

"He'll certainly be one tomorrow," Grace replied with a smile. "I haven't said a word to anyone—although Blythe knows, which means Harry knows."

"Raine knows I'm in town." He gave what he hoped was a casual shrug. "We have a business meeting tonight and she said no restaurants would be open, so she invited me over."

Arched brows rose higher. "Did she now? She's breaking her burger and glass of wine tradition?"

"No. I was informed that's the menu."

Grace gave a laugh of real merriment. "Only Raine would serve Mick Branson a burger. I love Raine but she is on the eclectic side. That's why I was surprised the two of you hit it off so well. She's right about Christmas Eve, by the way—we even close the restaurants here at the resort and the spa. Guests can pre-order special bags with gourmet sandwiches and salads that will be delivered via room service, but quite frankly, I just don't believe in making anyone work who would rather be with their family on Christmas. A few staff members would rather work for holiday pay, so the resort is open, but not the dining choices. In town everything is closed."

Vaguely he registered her words about the holiday, but his mind was caught on what she'd said about Raine. *Hit it off?* He chose not to comment. He could negotiate deals involving millions of dollars, but personal discussions were not his strong suit. "Los Angeles is a little different."

"Oh, I bet." Grace was definitely amused. Her phone beeped and she rose. "Excuse me, but that sound means something needs my attention. I'll see you tomorrow."

After she left he finished his toast and coffee, checked his email via his phone, and headed out to his rental car.

It was lightly snowing and briskly cold, the car dusted over in white, and he wished he'd thought about bringing some gloves. It wasn't something that occurred to him back in L.A. when he packed for the trip.

The wine shop was on the main street and someone had done an artistic job of decorating the windows with snowflakes. The bells on the huge wreath on the door jingled as Mick walked in. There were several other customers and he noted Kelly Carson, Slater's sister-in-law, was the one sitting behind the old polished counter. She looked cute wearing an elf hat and a surprised expression.

Good, his lucky day.

Or so he hoped, but it was yet another person to swear to secrecy. Her eyes had widened as she recognized him.

There was just no such thing as a secret in Mustang Creek. He'd heard that the last time he'd been in town and really hadn't believed it, but was now starting to feel like living proof.

"Merry Christmas, Mick," Kelly called as he approached.

"Merry Christmas," he said. "Let me make an educated guess and assume you're working because you wouldn't ask any of the employees to so they could be with their families."

She nodded and the fuzzy tassel on her hat bobbed. "You're right. Absolutely. We're only open until noon today anyway, holiday hours… I guess I didn't realize you were in town. No one mentioned it."

"No one knows." Well, not true. Grace, Blythe, Harry and Raine knew, and now Kelly. He smiled wryly. "Let me rephrase. I'd prefer if Slater didn't find out I'm here. It's about both business and friendship, so if you can keep it to yourself until tomorrow, I'd appreciate it."

She sent him a wink. "My lips are sealed."

"I knew I could count on you. Now, tell me, best wine to go with a burger would be…what?"

"I hate to disappoint you, but Bad Billy's won't be open."

The biker bar was legendary for its burgers. "I'm not actually getting my burger from Billy's."

She blinked. "Oh…oh! Raine?"

It was tempting to deny it, but…well, why bother? Clearly her Christmas Eve burgers tradition was well-known. "We have a business meeting tonight. What kind of wine does she usually buy?"

"The Wildfire Merlot." Kelly said it promptly, her expression alight with humor. "She also likes Soaring Eagle Chardonnay. Either one would be fine. At the end of the day, Mace always tells me to drink a wine you like with food you like. Don't worry about the rest of it. He thinks snobbish pairing is overrated."

"People all over California just fainted dead away because you said that."

"People all over California buy our wines," she countered with a mischievous elfin grin that matched her festive hat. "So he seems to know what he's doing."

Tough to argue with that. "I'll take a few bottles of each, plus some for the Christmas gathering tomorrow, including the new sparkling wine. Just give me a case."

2

IT WASN'T LIKE she didn't consider what she wore, but on a scale of one to ten she would rate herself maybe a five when it came to how much thought and time she usually put into her attire.

Tonight for some reason, Raine was on the higher end of the scale.

The long red skirt and clingy black blouse looked nice, but were not exactly hamburger-worthy, she decided with a critical eye before she changed into jeans and a teal blue silk sweater. Except it occurred to her that if she dribbled ketchup or spilled even a drop of wine the sweater would be toast and she'd have to toss it—she'd known at the time it was an impractical purchase but had loved it too much not to buy it—so she changed for a third time. Black leggings and a patterned gray sweater dress won the day, comfortable but certainly dressier than she'd usually choose for a night home alone.

Well, she wasn't going to be alone. She even set the table—which would never have happened on her traditional Christmas Eve—with what she called her December plates, white with tiny candy canes on them. Daisy had seen them when they'd been out shopping when she was six years old and begged, so Raine caved and bought them. Every year when the plates came out, it signaled the holiday season for her daughter and the sentimental value was priceless. Even though she'd been a classic example of a starving artist and had been trying to launch her business at the time, she'd also bought a set of silverware whose handles were etched with reindeer and a sleigh.

It was ironic in a good way to think someone as successful as Mick Branson wanted to meet with her on a professional level and would eat off the dishes that she'd bought when she really couldn't afford them. Now she was so busy she doubted she could accept whatever it was he wanted to discuss even if she was interested.

Mr. Bojangles wandered past with a feline yawn, headed for his food bowl, but stopping to be petted. It was like a royal decree when a cat of his size demanded to be scratched behind the ears. Raine stroked his head.

"What do you think of the table? Fancy enough for a hotshot executive?"

He yawned again, his gold-green eyes reflecting doubt. She said defensively, "Hey, I paid twenty bucks for those dishes."

His furry face expressed his skepticism that the plates were worth even that. She argued his point. "Daisy loves them."

He didn't disagree, just headed off to the kitchen to chomp loudly out of his bowl. His ample backside was normal for his breed, but his love of food didn't help matters. His vet, Jax Locke, had been diplomatic in suggesting she could maybe curtail the cat treats.

Raine agreed, but Jangles—as she called him face-to-face—was a contender when it came to getting his way. There was not much in the way of compromise on his part.

The snow was beginning to blow a little and she had started a fire in her fireplace with the push of a button. She liked ambiance and watching the flames, but as a single female didn't want to haul in logs, so she'd had a gas insert put in a few years ago. Bypassing Christmas music, she put on some soft classical in the background, and without the World's Largest Puppy—Samson—tearing around, the house felt downright serene. Daisy always took him with her to the ranch and he loved running free with the other dogs. The backyard at Raine's just wasn't as exciting as herding cattle with Drake and the other hands. Maybe when he got a little older Samson would be content to just bask in the sun. As it stood, he wanted to run amok.

Red, the head ranch hand, called the dog a log-legged galoot. That seemed about right.

When Raine saw the arc of headlights in the big front window and glanced at the fairy tale clock on the mantel, Cinderella's glass slipper was pointed right at six sharp. Mick Branson was right on time.

She, on the other hand, was perpetually late to everything. Maybe being awake at two in the morning was the only thing they had in common. She opened the door before he knocked and in return got a capricious swirl of snow blowing into the tiny foyer.

"Thanks," he said as he came in. "The wind is really picking up. A Merry Christmas with all the appropriate special effects." He studied her as he wiped his boots on the mat inside the door. "It's nice to see you again."

"And you as well." She shut the door, peering through the side panel of glass. "It is coming down out there, isn't it? So pretty."

"From safe in here, it's very pretty," he said with his all too fleeting smile. "The wine is in this bag, and where do you want my coat?"

She recognized the bag because she'd designed the print on it. The M for Mountain Vineyards was flanked by pine trees and a hawk sat on a branch on one side. "I'll take your coat, and the kitchen is through that doorway right there. It's impossible to get lost in this house."

"It's charming." He glanced around as he slipped off his wool coat.

She wasn't used to men who used the word "charming" in regular conversation, but he did have nice wide shoulders, so she'd cut him some slack. Actually, everything about him was attractive: dark hair, striking dark eyes, and what she'd define as an aristocratic face that spoke of a lineage that was Old World, probably Spain or Portugal. She had an admitted fascination for history, so she'd love to know his story. "I'll be right back. There's a corkscrew and glasses on the counter. Go for it."

He took her at her word, she discovered after she'd deposited his coat on the bed in the spare bedroom—one drawback to her quaint little house was no coat closet—and poured them both a glass of wine.

"Merlot," he told her as he set the bottle on the counter. "I took Kelly's advice and bought the wines I like best and didn't try to match hamburgers."

"She's pretty good at that sort of thing." Raine accepted a glass, looking at him as she did. "I've never had a business meeting on Christmas Eve, but you probably have. What's the protocol? I don't have a table in a conference room, but we could sit by the fire."

"I'm not all business, just so you know. Conference tables are overrated, and the fire sounds nice."

"I thought business was why you were here."

"Come on, Raine, I think you know that's not entirely it. I do have something I want to talk to you about, but I just wanted to see you."

Well, at least he was direct. She liked that, even as the admission surprised her. "The fire it is then."

She led the way and he followed, and as luck would have it when they passed the tree, Jangles decided on a drive-by attack to defend his territory. Maybe she should have issued a warning, but she was so used to the giant cat's antics she didn't think of it, and though obviously startled, Mick managed to not spill his wine even with claws in the hem of his no-doubt expensive slacks. She apologized as the cat unhooked and retreated back into his lair. "By the way, meet my cat, Mr. Bojangles. He has a perimeter staked out around the tree and he guards it. Sorry, I should have warned you."

"That's a cat? I would have guessed African lion."

"You should see the dog the Carson family gifted me. Mace made the mistake of suggesting Daisy help him pick out a puppy. She and that dog fell instantly in love. He's hers now. I think one day you'll be able to slap a saddle on that bad boy and ride out on the range. I have a sack of dog food in my pantry so big I need a furniture dolly to carry it in." In an attempt to be a proper hostess, she asked, "Shall we sit down?"

And get the business part done so we can relax a little. It was, after all, Christmas Eve.

Mick wasn't surprised at all by her house. Raine's taste showed, well…everywhere. It was so different from the elegance of his childhood home, he tried to restrain his smile. No settees, no polished tables, no imported rugs or pricey oil paintings…

There was a poster of wine labels she'd created above the fireplace and the mantel was a hand-hewn log of some kind. A ceramic frog sat on the brick hearth, and there was a rusted antique toy truck on the other side. Her couch was ruby red and suited the dark wood floors, and a coffee table with a distressed finish added an artistic touch. A craftsman glass lamp patterned with butterflies and brilliant flowers adorned a bookshelf. Nothing matched, yet the décor oddly fit together.

He liked it better than his own perfectly decorated house, which he'd hired someone expensive to put together. Raine's house was comfortable and lived-in; his place might look like it was straight out of a magazine, but it was hardly homey.

"This is nice."

"This is probably about a tenth of the space of your house, but thank you," she said drily. "Daisy and I don't need more. She can get that at the ranch. I'm not really into personal possessions, which is a good thing since she acquired that enormous puppy. Along with my favorite pair of shoes, the rug in the kitchen has been a casualty. I happened to like that rug but I had no idea it was a culinary canine delight. He chewed it to pieces when my back was turned for about eight seconds."

He had to laugh as he settled next to her on the couch. "Slater mentioned every time Mace went to acquire a pet, someone else in family became latched on to it and he had to try again."

"It's like visiting a zoo," she agreed, also laughing. "The moment the infamous Mrs. Arbuckle-Calder became involved, game over. That woman makes an executive decision over whether or not you might need a pet, and if you are deemed pet-worthy, she'll pick one out for you and just show up with it and drop it right inside your door. You don't really get to say yes or no. How do think I ended up with the lion?"

He liked the way she kicked off her black flats and propped her feet on the coffee table, wineglass in hand. A gust of wind hit the rafters, but the fire balanced it nicely. "I wasn't allowed pets growing up. My mother was opposed to the slightest hint of pet hair in her house, plus my parents traveled a lot, so pets were an inconvenience she didn't want to suffer."

Raine furrowed her brow. "No pets?"

"None."

"Daisy would be desolate without her cat and dog."

He'd had some moments of desolation, too, but he'd survived.

"Everyone is different. This is what I wanted to talk to you about. I know someone who produces Pixel motion pictures and I mentioned you were a graphic artist. I showed him your work, and he's interested in talking about it. He's fairly sure Wyoming is the end of the earth, but he's willing to come here to meet with you."

She stared at him. "What?"

Raine had the most beautiful unusual eyes. Not green and not gold, but a starburst mixture of of both colors.

"Pixel. Motion pictures. I—"

"I know what they are," she interrupted, groaning and briefly closing those eyes. "Oh man, I swore I was going tell you *no* to anything...but that changes the game."

"Anything?"

"Stop with the sexual innuendo, I'm processing here. I don't have the time in my day to add another thing, but I can't possibly pass that up. I thought you liked me. How could you dangle this in front of me?" She shook her head in disbelief. "I'm not even that qualified. I took some animation classes in college, but that's it."

He smiled. "My personal feelings about you aside, from what I've been able to see, you're really talented. I'd never have mentioned your name otherwise. But I'm glad I did, because the producer agrees with me. He thinks you could be a valuable addition to the team."

Raine glared at him from those vivid hazel eyes. "You knew this would be a graphic artist's dream. This is a calculated move."

"Of course I did. Never underestimate me." He had known. He understood a lot about being driven. Why else would they be exchanging emails at two in the morning?

"What kind of company are we talking about?"

She wasn't a fool, but he already knew that. "Let's just say you'd recognize the name."

She blew out a breath. "I knew you were trouble. I'm so busy right now as it is—"

"All you have to do is think about it and let me know if you want a face-to-face. I'm investing, so I want it to be topnotch. It's in my financial best interest to help him find the best artist possible." She opened her mouth again, undoubtedly to protest further, and he held up a hand. "That's enough business for one night, especially when it's Christmas Eve. I'm declaring the meeting portion of our evening officially over."

Raine blinked, then raised a brow. "In that case, I think it's time for the dinner portion of our evening. I hope you can stand spicy food." She got to her feet. "Bring the wine, please."

"I thought we were having hamburgers." He followed her toward the kitchen, bottle in hand. "But yes, I do like spicy."

Her kitchen was as interesting as the living room. A row of unmatched antique canisters sat on the polished counter. The appliances were modern but the vintage hutch in the corner held what looked like a beautiful set of old dishes and pink crystal glasses. A mobile made from tarnished silver forks hung over the farmhouse sink—another piece of décor that was quintessentially Raine and suited the room perfectly.

His mother would undoubtedly faint at the sight, but Mick again found himself both charmed and amused.

"Good." Raine moved efficiently between the refrigerator and the counter as she set down a plate and several containers. "Green chili cheeseburgers are my indulgence on Christmas Eve. Questionably traditional, I know, but I love them."

He grinned for what felt like the thousandth time that night. "Are you kidding me?" he said incredulously. "I'm from New Mexico. We didn't move to California until I was fifteen. My aunt and uncle still live in Las Cruces. I have done some self-analyzing to try and figure out if I go to visit them, or just for the food."

She gave him a surprised look that probably mirrored his own. "Are you serious? My cousin lives in Santa Fe. I love it there. She sends me the chilis every late August or early September and I hoard them like a miser."

"The real deal? From Hatch? Don't tease me."

"Oh yeah." Raine nodded, no doubt inwardly laughing at his expression. "I roast them myself and freeze them. I would save Daisy and the pets first in a fire, but I might consider going back in for my chilis."

He'd just gone straight to heaven. "You've just given me quite the Christmas present. If I can help, let me know. Otherwise I'll just stand here and drool."

She pulled out a cutting board from a side cupboard. "Somehow I suspect your culinary skills are limited to making reservations, but if you can slice an onion, you have a job to do."

"That I can do." She was right, he didn't cook often, but then again, he traveled constantly and home-cooked meals were hard to come by when one wasn't often home. Maybe that was part of what he liked about Mustang Creek—every aspect of the community felt welcoming and homey. If you walked into an establishment like Bad Billy's Burger Palace, you'd be greeted by name.

He hadn't even realized until recently that that appealed to him.

Maybe he was just getting a little restless in his life. Something was missing, and he knew he was in Mustang Creek for Christmas for more than just work.

Standing in Raine's kitchen, admiring the shapely curves of her body under that silvery sweater, he wondered again what it was about her that had caught his attention. It had served him well in the business world to play hunches and go with his instincts, and his instincts had started humming the instant he'd first laid eyes on her. Raine wasn't classically beautiful but she was one of those women who, whenever she walked into a room, unconsciously made everyone turn to look. Her vitality was part of the appeal, and since he himself was reserved and self-contained, he'd been fascinated from the start.

"Knife is in the drawer." She looked up and caught him staring. Wiping her hands on a towel, she looked down as a sudden faint hint of color bloomed in her cheeks. "What?"

"You're just so—" he cast about for the word "—alive."

"I hope so, since the alternative is pretty undesirable." The smile she gave him was quizzical this time.

He wasn't about to elaborate. "True enough, Ms. McCall."

"Knife is in the drawer, by the way."

"You mentioned that." He tugged open the drawer she indicated and found the object in question. "On the job."

Mick chopped onions while she dropped the burgers in the grill pan and in less than a minute, his mouth was watering from the tantalizing smell of sizzling meat. Outside, the snow was thickening, draping the trees and the wooden fence out back in a festive wardrobe of white. The whole scene was relaxing in a way he didn't often allow himself, a respite from the world, and the music softly playing in the background didn't hurt one bit.

Fire in the hearth, a concerto in the background, a glass of wine, a home-cooked meal and a beautiful woman...

The perfect way to spend Christmas Eve.

3

———✦———

"THAT WAS A real treat. I felt like I was home again."

For someone who obviously hit the gym, Mick could eat on a par with the Carson brothers, and that was a high bar. As Red, the head hand at the ranch would say, he could really strap on the ole feed bag. Raine was happy she'd decided to make three burgers instead of just two because that third one disappeared quickly. Mick's manners were meticulous, of course, but he had devoured his food with flattering enthusiasm.

"I warn you," she informed him when she got up to clear their plates, "I learned all about how to make dessert from Blythe Carson. Ice cream is going to be all you get."

"That sounds just fine to me."

"Once you taste Bad Billy's Lemon Drop Ice Cream, you'll be hooked for life." She wasn't kidding. "There's a reason I don't dare keep it on hand all the time. That would be a desire to keep my girlish figure."

He gave her a slow once-over as he rose, plate in hand. "There's nothing *I'd* change, trust me. Let me help with the cleanup."

She'd argue, but had a feeling Mick Branson didn't lose verbal battles very often, maybe ever. He was the epitome of cool, calm and collected, with a good dose of masculine confidence thrown in. It was telling that she wasn't sure how to handle his obvious interest, because she'd decided a long time ago to just live her life as she wished and that her untraditional approach was a healthy outlook on life, at least for her. She'd sat down with her daughter and explained that the reason she'd never married Slater was that they were too fundamentally different for it to work out, and Daisy seemed to accept that, perhaps because she saw how much her parents loved her and respected each other.

But no one was more different from her than Mick Branson, so Raine had to question why, when their fingers brushed as she handed him the ice cream scoop so he could do the honors, there was an electric flicker of awareness between them.

He wasn't her type.

She was definitely not his type. She wasn't sure what his type might be, but she imagined a cool, polished blonde who'd feel right at home in pearls and a stylish black dress. Someone who'd fit in at corporate functions and with the Hollywood set.

Mick interrupted her musings as he scooped out the creamy lemon mixture into the two Victorian glasses she'd inherited from her grandmother. "Daisy is a great kid from what I've seen. Spunky and self-confident."

She smiled. "That she is. It's hard to believe she's half-grown already. I don't know where the time goes."

He concentrated on scooping. "Have you ever thought about having more children?"

Raine's expression must have reflected her surprise at the unexpected question. He caught her gaze and for a moment she found herself trapped in those dark eyes. "I just meant you're a wonderful mother, according to Slater. You're young, so it just occurred to me. Plus I talked to Grace this morning and she told me her news, and also about Luce." He looked not exactly embarrassed but maybe off balance. "I didn't mean to get so personal so quickly. I officially recant."

Raine wasn't about to let him off the hook so easily. "I don't mind the question, but turnabout is fair play. So what about you? Kids?" He was, she'd guess, around forty or so. There wasn't a fleck of gray in that carefully tousled dark hair, but Slater had once remarked that he and Mick were about the same age.

"Do I have any kids? No. Do I want them? Maybe."

"I feel like I don't know that much about you. You've done a good job of keeping your private life, well… private."

"Checking up on me?" He didn't seem to mind—quite the opposite. "I keep it that way as much as possible."

"I might have checked a little when you first showed up in Mustang Creek, but Slater likes you, so I trust you. If I didn't, I wouldn't be wasting BB's Lemon Drop on you."

"In that case, I hope to prove worthy of the ice cream. Sounds like a high bar."

At least he had a sense of humor. She was discovering she liked that about him.

There were quite a lot of things she liked about him. Too many.

"It's an honor, trust me. I don't just give it away all the time."

Without a blink, he returned smoothly, "I didn't think you did."

Raine couldn't help but give him *the look*. "I thought I banned the sexual innuendos."

"Hey, you can take that remark any way you wish."

A man like him didn't look boyish often, but his unrepentant expression was pretty close. And those eyes…

"Just for that, I'm going to make you watch my favorite Christmas movie, unless you have other pressing plans."

"I'm all yours." He deftly wielded the ice cream scoop. "In case you're wondering—and I'm going to guess you are—my brother and his wife are in London for the holidays this year, my mother is in New York with friends, and since I have a little surprise for Slater, I decided Mustang Creek might not be a bad place to spend Christmas this year. I'm almost afraid to ask, but what's your favorite Christmas movie? Please tell me there isn't a lot of singing and dancing."

"Relax. There's none. I usually watch *Big Jake*. You know, John Wayne." She took two long-handled spoons from a drawer. "Not only is it a great movie, but it has sentimental value. My father loved it. I remember sitting on the couch watching it with him after my mother went to bed. Unlike you, she liked the movies with the singing and dancing and he needed a good dose of the Old West afterward. I was allowed to stay up as long as I wanted on Christmas Eve. I still do that."

"You are a big girl, so you can do whatever you want."

She was just going to ignore that. He was deliberately provoking her. "I always have done what I want. Make a note of it. Do you want a cup of coffee?"

"That sounds good. It'll keep me awake for the drive back to the resort later."

The reminder that their evening would come to an end caused an odd sinking in her stomach, one she immediately chided herself for. After all, it wasn't like she planned to invite him to spend the night, no matter how attractive she found him. The softly falling snow outside might be adding to the ambiance of the evening, but her guarded heart was resistant to even the most romantic of trappings.

She believed in love. In loving your child, your family, and of course, she'd thought she was in love with Slater what felt like a million years ago, but that just hadn't worked out.

It would have been easy to accept his proposal once he knew she was pregnant, to settle into a comfortable life as a Carson, but she'd known from the start that neither of their hearts would have been in it. They were friends—she genuinely liked the father of her child and was grateful for the good relationship they shared—but that wasn't the same as love.

For the life of her, she couldn't figure out why it was Mick Branson who apparently inspired more than friendly feelings in her. She couldn't have picked a man more different from her if she'd tried.

Not in a million years was she Hollywood. Not in a million years was he Mustang Creek.

Though when he settled next to her on the roomy

couch, ice cream in hand, he seemed comfortable enough despite the designer slacks and tailored shirt. He took a bite and gave her an incredulous look from those oh-so-sexy dark eyes. "You have to be kidding me."

"I told you. Billy is a burly, tattooed culinary angel."

"I might kiss him the next time I see him." Mick dug back in.

"And he might take exception to that." She took a spoonful from her own dish. The ice cream was smooth, creamy yet tart, and everything she remembered. Billy only made it once a year and she always put in an order early. Picking up the remote, she pushed a button to cue up the movie. "Here we go. The Duke."

"Pure Christmas magic in the form of an old western—sounds great to me. But I guess now would be the time to confess I've never actually seen it. Did you say *Big Jake*?"

"*What*?" She stared. "Never? That's…incomprehensible."

He shrugged. "If you met my family, well, let's just say John Wayne was not on their radar. I'm sure they would enjoy it, don't get me wrong, but they just wouldn't think of it. I believe I was dragged to a Broadway play as a child before I ever watched a cartoon."

That explained quite a lot. "Is that why you do what you do?"

"It might be. Why are you an artist? I doubt I'm going to get a straight-up answer. There probably isn't one."

She had to concede that one, so she changed the subject. "I can't believe you already ate all of that ice cream." He'd inhaled it. "Haven't you heard of an ice cream headache?"

"I've never had one, but for that stuff, I'd take my chances." He got up to go into the kitchen and she heard him rinse the bowl and considerately put it in the dishwasher.

Considerate? Oh no. That was trouble right there.

Mick Branson was larger than life in some ways. So was Slater, so maybe that accounted for the chemistry simmering between her and Mick. She was attracted to charismatic men.

She savored each spoonful as the opening movie scene unfolded, feeling oddly comfortable. Even though he wasn't a stranger, they'd never spent time alone together before this evening, so the ease between them surprised her.

Everything about the way Mick acted said he was interested and she wasn't positive she was ready for someone like him intruding on the life she'd so carefully built for herself and her daughter.

His life was all about reading signals. Meetings, the

stock market, international affairs, how the media was cooperating…

Mick was in tune with the business side of his life. The personal side? Not so much.

Raine was clearly a free spirit but there was a wariness about her that was impossible to miss. It wasn't like he didn't understand being cautious; he tended to tread carefully himself, or perhaps he would have had more long-term relationships rather than just a fleeting romantic entanglement here or there.

Her wary aura aside, he wondered if she had any idea how sexy it was to watch her eat ice cream.

He forced his gaze to remain on the screen rather than her lips. There was no way he'd take advantage of softly falling snow and all the rest of the ambiance to get her into bed, though he had a lot of enthusiasm for a night with the lovely Ms. McCall. Maybe more than one night, and that was food for thought right there.

He was afraid this was going somewhere, and Mick wasn't a man who considered himself afraid of all that much.

Luckily, John Wayne saved him along with everyone else on the screen. Well, not quite everyone, and with an analytical eye he admired the director's decisions on how the plot played out. It was his favorite kind of script, showing people as they really were—not all good, not all bad, but a combination of both. Slater tended to roll that way in his documentaries as well, with villains and heroes side by side. His characters weren't fictional, but balanced, and he made riveting dramas set in real places steeped in history.

"Good movie, but there's no love story," Mick pointed out when the credits rolled.

Raine sat easily with one leg folded under her. He'd already concluded she did yoga from the rolled-up mat tucked in the corner, so the agile pose didn't surprise him. What had surprised him more was when her giant cat had wandered out and jumped on the couch with remarkable grace for a creature of his size, then settled down next to her. "Isn't that what appeals to most men? All action and no sappy stuff."

He shook his head, a faint smile on his mouth. "I think you have it backward. Men are more interested in romance than women are."

"Au contraire, Mr. Boardroom." She waved her hand in dismissal. "Men are more interested in sex."

"I sense a debate coming. Who buys flowers and candy and dutifully mows the yard just to please the woman in his life?"

She shot back tartly, "A man who wants to have sex. I appreciate a thoughtful gesture as much as any woman, but let's not get confused about the motivation here."

"You can't put an entire gender in the same bracket, Ms. Artist. There are a lot of decent guys I know who would never walk into the bedroom of someone who they didn't have romantic feelings for in the first place. Brains and beauty are all well and good, but if a woman isn't also a nice person, no thanks. I can tell you, in the world I live in, there are plenty of women who use sex as leverage, so it could be argued that your assumption works both ways."

Raine stroked the cat's head and Mr. Bojangles gave a rusty purr. "I'm afraid you're right and I was just pulling your chain. People are too complex to reduce to stereotypes. I don't understand a lot of them, but I think I know more good ones than bad ones. It makes me glad Daisy is growing up in Mustang Creek."

"I've looked at some land in this area," he heard himself confessing. "I haven't found the right combination of house and location, but I have done some research."

She stopped petting the cat, her attention arrested. Mr. Bojangles sent him a lethal stare for interference in the petting process, clearly understanding the interruption was his fault. "Really?"

"It's beautiful country," he said noncommittally. "I have a vacation home in Bermuda, but while it's nice to have sun and sea, I get bored after about two days. I'm thinking about leasing it out or selling it, and building one here, or better yet, buying a place with some history behind it. There's more to do in Mustang Creek than lie on a beach with a drink in your hand."

Raine looked thoughtful. "I'm the same way. I've tried it once or twice, but I can't sit and do nothing for very long. I don't find it relaxing because I feel I should be doing *something*."

"We have that in common then."

"Why do I have the feeling that's about the only thing we have in common? Aside from a love of green chilis, of course."

"Not true," he told her, and gestured toward the TV. "We both like the John Wayne movie we just watched. We both like Mountain Winery merlot. We both would kill for Bad Billy's lemon ice cream. Mr. Bojangles clearly loves us both…the list just goes on."

"You were doing pretty good until the Jangles part. He's really picky. I can tell he hasn't made up his mind yet. He doesn't trust men that easily."

They weren't talking just about the cat, and he knew it. "He just needs to get to know me better. Let me prove how trustworthy I am."

"You want to prove yourself to a cat?"

"Well, he's a really big cat. I'm kind of afraid of him."

There was merriment in Raine's eyes. "His girth is

part of his charm, or so I tell the vet when he starts on me about Jangles' diet. Luckily, I feed him, so he adores me."

"He has impeccable taste."

"I doubt you're really afraid of him and I suppose he must like you to come out from under the tree and sit this close."

"I respect his opinion, one male to another."

"That's a good way to handle him. Otherwise Jangles might boss you around."

Mick had to raise a brow. "Maybe like his owner."

"Oh, come on, no one owns a pet. Have you really never had one?"

"I always wanted a dog, but it never worked out."

She only believed him—he was sure of it—because of his matter-of-fact tone. He wasn't shallow enough to ever complain about a privileged childhood but his mother hadn't approved of animals in the house, so they didn't have any. End of story. He'd begged for a dog and the answer was no.

"That's too bad. You missed out. But it's not too late to get one now."

"These days it's a timing issue. Once I was out of college, I immediately joined a firm that sent me to Japan for three years. When I came back to California, I started my own company, and trust me, with the hours I kept I didn't have the time for a dog and still don't."

"You need one." Raine said it firmly as if the whole matter was decided. "Buy the land, build your house, and you'll have no shortage of dog-sitters to pitch in if you're out of town. I can be one of them. Daisy would be thrilled, and Samson is used to other dogs from being at the ranch so frequently. When it comes to the land, do you want real Wyoming?"

It was a generous offer about the dog, and an impulsive one, but he already had the impression that despite Raine's wariness around him, she made a habit of following her instincts most of the time—not in an impractical way, but just acting from the heart. "Yes, that's the plan. Real Wyoming. Solitude and a stunning view. A place where I can sit and read, maybe write something that isn't a memo just for a change of pace, and relax on the front porch with a glass of wine or a cold beer and watch the sunset. I'm at a place in my life where I'm starting to realize that being driven has its perks, but working every second of the day isn't necessarily good for you."

"Write something? Like the great American novel?" She was looking at him like he'd sprouted a second head.

"Believe it or not, Ms. Artist, I do have some imagination." He didn't add that he could easily imagine her soft, warm and naked in his arms, but it was getting harder to banish those images from his mind.

"I have no trouble believing that, actually. Excuse

me, Jangles, your new friend and I have someplace to go." She gently scooted away from the cat and stood. "I'll get your coat, Mr. Boardroom. Time for a scenic Christmas Eve jaunt."

"Now?" He glanced at the clock, which had wands for hands and glass slippers in varying colors to represent the hours. Which made him think she'd designed it. It looked like, if he could read it correctly, it was nearly eleven o'clock.

"As good a time as any, right? Snow falling, the mountains in the backdrop and winter magic in the air... I want to show you something. No, now I *need* to show you something."

He had absolutely no idea what she was talking about, but was willing to play along. "Okay, I'm game."

"You might be when you see what I'm going to show you. I'll drive."

"Drive? Where—"

"Let's go." She opened a hall closet and took out a coat, then disappeared to return with his, pulling on fluffy white mittens as he did up his buttons. "This is perfect."

Mystified, he said, "I'll take your word for it. Care to give me a hint where we're going?"

"I'm a show-not-tell kind of girl. You'll find out."

Two minutes later they were in the car, driving toward a destination unknown.

The place looked as she remembered it the day she put it up for sale, but was also lit by the moon now that the snow had subsided to flurries, and she spotted the twinkle of a star or two as the clouds moved overhead in the brisk December wind.

Maybe fate had smiled on her twice this night.

Raine took in the weathered structure before them and tried to stifle a pang over the prospect of it being torn down. She warned herself that a man like Mick Branson probably wouldn't want the dilapidated wreck, and she could hardly blame him for that, but the setting was incredible.

"If you want Wyoming, this is it," she said as she parked the SUV. "There's a small lake behind the house, fed by a spring. It's so crystal clear, fishing should be a crime there because you can drop a hook right in front of a fish. I know it's frozen over right now, but in the warmer weather it's perfect for swimming in. And you have never seen anything so amazing in your life as the view from the back porch when you sit and watch the sun come up."

He was diplomatic, but she expected that. "The cabin looks really old."

"That's the understatement of the century. The house is falling down." She shut off the vehicle. "It was once just one room, but sections were added on here and there over the past century. Keep in mind the location. It isn't a lot of land, just a hundred acres, but you don't want to run cattle, correct? Just have a place to get away. Let me show you the inside."

"One hundred acres in L.A. isn't even a possibility. Neither is me running cattle, since I'd have no idea what to do. I do just need a place to get away... Raine, why do you have a key?"

"You can tear it all down as far as the buildings go, though I wish you wouldn't, but this is really a nice piece of property."

"That doesn't answer my question."

She sighed and turned to face him. "It belonged to my grandfather."

He paused. "Okay."

"And it belonged to his grandfather before him."

His jaw dropped. "You're joking, right?"

She wasn't. "It was built a very long time ago obviously. Don't those old pictures you've seen strike a chord? Slater featured a before and after of this place in his documentary. I have to say, he made his point about continuity across the generations. It hasn't changed."

Snow was still drifting down as she stood there, reminded powerfully of Slater's film. Mick said, "I re-member. He didn't tell me this belonged to your family."

Drily, she remarked, "When Slater is in work mode, the rest of the world just goes away. Plus I doubt he thought it'd matter to you one way or another. Wait until you see the inside." She pulled out the flashlight she'd brought, the powerful beam catching the sagging facade. "No electricity. The water is piped in straight from the lake with no filtration system whatsoever, but since my grandfather grew up here, he just drank it anyway and swore it was better than any city water could ever be. I'd skip that top step—it was dicey the last time I was here and I doubt it has improved any."

Mick had a bemused expression on his face. "This has certainly been an interesting first date. Lead on."

She slanted him a sidelong look and hopped up over the tricky step. The entire porch creaked, but it had done so for as long as she could remember. "Daté, huh? I thought it was a business meeting."

"I guess now's the time for me to confess that that was a ploy to get you to have dinner with me. My reasons for talking business with you were genuine, but the min-ute that discussion was over, it became a date." He was tall enough to step smoothly over the dicey step. "See how devious I am? You fell right into my wicked trap."

"Or you fell into mine." She jiggled the key in the

ancient lock. There was an art to cajoling it to cooperate. "Have I mentioned this place is haunted?"

"No, but what would Christmas Eve be without a snowy haunted old cabin? If it wasn't, I'd be disappointed." His tone was dry, but he looked intrigued.

She liked his understated sense of humor. To her that was more important than good looks or money. The door finally decided they could come inside and obediently creaked open. "Here's your slice of history."

4

THE INSIDE OF the cabin was like a time capsule.

Mick couldn't believe what he was seeing. Old wooden armchairs around a table made from what looked like an old trough turned upside down, an ancient washtub in the corner, a very old rifle over the hearth of a fireplace he suspected had been the only source of heat for the place. There was even a tin cup sitting on the table like it had been left there by the last occupant.

And everywhere there were books. In homemade shelves against the walls and stacked on the floor. An ancient dry sink was part of the kitchen area, as was a rusted metal work table and several shelves with some significantly old dishes. In the corner, a wooden bucket right next to it was probably the way to wash them.

Raine stood next to him, her mittened hands in her pockets, and said neutrally, "No electricity, no heat, and if you look around for the bathroom, it's out back. My grandfather was a minimalist. He read Walden and never glanced back. Maybe you've heard of him. Matthew Brighton."

Mick about fell over. "The author?" It would certainly account for all the books…but really?

"That's the one."

"*He* was your grandfather?"

"Yes." She'd put on this cute white knit hat before they left the house and it set off her dark hair. Her nose was tinged pink from the cold.

He couldn't believe it. "My father had some of his books. I read them as a kid. That's how I got hooked on Westerns. Are you serious?"

"Would I lie?"

He didn't think she ever would. In his estimation she was probably as honest as it was possible to hope for a person to be.

He found himself grinning. "I loved those books. My favorite was *Paintbrush Pass*."

She smiled. "Mine, too. Do you realize that was set right here?"

"Here…here? Like on this property here?"

"Exactly."

Oh hell, that intrigued him. "I knew Slater's film emphasized the legacy of a famous Western author and it was Brighton. I liked seeing the town through that lens."

Her eyes suddenly glossed over. "This is where my grandfather wrote. He sat right at that desk." She pointed to the corner. "Impressive, right?"

It wasn't, certainly not by modern standards. But it was perfect—an old wagon wheel on a post covered with pieced together lengths of hand-shaved wood no one had ever bothered to finish other than to roughly plane it with a tool that gave it a moderately flat surface. Brighton's typewriter was still there and should probably be in a museum.

"He told me once that was all he'd asked for in his life. Solitude and a place to write suited his needs perfectly. Central air was an option he didn't worry about, he'd just open the windows. He didn't need a dishwasher since he had two perfectly good hands and that old bucket."

Mick walked over and ran his hand reverently over the surface on the typewriter, coating his fingers with dust. "I can't believe this."

Raine still missed her grandfather. He could hear it in her voice. "He was a rather salty old character, but all in all, a happy man."

"I can imagine. You know, thanks to him I wrote a couple of short stories in college that actually got published. My major was business, but my minor was

English. I started a novel, but then I got that fairly high-powered job right after graduation." He lifted his shoulder in a negligent shrug, but life was full of what-ifs and he knew that. "Going that direction certainly made more sense at the time."

"This property would be a great place for a house." She looked him in the eye. "I swear you'd get a bargain price if you'd just let the cabin stand. There's lots of space to build. I've tried the Bliss County Historical Society, but they think it's too remote to really be a tourist draw, so they can't justify the funding for a decent road and maybe they're right. Not even Mrs. Arbuckle-Calder can whip up some support. I want someone to enjoy the place and not tear down the cabin. If you want a scenic spot, this is it. Just tell me you won't raze the cabin and I'll practically give it away."

So this was why she'd dragged him halfway up a mountain in the middle of a snowy night. He sensed from the way she looked at him that she was somehow confident he was the man who might be worthy enough to take on this legacy that mattered to her.

He had to admit he was flattered—and humbled. It mattered to him, too. He'd devoured Brighton's books, reading a lot of them in one sitting. He couldn't agree more that the place should stay exactly as it was.

"I'm not quite ready to sign on the dotted line, but

I'm definitely intrigued. Second date? We can come back and you can show me the property in the daylight." It was difficult not to confess he'd see footage of it tomorrow, but especially now, he wanted her to be as surprised as Slater and the rest of his family when the documentary aired.

"Second date." Her smile was tremulous and he doubted that happened often with her. "I never wanted to sell it in the first place, but taxes are expensive. And though Daisy and I come up here for a picnic now and then, as ridiculous as this sounds, I think the cabin is starting to get depressed about being abandoned. I want someone who appreciates the history and doesn't just see a dilapidated wreck. If you didn't have vision, you and Slater wouldn't get along."

He needed to set the record straight. "If he wasn't a brilliant filmmaker we wouldn't get along on a business level, but he is, and as a person I like him very much. It has nothing to do with me except I help other people believe in what he has in mind."

Her breath was frosty as she blew out a laugh. "He'd so disagree. I believe he calls you 'the driving force.'"

"Maybe I am, of the funding of the production. He's the inspired one. It's collaboration, a sum of the parts."

"Slater Carson doesn't collaborate with just anyone Take my word for it. I've known him for a while." She suddenly put those fluffy mittens on his shoulders and rose up to give him a light kiss that was very nice but not nearly all he wanted. Her lips were warm and smooth. She whispered, "I'm glad you're here. Merry Christmas."

At that moment a breeze brushed by, ruffling a stack of old, yellowed papers still sitting on the cluttered desk. Startled, he looked around, but the door was firmly shut and so were the windows. She said blithely, "I told you it was haunted. I think he likes you. Let's head back."

One of the pages had floated to the floor and she bent to pick it up.

Well, there was no question she was an idiot.

A sentimental idiot, but so it went. The minute Raine heard Mick Branson was looking for property in Wyoming, she thought about her family legacy. That he knew her grandfather's name blew her away. That he'd read his books made it even more special.

Fate, plain and simple.

She was a great believer in spiritual signs, no matter if it was labeled *fate* or attributed to some divine power. If Mick bought the property, maybe he *would* leave the cabin standing. She'd resigned herself to saying goodbye to it someday, and Blythe had kindly offered to have the Carson Ranch pay the taxes, but Raine wanted someone to use the land, to enjoy the breathtaking views, to appreciate and find joy in it like her grandfather had his whole life. She'd thought about someday building a house on it, but it would have to be after Daisy was out of school. Their modest little house suited them perfectly for now.

"Two people have looked at the property in the past three years," she told Mick when they were back in the car and bumping along what didn't even resemble a lane. "Both thought it was too remote and the cost of bringing electricity and making a decent road was prohibitive. The road has to be built in order to bring in supplies for building and fuel. I'd put in a generator and call it a day. Internet might be a bit dicey, too."

Mick was hanging on to the strap on the passenger side. "How did your grandfather handle it? I mean, everyone needs groceries."

"He rode a horse into town. He used saddlebags."

"Of course," he murmured. "I just take the freeway or get on a plane. I guess I forget sometimes where I am. So he didn't just write about it, he lived the life."

"There's something to be said for convenience, but on the other hand, the middle of nowhere is pretty peaceful. There are sacrifices involved in both, I suppose."

"It's tough to get what you want without sacrifice," he agreed quietly. "I'm living proof of that. I worked very hard to please my parents when I would have rather have been one of those daring cowboys in your grandfather's novels."

"Those fictitious cowhands would have thought you were the glamorous one. Ranch life is cold, it's lonely, and you definitely don't get any thank-you notes from the cattle. At least in your line of work you get invitations to the Oscars."

Mick had the grace to laugh. "I wouldn't exactly call my life glamorous, but I get what you're saying."

"I never thought I'd say this, but I really see why Slater likes you. You're very real."

"As compared to being fake?"

"As compared to being a snob because you probably own suits that cost more than some of the pickups people drive around here. I'm surprised the cabin didn't collapse when you walked in wearing a cashmere coat and loafers instead of boots."

"There's a part of me that would rather walk around in worn jeans and a flannel shirt. It's all based on what we get used to, and what works for us." He took a deep, appreciative breath as he looked out the window. "Man, it *is* beautiful here. Aspens in snow are about as Christmas as you can get."

She smiled to herself. He'd mentioned the aspens. That was a sign.

It did look like quite the winter wonderland outside,

the trees glistening and, now that the weather was clearing, a moon that illuminated the snowcapped mountains. Something slunk by in the shadow of the trees and disappeared before she could get a clean view beside the gleam of feral eyes. *Big wolf or small mountain lion?* Out here, either was a possibility.

Mick noticed it, too. "What was that?"

"Not sure." The increasing wind picked up some snow and flung it at the windshield. "But I'm fairly certain we'd just as soon avoid it on foot if possible."

He muttered, "Me, too. I don't see how the ranchers out here do it. Drake Carson in particular, riding fence lines after dark every single night."

"Not that I've ever known him to use it, but he carries a rifle and rides a really big horse. And I'm sure he doesn't understand how you're able to endure traveling the crowded L.A. freeways on a regular basis and having three-martini lunches in fancy restaurants."

Lightly, Mick said, "I usually keep it to just two martinis, no olive, just a twist of lemon." She caught his grin in the darkness of the car. "Actually, I tend to stick to a glass of sparkling water. I work long hours. A drink at lunch, much less three, is just bad for productivity."

"I might do business with a winery, but I agree."

"You see? We have another mutual philosophy. What time are you headed out to the ranch tomorrow?"

She turned on the county highway and it felt smooth as glass compared to the rutted, overgrown and disused lane that had never been graded in her memory. "About ten or so. We don't open gifts until the morning chores are done and everyone rides back in. Cattle still need to be fed and the horses taken care of, even on Christmas day."

"I was told dinner was at one sharp."

"My advice is don't be late. You've met Harry." The Carson housekeeper, Harriet Armstrong, was a legendary cook, but also an unstoppable force of nature. All three of the Carson sons considered her a second mother. "If you're late, you get to do all the dishes. Take it from someone who has made that unfortunate mistake. I'm habitually running behind, but not if Harry is involved. I toe the line around her."

"Don't worry, I'll be prompt. I'm really looking forward to tomorrow."

She glanced at the time display. "Today, actually. I'd apologize for dragging you out so late, but I happen to know you're also a night owl. I just forget what time it is. A personal flaw."

"You can get a lot done when it's quiet and your phone isn't beeping, and no one is sending emails."

"*You* emailed *me* at two in the morning."

"I didn't expect you'd be awake."

"I certainly didn't expect to get an email from you, either. Slater had some part in that, didn't he? I know you've never asked me for my email address."

"I asked if he thought you'd be interested. He said you were definitely a woman who made her own decisions, but if an animation film fell into your lap, you might jump on the idea."

"I see."

"There's a firm rule in business. It never hurts to make a proposition."

"Just in business?" She raised her brows, knowing it was probably more than a little dangerous to flirt with this man, but somehow unable to stop herself.

"Timing is everything."

At least he was reading the signals with unerring accuracy. She wasn't ready for a holiday romance when he would just get on a plane afterward and head back to California.

He wasn't serious, she told herself; he was just casually interested. She'd run across that before. Careless bachelors that came around, most of them shying away when they discovered she had a daughter, but Mick knew about Daisy already so she wasn't sure exactly what he wanted.

Mustang Creek definitely looked festive, with the streetlights adorned with wreaths and holiday lights strung in the windows of the closed shops. The streets were utterly deserted and no doubt everyone was snug in their beds. Her eclectic tree looked good from the street, she noticed as she pulled into the driveway. At the sound of the car, an indignant furry face appeared in the window, Mr. Bojangles monitoring—as always—her every move.

Had to love that cat. He was spoiled since she worked at home, but they were definite roomies.

"I think someone believes you've been out past your curfew," Mick said with a laugh. "He probably scared Santa Claus half to death while we were gone when Santa tried to put presents under the tree."

"Jangles wouldn't hurt a fly. He just looks fearsome." She'd invite him in, but it really was late, and he still had to drive to the resort.

"I won't argue that point." Mick studied her for a moment, as if reading her mind. "I had a very nice evening. Thanks again for the burgers and ice cream, and for introducing me to *Big Jake*. See you later today."

He walked her to the door and then everything changed. "By the way, nice kiss earlier but I think maybe we could go it one better." His dark eyes really could smolder, and she'd thought that was just a creative myth.

It was irrefutable that his kiss was more memorable than her brief impulsive peck back in the cabin. He was really good at it too, but then again, he was probably good at just about everything.

However, he seemed almost more off balance than she was when he finally let her go. He left without a word, getting swiftly into his rental car and backing out of the driveway, and she was almost amused as she watched him drive off. Raine went inside and sat down on the couch, Jangles immediately snuggling close. She remembered the piece of paper that she'd absently picked up in the cabin, and retrieved it from her pocket, wondering what it would say.

It was the end of a chapter.

The old man tentatively approved of the greenhorn, though he wasn't sure city folks were quite his type. Maybe he had real promise.

Raine laughed and scratched under the cat's chin. "You see," she whispered, "I knew Grandpa liked him."

5

FOR GIFTS, RYDER had been easy. Mick had once been a teenaged boy, so he had a fair idea of what they liked, but times changed. He'd opted for a gift card to a very popular online store.

Daisy had been more of a challenge.

He really knew nothing about a girl her age, and his childless sister-in-law was no help. In the end, he'd asked his mother's opinion.

"A purse," she announced promptly. "I have plenty of friends with granddaughters, not that I have any yet, so I will ask what brands are popular right now."

He ignored the implied criticism. "I'd appreciate it, but I can't pick out a purse."

"Sure you can. You have wonderful taste."

Well, he *had* asked, he thought as the call ended. The idea was better than nothing, which was all he'd had before. So he'd gone into the closest trendy store and asked the young clerk if she was Daisy's age what she might want. Directly she went to a rack, selected a purse he would never have picked out in a million years, and handed it over. "She'll faint over this," she informed him. "If we hadn't gotten a shipment in today we wouldn't have it on the shelf."

He took her word for it and had it gift-wrapped, along with some nail polish the knowledgeable clerk promised with a dimpled smile was popular with girls Daisy's age. For Blythe, a small Victorian tabletop greenhouse because she was the ultimate gardener, and for Harry, who always had a cup around as far as he could tell, a genuine English antique tea set. Grace and Luce were getting robes his sister-in-law swore by, since she claimed they were just the right weight, yet warm and cozy, and the Carson men were getting handmade leather gloves.

Raine had taken some thought. He wasn't trying to impress her; he was trying to show he was thoughtful enough to understand what she might like. In the end he'd stumbled upon the perfect gift—or he hoped it was, anyway. He'd found an obscure but original print of the infamous Sirens luring sailors to their demise when he was recently in Athens, the color faded because he had no idea how to date it. But the detail was so beautiful he thought she'd love it. He'd had it framed, and after seeing her house, he was sure it would fit right in. He'd liked her imaginative décor.

Packing up the gifts he'd had shipped to the hotel, Mick got in the rental car, checked his phone one last time, and shut it off. It was Christmas Day. London was hours different, his mother was in New York so he'd call her later, and no one else needed to talk to him in Wyoming.

The resort really was quiet, but Mick noticed the bar was full as he walked past, and there were a lot of skis in the lobby propped against the wall and a fire going in the giant stone fireplace. It made him reflect on how the season was celebrated, and if one person wanted to sit by a fire and another wanted to brave the slopes because the powder was perfect, that was the quintessential to-each-his-own. Both of those sounded pretty good to him, depending on the company. The Alps at Christmas that year he was sixteen had been an experience, but he preferred this homey atmosphere hands down.

He was very much looking forward to the company he would be in today.

The Carson ranch looked festive as he pulled up, the veranda of the big house decorated with twinkling lights and a garland, and there were two small trees complete with ornaments on either side of the doors. The row of cars spoke of a gathering in progress.

It was overcast and a few flakes floated down, landing on his shoulders and hair as he walked up the steps. Blythe answered the door, her smile gracious. "Mick, Merry Christmas. It's so good to see you."

"And you. I hope I'm not late."

"The fear-of-Harry factor is a powerful thing." Blythe took his coat. "You come bearing gifts. How nice of you. We were just about to start the gift exchange. Brace yourself for the usual male Carson competition. They are ridiculous. It isn't a monetary thing at all, it's just their nature. They have a built-in need to outdo each other whether it's through throwing a rope on a horse or buying a toy for a child."

"Hopefully I'll be a contender, since I made a few educated guesses." He stepped farther into the foyer. "But I make no promises."

As it turned out, he won the competition.

At least with Daisy. The purse was a leaping-up-and-down hit. She gasped as she opened the package and came over and gave Mick an exuberant hug, clinging to that purse like it was made of pure gold.

He made a mental note to thank his mother later.

Grace poked him in the shoulder with an accusing finger. "How'd you manage to find that? I tried to order one online three months ago. I'm still on a waiting list."

Raine studied him, clearly equal parts intrigued and

annoyed. "Four months ago for me. Stop showing off, Branson." She wore dark jeans and a yellow top that brought out the gold in her eyes, and looked delicious against the sweep of her hair at her shoulders.

"I probably shouldn't tell you that all I had to do was walk into a store and there it was." He grinned as he sat back carelessly in his comfortable chair and took a sip of the smooth merlot Blythe had handed him. He had to admit that the spirited gift exchange had been much preferable to the stuffy country club dining room where he usually spent his holiday.

Both women glared at him.

Slater told him flat-out that if he would give up his shopping secrets, they'd be friends for life. "I don't think her first car is going to make her as happy as that purse did."

"I thought we already were friends for life." Mick was going to go back and give the clerk the bonus of her life. The joy of giving was defined by Daisy's excited smile.

Slater acknowledged that with a nod of his head and a chuckle. "At least you beat out my brothers. For that, I'll forgive you. They would create a favorite uncle pendant and ride around an arena brandishing it until next year. Boys are simple. Give them a video game or some sports equipment and you're good to go. If Grace has a girl this time, the games will begin again. If Luce has a girl there might be an amusement park in the front yard with spinning teacups and a roller coaster."

Mick could envision it. "A unique addition to a working ranch. And maybe worth a brand-new documentary on how fatherhood can soften even the toughest cowboy."

"What can I say? We like to please our ladies."

"Having gotten to know your ladies pretty well recently, I can't say I blame you."

Slater caught his eyes drifting to Raine and said neutrally, "My wife didn't tell me until this morning you'd be here, but she was all too delighted to tell me about your Christmas Eve dinner plans. So how'd last night go?"

"Well. I told Raine about the animated film. She seems interested."

Slater rubbed his jaw and laughed. "Not quite what I was asking, but that's good."

"She also showed me her grandfather's cabin. I can't believe she's related to Matthew Brighton. I've been thinking about buying property here, but it was pitch-dark so I couldn't get a feel for the view or anything else. You know the territory. Give me your opinion."

"That's so Raine. She took you there on a snowy Christmas Eve when there isn't even a real road to the place? You two could have easily gotten stuck there."

Mick couldn't help it. "That would have been just fine with me."

"So I gathered," Slater said drily. "As for the property, it's a wonderful piece of land but you can't run cattle there, it needs a road, there's no electricity, and that old cabin is supposed to be haunted now. That's nonsense I usually don't believe in, but I was up there once because Raine asked me to check on it and I'll be damned if I didn't hear someone say in a deep male voice: *Howdy, Slater.* I knew I was alone, so I about jumped out of my skin." He shook his head, chuckling at himself. "On the positive side, that lake is so scenic you could make a fortune just selling postcards and the view of the mountains just can't be beat. You'd wake up to bears and elk wandering past the decaying front porch, but when it comes to peace and quiet, if that's what you're after, you'd have it in spades."

Mick refrained from mentioning the sudden breeze that had swept through the cabin last night. He was also a skeptic but that had been an odd moment. He took a sip of wine and studied his glass thoughtfully. "I don't think I'd mind sitting on a porch with a cup of coffee in the morning and waving hello to a bear. I'd build a house with all the modern amenities, but the cabin would stay."

"That would make Raine really happy, but I think you just did anyway." Slater pointed.

She'd unwrapped the illustration and her rapt attention was emphasized by the reverence with which she ran a finger over the glass, tracing an outline of one of the figures. Raine was sitting cross-legged on the floor by the enormous tree. She looked over at him. "Mick, *where* did you get this?"

"Santorini. I was in Athens on business. I couldn't skip a tour of the island while I was already in Greece."

"It's gorgeous."

He held her gaze for a beat. "Maybe that's why I thought of you."

Well done.

Raine was fairly sure that smooth compliment was overheard by almost everyone in the room. If nothing else, Mick Branson had style down pat.

It was unsettling to be under the Carson microscope at this particular moment. She was grateful for the extended family for both her daughter and herself, but the scrutiny that accompanied it was a bit much. Slater was fine, they'd come to an understanding a long time ago, and she was genuinely happy he was married to Grace. She loved Drake, Mace and their wives as well, but she wished they'd focus on their own gifts right now.

Instead, all eyes were on her and Mick.

She was keenly aware of it, and so was he from his expression.

The framed print he'd given her was simply priceless. No matter what he'd spent—and she didn't want to think about what it had probably cost him—it was the fact that he'd seemed to know exactly what she'd love that moved her the most. She figured she could forgive him the purse triumph. She was touched he'd thought of Daisy at all.

Both gifts were the perfect choice.

The same was true for what he'd selected for Ryder, and everyone else; he'd clearly put some time into it, and no small amount of thought.

No one had ever managed to gain her attention in quite this way. It wasn't his money. She was fine all on her own. For that matter, if money was a draw for her, she'd have married Slater all those years ago when he asked.

Mick had read her grandfather's books. He could easily name his favorite, and since it was hers, too, well…

A small voice in her head said: *Watch yourself, McCall.*

"And now yours." She took a box from under the tree, wading through the sea of wrapping paper. Drake and Mace were supposed to be keeping up with gathering the discarded colorful paper and putting it into bags as each gift was eagerly unwrapped, but there was quite the crowd, a ridiculous amount of gifts, especially for the kids, and they'd finally looked at each other and declared jointly they'd pick it up afterward.

"Mine?" Mick raised his brows. "You didn't have a lot of shopping time."

"I didn't need it." She perched on the edge of his chair, sharing it with him. She wanted to see his expression when he opened it.

Delilah, Ryder's little long-haired mutt, had taken a shine to Mick and was currently draped over his expensive shoe and his gentle attempts to dislodge her merely made her wag her floppy tail, so he'd evidently resigned himself to her adoration and the amount of hair being deposited on his tailored pants. Samson was having a ball attacking discarded wads of paper, while Drake's two well-behaved German shepherds watched with superior resignation, as if inwardly they were shaking their heads. Blythe's cat was used to the turmoil enough to doze on the top on the couch, having an afternoon siesta.

A man like Mick Branson probably thought he was having Christmas at a zoo. He accepted the box with a look of protest. "You didn't have to—"

"Give? None of us *have* to, we want to. Now open it."

He obligingly tore open the paper and lifted the lid on the box. His expression went from curious to stunned.

"You're kidding. An original manuscript? I don't recognize the title."

"It's never been published," she explained as he stared at the manuscript, reverently touching the title page. "Grandpa started it right before he died. *The Aspen Trail* was something he thought about for a long time, one of the books that run circles in your head, he told me once. He still used that old typewriter, so you'll find some penciled-in corrections."

He tore his gaze away from it to look at her. "You can't give me this. It's probably worth a small fortune."

"I just did. But, well, it comes with a catch."

"What?" He was understandably wary.

"Could you maybe finish it?"

"*What?*"

"Read it. I want to know what happens next."

"I can't possibly—"

"Put that English minor to good use. You said you have imagination. So prove it."

Harry emerged from the kitchen right then and saved Mick by making the grand announcement. "Okay, ladies and gents, it's time."

The males in the room rushed to help her carry in food, which wasn't surprising since they would eat most of it. And it wasn't like Harry just roasted a turkey; she'd made prime rib, Swedish meatballs, ribs, fish…a variety of side dishes in order to please everyone, and Blythe had baked her legendary rolls, so it was quite a varied feast, as Raine had come to expect. Ask for it, and you got it as a special Harry gift. Dessert was a miracle, too, with everyone's favorites on the table, but then again, with all the leftovers, Harry would get a few days off to balance all the marathon baking and cooking.

Today, she also got another special gift.

When Harry sat down with the inevitable cup of tea, she picked up the envelope that had mysteriously appeared on her placemat during her last trip into the kitchen. "What's this?"

It was almost as much of a pleasure to see her open that envelope as it was to see Daisy sitting with her precious purse at the table, trying to eat one-handed because she didn't want to let go of it.

Harry's eyes widened. "A European River cruise? Airline tickets?"

"For you and your sister." Blythe smiled. "It's from all of us, so don't just thank me. You've always said you wanted to go, so go. I can manage this house alone for a couple of weeks and Raine is going to do lunches for the hands. Everyone is pitching in so you can just relax and enjoy. Take pictures of the castles, please."

"Stephano has volunteered to cook," Grace added, as Harry continued to look stunned. "I'm bringing home dinner from the resort's restaurant every night. You do realize he'll try to outdo you, right?"

"I'm making my famous chili on the weekends," Luce said. "In exchange for river pics. I hope you'll throw in some vineyards snaps for Mace."

Kelly piped up, "Yes, do. I'd like to frame one for the store. By the way, I'm in charge of dessert. If you'd leave out a few recipes I'd appreciate it."

"I will." Harry looked endearingly touched, maybe even teary-eyed, as she opened the brochure. "My sister is going to love this."

That translated to Harry loving it. Raine suspected Harriet Armstrong could be the most sentimental woman on this earth, but she was too stubborn to admit it.

Seated next to her, Mick whispered, "Is she a wizard or something? How many people does it take to fill her shoes?"

Raine whispered back, "A tyrant wizard. I believe that's her official job description. You've eaten her food, so you know she has magical powers."

He was way too handsome, especially when he smiled. Hearts probably fluttered all over California, and apparently in foreign countries as well, since she assumed business didn't take up all his time there.

But he'd evidently thought of her on his travels.

"I agree."

"Why do you keep checking the clock?" She had to ask because she'd seen him keeping a close eye on it. Not that she was watching him or anything like that... no, not at all.

Right.

Mick just said in a neutral tone, "I have a good reason, and no, I won't explain. Trust me, it will be worth it."

"Promise?"

"Yes, and I always keep my promises. Just wait."

6

IF THERE WAS one thing Mick knew, it was that surprises didn't always go according to plan. Still, he was pleased with the way his unfolded.

Dinner was over, the table cleared and the adults sipped wine. Snow had begun to fall again, so the ranch looked like an idyllic cowboy poster.

"Slater!" Ryder rushed in, waving his hands. "Dude, your movie is about to come on."

Mick smiled. It would've been fun to spring the news himself, but the teen's wide-eyed announcement added a nice hint of drama.

Slater, by contrast, was calm when he replied, "Don't call me *dude*, Ryder. I don't play on your basketball team and have the locker next to you. And what film do you mean?"

"*Wild West…Still Wild*. Your documentary. I just saw an ad for it."

Mace perked up. "Really?"

Mick hoped he was pleased. There was a short ad for the winery at the beginning of the film, and also an ad for the resort and spa Grace managed.

"Yeah, du… I mean, Uncle Mace, really."

"But it isn't out for another month."

Mick cleared his throat. The cat was officially out of the bag. "Actually, it might be premiering in…oh, about twenty-eight minutes."

It wasn't surprising Slater was visibly taken aback. "Mick, that's why you're here?" He turned to his wife, who was beaming smugly. "You knew, didn't you? And you didn't tell me?"

Grace, looking unrepentant, lifted her slim shoulders. "If you think I'd spoil a great surprise, think again. Surprise!"

"Christmas Day?" Slater looked floored, staring at Mick. "How'd you pull that off?"

"I have strings I tighten now and again." Mick wasn't lying about that. Those were some hard-won tug-o-wars.

"It isn't possible. Not for a documentary."

"Tell me that again in twenty-seven minutes."

"I just saw the ad. Like a major commercial!" Ryder was jacked up, his thin face alight. Mick could swear the kid had grown about four inches since his last visit to Bliss County and when he filled out, he was going to be quite the broad-shouldered man. "I was watching football."

So far the films had all made a good profit and that's why Mick could still get investors on board, but that ad had taken a lot of money and some true finesse. Everyone involved had agreed that maybe it was time to notch it up, especially once they'd viewed the film. They'd thought the investment would pay off.

"During a football game on a major network?" Drake wasn't a wine drinker so he lifted his bottle of beer in a salute. "Look at you, Showbiz."

I think you're the one we'll be looking at," Mick informed him, enjoying the moment. "Remember how the film opens? I think millions are about to get a peek at you kissing your lovely wife."

"Oh, hell," Drake muttered in obvious chagrin. "I'd either forgotten or blocked that out of my mind. Tell me you aren't serious."

Luce laughed. "Relax, you're not being rocketed into instant stardom, honey. In that footage no one can really tell it's us, and besides, they'll all be looking at the wild stallion in the background. I'm sorry, but I think Smoke is the one who will steal the show."

"He's welcome to it," her husband responded darkly.

Maybe it was the Hollywood in him, but Mick had always thought each of the Carson brothers would make a fascinating leading man in his own way. All three were intense, but he'd describe Slater as artistic, Drake as the quiet cowboy, and Mace the wildcard.

What was he?

Focused, maybe. Not artistic, that was for sure. Though he appreciated art in all forms, he couldn't draw so much as a square. "The gloves were just for show, Showbiz," he told Slater. "Your real gift is going to be the next couple of hours. I don't know how you're going to outdo this one, but you should have the opportunity if this doc goes over like I think it will. The backers loved it enough that the commercial was a sell."

"They loved it?"

"Of course. I held a showing. This is business, Carson. Don't look so surprised that they enjoyed it."

Raine was the one who elbowed him. "I'm with Slater. This is like having someone tell you if your child is ugly or pretty, Branson. It's nerve-wracking stuff."

He did get that. He really did, at least on an intellectual level. Defensively, he murmured, "He doesn't make movies just to make them. He wants people to watch them. Slater knows what he's doing."

"Yes, but no," she corrected. "He really does make movies just because he loves them. Having people watch and enjoy them is a bonus. But without someone like you, he could never do it on this scale."

Raine was an intellectual challenge at times. Maybe that was why he liked her so much. No agenda. "What's the point of doing it if no one sees it?"

"Because of the sheer joy of creation. I have artwork I've done I wouldn't sell even if offered a fortune for it."

"A private showing of those pieces would interest me a great deal." He made his tone deliberately suggestive.

Raine looked amused. "Please tell me you're usually more subtle when you flirt, Branson."

"You're harder to flirt with than most women, Ms. McCall."

"I'd like to think I'm not most women."

"You've got that right."

Her beautiful eyes softened. "That's improvement right there. I'm going to help clear the table. I think we all have a movie to watch."

The film was brilliant, but Raine had expected that. Though she and Slater hadn't ended up on the same page in life, they certainly connected on different levels, and one of them was their mutual understanding of the emotional significance of vision.

The documentary was a love letter to Mustang Creek, taking viewers on a journey through its rich history.

There were pictures of the old hotel that was there before the new resort, and video of a snowboarder in mid-air doing an Olympic-style flip, and then photos of cowboys digging a path for their horses out of the snow. Ranch hands around a table wearing chaps and drinking coffee from tin cups, and the same table a hundred years later, same cups, different men. The main street of Mustang Creek back in the day, and the similarity to the modernized version, including the wine store, before and after. Elk grazing next to cattle, the wild horses at full gallop, fluttering fall leaves and an eagle soaring above, a mountain lion perched above a walking trail…

And her grandfather's cabin, so unchanged from when it was built except for the slow process of aging. She drew in a breath at the picture of him when he was a boy happily playing on the steps, and later a picture she'd provided of an old man sitting on the front porch smoking a pipe—that child grown and weathered by time but still content. In the latter photograph there was a book on a simple table next to him; one of his, of course.

Her mother had taken the picture and Raine wasn't immune to a nostalgic moment. It was telling that even the kids didn't get restless, but watched intently. When it was over, there was a resounding silence.

Then Blythe began to clap, Daisy jumped up to run and kiss her dad, and everyone was talking at once.

The beginning of the film had been fantastic, with an unintentional shot of Drake leaning in to Luce for a passionate kiss, accidentally captured by remote cameras but, fortunately for the couple, entirely in silhouette. Luce had been right—the setting took over.

But the ending was astounding.

The wild horses were being herded off and Slater had taken gorgeous footage of the warrior stallion stopping to nudge a gangly colt, gently urging the youngster into the herd because he wasn't quite able yet to keep up.

It was so well done, emphasizing the continuing cycle of life.

"Let's hope the ratings reflect the quality of the work." Mick sounded optimistic, his long legs extended, Delilah yet again camped out on his foot.

"They will." Raine was able to say it with utter conviction.

Mick didn't hesitate. "I loved the idea, loved the execution, and Slater's style and his sense of timing are distinctive. I could tune in and know right away who ran the production. That isn't easy to come by."

"He's a bright man," Grace interjected, snuggling into her husband as he grinned and ran a hand over Daisy's hair.

"He has excellent taste," Raine agreed. She glanced at Mick's feet. "And apparently so does a certain small, floppy dog."

"Thanks." Mick eyed his snoozing new best friend, and the sleeping giant at *her* feet. "Raine, you do realize you're going to need a larger yard for that beast."

Samson had come over and collapsed at her feet midmovie and, even at his young age, he already snored. His head was significantly bigger than her foot. She offered helpfully, "If you decide you want my grandfather's property, I'll throw him in for free. Problem solved. That's one big yard."

Mick chuckled. "Oh yes, I bet your daughter would let that fly. And I might have always wanted a dog, but I'm not sure about a rambunctious horse in canine form."

"Yeah, I guess I'm stuck with him. But there's one thing I can give you." She was impulsive and she knew it. It was exactly how she ordered her world. Follow the heart. If she had a motto, that was it. Raine took a breath and blurted out, "What if I just deeded the property to you on the proviso you keep the cabin as it is? Yours, free and clear."

It wasn't hard to see Mick was flabbergasted. He looked at her like she was insane. "That is the most ridiculous thing I've ever heard."

She stood her ground. "I don't agree. I think it makes perfect sense."

"Raine...the property is like what I'm looking for and I can afford to *buy* it."

"I believe I already told you that I want someone who appreciates it to have it. If you can afford to buy it, you can afford the taxes and to put in a decent road. Fix that top step on the porch, too, will you? Say you'll keep the cabin. We'll call it even."

It seemed like he was searching for words. "You...you can't *give* a hundred acres and a historical cabin away."

The more she thought about it, the better the idea seemed to be. "You want land in this area, and you'd have it." She needed to make her position clear so she chose her next words carefully. "I'm really being self-ish. Mick, I don't want to sell it. But I can't justifiably keep it either and let it fall apart. This seems a lot more right to me. You'd be doing me a favor. The guilt of having it on the market has been eating away at me. I think, given your friendship with Slater, you'd let Daisy come out there every once in a while to visit the cabin. That's so much better than a stranger buying it and not caring that he was Matthew Brighton, the author, and getting rid of it."

"If you get that animated movie deal I mentioned, *you* could afford all of that."

"That's a big 'if.' And I assume these things take time. I would have given it to the Carson family, but they really don't need more land. For them, it would just be taxes and something else to manage. They would do it, but it would be an imposition on my part."

"You *are* part of the Carson family."

He was right, and he was wrong. "My daughter is. I've been made welcome, no doubt about it, but there's a reason I spend Christmas Eve on my own."

"Not this year."

She held his gaze, remembering that brief kiss that was still a spine-tingling experience, the second one even better. "No. I want you to know I don't share my green chilis with just anyone."

"That was a Christmas gift all its own. If a genie had popped out of a bottle and asked what I wanted for dinner, that selection would have been my choice."

There came that heart-stopping smile again. She pounced on the moment. "So we have a deal then? Take the land, keep the cabin, and I'll make you green chili cheeseburgers every Christmas Eve if you want."

"Okay, we have a standing date."

"Mom, Mom." Daisy rushed in and flopped down on the floor next to Samson, who promptly rolled over to get his belly rubbed. Her blue eyes were alight. "Dad and Uncle Mace are going to take me and Ryder for a midnight ride in the snow tonight. Is that okay? I can just stay over again, unless you mind."

At least they'd spent the day together, and it was

Christmas after all. "I don't mind." But Raine had to ask, "Are you going to take your purse on the ride?"

Daisy was appalled. "No. What if snow got on it?"

"Oh no, hadn't thought of that. It would be a tragedy." She bent to kiss her daughter's head. "Go and have fun."

"Thanks, Mom." She jumped up and ran off, and Samson decided maybe something was afoot and followed in a lumbering gait, clumsy but somehow still cute despite his size.

"Don't look smug," Raine informed Mick. "She loved my gift, too."

"I'd love to take credit but I can't." He didn't heed her request but looked smug anyway. "There's a very efficient clerk who understands both retail and young girls and does an excellent job for her company. Daisy should really thank her for the purse. So now you're free for the evening?"

What she said next might be life-changing. Raine thought it over—letting him know she wasn't *always* impulsive. She trusted him absolutely with her grandfather's property. Her heart was a different matter, because it also included her child. So when she spoke, her tone was cautious. "It seems like I am."

"Can we spend it together?"

"Are we talking the entire night?" She looked him squarely in the eyes.

He looked right back. "You just don't pull punches, do you? I'm talking whatever you want."

"I hope you can accept I'm not sure."

"I'm fairly aware there's a guarded side of you. Kind of like a prickly pear cactus."

"Those plants have beautiful flowers, so I'll take that as a compliment." She shot him her sweetest smile.

"I meant it as one," he replied. "I know you have reason to be cautious, and that you're used to being independent."

"I think learning to rely on yourself is a very valuable lesson. I remember as a child once asking my grandfather if he wasn't lonely sometimes, all alone in that old secluded place, and he answered that it never even occurred to him. He was happy with himself for company. I think I took to that mentality."

Mick regarded her intently. "You certainly seem to have done just that."

Maybe it was the season, because she wasn't usually that open with her feelings. "I'm not very conformist. I've met handsome men I would never give a second glance because they just aren't my type. I don't like them shallow, and I don't like arrogance. I'm not into cocktail parties and getting a manicure, but would rather mow my yard or tackle fixing a leaky faucet. That's not very feminine, I guess. If you're looking for someone who will put on a little black dress and stay on your arm at Hollywood parties, you'd better move on."

He just seemed amused. "If you think for a minute I haven't already figured that one out, you underestimate me. I hate to disabuse you of the notion that all I do is rub elbows with the elite, but I like quiet evenings in even more."

"Then how about a fire and a glass of wine?" She really wasn't sure what she was getting into, but it was going past the ankle-deep level and she might be up to mid-calf. "Maybe some philosophical discussion about life, and I'm sure Jangles will want to give his two cents. He might even think about sitting on your lap."

Mick lifted his brows in mock alarm. "I think I've had enough of animals sitting on me for one day." Then he added, "Otherwise, it sounds perfect."

7

HE COULDN'T VERY well tell the truth, so Mick said neutrally, "It's certainly been an interesting trip so far. How's New York?"

His mother answered, "Busy, brilliant, definitely full of holiday spirit. There's nothing like seeing The Nutcracker at Rockefeller Hall. What was so interesting in the wilds of Wyoming?"

Well, he should have known he wouldn't get off the hook so easily. "A certain woman that, oddly enough, I think you might like."

He was sitting in his car outside Raine's house, gazing at her enchanting but unusually decorated tree through the large front window.

"Why would it be odd if I liked her?"

"She's definitely a small-town girl, an artist, and though I bet she could catch one without any problem,

I doubt she owns a set of fish forks to serve the trout. By the way, thanks for the tip on the purse. Her daughter is now my biggest fan."

"She has a daughter?"

"She does."

"So she's divorced."

"Actually, no."

There was a judgmental pause. He expected nothing else. Better to get it out in the open now.

"I see."

"No, you don't. Raine turned down Slater's proposal because she thought in the long term that a marriage between them wouldn't work. They parent together and have remained friends. It seems like a reasonable arrangement and Daisy is a happy, well-adjusted kid."

"Slater...as in Slater Carson?"

"He's Daisy's father, yes."

"That's sounds complicated, Michael. Don't you handle a lot of the backing for his films?"

To his friends he was Mick, but to his mother he would always be Michael. As patiently as possible, he said, "He's happily married, has another child, and in fact, a third on the way. He cares about Raine as the mother of his daughter but he doesn't have an issue with my having feelings for her."

"You sound definite enough," she said, but it was grudgingly. "I'll have to trust your judgment."

Considering he'd been a grown man for over two decades, he could point out that she had no say one way or the other—but then again, he'd always believed that it was a mistake to become involved with someone your family disliked. It added an unwelcome dimension to something that was supposed to enrich your life and make you happy.

It surprised him that the big, sometimes boisterous Carson family was comfortable for him when he'd grown up very differently. It also surprised him that he was so attracted to Raine when she was the antithesis of the women he'd dated before, and it surprised him even more that she seemed to feel the same way about him. He wasn't a free-spirited artist, or a tried-and-true cowboy.

"She's—" he sought the right description "—like a warm breeze on a sunny afternoon."

"Oh no, now you're getting poetic? It must be love. Darling, have a wonderful evening. Now I need a martini. Merry Christmas."

He couldn't help laughing at himself all the way up the snowy sidewalk, but he thought it was a good description and would stand by it. When Raine opened the door at his knock, she gave him a quizzical look. "What's so funny?"

He smiled. "Let's just say I think my mother likes you."

"Um, I'd ask why you were talking about me to your mother, but something tells me I'd rather not know. Come on in. Fire and wine are in place. If I eat again in this lifetime I'll be surprised, but Harry sent cookies and turkey sandwiches. If you get hungry, speak up."

"I will." He was certainly hungry, but he wasn't thinking that much about food and he had a feeling she knew it. He really wasn't like this with women, more pursued than the pursuer most of the time, but there was some serious chemistry going on his part anyway.

He was lucky that the lion didn't have an entire pride waiting for him. Mr. Bojangles barely let him get in the door before he launched a sneak attack, darting out from his super-not-so-secret hiding place and nailing his ankle again. It added comic relief that when the critter went back under the tree, his bushy tail was fully visible, even if his ample body was hidden.

"He must have trained with the special forces. The ambush was perfect, but he may have skipped class on hiding day."

Raine observed wryly, "He's not quite figured out that his size is a problem. I've thought about getting a bigger tree just to make sure he doesn't get insecure about his ability to be stealthy."

"That would be the compassionate thing to do."

She'd changed into soft, drawstring pajama pants, a flowing top with the same pattern, and slippers with raccoon faces on them. How that could be sexier than a slinky nightgown he wasn't sure, but it worked for him. There was a nice fire, and two glasses of wine on the coffee table.

The mixed signals were driving him crazy. He was invited—or maybe he'd invited himself by suggesting they spend the evening together—and yet she was dressed like she was going to a sorority slumber party. She'd told him flat-out she was unsure how she viewed things between them, but agreed to have him over again anyway.

The agreement was good. The rest of it was up in the air.

"What smells so good in here?"

"That candle from the local store that Grace bought for me. She knows I love vanilla." Raine sat down and visibly relaxed, cradling her wineglass in her slender fingers, propping her feet on the coffee table and wiggling her toes in those ridiculous slippers. "I love Christmas at the ranch, but a little peace and quiet afterward is nice, too. I always manage to forget how exhausting a big crowd can be. I go out to lunch with friends now and then, but mostly I'm by myself all day, at least during the school year." She smiled. "I love my daughter—that goes without saying—but the quiet is nice. Feel free, by the way, to take off those Italian loafers and put your feet up. *Formality* is almost a dirty word in this house."

"My mother would faint if I put my feet on your coffee table, but taking off my shoes sounds great." He slipped them off. "Solitude can be a friend or an enemy, depending on the person. I know far too many people who can't stand to be alone, almost never eat at home, and in general love the bustle of a big city." He relaxed, too, just enjoying the view, and he wasn't looking at the sparkling tree or the fire. "Is this the beginning of our deep philosophical discussion?"

"Or maybe just two people talking. You still worry about what your mother thinks of you?"

"I wouldn't say worry, exactly. But I try to keep on her good side."

"Good for you." Her tone was approving. "I like that."

"Hopefully that isn't the only thing you like about me."

"No." She smiled playfully. "You have great hair."

He shot her a look. "Not quite the compliment I was angling for. I was hoping to hear my intellect amazes you and my charm is unsurpassed in your experience."

"Both those things could be true, but I just can't get past the hair. Do you have a stylist?"

"You think you're so funny, don't you."

She laughed, hiding her mouth behind her hand. "Kind of."

"No, I don't have a stylist. I get it cut and I wash and comb it. Surely there's something else you like."

She pretended to think it over. "Now I suppose I have to mention those gorgeous movie-star eyes and high cheekbones. Nice shoulders, too, unless there's padding in your shirts."

"And here I thought I wasn't in Hollywood...throw me a bone here." He was laughing, too, but also serious.

Her smile faded as she held his gaze. "I trust you are a good man. If I didn't, you wouldn't be sitting here right now."

It was exactly the type of compliment he might have expected from Raine—frank and straightforward—but he was aware that she meant what she said. "And you wouldn't be giving me your grandfather's property. We'll have to talk over that one again later. You really can't do that."

"I talked to Slater. He said it was a sound idea. Drake agreed and Mace was with it, too. One of the reasons I like you so much is that they all trust you. Those are some pigheaded, stubborn men, but they're some of the best judges of character that I know. And lucky for me, they don't even think about your hair."

"But you do?"

"In the context of maybe running my fingers through it, I do."

"Feel free." He certainly meant that. *Time to carefully consider your next words, Branson.* He studied the flames in the fireplace for a moment. "I don't think it's a secret I'd really like to spend the night making wild, passionate love with you, but that's entirely your call."

"Are you wild and passionate, Mr. Boardroom?"

"I was more thinking about *you* being that way. I've thought about it quite a lot. After making a spreadsheet detailing your personality traits and comparing them to mine, I've come to the conclusion that you are in the lead in those departments."

She almost spat out her sip of wine and swiped her mouth with the back of her hand, laughing. "Damn you, Branson, don't do that to me."

"Do what?" He put on his most innocent face, but he was laughing as well.

"We could be the most unlikely couple in the world."

"Maybe," he acknowledged. "But I never did like doing the predictable."

She set aside her wine. "I think your hair might be pretty messy in the morning."

What *was* she doing?

It could be foolish, but it didn't seem like that. Maybe

she'd regret it in the morning, but Raine really wanted to lie in his arms as the snow fell softly outside.

And tumble head over in heels in love.

Not too much to ask, right?

Maybe it had already happened.

She had to admit that Mick was deliciously male lounging on her couch, and she'd never before been tempted to stray over the line she'd drawn for herself.

Nothing casual.

No males who would love her and leave her. That was for her own well-being.

No long-distance relationships. They didn't work as far as she could tell.

No one who would break her daughter's heart if he decided to decamp. It wasn't like Daisy didn't have a grounded support system, but still she had parents who lived separate lives and introducing Mick into the mixture was a risk. Mick could be all of those things. A love-'em-and-leave-'em sort, a potential scoundrel, as her grandfather would have put it, but maybe something else also…

"Do you have the manuscript I gave you in your car?"

"Of course." He looked like Daisy had when Raine had asked about the infamous purse on the snowy ride. "Why?"

"I need to see it."

"Sure, fine, if you've changed your mind about giving it away—"

"No, I haven't changed my mind. I just need to look at it."

He seemed baffled but obligingly went out in the snow and a minute or two later returned with the box. Flakes of snow glistened on his hair and dusted his shoulders. He set the manuscript on the table. "It's still just coming down lightly and there isn't even a breath of wind but I get the feeling it's going to really snow. I think they'll enjoy their midnight excursion."

Daisy would love it. Her sense of adventure had made her a handful as a young child, but Raine had that same enthusiasm, so she could hardly fault her daughter for her eagerness to experience new things and maybe take a risk now and then. "I would bet on it. She's a pretty happy kid and Slater is a wonderful dad." She gestured to the box on the table. "Pick a page."

"What?"

"Just pick one at random out of the manuscript and hand it to me."

"Raine. Why?"

"Because I asked you to?"

"Fair enough." He shuffled through the manuscript. "Any page?"

"Yes. Just pick one."

He flipped through the manuscript, selected one and shrugged. "Here."

She stepped to him, plucked the page from his fingers and read the first line: *He kept his emotions close, like a beloved jacket, worn and well-used, the one he would wear out into a howling storm. He was not a man easy to read, yet she trusted him.*

So she should.

Raine handed back the page. "That was what I wanted to see."

"A random page?"

"It sure seems that way, doesn't it? Kiss me."

He'd fallen into a dream.

There was Raine, pressed against him, her mouth soft against his, warm arms around his neck and he couldn't be more enthusiastic about the idea. This wasn't like the brief kiss at the cabin either, or the more arousing one as he'd left the night before. It was hot, and he didn't need the encouragement.

At all.

What made her go from wary to passionate he wasn't sure, but he wasn't going to argue, either. She kissed him back with sensual promise and he didn't miss the signal.

He tightened his arm around her waist to bring her body more fully against his so he could feel every curve, every nuance. She did like vanilla. Her hair held a sweet scent of it, and was like fine silk under his fingers.

"Bedroom?" he murmured against her mouth when they both came up for air.

She whispered back, "I think that's the best idea you've had all day."

"You lead the way."

Her choice the whole time. This was what he wanted, hands down, but she needed to be on the same page.

She was. She ran her fingers through his hair. "Um, we do have one problem though. I'm not on birth control. I think I mentioned I'm kind of a hermit most of the time."

He traced the curve of her cheekbone with a finger and figured he might as well confess. "I have condoms. I'm not saying I thought this would be a sure thing, but I was hopeful anyway. Boardroom executives are master planners and always arrogantly anticipate the best outcome possible. I took two flights and endured a four-hour layover just because I was hoping for the kiss of a lifetime. I got it."

Oh, whoa, did I just say that?

"Of a lifetime? No pressure." Her eyes held a knowing look.

He was used to calling the shots, but she was definitely in charge. "Trust me, you didn't disappoint."

"Bedroom is this way."

He followed her. She could have been leading him off a cliff and he probably wouldn't have noticed anything besides the sway of her hips and her fluid stride.

As she walked in front of him, she took off that loose, less-than-sexy pajama top he found so inexplicably arousing, then tossed it down on the hallway floor. The graceful curve of her back almost did him in right then and there.

"Raine." It was said on a groan.

She glanced back. "Don't lag behind."

"Are you kidding? I'm following at warp speed."

Her laughter was warm and infectious, and he couldn't help but think that this was what life should be about. The joy of another person's presence, and definitely the magic of their laugh.

Raine's bedroom was a reflection of her personality, from the colorful artwork on the walls right down to the unusual black bedspread that was patterned with bright red poppies. The headboard looked antique, intricately carved, and he'd examine it later but right now that wasn't his focus at all.

Raine was shimmying out of her drawstring pants. "You seem kinda overdressed to me, Branson."

She was stunning with every stitch on, and naked…

he'd dream about that image. Long legs, firm breasts, a taut stomach…heaven.

His hands had forgotten how to follow brain signals. Mick fumbled with the buttons on his shirt and finally got enough undone to be able to strip it off, though he was fairly sure at least one button went rolling. Socks next, then pants, and by this time Raine had pulled back the exotic bedspread and her dark hair was spilled enticingly over the pillow.

He even surprised himself when he said, as he joined her on the bed, "This is what falling in love should be about."

She brushed his hair back. "You didn't just say that."

"I think I just did."

"I'm so not ready for your direct approach."

He nuzzled her throat. "You aren't ready for us, and I'm not either, but I'm ahead of the game as I've been thinking about my options for quite some time. I can pretend you haven't captured my interest like no woman I've ever met, but it doesn't work. The first time I saw you I was sixteen again and my locker was next to the one of the prettiest girl in school."

"Do you say that to all—"

He stopped her with gentle fingers on her lips. "Raine, you have it all wrong. There are really no 'all.' I'm not wired that way. I'm selective. I always have been. Sex should mean something intimate and special between two people. If you think differently then you're not the person I thought you are, and I'm usually a pretty good judge of character."

"You know the right things to say, don't you?"

"I'm just speaking from the heart. Really."

She bit his shoulder lightly. "Then seduce me right now or I'll haul off and slug you. I don't know what I want long-term, but I do want you right this red-hot second, so you'd better make a note of it."

"Slugging is legal in Wyoming?"

"Probably not, but we like to make our own rules out here."

"I believe I just watched a film about the Wild West, so I'm going to take your word for it, ma'am."

"Hold on a second." Her eyes were luminous. "I have something I want to do first."

Her fingers ran through his hair again. How that could push him toward the edge, he wasn't sure, but it certainly did, even though he knew she was just teasing him.

Two could play that game.

He started with her breasts, firm and luscious, her nipples already taut, and when he drew one rigid tip into his mouth she shivered and let out a small moan of pleasure. He explored the valley between them with his tongue, gave due attention to the other nipple, and kissed his way downward.

She liked that too and wasn't shy about expressing it.

He discovered she wasn't really shy about anything and that just tipped fuel right on the fire to create a skylight blast. The dance between them was natural and beautiful; when he moved, Raine did too, and the heat level started to scorch the roof.

Her climax involved a small scream and then it was his turn. He managed to remember the condoms he'd brought so carefully at zero hour, slipped one on, and then there was nothing but pleasure and deep satisfaction as he joined their bodies and sank deep inside her.

Mick had been waiting for her his entire adult life. There was no question. He knew it all the way down to his heart.

8

SHE WAS IN his arms, he was in her bed. Jangles had decided to join them at some point and was sleeping peacefully in a large furry ball at the foot, taking up a good deal of space. Outside the wind had begun to pick up; she could hear the whisper under the eaves.

Raine was physically content, no doubt about that, but emotionally she wasn't yet she'd made the right decision. Mick had lapsed into a deep sleep, and was breathing peacefully, his tanned chest quite the contrast to the stark-white sheets she preferred.

There was no way she considered her relationship with Slater a mistake because it had given her Daisy, but it had made her cautious about choosing future partners. This man was far more dangerous because he didn't live nearby, and she liked him too much. Maybe gifting the property to him hadn't been an act of altruism but a selfish move to get him to spend time in Wyoming.

This relationship was evolving too quickly for her comfort. Mick Branson was a wild card she hadn't seen in her hand. How to play that hand was the real question. Discard him? No, he didn't deserve that. Up the ante? That was a definite possibility.

He was intimidating in many ways, but she was used to men like that. All the Carson men were confident, forthright and driven, and she was around them often. Mick was more understated, but he got his way just as effectively, even if he used a memo and not a lasso.

There was more than one kind of cowboy in this world.

She looked at Jangles, who sensed her uncertainty and lifted his head. "What am I supposed to do?" she whispered.

He answered with a very obvious reply by lowering his head and closing his eyes: *Just go to sleep.*

Sage advice. She took it by relaxing next to Mick and nestling in closer.

Snow. Overnight? Nearly two feet of it. Mick had obviously rented the wrong type of car. He had to admit he wasn't used to shoveling snow in L.A., so the waist-high drift by his luxury car wasn't a very welcome surprise. He wasn't positive a big truck could handle it, either.

He accepted a cup of coffee—Raine informed him it was something called Snake River Chocolate Peppermint blend, but it tasted just like coffee to him so he was fine with it—and he settled into a chair in her homey kitchen and took a sip. "I could be snowed in for a bit."

"No way." She looked cozy in a long soft pink sweater and worn jeans, her eyes sparkling. "I have backup. I *want* you to see the cabin in the deep snow like this. We aren't staying put because of a little snow."

"A *little* snow?"

"Hey, it happens here now and then."

It definitely qualified as the classic winter wonderland outside. The tree in her backyard was like a giant white sculpture. "You're serious?"

"I am. If it doesn't move you to see the place after a fresh snowfall, you aren't the man I think you are."

"What kind of man do you think I am?"

She put both elbows solidly on the table. "I've already pointed out I trust you. If I didn't, last night wouldn't have happened."

It was easy to say softly, "Then I'm glad you do."

"Me, too."

That was the response he was hoping for, and damn if this Snake River Chocolate stuff wasn't pretty good.

He'd woken first and Raine had been half draped across him, deliciously nude and disheveled. The lion had been curled up at the foot of the bed and gave him the old stink-eye, but he interpreted approval there, so there had been a telling sense of contentment. Mick smiled lazily. "So, how do you propose we get out to a place that has no real driveway?"

"I have Alice for a reason."

"Do I even want to know who Alice is?"

"More like a what than a who. My snowmobile. It's very handy around these parts." She daintily sipped her peppermint coffee.

"You named it?" He was amused but not surprised. Raine would do something like that.

"Of course. We'll go look at the property in the daylight and then we can go pick up Daisy."

It wasn't his usual mode of travel but he wasn't without a sense of adventure. "I assume you know how to drive one, since I don't."

"I was practically born on one. I'm a December baby. My father took my mother to the hospital on a snowmobile. I can drive it in my sleep."

At least he was in good hands. "I bet she enjoyed that."

"I'm sure she enjoyed getting to the hospital, either way."

"There's a valid point."

"How would you know? You're male."

No way was he going to let her get away with that. "I have feelings, too. Male and childbirth translates to helpless in most cases to control the situation. We'd love to fix it, but we can't always, and it makes us crazy."

"You all are crazy anyway, and what would you know about childbirth?"

"I lost a child once." It was the truth, but he kept it as low key as possible. "That was tough. Like you and Slater, apparently we weren't meant to be together forever. She got pregnant then miscarried. Our relationship didn't weather the storm. The child certainly wasn't planned, but I'd gotten used to the idea of fatherhood, gone to a few appointments, even heard the heartbeat. The sense of loss was acute."

Her eyes were full of sympathy and she reached over to touch his hand. "I had no idea. I'm so sorry."

"I don't tell anyone. But you aren't just anyone. I thought maybe you should know."

Raine was predictably direct. "Is that why you asked me if I'd ever considered having more children?"

Was it?

He still wasn't sure why he'd asked that personal question out of the blue. He did what he did best and equivocated. "I asked because you and Daisy seem to have a wonderful relationship. I wouldn't mind a second cup of coffee, but I can get it for myself." He stood, cup in hand. "When's your birthday?"

She clearly knew he was deflecting, but went along with it. "The thirtieth."

He hadn't planned on staying that long, but maybe he should change his mind. "We need to do something special then."

"Like?" Her brows went up.

"Paris? Rome? How about Key West? We could watch the famous sunset over the ocean, and escape the snow. You choose."

No one should look so gorgeous in the morning, bed-head and all.

Mick could be stuck on the cover of a magazine in just his boxers and it would sell a million copies. She'd be the first one in line to buy an issue.

Raine waited until he returned with his coffee before she'd formulated her response. "Those are all nice options, but I can't just pick up and jet off with you, so right here would be better if you have the time."

She was touched.

In the head.

Don't fall in love with this man.

Too late.

"I can make the time." He leaned back and his smile

was boyish. "I certainly have it coming to me. And it doesn't hurt being my own boss, I suppose."

"I work harder than most people I know and I'm my own boss, too. I don't think I could make the time."

"Sweetheart, if you don't think I work hard, think again."

It wasn't like she didn't know he did. This was a pointless argument, and probably one she was instigating in order to distract herself from worrying thoughts of love and forever after. She smoothed her fingers across the fringe of the placemat. "I know for a fact you do. What I don't know is what you want from our…er…friendship." She'd searched for a word and settled on that one, though as soon as she said it she was fairly sure a kindergartener would have chosen something more sophisticated.

Apparently he agreed, his mouth curving in amusement. "I think after last night we're a bit more than friends, don't you? I'm not positive what you want either, so we'll have to figure it out together."

He'd done a lot better than she had in the words department.

Jangles strolled into the kitchen and made a familiar sound. It was something between a growl and a screech. Mick looked startled and slightly afraid for his life. "What was that? Is he sick?"

"He wants to be fed. He's very vocal about it and

emits that special noise so there's no misunderstanding. If it's any consolation, I wondered the same thing the first time I heard it. I assume, Mr. Boardroom, you can use a can opener? While you do the honors, I'll go get Alice. The food is in the pantry and the opener in that drawer right there." She pointed and got up. "I'd move fast if I were you. He can get cranky if it takes too long. I'm going to go put on my coat. When you're done, put on something warm and meet me out front."

"Cranky?"

"Very."

The smooth, urbane Mick Branson could get out of a chair and scramble across a room with impressive speed when faced with a large demanding cat. Jangles had his solid behind already on the floor by his bowl and his body language said he meant business. Raine was still laughing when she slipped into her favorite parka and went out back, wading through the snow.

The sleek snowmobile started sweetly. She'd gotten it from a friend of Blythe's whose husband had unexpectedly passed away, and much like her grandfather's property, the woman wasn't going to use it, but didn't want to sell his beloved possession. When Raine mentioned to Blythe that she was thinking of getting a sled—it was what her father had always called his snowmobile—suddenly she had one. The woman refused money for it, so Raine had done a graphic image of the vehicle and framed it as a gift.

She understood entirely not wanting to place monetary value on a possession so near and dear to someone you loved, but giving it to someone who would appreciate it was completely different.

Mick would appreciate the cabin property, especially on a day like this that Mother Nature had handcrafted to show it off. Brilliant blue skies, deep snow, and the mountains looked surreal, like something from a fairy tale. The skiers would be in seventh heaven, that was for sure. This was pure powder, the kind they lived for. Grace would be busy today, with the week between holidays and the resort always jammed full in this sort of weather.

When she pulled around, Mick was already on the sidewalk—probably to escape Jangles—and when she stopped he came down the steps and jumped on behind her. "Why do I think I'm going to need to hang on for dear life?"

"I like speed," she said. "Remember last night?"

He wrapped his arms around her waist and said exactly the right thing. "I'll never forget it. I trust you, so go for it."

She'd said the same thing. Trust was very important

to her. Then he swept back her hair and kissed the nape of her neck just as she hit the throttle.

He had good technique and timing, she'd give him that.

Excellent technique, she recalled, thinking again of last night. Her burning cheeks appreciated the cold bite of the air as they took off. They were clearing the streets now, but not with big plows, more ranchers with trucks and blades, and they blew past without effort and were hardly the only ones on a snowmobile. The minute they were out of town she hit the back trail. Of course her phone started to vibrate and she fished it out of her pocket and held it over her shoulder. "Mind answering this?"

Mick objected. "It's your phone."

"I don't have a lot of secrets and it could be my daughter. So please do it with my complete permission."

He did, though she couldn't really hear the conversation too well, but she had the feeling he'd just met her grandmother.

Clara was not a Slater Carson fan, which was much more a reflection of her old-fashioned values than the man himself, and Raine had patiently explained time and again that he'd offered marriage. The opinionated woman didn't like the fact they'd slept together before Raine had stood in a frothy white dress in front of an altar, wearing a lacy veil and flanked by six bridesmaids as a grave minister made her repeat vows.

The truth was, Raine hadn't ever really coveted that scenario. An image of Mick in a tux flashed into her mind and she quashed it as quickly as it appeared.

"Tell Gran I'll call later," she said over the sound of the engine.

A minute later he handed back the phone. "She said she liked the sound of my voice."

"She *did*?"

"What? I don't have a nice voice? She asked me to tell you Merry Christmas."

This wasn't the moment when she could go into a long convoluted explanation about how her grandmother formed opinions first and asked questions later. Instead she said, "Look at that view."

The soaring vista before them was incomparable, and just one of the many reasons she loved where she lived. The streets of Mustang Creek gave way to a county road as they breezed through, and within fifteen minutes they were gliding along toward her grandfather's property.

Trees; leafless now but he should see them in the spring, summer, and fall. Even now their branches were decorated with white, making them graceful and glistening. The background behind it all was beyond imagination. The Grand Tetons were very grand indeed after a snowfall like last night's.

His arms tightened briefly. "You're beautiful. The mountains look wonderful, too."

Well, he'd survived feeding Jangles and talking to her grandmother—sometimes a lesson in patience—so she'd skip pointing out that that was a tired line. The man was probably just plain frazzled. "Wait until we go around the curve."

They crested the hill where she'd put the lane to the property if it was her decision, even if it was a steep incline and there would be a curve. Although the snowmobile was loud, she had the satisfaction of hearing Mick catch his breath.

So he should. The unobstructed view of mountains, a frozen lake, and the quaint little cabin could have been straight out of one of her grandfather's books. She was fairly sure the chimney needed to be rebuilt and cleared, since birds considered it a wonderful place to nest and over time part of it had toppled over, but it was definitely picturesque.

If Mr. Boardroom had ever wanted to be a cowboy, he could fulfill that dream right here.

"Raine."

"I know, right?"

"You could get a million dollars for this."

"I don't need a million dollars. I need someone who will keep it intact and let my daughter come visit. I need someone who won't develop it, won't tear down the old corral and won't destroy the cabin." She stopped the sled in a flurry of disrupted snow. "Call me crazy, but I think that person could be you."

9

—◆——————◆—

THE VIEW FROM the Carson ranch was spectacular.

This view might very well be better, if that was possible.

Mick had to admit he was wowed. Yes, the cabin was beyond quaint with its sagging porch and drooping, snow-laden roof, like a framed picture of a holiday card you might pick up at a boutique and mail to your friends, but the lake and the mountains took his breath away.

Stately firs stood in stands sprinkled with the aspens that had no doubt inspired Matthew Brighton's manuscript, and there was no one around for literally miles.

And miles.

Taking in the spectacular scenery, sensing the peace that came from such solitude, Mick knew Raine was right about this place being perfect for him. He'd been thinking for a long time about a change in venue to Wyoming, and certainly Slater's documentary influenced him, but he'd never quite envisioned anything quite like this. He could build the house of his dreams right here. They got off the snowmobile and stood knee-deep in drifts and he inhaled the quiet.

"Thoughts?" Raine read his expression perfectly. It was there in her eyes.

"I'm afraid that you already know what they are."

"Does it get any better than this?"

"I'm doubting it."

"You accept my terms then?"

He huffed out a breath. "Raine, you essentially have no terms. I'd walk over thin ice to save Daisy with or without the property, and your grandfather is a hero of mine. I'll leave the cabin as it is, of course, if you're serious about this."

"That will be all you need to do then."

"Why is it I think arguing with you is just a lesson in futility, but let me try one more time. This is exactly what I've been thinking about and then some, but let me have an appraiser put a fair price on it and—"

"No." She shook her head vehemently. "It's cathartic, giving it to you. Here, let me show you where I'd put a house."

They waded through the snow for a few hundred yards and then she pointed. "There."

The spot was idyllic to say the least, with a stream that was partially frozen right next to it, groves of trees, and a level area with a view that would support a house the size he was considering. A big one. Wraparound porch, a hot tub in the back, second level deck, and maybe three guest suites. He wanted to invite his family, but also use it for business purposes, and inside he wanted the real deal. Log detail, soaring ceilings, stacked fireplace, ultimate bathrooms...

"I agree it's perfect." He wanted to invite her to live with him and that was telling of itself. But he wasn't necessarily there yet, and his spidey senses said she wasn't either, so he left it alone.

"I assume you won't go modest, so this would be perfect." Raine nodded, her cheeks rosy from the cold.

It would be. "Lots of space...yes."

Only perfect if you choose to share it.

Dangerous thinking for a confirmed bachelor, but the image was still in his mind. "You have artistic vision, so maybe you could help me design the house."

That brought her head around. "I did study architecture in college. Just a few classes though. Are you serious?"

"Unfortunately, make a note. I'm always serious."

That was true. He could kid around, but didn't do it often or spontaneously.

Raine considered him thoughtfully. "If I have artistic vision, you have an artistic soul. Otherwise you wouldn't catch on to what Slater wants to do so easily. I would love to help design your house here. It's a dream come true for me. You'll still need an architect, but we could at least draw up the idea of what you have in mind."

We have in mind.

He wanted nothing more. "Let's do it together. That aside, this is my night. Let me cook for you. I'll have to borrow your kitchen, of course. I asked Harry if Daisy would eat lobster mac and cheese. She seemed to think that would go over very well."

Of course she argued. "Lobster? You can't get lobster in Wyoming in December. Last I checked they don't abound around these parts. The local grocery certainly doesn't have them."

"I haven't been in there but I'll take your word for it. On the other hand, you can get it if you know the right people." He tried to not sound smug and failed.

She pounced on it. "Grace."

"Not Grace so much as her chef."

"Stephano? He's making it... Well then, I'm in."

Such confidence. She was right, of course, Stephano adored Daisy so he'd been right on board when Mick had called. He said with mock indignation, "First you doubt the quality of my voice, and now this. How do you know I can't cook?"

Raine gave him a gamine grin. "I know *he* can. You haven't proven yourself."

Mick just gave it up with a laugh. "I can't cook usually but I spent a week in Maine when I was in college, hiking Acadia National Park. One of the rangers recommended this little restaurant and I had lobster mac there for the first time. The owner gave me the recipe when I ordered a second helping and she learned I lived in this godforsaken place called California. She felt sorry for any young man that didn't live in Maine. The recipe is apparently an old family favorite."

"My daughter loves lobster *and* she loves mac and cheese. Daisy will be thrilled."

"Can we pretend it isn't the only dish I can make?"

"Um, if you think you can fool her, think again, but go ahead and try. She's a smart cookie. That kid figured out the Easter Bunny, Santa Claus and the Tooth Fairy way before any of her friends. I'm proud to say she let them go on believing but she sure was on to me. When asked flat out, I cannot tell a lie."

"Good to know." He said it lightly, but didn't mean it lightly. Honesty was important to him. He kissed her cool cheek. "I mean that."

"I take it we need to stop off at the resort before we

pick up Daisy. The road crews will have been out by now."

"We do." He said it with a straight face. "A lobster waits for no one."

Raine burst out laughing and picked up a handful of snow and tossed it at him. "Okay, now you *do* win for the worst line ever."

He reached down and retaliated. "If you want a snowball fight, I'm in."

"In that case, I should probably warn you I'm vicious."

"I have good aim."

Raine pelted him with another snowball. "Good luck, cowboy. I was born in snow country."

He needed luck. She was pretty accurate as well. After the third one caught him right in the chest he surrendered, arms in the air. "Mercy."

Of course she pelted him again.

He tackled her and the resulting kiss made him forget about the cold even though they were both lying in the snow.

"I'm falling in love with you." He definitely hadn't meant to admit that, but it was true and she already knew it.

"If you haven't figured out we have the same problem, then you aren't paying attention." Raine looked reflective lying beneath him. "We're both idiots."

"I don't think I am."

"I don't think I am, either." Her eyes were suddenly shiny. "But I've been wrong before."

"Raine, do you really think Slater was a mistake?"

She sat up and shook snow out of her dark hair. "No, of course not. I wouldn't have Daisy if it wasn't for him, and I'll always care about him. It's just that I keep hoping to find gold in a muddy river bed, but I haven't had a strike yet."

He probably had snow in his hair as well but didn't care. "You sure about that? I'm going to finish that manuscript, by the way. I don't know if I can do it justice, but maybe *I'll* get a strike."

She kissed him then, snowy mittens on his cheeks but her mouth was warm and giving. "I'm so glad."

"I won't know what I'm doing."

"You'll do great. I feel it."

"I'll trust you to tell me if it's terrible."

"Oh, don't you think you'd be the first to know?" Raine gave him a merry glance before getting to her feet. "I'm not shy with my opinions in case you haven't noticed. I believe *blatantly outspoken* is the Carsons' preferred term for me. I have bad news for you, though. Their head ranch hand, Red, is a die-hard Matthew Brighton fan. It's his opinion you really need to worry about, because he won't pull his punches if you can't tell a snake hole from the Grand Canyon."

"Great. Well, I guess I know who my expert consultant will be if I need help with research." Mick got up also and tried to brush off his jeans. "I'm probably nuts even to try this, but I do like a challenge."

The look she gave him was only half-teasing. "Is that why you fell for me? Because I'm a challenge?"

"Maybe it started that way," he admitted, catching her hand as they made their way back to the snowmobile. "You do keep me on my toes. But if you haven't figured out that I'm crazy about everything that makes you you, then you're the one who's not paying attention."

"Likewise, cowboy." She started the snowmobile again. "Climb on board. Isn't there a lobster with your name on it?"

Cream, cheese, pasta, garlic…there was no way to go wrong with a meal like that, so Mick was cheating. He did let Raine do the salad and got the bread from the restaurant, but otherwise he prepared everything himself. And if the purse he'd given Daisy had won her over, the dinner he served them made her his devoted fan for life.

That was so important to her, Raine thought as she watched her daughter interact so naturally with Mick. Daisy's face was animated as she described the midnight ride in the snow, and she'd definitely cleaned her plate so his dinner choice had been about as popular as Harry's cooking, which was saying something.

Clever man.

"Remind me to kiss Stephano next time I see him," Raine declared during a lull in the excited conversation. "That lobster was the perfect touch."

"How about you kiss the actual cook, not just the ingredient-supplier?" Mick gave her a look of mock reproof. "Besides, I'm way better looking than he is."

"Maybe a tinge." Raine gave him a dreamy smile. "But he has that Latin air, you know?"

Daisy joined her mother in giggling at the expression on Mick's face. Raine knew she was taking it all in—their unexpected guest, the overt affection between them. What Raine wanted her daughter to walk away with from tonight was a sense that love was supposed to be fun. It wasn't supposed to be easy all of the time, but fun was very important.

Mick threw up his hands. "In that case, how's an ordinary guy supposed to compete?"

She shouldn't say it so softly, but she did anyway. "Oh you aren't ordinary by any means."

"No?"

"No."

Enough said. Daisy was clearly paying attention to the nuances of the conversation, listening avidly. The good news was that purse aside, she seemed to really like Mick. That hadn't been the case last time she'd introduced her daughter to a man she'd briefly been dating, a doctor from a nearby town. Daisy had instantly pronounced him boring and that put an end to that. She might not have known him long enough to give him a fair shot, but Raine trusted her daughter's instincts. Besides that, any man who was a part of her life would be part of her daughter's as well. Her opinion counted.

Daisy jumped up. "Who wants ice cream? I'll get it." She began to eagerly stack the plates. They had an agreement. Raine cooked and cleaned up the kitchen, but Daisy cleared the table.

"Her grandmother is Blythe Carson," Raine confided. "According to Blythe, ice cream is an essential food group all by itself. Beware."

Mick lifted a brow. "Beware? I love ice cream."

"Good. Get ready to prove it."

He ended up with brownie fudge with cherries and marshmallow topping in a massive bowl, not to mention various kinds of sprinkles in rainbow colors. Before he dug in he muttered, "Beware. Now I get it. I'll have to go to the gym fifteen times to work this off."

"I'll go with you." Her bowl was half the size.

"You can go with me anywhere."

There was that smooth Hollywood charm again. She scooped up marshmallow and cherry on her spoon. "You see, our problem is I'm *not* going anywhere. I can't. That's why I want to contact my Realtor's office the minute it's open, yank the cabin property off the market, and tell them to set up a closing."

"Cabin? You mean Grandpa's house?" Daisy had seemed to be focused on her own heaping spoonful, but Raine knew she was listening to their every word.

"That's right. I'm giving it to Mick."

"That's a pretty good idea."

Raine smiled. "Mick is a writer. He'll love it there."

That was a full-out dare. Daisy actually stopped eating ice cream, and that was something. Her eyes were wide. "You are? Like him?"

He blinked. "No." Then relented. "Well, I'm afraid I'm nowhere near as talented as your great-grandfather, but I've tried a time or two."

"He's been published in literary magazines." Raine couldn't resist imparting that information and ignored the quelling look from the man across the table. "And he's read the Matthew Brighton books."

"Have you really?" Daisy grinned, obviously delighted. "My favorite is *Mountain Sunrise*."

"I liked that one, too." Mick acted nonchalant, but Raine sensed his passion for finishing the manuscript. No matter how it turned out, she was glad to have played a small role in encouraging him to explore the creative side he didn't often get to give free rein to.

Raine got up. "I'm going to go clean the kitchen. I truly can't eat another bite. I might need to go for a walk but someone should probably carry me."

Daisy pointed out, "Then it wouldn't be a walk."

"I'll help you clean up since I made the mess, and then I'll take you on that walk." Mick rose as well. "Beautiful moon out there."

Raine probably should have predicted the total chaos that ensued when Mick took a step toward the kitchen.

Jangles did a daring guerilla move and went for his ankles, but now Samson was back in residence and wanted part of the action. Raine was almost swept off her feet— not in the romantic sense—as a giant puppy chased a giant cat and both of them nearly took her out, the cat dodging right in front of her and the dog accidentally slamming into the back of her legs. Mick managed to keep his balance during the mayhem and caught her shoulders, steadying her at the last second as the animals dashed past.

"Such a peaceful household," she said darkly. "Bunch of wild critters that don't realize if they break your leg you can't get to the grocery store to buy them more food."

They went by again at full speed, careening into walls and not caring, playing a classic game of circling the house. It was endearingly funny, but she made sure her computer wasn't plugged in when they really got going because Samson could easily catch that cord. One day he might not be so clumsy, but for now she was taking precautions.

"I like it," Mick said and kissed her swiftly out of Daisy's sightline. "Full of life. I'm starting to think my house in California is entirely too quiet."

"Then move here. I promise no peace and quiet at all."

She was really losing it if she'd just said that. So she just blundered on. "You can't live in the cabin while the house is being built."

"Sure I could. I've also read Walden."

"You wear Italian shoes."

"So? Stop harping on my shoes and focus on the man." He caught her playfully around the waist. "But invitation accepted. Where would I sleep? With you?"

"I'm thinking that might be the case." She went serious because she might as well make her position clear. "But only on the nights when Daisy is at the ranch. I'm not so naive as to think she hasn't cottoned on to the fact that there's something going between us, but I also know

Slater and Grace kept their feelings for each other off her radar until they understood where they were headed, and I appreciated that. Daisy likes you, and so do I—"

"Glad to hear it." He was busy nuzzling her neck. "I can always stay at the cabin."

"Don't you have business on the West Coast?"

"That's the beauty of modern technology. I can work from anywhere, to a certain extent." He kissed her again.

"No plumbing." She whispered it against his mouth, not quite sure why she was trying to warn him off when she so badly wanted him to stay.

"Versus no you? That's hardly a contest."

"I have to think of my daughter."

"I will always think of her, too, I promise. And then there's the other females in our lives to think of. We'll have to handle my mother and your grandmother, Blythe, Harry, and the rest of the bunch."

"The interferers. Grace, Luce and Kelly will be just as bad."

"Exactly."

She couldn't help but laugh at his grim expression. "They'll be fine. They interfere, but mean well."

"Women just don't operate like men."

"Do you think?"

His grin was instant. "Think? Your presence seems to impair the process. No offense intended."

"None taken." She disengaged from his embrace. "If you can rinse dishes and hand them to me while I load the dishwasher, I'll be yours for life."

"Hey, I thought I was the one that made the deals. Don't try and show me up." He picked up a plate and flipped the lever on the faucet. "Obviously I accept your terms. We can negotiate the details."

10

THE SKIERS WERE out in full force and Mick sat in a comfortable chair and watched out the window of his room as they careened down the slopes while he sipped a cup of coffee. It was clear and brilliant outside and he was in a reflective mood, watching the sunlight bounce off the sparkling snow.

I'll be yours for life.

Now that was a thought.

She'd probably meant it in a different way than he took it, joking, not serious at all, but it had certainly struck a nerve.

He sat there and seriously considered marriage for the first time in his life.

That word had always scared him. It wasn't the permanence of it, since half the people he knew were divorced—it was the emotional investment. Yet the true problem was that he was convinced it scared Raine even more. She'd opted out once already. Slater was a great guy but she'd given him a firm no when he proposed, and changing her mind was going to take more than the two of them enjoying a night in bed together.

So he really considered it over a second cup of coffee, and then called his brother. Ran answered pretty swiftly but he lived by his phone, even at this time of the year. Mick said, "Hi. How's London?"

"Covered in white. Snowed last night. How's Wyoming?"

"Ditto."

"An ocean away and the same story. It must be Christmas. So what's up?"

"I think I need a ring and Ingrid is no slouch in that department. Could you ask her to pick one out? I'll write you a check when you're back in the States, or I can send you the money now. We can get it sized here."

His brother's wife had been a jewelry store buyer before the two of them got married and remained a consummate gem shopper. They kept her jewelry in a safe.

"What kind of ring?"

"Engagement."

"Are you joking around?" Ran sounded stunned. "*You're* proposing to someone?"

"I'm going to give it a try. And if she says yes, moving

to Wyoming full-time. I do half my business by phone or email, not to mention I have to fly from Los Angeles all the time anyway for meetings. I can do that from here."

"You'd *live* in Wyoming?"

He chuckled at his brother's horrified tone. "I realize Mustang Creek doesn't have a ballet company or symphony orchestra, but the scenery alone makes up for that, and yes, I'd live here because she's here and isn't going anywhere and I wouldn't ask it of her. I like it here anyway, you know that."

"I know you keep going back and now I finally understand why."

He thought about Bad Billy's Burger Palace and Harry's cooking, not to mention the resort. "Lots of good food choices, great schools, all the peace and quiet a man could want, and I doubt the sunsets could be beat by any place on earth. No shortage of beautiful women, either." Grace, Luce, and Kelly certainly qualified, as did the wives of Slater's friends he'd met. Not that he had eyes for anyone but Raine. "And I'm talking the type that don't need a salon and expensive make-up artist to make it happen."

His brother wasn't without a sense of humor. "I might just visit then, to check out the scenery."

"You'll be welcome anytime. Tell Ingrid that Raine would probably like something different for the ring. She's an artist. I don't think she'd go for a two-carat marquis. She might turn me down on that one. Something really eclectic would work. Tell Ingrid I implicitly trust her and Raine has hazel eyes and dark hair."

Randal Branson had never been all that imaginative. "The color of her hair and eyes matters…why?"

"I have no idea, but I figure it doesn't hurt to arm Ingrid with enough information to find the perfect ring. Tell her to make it unusual, one of a kind even. Just like Raine."

"I thought the romantic ideal was the man should pick out the ring."

He wasn't easily fooled. "Who picked out Ingrid's? I've seen it. It's tasteful, so don't try to claim it was you."

"Okay, you got me. She chose it herself and I was happy to let her."

"I rest my case," Mick said. "You'll bring the ring back from London?"

"Ingrid has a lot of associates here. I think she'll enjoy shopping for it and be really picky about the stone and setting. I've seen her in action. We fly back tomorrow and she wants to do some last-minute shopping so we were going out anyway. We're invited to the Austins' famous annual New Year's party."

Mick had been, too, but he was spending the holiday right where he was. Those glitzy affairs had lost their gloss even before he'd become so involved with Raine.

"I was thinking New Year's Eve is the perfect night to propose."

"Not waiting around."

"I thought you'd just intimated I'd waited around too much in my life already."

"I'm just happy for you." Ran sounded sincere. "Ingrid will find you the perfect ring and I'll have it insured and overnighted."

"That's all I could ask for. Tell Ingrid thanks in advance from me."

They ended the call and he settled back, amazingly content with his decision. He was used to such a fast-paced life he found he liked just sitting there and watching the ski runs. It was interesting to take time to contemplate the life-changing curve in the road of his future.

He'd have an instant daughter if Raine said yes. Maybe more children; a subject they would need to discuss later.

If she said yes.

It would certainly affect the plans for the house he was going to build.

If she said yes.

It was going to completely change his life.

If she said yes.

Not a given.

Suddenly restless, he got up to pace the length of the room. He'd always considered himself more a man of controlled contemplation than action, but right now he needed to walk off this unexpected insecurity. It was probably a good sign it meant so much to him, but he wasn't enjoying the myriad emotions. He was nervous, a concept that was foreign to him. Usually, when awaiting the outcome of a deal he'd negotiated, he was confident and straightforward, and if it fell through—which happened now and then for various reasons—so it went.

He couldn't shrug this off if Raine decided he wasn't the one.

The break-up after the miscarriage had been painful, but they would probably have only stayed together for the baby, so that was something else he and Raine had in common. Like Slater, he would have offered marriage, but if his ex-girlfriend had said yes, he wasn't sure at all it would have lasted. The experience did teach him something about himself and that was that he was much more traditional than he thought, but it also made him realize he valued relationships in a long-term way.

Double-whammy right there.

He wanted a wife, family, and roots.

Speaking of roots…if he was going to make good on his promise, he might as well get started on reading *The Aspen Trail*. What better way to spend a snowy morning, especially since he knew Raine was working, though she'd agreed to lunch. She'd already had plans to meet with friends for dinner. They sponsored a college scholarship at the local high school and between them formed a committee each year to review the applications and select a recipient. The Carson Ranch matched their contributions and people from all over the state applied for it, and Raine had said with a definite tinge of emotion in her voice that it was wonderful to support higher education. He agreed. Already it had occurred to him to maybe set up a college fund for Daisy in her grandfather's name to offset the property gift.

So he sat back down, told himself to forget everything else for the moment, and he started to read.

Chapter One

The haze of the sun hit the leaves in a slanted light and cast shadows on the ground. The cowboy nudged his horse forward with his heel, the silent communication as natural as words between them. They understood each other without effort.

The cowboy wished it was half that easy with women.

His sweetheart was an independent sort with

a mind of her own, and had little use for him unless she was so inclined.

He needed to win the lady but wasn't sure how
to go about it.

Mick laughed quietly and sat back, his feet propped
up. That seemed all too appropriate to his current situation. He'd won his way into Raine's bed, but he wasn't
sure about her heart.

That dark-haired beauty didn't want his help,
hadn't asked for it, and was as dangerous as a
loaded pistol ready to go off. Part of him admired
her feisty spirit, but a bigger part wished she'd
agree to lean on him just a little more. Maybe his
days as a drifter were coming to an end, because he
wasn't going anywhere. This valley felt like home
and whether she admitted it or not, she needed
someone like him around.

There was a reason for the price on his head in
Arkansas. He was damned handy with a gun. A
man needed to be able to defend himself, and others if it came right down to it. Maybe someday he'd
even tell her that story. But now there was trouble
coming. He could smell it in the air and hear it in
the whisper of the aspen leaves.

Could he write in a voice like Brighton's, one that was all the more powerful for its simplicity? Mick wasn't sure, but he *was* sure he was interested to find out what trouble was coming and how it worked out with the dark-haired beauty and the cowboy. What was the danger?

He was taking mental notes.

So he read on.

"We need more details."

Hadleigh Galloway, Melody Hogan and Bex Calder all stared her down. They'd known each other since childhood, and the tight-knit threesome were the first people Raine had thought of when she'd come up with the idea of the scholarship. All successful businesswomen and mothers, they'd done what she hoped and, despite their busy schedules, embraced the idea. Bex's wealthy in-laws had handed over a large sum of money as well.

It was no longer just one scholarship, they'd decided over appetizers and then an array of salads varying from shrimp to garlic chicken. They could now safely give out five from the current endowment. They had their usual table at Bad Billy's and the place was hopping due to the influx of skiers. The old jukebox was getting a definite workout, with an emphasis on Patsy Cline and Willie Nelson.

"Details?" Raine tried to look like she didn't under-stand the demand. "Of what?"

"Nice try," Hadleigh said after a sip of iced tea. "Let's talk you and Mick Branson. Don't ask how we know, because of course we do."

Drake was probably to blame, since he played poker with Tripp Galloway and Spence Hogan once a week, and he regularly bought horses from Tate Calder, so all their husbands were probably a font of information.

"I'm not sure what you want to know. He's…nice." Raine took another shrimp and popped it in her mouth to avoid the conversation. Billy's poppyseed dressing was so good it should probably be illegal.

Melody wasn't letting her off the hook. "In the looks department, I agree. Better than nice. Let's upgrade it to deliciously handsome. And there's no doubt he's suc-cessful. He seems to be spending a lot of time here in Bliss County all of a sudden. He spent Christmas Eve at your house and I'm guessing there was mistletoe in-volved. What's up?"

"He just came so he could see Slater's movie with the family as a surprise Christmas gift."

"I watched it, of course. It was fabulous. But nope." Bex shook her head. "A phone call at the right moment could have done the trick. Speculation has it he came here to see *you*. I have it on good authority."

"Whose?"

"Blythe's, via my mother-in-law. The networking around here is incredible."

Lettie Arbuckle-Calder *was* connected. "Like I don't know that," Raine muttered.

"I'd say he's not your type, but maybe I'm wrong." Melody, a jewelry artist, spoke thoughtfully. "I've met him and he has a soulful aura."

Hadleigh snorted. "You should have been a hippie, you know that? A soulful aura?"

Melody wasn't one to take anything from Hadleigh without arguing, even if they were fast friends. "Hippie, huh? Let's talk about someone who makes quilts for a living. There's hippie for you. I think you're the only person I know with an incense burner."

"That's an air freshener."

Bex said mildly to Raine under her breath, "I'll put a stop to this. Been doing it for years now. Otherwise it could go on for an hour." Loudly, she interrupted, "I think we were talking about Mick Branson, right? Tell us about him."

Too bad putting a stop to the bickering meant shining the spotlight back on Raine. "He's creative and imaginative, once you see beneath that corporate businessman image. Yes, he raises money for Slater's films, but that's because he sees the vision."

"Or the money." That was Bex, so practical.

"Nope. To see his face when the documentary came on at prime time on a day that isn't easy to secure was priceless. Mick did it for all of us. I'd say he moved heaven and earth to make it happen."

"You're in love with him." Hadleigh looked delighted. "I can see it."

"You can't see love," Raine argued, sidestepping an actual answer. She'd only just begun to admit her feelings to herself and to Mick. She wasn't quite ready to share them with others yet, not even friends.

"Yes, she can," Melody disagreed, jumping right into Hadleigh camp. "She has a special magic."

"She can. She's a wizard." Bex pointed a finger at her friend. "She's got a potion or something she takes."

"I do not," Hadleigh protested despite her grin. "There's no simmering pot, no incantations."

"Wizard." They said it accusingly in unison.

"I'm empathic and gifted with insight," she corrected loftily, then turned to Raine. "Do we have wedding plans yet?"

"No!"

"We will soon," the wizard decreed. "The resort will be perfect as a venue. Elegant enough for out-of-town guests, but convenient for everyone else. Blythe wouldn't dream of anyone else doing the bridal shower but her."

"He hasn't asked me." Raine had to point it out.

"What would you say?" That was Bex.

"It doesn't matter, he won't ask. If he wanted to get married, he would have by now."

The three of them looked at each other, and then burst out laughing. Melody was the one who said, "Honey, take it from three married women, it doesn't work that way. They only cave when they find the right woman."

"And once they do, they're pretty wonderful," Hadleigh informed her in a theatrical whisper. "Don't tell Tripp I said that because I'll deny it. Those cocky pilot types are full enough of themselves already."

"I agree." Bex's husband had also been a pilot before he decided to become a horse breeder. "And they're wonderful, only if given some instruction," she explained with a cheeky smile. "They need guidance."

Raine needed to rein in all this speculation. "Mick's well beyond the time in his life when he's going to ask without careful consideration, and he certainly would not ask *me*. I come with a daughter, a giant cat and a big blundering dog. Most of the time I live in faded jeans that are genuinely faded from being washed like a million times, and a handful of T-shirts. I decided when I was about twenty that high heels were overrated and haven't looked back. Besides, I live here and he lives somewhere very different. I will never be glamourous and I don't apologize for it, but he could get glamour-ous if he wanted it."

"Do you think that's the type of woman he wants?" Hadleigh considered her carefully. "It doesn't seem to me it is. He could have had that at any time. He's dated actresses, debutantes, and if I remember correctly, a very famous professional female athlete."

Raine weighed her words. "He's fallen in love with Wyoming."

"Or you."

Bex added, "Or both."

She wasn't convinced yet, despite his earlier declaration. "Maybe. I could be a passing fad, like when we were in high school and decided blue mascara was the way to go. That didn't last too long."

He'd said it though. *I'm falling in love with you.*

Her artistic bent seemed to fascinate him, and his desire to write did the same for her. Mick Branson had layers, and she needed that. He wasn't just Mr. Boardroom, he was also polite and thoughtful. That he'd wanted to make dinner for both her and Daisy was a winning strategy, that was for sure. He'd earned some definite points there.

She added, "He did fix me dinner."

All three of her companions glanced at each other and said in unison, "We know."

Of course they did.

Melody commented, "He's a goner. Ask the wizard."

"Goner," Hadleigh confirmed sagely, and Raine smiled, shook her head and gave up.

11

MICK READ THE entire manuscript in one day. Other than an extremely quick lunch with Raine that had ended with a brief and unsatisfying goodbye peck on the cheek because she was in a hurry and they were in a public place, he'd spent the rest of the time reading in his room. Dinner was room service, eaten almost absently as he read.

It was an indulgence for him and the unfinished work was fantastic.

No pressure.

It brought him back to his childhood when he'd read those first Matthew Brighton books. Being reminded of his father was welcome when he was now committed to changing his life.

Loyalty. Fidelity. Integrity.

He'd absorbed those lessons without need of a lecture.

He'd bet most people thought his parents were frivolous due to their wealth, but they absolutely were not. His father had been demonstratively diligent as a family man, and as a businessman. Both he and Ran had learned a lot from him. Their father wasn't successful because it came naturally, it was because he worked at it, and his example had stuck.

Don't ever screw someone over and think that's okay.

They didn't.

When it goes south, regroup and think about how to fix it. It might seem like the end of the world, but it isn't.

Deal with hard guidelines but make them fair. No one loses that way.

Take time every single day to make sure you appreciate what you have. Ambition is fine, but avarice is not.

Raine was 100 percent on that one. It was clear she liked her life. Mick liked his, too, but recognized that the missing elements had nothing to do with money and everything to do with taking more time to simply enjoy himself. He didn't like busy airports and congested freeways yet had to put up with both on an almost daily basis and both of his houses were nice by any standard and luxurious by most, but a waste since he didn't use even half the space.

It was time to just sell them and move on. He realized now he'd been thinking about it for some time, even before his keen interest in this part of Wyoming had arisen. Maybe ever since he'd picked up his first Matthew Brighton novel and sat down to read.

His father would no doubt approve.

The last paragraph of the manuscript was: *He was a man of action and it wasn't in his nature to sit idly by and just let things happen. They happened on his terms and that was that.*

Mick dealt with talented people on a constant basis. That was his job, to win sponsors, to create backing for plays and films like the ones Slater did so well, to decide what was innovative and new, and what wasn't going to go over with a large viewing audience.

Now the tables had turned and he was the one sitting there on the creative edge…

Tentatively he opened a document on his computer and began to type. He was daunted, yes, but it was out of the question to not at least give it a try. Two hours later he had some words down and wasn't displeased with the result—not that he was impressed with himself, but it had come far easier than he imagined.

He sent Raine an email. Mission Aspen Trail conclusion has begun.

It was now after midnight, and of course she typed right back immediately. You've been busy.

How was the meeting?

It was good. We're all pleased with the number of applicants.
The scholarship is evolving into more than we imagined.
There are a lot of good students out there who deserve the
chance to make their dreams come true.

A very Raine sort of sentiment. The woman who
preferred to give away an expensive piece of property.

Good cause, he typed back. I'll help, of course. You
should get my mother involved.

Had he really just said that, in writing, no less?

Instantly he recanted. He loved his mother but she
had a tendency to take charge and definite ideas on how
things should be done. *Or maybe not. She might take over.*

We were talking about how we need someone to maybe run
a foundation. Do you think she would?

Oh, I think you'd maybe raise a monster from the depths,
but if you want meticulous management, she's your woman.
That was honest.

Monster or not, she could be just what we need.

I can obviously get you in touch with her. Can we have dinner tomorrow?

We can but I have something else in mind. Call me in the morning.

Like?

Just call. And sweet dreams.

She didn't write anything further.

If he knew Raine she'd gone right back to work. He did the same, not returning to the manuscript but instead answering emails and checking his messages since he'd basically taken the day off. No news, no stock market updates, none of his usual routine, just moonlight on the snow and a sense of personal well-being.

He had no illusions that this was all going to be simple. Making a major change never was an easy process, but if he trusted his instincts at all, he had to accept that it was time.

Occasionally she got some pretty harebrained ideas.

Raine had to admit this could be one of them. She strapped the toboggan to the top of her SUV and Daisy clapped, her eyes shining. She was going to be taller than her mother, Raine had already figured out, taking more after Slater in that regard, and had that coltish lack of grace that would change as she matured. In any case, she was young enough to still think sledding was big fun, and maybe Raine was too, since she agreed. Samson seemed just as excited, romping through the snow.

Some kids never grew up.

Some grown-ups—namely her—just wanted to see Mick Branson rocket down a wicked hill on a toboggan. She could probably sell pictures of that. She knew the steep hill, and since she doubted he had a proper coat for this experience, had asked Slater if she could borrow one. They were very close to the same build. Of course the answer had been an amused yes once she explained why she was asking. He even said he'd love to film it, but his crew was all off on Christmas break.

"That's what my phone is for," she'd assured him. She could catch a short video of the urbane Mr. Branson careening down the slope if he had the fortitude to accept the challenge.

She somehow thought he would. So far he'd proven to be unshakable, even in the face of the entire Carson family, Jangles and his sneak attacks, talking to her grandmother, whipping up a dinner extraordinaire...

She'd see if those nerves of steel held up.

Red called it Dead Man's Hill and it was certainly a

wild ride. He was the first person to point her in that direction with the admonishment it was not for the faint of heart. He was right. But the snow was perfect and it wouldn't be winter if she didn't at least go down that hill once a week, and Daisy loved it. Mick could decline if he wanted, but she had a feeling he would be game.

Raine doubted anything tripped him up, but she had to admit she was eager to see the look on his face when he first saw that slope. If a person didn't have a moment of doubt, then they just weren't sensible. What they decided after they stared down that 45 degree angle and thought it was maybe a bad decision but looked like it might be really fun, well, that was up to them.

Red had wisely counseled that if you didn't panic like a sheep that had eaten loco weed then you would be fine. Raine was uncertain how a sheep that had ingested that plant did act, but it sounded like solid advice to just enjoy the experience.

Mick pulled up, right on time as usual, and got out of his fancy rental, eyeing the contraptions strapped to the top of her car. "You've been out sledding?"

"No. Not yet."

"I'm beginning to see the light. This is why you told me to wear jeans."

"Yep," she responded cheerfully. "Hop in. I have the right kind of coat for you and Mace offered up a spare pair of snow boots since some hiking is involved. The good news for you is you get to carry the big toboggan. Don't worry, I have a thermos of hot cocoa."

"It had better have some whiskey in it," he said darkly, but gamely climbed in the passenger side on the car.

She jumped in and started the vehicle. "Has Mr. Boardroom ever been sledding?"

"Maybe when I was about thirty years younger. Are you sure my feeble body can take this?" He buckled his seat belt.

She eyed his muscular frame and broad shoulders with true appreciation. "I think you'll survive."

"I guess I have no choice but to find out. I'm being… what's the expression out here in the wilds? Railroaded?"

"That's the one." She pulled out onto the street, which was clearing nicely after being plowed. The abundant sunshine helped, too, even though the temps were still below freezing.

Samson woofed from his spot next to Daisy in the back seat. "We're bringing the *dog*?"

"He loves it. I think he can ride down the slopes with you. At the bottom you get a special bonus since he always licks your face in exuberant gratitude."

"That takes dogsledding to an interesting level." He looked resigned. "This just gets better all the time. I was thinking a fire and maybe a glass of wine."

"We'll get to that. I'm making homemade pizza, by the way."

"That sounds fabulous." Mick scooted his seat back a few inches, careful not to jar Samson, who was curled up on the seat behind him. "Let me guess—smoked salmon and caviar on crème fraîche."

"This isn't Beverly Hills, hotshot. How about sausage, pepperoni, onion and green pepper."

"Or sardines, Gouda and watermelon." His tone was so serious she heard Daisy draw in a disbelieving breath from the back seat. "It's my favorite."

"Be careful," she said as she turned onto main street. "Or I'll get Stephano to fix that just for you."

"You guys are joking, right?" Daisy asked suspiciously from behind them. "Sardines are fish. That doesn't go with watermelon. And I've never had watermelon on pizza. It sounds gross."

"We're definitely joking." Mick gave a mock shudder. "I tried sardines once in college. I still have nightmares about it. Cans of sardines are following me around on tiptoe, begging me to give them a second chance."

"You're funny," Daisy informed him with the giggle Raine never got enough of hearing.

He did have a good sense of humor once a person caught on to the droll delivery. Raine was happy about that. Raine was...*happy*, she realized. Before he'd come breezing back into town she'd been very content. After all, she had a wonderful daughter, friends, a satisfying career…but this was different. She had to tamp down the hope that maybe Hadleigh the Wizard was right, and try to stay practical.

Even with the property and cabin he wouldn't be around much because he was a busy man. For that matter, she was pretty busy, too. So did their lives collide in the right way?

They might.

Let's see how he handles Dead Man's Hill.

"We're getting close." She headed for the road opposite the ski slopes. "You might want to try on the boots."

He toed off the loafers and picked up the boots she'd left on the floor on the passenger side. "I take it this will be an Olympic event of some kind. Call it a hunch."

"Depends on the snow. There's fast snow and slow snow."

"You'll have to teach me the difference."

"One will cause a sardine-like experience and the other is just fun."

"More nightmares?"

"Only if it's the fast snow."

He sent her a keen glare. "You're deliberately trying to scare me, aren't you?"

"Shoot, you found me out. Let's see if you're up for it."

The drive was scenic by any standards, and right there it was an especially high bar. The curvy road wound up toward the mountains and was crowded by trees, and for most people that alone was harrowing. Luckily she'd driven it enough times to know just when to slow down and take it easy. Some kindly good-old boy had plowed one lane with the blade on his truck and she hoped they wouldn't meet a car coming the other direction, but otherwise the climb was breathtaking. They parked at a scenic outlook the state had put there years ago, and turned to Mick. "Here's the hard part. It's easy to walk to the hill, but we have to hike back up towing the toboggans."

"It seems to me you've done this before, so we can certainly handle it together. I don't really see a hill though."

She sent him a mischievous grin. "You will."

12

THE WOMAN WAS trying to kill him.

That wasn't a hill. That was a champion alpine slope. Mick pointed at the bottom. "There's a stream down there."

Raine was blasé about that observation, looking absurdly attractive in earmuffs and a scarf. "You're going so fast and with the angle you sail over it, that's part of the fun."

"Uh, I think I weigh a little more than you do."

"No problem. I've seen Drake, Slater and Mace float right over it. Just brace yourself."

"Is this some kind of Grand Teton test?" He hefted the biggest toboggan off the roof.

She flashed a mischievous grin. "Trial by fire."

"I'm going to trust you."

"I think we've already trusted each other quite a bit."

She certainly had a point there. They had. She'd slept in his arms and he wanted a repeat performance in the worst way.

Daisy had bounced out of the car and was impatiently waiting. Samson seemed equally trusting this wasn't a suicide mission and was gamboling in the snow, so Mick had no choice but to take it on faith as well.

That was one hell of a steep mini-mountain. It looked neck-break worthy. "People have survived this?" he asked dubiously.

"You're looking at some of them right here."

"How many dead bodies buried at the bottom of Dead Man's Hill?"

"Hard to say. Headstones are covered with snow. You gonna chicken out?"

"Never." He wasn't about to give up that kind of dare. "Promise me a night together if we both survive?"

"Deal." Her hazel eyes held a teasing light.

"I'll risk anything for that."

"Then hop on for the ride of your life."

"I thought we were just negotiating for that to come later."

She gave him the look he probably deserved for that comment. Daisy had already gotten on the smaller sled with the ease of someone who had definitely done it before. Samson had climbed on behind her and was furiously wagging his tail, a canine grin on his face, and she gave a whoop and pushed off.

"She's going to lord it over us if they win. Hurry."

Raine sat her very shapely behind down on the bigger toboggan and waved him on. Mick had to admit that despite having scuba dived off the Great Coral Reef and canoed on the Amazon, this had to be up in the top ten of adventurous things he'd done in his lifetime. He gamely got on behind her, wrapped his arms around her slim waist and said a small prayer she knew what she was doing.

The snow was deep enough they had a smooth trip, but they picked up speed at a blood-racing rate and he was pretty sure he didn't need the parka she'd provided because he broke out in a sweat. Their sled was heavier with two adults so they caught up with Daisy and passed her, Raine giving her daughter a cheery wave, and when the slope flattened out, they finally came to a halt in a swoosh of snow and triumph.

Daisy arrived about two seconds later, spinning around in a circle as she too came to a halt, breathless but laughing. "Hey, that's not fair. You had ballast."

Mick wasn't sure if he was more surprised she knew the word and could use it, or if he was insulted. "Big word for a small fry. And you had a little ballast yourself."

His mistake was to point at the dog. Samson took it

as an invitation to come leap all over him, his enormous snowy paws dancing with such enthusiasm Mick actually staggered backwards.

Raine didn't quite succeed in hiding her merriment with her mitten clamped over her mouth.

Daisy was as saucy as her mother. "I may be a small fry, but at least I know how to handle a big dog."

He burst out laughing, trying unsuccessfully to fend off the dog's burst of affection. "You have a point there. Too bad he didn't help you win the sledding race."

"We'll see what happens next. Have fun carrying that big toboggan up that hill, Mr. Branson. Come on, Samson."

It *was* imposingly steep. "We have to walk up that? Maybe I should have ridden up on Samson."

"Great cardio workout," Raine replied without apology, handing him the rope to the toboggan. "Think about your heart."

"I have been lately." He gave her a meaningful look.

"Don't do that." Her gaze softened. "I'm already afraid I'm in too deep."

"Why be afraid?" It was hard to believe he was standing knee-deep in snow having this conversation.

"You don't even live close."

"I'm considering selling both my houses and moving here. I have a cabin apparently. I'm going to build a house. Remember, you're going to help me design it. I'll even buy myself a parka. Talk about *in deep*."

"A parka? That *is* deep."

"Almost like a promise ring with weatherproof lining."

"Those are the best kind. That way you don't get cold fingers."

"I thought it was cold feet."

"What are we discussing?"

"You tell me."

"Branson," she said, starting to trudge up the hill— and it took some trudging; he definitely had his work cut out for him carting up that sled, "your love of talking in circles has to go. I'm sure that works well in Hollywood, but in these parts we prefer a more direct approach."

"You want direct? I'll give you direct. We might be too old for promise rings, but not for a more committed relationship. I'd like you to start thinking it over."

He wasn't quite what Red would call a straight-shooter. The kind of man who slapped down his glass on the counter and asked for more red-eye, straight up.

He was tailored slacks, a linen shirt and a persuasive voice.

Well, he had on jeans at the moment, but he looked great in them. His dark hair was every which way, thanks to Samson, and he hauled up the toboggan without missing a breath, so he clearly had more facets to him than just boardroom suaveness. If she had to label his style, she'd call it tousled elegance.

He was also the creative, sensitive man who would finish an old Western novel.

Trouble on the horizon.

She thought maybe he'd just proposed. Or suggested it anyway.

The wizard was perhaps spot-on.

Raine pointed out softly, "We've slept together once."

"It was more than just sex, at least to me."

She was instantly out of breath and it had nothing to do with the steep slope of the hill. "To me as well, but—"

"I'm bringing to the table that I have some social and historical connection to this area. I like your daughter, I even like your beastly dog and that lion of a cat."

"This isn't a business meeting," she said, laughing. "Mick, we're walking up a nearly perpendicular hill in knee-deep snow. You really don't have to sell yourself at this moment."

"Hey, I'll have you know just coming down Mount Everest was a demonstration of my affection for your comely person."

"Comely?" Her brows shot up.

"I've reading some old-fashioned Westerns lately.

They use *comely*. That's a word that needs to be brought back. I'm just the man to do it. Consider yourself comely, ma'am."

"You might want to work on your Western drawl, cowboy."

"I can't fire a six-shooter, either. Never touched a cow in my life, and oddly enough I don't have the desire to herd one anywhere. I think you'd better go back to Mr. Boardroom."

It was quite the hill to climb, so her laugh was just an expulsion of frosty breath. "Please tell me you can ride a horse."

"That I've done. In several countries, including Argentina. And in Patagonia those vaqueros are a critical bunch."

"Where haven't you traveled?" she asked curiously as they soldiered up the incline. "Somehow I think that's a shorter list than the opposite question."

Blithely, he said, "I've skipped Siberia and Antarctica. Too cold, though Mustang Creek in winter might just give them a run for their money." He sent her a wink. "I'm joking, but in reality, my parents dragged me all around the world. As I got older, I had to travel for business, so I ended up pretty much everywhere at one time or the other."

That was so different from Raine's conservative upbringing of childhood church camp and the occasional spring break vacation when she was in college. He came from money and she certainly didn't. Her parents were just hardworking middle-class people who weighed their finances based on what they could afford and what they couldn't, were practical and dependable and always there for her. What more could she ask for?

"We really couldn't be more different."

"So?"

"Would it work with you here?"

"My business schedule? Not all the time."

At least he told the truth. "I can't ask you to make that commitment."

"I think I'm asking *you*." He plowed through a deep pile of snow. "I've never asked anyone before, so maybe I mean it."

"Maybe?"

"That was ill-phrased. I meant, you should consider maybe I really mean it."

"Do I seem hesitant?"

"Do I?" He tugged the sled over a big rock. "Glad we didn't slam into that on our way down."

"I knew it was there." Raine only wished she could avoid emotional pitfalls so easily. "No, you don't seem hesitant. That might scare me the most."

"On the same page then?"

"We could be."

She felt her heart warm despite the fact that there was snow in her boots and her toes were cold. Was it possible she'd just gotten engaged?

No.

Well, maybe. After all, the man *had* slid down Dead Man's Hill because he trusted her. He was going to *move* to Wyoming.

"Oh, I say 'maybe' and get in trouble, but you can say 'could'?"

This wasn't best time for verbal sparring because she was getting out of breath. Deep snow was great for sledding, but it was hell on wheels trying to walk through, especially up an incline like this one. Five seconds to get down and twenty minutes to climb back up. "We'll debate that over the glass of wine by the fire, okay?"

"I think we just came to an agreement on something."

"Can we agree on resting at the top of the hill for at least a few minutes before we attempt to become professional daredevils again? I felt like I was fleeing the bad guys in an action movie."

"Would we have escaped?"

"Oh, definitely. No one would be stupid enough to follow us down this hill, not even bad guys. At least we didn't crash into any of the headstones."

"Like the rock, I know where those are, too, but I admit with ballast it is a little harder to steer."

He laughed and hauled the toboggan the last length of the climb. "Maybe I should sit this next trip out then."

"Not on your life, Mr. Boardroom."

13

WARM, COMFORTABLE AND there was no harrowing hill right in front of him. True, a very large and still-wet dog sat at his feet, not to mention the giant cat beneath the tree, but he'd started the fire while Raine made her pizza dough, and he had a glass of merlot in his hand.

When he'd gotten back to the resort, he'd even managed to write a few pages, including the ending paragraph to a chapter: *Her adventurous spirit never failed to captivate him, and the fascination didn't end there. She was comely, but he'd met other beautiful women. She was intrepid.*

If going down that slope at warp speed wasn't intrepid, he didn't know what was. He felt somewhat intrepid himself, so Raine definitely qualified.

He was starting to wonder if Matthew Brighton hadn't

modeled this last novel's heroine after his lovely grand-daughter.

It sure seemed like it.

Was Mick the hero?

A tall, dark-haired greenhorn was the main male character. He was starting to wonder. He didn't really believe in premonitions but he was changing his mind. These days, he couldn't help but feel that something was going on and he might be a part of it.

And he got to write his own ending.

Raine came in from the kitchen. "I didn't have watermelon. Or Gouda or sardines. I'm afraid you're stuck with my original recipe."

"I suppose I can live without sardines just this once."

"Harry makes the pizza sauce from scratch. Just wait. She could bottle it and retire. We all just hope she never will."

He couldn't see the always-bustling Harry ever content with retirement. "Was she ever married?"

Raine settled in next to him on the couch. "Harry? I think so. She's like Red. You can't ask too much. I skirt around those subjects like they're a rattlesnake ready to strike."

"Interesting analogy. Maybe you should be the one writing the rest of this book."

"I'll stick to graphic design, thanks. But my philosophy has always been that if something is private and a person doesn't want to talk about it, then they shouldn't have to. Life's too short. Don't stir the pot if there's no need." She planted her bare feet on the coffee table and wiggled her toes. She'd changed into plaid pajama pants and a faded shirt with a picture of Goofy on the front. "The fire is nice."

"After practically flinging myself off a cliff three times, I agree. I felt like I was competing in the luge at the Olympic Games."

Raine elbowed him. "Admit it, you had fun."

He slipped his arm around her shoulders. "As long as Samson enjoyed himself, that's what matters most."

"He did. Jangles is jealous. Look at him, all out of sorts."

"No offense, but he always looks all out of sorts." A pair of unwinking amber eyes was watching them stealthily through the branches of the Christmas tree. "I think he's spying on us."

"Probably wondering if we're going to make out on the couch, just like a suspicious father. That isn't a bad idea by the way. Daisy's not going to venture out from her room until her movie is done playing."

He'd never heard a better idea in his life. "I don't know if I have the strength after walking up that hill three times, but I'm willing to give it a try."

Raine's mouth curved. "I somehow think you'll manage."

He wanted one hell of a lot more than a kiss—or two—but would take what he could get. A beautiful woman in his arms and a crackling fire was his true idea of holiday cheer, and Raine kissed him back with her usual audacity, her fingers trailing along the back of his neck with tantalizing slowness.

If Daisy hadn't been in residence, and Jangles watching their every move, he might have at least tried to slip off her shirt and caress what he knew to be very lovely breasts, but he settled for just pulling her closer so he could feel them against his chest.

Naturally Samson decided to join them then, bounding onto the couch with great enthusiasm, not exactly adding to the romance of the moment, and both he and Raine were the recipients of kisses of the doggie variety.

So much for the romantic mood.

"It's a zoo here." She laughingly pushed Samson away to prevent another attack of affection. "I warned you."

"There are worse things than to be loved." He picked up the dog—no small feat—and set him on the floor. That animal weighed about a ton and it wasn't done growing. Samson was a fitting name.

"I couldn't agree more." Neither could Samson, who decided to join them again. Mick gently but firmly set

him back on the ground, avoiding another slobber-
ing sign that the puppy stood behind him one hundred
percent. "Don't get too flattered," Raine warned him
wryly. "He loves everyone. Now if Drake's dogs love
you, you're part of a special club."

"I want to be a part of a different club entirely," he
told her quietly. "The 'If Raine Loves You' club."

She met his gaze squarely. "Aside from Daisy, I'm
starting to think you could be the founding member."

"What about Slater?"

She considered the glass in her hand. "I'll always care
about him. But we were more in lust than in love. When
he offered to marry me it was just because he's a good
old-fashioned nice guy. We'd already mutually gone our
separate ways when I discovered I was pregnant. Luckily for both of us, I'm not an old-fashioned girl. You've
seen how happy he is with Grace."

He had, and he wouldn't mind that for himself at all.
He thought about Grace and Luce and the serene glow
that currently seemed to surround them both. He'd always thought that was a myth, but had changed his mind.
Their happiness came through loud and clear.

"I want children." Those were his cards, right on the
table. A straight flush, no request for more of the deck.
He was afraid to be so blunt, but she deserved to know

it. Besides, she had encouraged him to be more direct out on the hill.

Raine didn't bat an eye. "Slater and I...we were really young when I had Daisy. I've been thinking about it more closely now than I did then. I'm past thirty. I might not *get* pregnant. Can you live with that?"

"Of course." He squeezed her hand. "Life is a gamble. But one thing that's certain is how I feel about you. I risked Dead Man's Hill just to gain your admiration. I bought a purse to win over your daughter. When a grown man is willing to buy a cute purse, you know he's serious."

With a straight face, she agreed. "We'll put the purse in as exhibit A."

"Exhibit B might be making out on a couch like a teenager. That isn't boardroom behavior. You might be a bad influence."

Raine's eyes sparkled. "Just wait. Now, tell me about the book. Gramps was working on it when he passed away, so I haven't been able to bring myself to read it. I'm not going to ask if it's good, because I know it must be. What's the storyline?"

She was admittedly curious.

Mick sounded very neutral. "A Tenderfoot imagines he's a cowboy and falls in love with a dark-haired independent woman and is determined to win her heart.

There's some conflict with a neighboring rancher who wants her land. Sound familiar?"

How was it she'd imagined something exactly like that? Tears stung her eyes. "I miss him. It would have been so nice if you could have met him."

"No one could agree more."

"He would have thought you were a fine man."

"I hope he would have been right."

She smiled through her tears. "I know he would."

"That might be the best compliment I've ever gotten." He lifted her hand and kissed it. "I might comment that you now smell vaguely of giant puppy, but I think I might too, so I'll let it go just this once."

Raine was conciliatory. "You might want to get used to that. I don't think Samson will improve as he gets older. Plus your dog will be added to the mix. What were you thinking about? Giant dog, or a small one? Medium breed? What's our plan?"

"I can't ask you—"

"You didn't. I offered." She raised a hand. "So what was that boyhood dream?"

"Collie."

"Done." He seemed like a collie sort of man. It fit. "Long hair, just my luck. I'll tell Blythe, who will tell Mrs. Lettie Arbuckle-Calder and you'll have a collie rescue pup in no time. That woman will scour the state for one. She's a wonder. And don't tell me how you can afford to buy one, because rescue it is."

Mildly, he said, "You can be on the bossy side at times. Just an observation."

He was right. "I'm really used to running my life all on my own, and also making most of the decisions concerning my daughter. If it's anything big, of course I ask Slater, but we don't have a custody agreement because we've never needed one. Ultimately it falls to me to make the day-to-day choices. I warn you, like your heroine, I'm used to being independent."

"If you weren't, I doubt I'd be so interested. Not only do I have my hands full running a company and my own life, no matter how *comely* she might be, I don't want someone who just wants me to take care of her."

Raine practically spit out her sip of wine laughing but managed to swallow in the nick of time. "*Comely*, again. You and that word."

He shrugged. "A man on a mission, I tell you. Soon teenagers will be using it, nudging each other in the football stands on Friday nights. *Dude, look at that comely girl over there. Check her out.*"

"If anyone can do it, I think you can."

"Thanks for the vote of confidence." He was looking gorgeous, and cowboy-like in his denim shirt and jeans. Except for the hair. He needed a hat to really mess it up, and a set of boots and a horse. She'd get Tate Calder to help her with that last one.

Wedding present?

What else to give the man who probably had everything? She couldn't top that beach house in Bermuda.

An old six-shooter?

She did know Bad Billy had a friend who dealt in antique guns. Maybe she'd see what he could negotiate for her. Billy knew everyone.

If Mick finished this book, he certainly deserved something like that...unique and special. Very Old West. Something to hang on the wall of his new house.

She thought he'd love it. Hat and boots aside, he'd really go for the six-shooter. Raine got up. "Let me check on my pizza dough."

"It will have risen about two millimeters, Raine." He captured her waist and pulled her back. "Stay here with me."

She traced the line of his nose with her fingertip. "You are entirely too dangerous."

"I'm entirely yours if you want me."

"Mick." Her voice was hushed.

"I'm right here."

"I know. Your hands are doing interesting things."

"Nice?"

"Too nice. Jangles is still watching us."

"I'm going to have to get used to him giving me the stink-eye, right?"

"You are taking some risks. I wish I could invite you to stay the night, but like I said, I can't. Daisy is certainly old enough to understand why you would. I need to talk to her before anything like that happens."

It was almost disappointing that he immediately let her go and settled back into a more relaxed pose with a sigh. "My intellect is telling me I agree one hundred percent, but another part of me has a different take on the situation. Maybe you shouldn't dress so provocatively."

"These pajama pants and the T-shirt really are a little over the top. I'll try to tone it down."

"See that you do if you want me to behave. Maybe you could shave your head or get a giant tattoo of an elf on your forehead. I'm not positive even that would turn me off, but it would be a good start."

Raine laughed. "You've got the holiday spirit, I see. The elf might look strange in July, so I think I'll skip that one, and I happen to like my hair right where it is."

"There lies the crux of the problem, so do I."

At that moment Jangles prowled stealthily out from beneath the tree—which really meant he lumbered out, because he definitely could not pull off a quiet approach—and launched himself onto the couch between them, but couldn't quite fit. Mick reached for his wineglass and scooted away enough to give the cat room to settle down. "I think he's decided to help us out with the self-control issue."

"He's a very wise feline." He was. He definitely liked Mick. She did, too. "So what's Slater's next project? I haven't asked him yet."

"Becoming a father for the third time comes first, I think, but I've heard some musings about the Snake River. After this last film, he'll be able to choose just about anything, I'd guess. Backers will be lining up."

"I like the idea." Raine was sincere. "It's beautiful country there. He'll absolutely remind people we moved west gradually."

"And the setting will win the day."

"I think so. His films work that way."

"He does have an eye for beautiful things. I'm looking at one of them right now." He held her gaze.

It was a nicely done compliment. "Thank you, but I'm hardly beautiful."

"Maybe not in a traditional blonde bombshell sense, but you're striking, and your eyes are unforgettable. I know I couldn't stop thinking about you. Slater is a smart man, so I was surprised he ever gave you up, but I didn't really know the whole story."

"I'm glad I got to share it with you." She hadn't been able to get him out of her mind, either. "Now, if you can chop some onions and green peppers, we'll really be on the same page. Follow me."

He could and he did, and she liked the sight of him in her kitchen, the Hollywood executive with a knife in his hand, frowning over the cutting board in concentration.

It might be a different kind of board than he was used to, but she was starting to think he'd adjust to the change.

14

She bent over to dip water out of the river, her hair in a makeshift knot that had come half-loose, her skirt hiked up over a pair of the prettiest ankles he'd ever seen as she waded in.

He'd die for her.

It was a possibility. There was a small local war going on as the ranchers squabbled over their land and she was vulnerable, a woman alone with a child, a lovely widow doing her best to hold on to what she'd fought to build. He wasn't about to let her lose it all.

Maybe he wasn't a fast draw yet, even though he'd been practicing, but he was a fair rifle shot, he'd discovered, and he could put food on the table. She'd made venison stew the night before that was so tender it melted in his mouth, and despite her guarded stance, he could tell she was starting to trust him. He now had his bedroll on that old front porch.

He felt like he'd gained something special right there.

The war wasn't over, but a skirmish had been won.

MICK EYED HIS computer screen thoughtfully, read it over again, and decided it fit the voice well enough, but wondered if it was too sentimental.

Maybe not. Men were every bit as sensitive as women were, they just didn't express it in the same way. His father had refused to get rid of the old rocker in the corner of the living room because his grandmother had given it to him, despite his mother's objections to the impact on her otherwise perfectly furnished space. It did stick out like a sore thumb, but he'd stood firm.

Though she came off as highbrow most of the time, Mick had certainly noted his mother had left it there even after her husband had died. That antique rocker stayed put. Maybe she was more sentimental than he thought.

So maybe he'd leave the writing as it was for now. He liked it. If a man would sleep on a woman's front porch, he was really into her, and willing to protect her. Hopefully Matthew Brighton would agree.

Especially on a day like today. The wind had picked up, he could hear it whistling by the windows, and even the ski slopes were empty. It was getting later, or maybe just felt like it because the skies were so gray.

He was trying not to crowd Raine too much, but he slipped out his phone and thought about it and then touched the screen. She answered almost at once. "Hi. What do you need? I'm swamped."

He grinned at her tone. Even clearly distracted, she was appealing. "This might sound crazy, but what if I asked Stephano to make a few sandwiches and throw in whatever other genius side dishes he has and we took dinner to the cabin? Daisy could come, too, of course, but I need… I don't know, a sense of place. You said the woodstove still worked, right?"

"There's probably a zillion nests in the chimney, even though I had it cleaned, so the whole place could go up in a plume of smoke, but as far as I know, yes. Slater just picked Daisy up so she can't come along, but I'm up for it. I need a break. Tell Stephano I'd love some of that garlic artichoke dip he's so famous for. I'll come get you. What time?"

He glanced at his phone. "Is two hours too soon?"

"No, perfect."

"Great. I'll call when I'm on my way."

He then phoned down to the room service number and asked for Stephano himself if possible. Probably thanks to his association with the Carson family, it was. "Can you make me whatever you think is your best sandwich, the artichoke dip Raine apparently loves, and anything else you'd add to an alfresco dinner for two in an old cabin? I'm putting myself in your hands."

"You have chosen wisely." Stephano sounded delighted as he announced, "I will wipe your socks off."

Mick almost mentioned that "knock your socks off" might be the more appropriate description, but he refrained. Stephano's English was sometimes as creative as his cooking. "I look forward to the meal."

"You should."

He hung up with an inward shake of the head and a grin. There was nothing wrong with self-confidence. Mick normally had a decent dose of it himself, but lately he couldn't count on it.

It didn't help that the front desk called and said a special delivery had arrived for him via special courier, and as he went down and signed the confirmation of delivery he knew that his life had just changed forever. Raine had turned down Slater flat. At the moment Mick was decently hopeful that that wouldn't happen to him. Although she'd pointed out how different they were, an observation he didn't disagree with, they'd then discussed marriage, even children and some future plans, so he took that as an encouraging sign. But he hadn't actually *asked* yet.

He'd implicitly trusted Ingrid to choose a stunning ring and he wasn't disappointed. Nestled in the satin lining inside the small box was a chocolate diamond exquisitely cut and anchored on a platinum band. The name of the jeweler making him lift his brows. The assumption she'd spent quite a chunk of his change on it was a given, but he planned on only doing this once in his life.

He felt Raine would love it. He sent off a quick text to his brother. Tell Ingrid I'm smiling. Thanks.

Ran texted right back. Good luck, loverboy.

He went back to his room, wondered what a man wore to propose at a haunted cabin at night, and finally decided maybe he should go shopping at some point because the best he could do was dark, tailored slacks and a white shirt along with his infamous loafers. Definitely vintage Mr. Boardroom, but then again, he was living out of a suitcase at the moment. He hadn't known exactly what to expect from this visit to Mustang Creek.

More writing was out of the question. Instead he paced, tried to watch the news and turned it off since it was the wrong night to hear about what was awry in the world, and instead turned on a classical music station and checked his email. Not much going on during a holiday week and he was enjoying the respite from his normally hectic schedule, so that was just fine with him.

It was ridiculous, but he was nervous. Like he was seventeen and about to pick up his first prom date.

But he was far from seventeen, he reminded himself as he clicked off the computer screen. And he needed to get a grip. He took a calming breath, deep and slow.

He could handle this. Ask the question, hopefully get the right response, and if she chose to be as pigheaded as a feisty mule—a description he'd undoubtedly picked up from Red somewhere along the line—he'd reconsider his tactics.

The elegant bag with Stephano's latest masterpieces was delivered right on time and he was more than ready to make the call. "I'll be there in a few minutes with the requested dip in tow."

"I'll be ready."

I'll have the ring and the question.

He didn't say it, but he certainly thought it as he left the resort and got in his car. He did make one stop in town before he drove to her house, and when he pulled up the light was a warm, welcoming glow in her window.

He knocked and walked in when he heard her call out a welcome. Jangles of course went in for the kill, but by now Mick was ready for it and dodged away. Raine was smiling. "Nice move for a city boy. But he's going to mope. Give him a couple of treats to make him feel better while I grab my keys."

Of course, the cat understood every word. He followed Mick into the kitchen and stared unwaveringly at the correct jar on the counter.

Message received.

He got out a handful of treats and put them in the bowl. Jangles devoured them in about two seconds. Mick had an impulse to deal out more, but Raine came in then and said, "No, that's enough, he's playing you. He does that. Let's go."

She jiggled the keys.

He wasn't positive he was composed enough for this evening, but he decided to take his cues from Jangles, who had collapsed into a relaxed sprawl on the floor, his eyes half closing. His pose screamed: *stop worrying.*

Mick escorted Raine out the door. "Let's go while the food is still at least semi-hot. It smells like heaven."

"What is it?"

"No idea."

"You ordered it, right?"

He held her elbow as they made their way down the snowy sidewalk. "I gave Stephano carte blanche, though I did specifically request the dip you wanted. He promised I would be impressed—at least I think that's what he was saying."

"He does have a way with words, doesn't he?" She pushed a button to unlock the vehicle. "One of the many things I love about him."

He set the bag in the back and got in. "You don't mind driving in this weather?"

"No." She didn't, he could tell. "Wow, it does smell amazing in here."

"That man loves you right back. Whatever is in there is because I mentioned your name. I can take zero credit."

She backed up the car and they tackled the street. "I'm already starving. The cabin, huh? I appreciate your enthusiasm but you should be forewarned this could be an interesting journey. The snow has somewhat melted off, but it's blowing around more than a little. Luckily this little buggy can handle just about anything." She patted the steering wheel. "I've been there a thousand times. I think I could find it blindfolded."

Maybe she'd been optimistic.

It wasn't whiteout conditions, but it was very near, and in broad daylight it was a challenge without a road of any kind, so in the dark it was close to impossible.

Mick seemed pretty determined that the cabin be their destination though, and she sensed it had something to do with the manuscript. She was pretty good at reading people and more in tune with him than most—and Mr. Cool, Calm and Collected was wound up about something. There was tension in his shoulders and a set to his jaw that said something was certainly on his mind.

Maybe it was just that he was making some big decisions, but she didn't think so. Mick Branson did that every single day and didn't even blink about it. He made up his mind and sailed on that ship full-steam ahead.

"There's a big drift by the porch," she noted out loud. "We'll be walking the last bit. Luckily there's still firewood piled inside. I brought a lighter for the lantern in case all the matches are damp and you should put on those boots Mace gave you."

"I bought some for myself, and a sleeping bag, some candles, and a fire log to get things going for our impromptu camping trip."

No wonder he'd loaded several bags besides the food into the back of her car. She'd wondered if they were going off to safari in deepest Africa.

Snow swirled around them in ghostly forms, circling the windows, brushing the hood, occasionally obscuring the entire structure. Raine put up her hood. "I'll go unlock that reluctant door if you'll bring the stuff in. I've got the food, so don't take too long, or it will all be gone. Just a friendly warning."

"Consider me warned. Stephano would never forgive me if I moved too slowly to sample his latest creations."

"The artichoke dip alone will make you weep with joy."

"I'm going to take your word for it, and get inside as soon as possible."

The first blast of wind hit her square in the face. She'd watched the forecast and knew it was supposed to calm down, but it about knocked her over. She scrambled for the doorway, almost forgot the bad top step, and then struggled with the key.

The door opened like magic and she practically fell inside, first because she'd braced for its usual resistance and was caught off guard by its easy surrender, then because another gust propelled her from behind.

By some miracle Raine managed to keep her balance as she stumbled in, and despite the dark, she avoided the old couch that undoubtedly had mice in it and made it to the table. The lantern helped as soon she managed to get it lit, and just then Mick came through the door like a pack mule, loaded down with everything a man could carry and maybe more.

He panted, "I thought the wind was going to die down. I think it's getting worse."

She watched him dump the bags on the floor. "It is

supposed to calm by dawn. I think we're spending the night right here."

"Well then, let's get the fire started."

Her grandfather never would have dreamed of using anything as modern as a fire log to light that old wood-stove, but then again, it was remarkably handy. Mick knelt there, dusted in snow, and the log caught with one touch of a match. She was happy to see it seemed to be venting properly because the room didn't instantly fill with smoke.

"I brought a tablecloth from home. For all I know there's a bear hibernating in the single closet where things like that are kept, and I'm not going to look. Clean utensils and paper plates as well, since everything gets so dusty when it isn't used."

Mick agreed. "Let's not go bear hunting."

He was a typical man and had brought candles, but nothing to put them on, so she dug out a couple of old plates, and set the table and it was…well, nice. Ta-blecloth, candlelight and an undeniably attractive man. What more could a girl want?

Food, for one, and maybe some heat. Fortunately, the stove was starting to take care of the temperature, and the howl of the wind outside did add to the cozy ambience.

She was even able to take off her coat as they sat down to discover what wonders Stephano had prepared for them. One sandwich consisted of watercress and smoked salmon with aioli on French bread, the other one roast beef layered with what had to be artisan cheese and served in some sort of homemade rye that had flecks of fennel, too. There was also a pasta salad with tiny shrimp and Kalamata olives, not to mention Raine's prized artichoke dip, and to top it all off, a key lime cheesecake.

It looked delicious.

Quite the alfresco picnic. It was hardly a wild guess that food like this had never been eaten in the cabin before. "I suspect my grandfather subsisted on pemmican or something similar," she told Mick jokingly. "He did like good whiskey and believe it or not, applesauce. There are several groves of apple trees on the property. I remember the smell of applesauce simmering on the stove from my childhood."

"That stove has to be from the Civil War era. I've never seen anything like it."

"It isn't new, that I can promise you. But it works just fine."

"I can tell, since it is warming up in here."

The candlelight played nicely off the masculine lines of his face. If she hadn't seen him interact with Daisy and Ryder, holding babies, laughing with Blythe and Harry, and joking with the Carson brothers, she might worry more that she was influenced by his good looks. Being her, she blurted out what she was thinking. "Don't get all full of yourself, but you're as handsome as this dip is delicious."

Amusement lit his eyes. "Now there's a rare compliment. Because you made a really good call on the dip."

"I always make good calls." She shamelessly took another helping. "But lucky for you, there's plenty. Even I can't eat all of this. Stephano must like you."

"I'm starting to believe that. Just try the pasta salad. I want that at our wedding."

She was still mid-bite when he slid a small box across the tiny table. His smile was wry. "I would be on bended knee, but have a feeling that part isn't as important to you as the question itself. I would love it if you would agree to marry me, Raine. You'd have the last vote on the pasta salad being served at the reception, of course. The dip is a given."

"Yes." She didn't even hesitate, which spoke volumes to her.

And to him, which was reflected in his expression.

"You're sure."

"I didn't sound sure just now? What about you?"

"Absolutely. Now that's settled, maybe you'd like to open that." He nodded toward the box.

She complied and took in a deep breath. The ring was both gorgeous and unusual, and in the candlelight the gem in the exquisite setting winked with tones of brown and bronze. It was Mick Branson–style over the top, and she had no idea what to say.

"Mick."

He reached over. "I take it you like it. I think I'm supposed to put it on your finger, but I've never done this before. If I mess it up, let me know."

He definitely didn't mess it up.

He must have slid the ring on the right finger and said the right words because he was engaged.

Officially.

"Wedding date…when do you have in mind? Just wondering since I'm one hundred percent certain my mother will ask that question."

For the first time since he'd proposed, Raine looked uncertain. "I haven't even met her."

"Oh, she'll consider that an unimportant detail. She'll be so thrilled I'm finally getting married that she'll get immediately involved. I, for one, would like something very understated. But it's your day. I'll just be tagging along."

"Not so. You've promised to bring the dip. You'll be the star. As for the date, I'd like mid-May. It's so gorgeous here at that time of year."

"Done. Stephano can cater. Perfect. That's settled."

"I loved Bex Calder's wedding dress. I might count it

as my borrowed item, if she doesn't mind. We're about the same size."

"Food, dress, ring, date. Our work is done. As for my wardrobe, I'll wear pants, I promise. No one will be looking at me anyway, not with you in the room. My brother as best man, Slater, and Ryder as grooms-men and I think we have a wedding all planned. Let's keep it simple."

"You do remember you're Mick Branson, right?" She laughed and shook her head. "I somehow think it won't be simple. I believe celebrities will be invited and Ryder would be the most nervous groomsman on the face of the planet, and Drake would bring his dogs. My brides-maids would all be pregnant—"

"So how about we set the date for sooner, with just me and you instead? I'm good with that." He was more than good with it. He'd marry her standing in a muddy field in a rainstorm. "Apply for a marriage license at the Bliss County courthouse and have it over and done?"

It was what he wanted. Simple. The fanfare held no appeal. If she wanted the big event—then of course, yes, every bride was entitled to that—but if he was given a choice...

He'd keep it low-key.

Raine put the last scoop of dip on his plate. "How offended would your family be? No movie stars, no corporate executives except you, not even them."

That he could assuage her on. "You do realize that being Mick Branson really isn't my agenda."

"You know, I do. I *love* that about you."

"There will be a party." He confessed that tidbit almost reluctantly. "My mother will want to throw a reception at some point, but quite frankly, everyone in my family travels so much that getting them all together at the same time probably means planning the wedding out a year or so, and I don't want to do that. I have zero desire to wait."

"If you think Blythe and Harry won't throw a shindig, you're dreaming, cowboy. So we're looking at two parties, and I doubt they'll be quite the same. I'll have to buy heels for one, and will be able to wear my favorite pair of comfortable old flats to the other. They could do that in May instead."

"We could just not tell anyone and let them believe we're living in sin."

"If you think Daisy wouldn't spill the beans, then think again, and I would tell her the truth." She took a bite of her sandwich and after she swallowed, said, "Oh my gosh, Stephano must *really* like you. We might have to set the cheesecake out on the front porch to save it for breakfast."

Raine would do that. She'd eat key lime cheesecake for breakfast without a thought.

She'd accepted his proposal in a run-down cabin in Wyoming during what he expected was now a white-out snowstorm. The entire structure shook with the next gust of wind.

But unlike in the book he was writing, Mick mused with a private grin, he was not going to have his bedroll on the front porch this particular night.

15

HE WANTED TO *marry her.*

She wasn't every man's ideal of a perfect bride. She had a child, a past, and her unconventional approach to life was hardly traditional.

But he had no doubt he loved her and that was all that mattered.

She'd said yes.

He didn't ask her the traditional way but while they were eating dinner. He didn't mean to quite blurt it out like that, but his emotions got the best of him.

It was every girl's dream.

A beautiful ring, a romantic proposal and killer artichoke dip.

Not to mention a wind velocity that measured off the charts. It was amazing that she couldn't envision a more perfect evening. If the roof stayed on she'd be amazed at the workmanship of those long-ago craftsmen that nailed it on.

While there was the probability of a rodent drive-by, and Raine wasn't unaware of it because they'd heard rustling all evening, the room was nice and toasty, and when Mick rolled out the sleeping bag and started to undress her, she was willing.

Extremely willing.

He shucked off his clothes just as quickly, joined her under the warm folds of the sleeping bag and kissed her softly. Not passionately, but with a gentleness that melted her heart. He said, "I've waited for you. I don't think I knew what I was waiting for. Now I understand."

She'd waited for him, too. "Right there with you. A man with good hair in a haunted cabin is a rare find. You're so warm. Hold me closer and protect me from the possible rodent population."

"I'm your knight on a white steed. No mouse will bother you on my watch."

He was a very aroused knight. She wasn't at all averse to that, either. "I'm petrified, but with you to save me from fearsome rodents…say no more."

"No problem there. And warm? I'm alone with you, so call it what it is. I'm on fire. Can we stop talking and do something else entirely? I want to make love to you and I suspect your car will be blown away at any minute and the cabin will fall down around us and I won't care."

No condom. She didn't ask for one and he didn't use one. They'd had that conversation. He was…perfect. Insistently passionate but not less than thoughtful and understood her every response to each touch and whisper, and afterward the wind keening outside was almost as sexy as the way her leg sprawled over his thigh when it was said and done.

Raine rested her head on his damp chest. "I do love you."

"I hope so, since we're engaged."

"That part doesn't matter to me as much as that I *love* you. I can't believe it."

"Can't believe it? I'm trying to decide if I should be insulted or not. You sound uncertain."

"About my feelings, not about you." She gave him a playful slap on the shoulder. "Give me some latitude. This hasn't happened to me before."

"Never found the right man? I, for one, am pretty glad of it. You waited for me." His fingers sifted through her hair. "I'm going to christen you my best Christmas gift ever."

"I intend to be."

"Good, because you succeeded."

"How are you going to finish the book? The last I

read, our hero was sleeping on the front porch in a raging snow storm."

"I think he moves inside. She would never leave him out there in the cold."

"Of course not. I bet he likes it better inside."

"They hook up."

"I think you need to put it more eloquently than that." She nestled closer, knowing he would take her words for the teasing they were. Mick would never be crude.

"Easier said than done, especially for a rugged, solitary cowboy like him. He likes the fact that he found her—he likes it a lot. He just isn't too good at saying it."

"She needs him to say it."

She heard him take in a breath. "I'm guessing you're talking about us. I honestly think the moment I met you I knew I was falling pretty hard."

"I was talking about the book, Mick. I would never play you like that. You made a distinct impression as well, I might add. As far as I can tell, everyone in the entire Carson camp immediately cottoned on to how we were feeling. I don't think we should play poker with them until we work on our technique. Now, back to the book. How does it end?"

"I'm not going to tell you, because I don't really know yet. You'll have to read it yourself when it's finally done. I don't know if my writing is on a par with your grandfather's, but I'm really enjoying it. It's coming more naturally than I might have guessed, probably because I've read pretty much all his books. He's so descriptive. Maybe that's why I have such a connection with this part of the country. I'd been here in my imagination often enough before my first visit."

"Well, this cabin certainly qualifies as the real deal. I'm surprised there isn't a musket mounted on the wall somewhere. On a night like tonight I'm surprised there *are* still walls."

It was wicked out there. She was warm and cozy enough in the afterglow, but the weather wasn't very friendly. Raine was glad Daisy was safe and sound at the ranch. If she had to call it, she suspected they might be stranded for longer than anticipated—the drift by the front door wasn't getting any smaller. "We could have a hard time leaving in the morning."

"Fine. I'd stay like this forever."

That was as good as *I love you.*

"This is a nice sleeping bag."

He chuckled. "I forgot pillows. I didn't think of it. I don't camp too often."

"I'll use you as my pillow. You're actually quite comfortable."

"That type of high praise is likely to win my heart."

"I had that in the bag already, right?"

"I thought that went without saying."

Raine rolled on top of him, which was very easy to do since they were sharing a single sleeping bag. She said simply, "I'm happy."

"That's what we're supposed to do for each other."

"I hope I'm holding up my end of the bargain."

"You have no idea."

She touched his lower lip, their mouths just inches apart. "Oh, I think I have some idea. Otherwise I'm guessing you wouldn't be quite so enthusiastic about one small sleeping bag with two bodies and no pillows."

"I thought I was your pillow." He held her closely, lightly stroking her back, those long fingers taking some definite liberties.

"And you're a good one. If you could market you, the stores would sell out. Women would flock in."

"Unfortunately, I think I'm taken, correct?"

"You got that right, mister."

Hands down, it was the most erotic night of his life.

In bed—well, technically in a sleeping bag—with a very sexy woman, and she'd fallen asleep all draped across him, not that she had much choice because there was nowhere else to go. It gave him some time to reflect on his recent life decisions.

If he sold both his other houses he could build her

the house of any woman's dreams, but he didn't think she'd go for it. Raine would probably prefer something modest, but a dream artist's studio was a definite must. Maybe after Daisy graduated high school Raine would be willing to move to the cabin property full-time.

His wife. He was starting to get a real charge out of the notion.

Water, electricity, internet, a decent road… He could arrange all of that.

He had an idea forming in his head about the floor plan. As long as Raine basically agreed with it, he was in a very good place. She was focused on details and he was focused on what would work. A one-time-only construction project was his goal and he thought it was hers, too.

He liked pairing the right backer with the right film, and the right artist with the right project, because he could spot solid worth. He'd probably shot himself in the foot by even proposing that Raine consider doing the pixel film. She would be busier than ever, but *he* was ready to slow down and take a look around. His frenetic working pace couldn't go on forever, he'd always known that. If he cut back, he could be there a lot more of the time for Raine and Daisy—and any kids he and Raine might have together.

It seemed to him they'd started working on that to-night.

Those select casual relationships he'd had in the past amounted to nothing and he knew why now. He'd known something was missing, but just not how to define it.

Raine had settled all that.

And now he knew how the book ended.

"I did something wrong." He knew he had. She was quiet, and maybe not distant, but certainly distracted.

"No," she told him in a resigned voice, "you did something too right, I'm afraid."

How was that possible? he argued in his mind, but the spitfire was good at calling his hand. "The land dispute is settled. That varmit won't ever threaten you or this place again. What now?"

She put her hands on her hips, but at least now there was laughter in her eyes. "*Varmit*? Eastern boy, you need to learn a great deal about how to say a word like that. You can't pull off cowboy just yet, but you're pretty good, I'll grant, at solving a real problem without just taking out a gun."

"A man can use his brain now and then instead

of force. I still don't understand why you're mad at me."

"I'm not mad, just pretty sure I'm going to have a baby."

He'd known it was possible, but he was still stunned. "What?"

"That isn't necessarily all your fault, I was there too, but in case you haven't noticed, we aren't married."

He recovered after a moment. And he could solve that problem, too. "There's a preacher in Mustang Creek. Let me hitch up the horses. We can pay him a quiet visit and take care of that right away."

She was going to be stubborn to the last minute, but was so beautiful every time he looked at her she took his breath away. "The last time you did that it didn't work out so well. I seem to remember sitting in the buckboard and watching you jump out to chase the loose horses down."

"Sweetheart, I remember. Thanks for reminding me you were laughing so hard I thought you might fall off the seat."

"I'm not sure I should marry a greenhorn."

He went over and kissed her. "I'm positive you should."

Her smile was predictably saucy. "I think I will. I'll hitch up the horses."

EPILOGUE

❖

December 24th, one year later

WAS THIS A MISTAKE?

Maybe it was—it was going to be hard to tell until it all settled out, but still Raine had fingers and toes crossed.

It was official, she was nuts for even thinking of this, but then again, Stephano and Harry had done most of the work. In a rare truce, they'd coordinated the menu and though they hadn't necessarily cooperated with each other, they'd grudgingly come to an agreement on what to serve.

The new house was complete, if not quite ready for guests since she'd been more than a little busy, but Hadleigh, Melody and Bex had put up decorations and Grace, Luce and Kelly were on kid patrol.

Mick had mentioned he was looking forward to green chili cheeseburgers and an old Western movie.

Not this year. His entire family had agreed to come.

Was she nervous? Oh yes. Not because she was worried the party wouldn't go smoothly, but because she wasn't sure how her surprise was going to be received. Mick seemed to accept just fine that his family didn't spend Christmas together, but she wanted to give him this special gift.

A really wonderful gift hopefully, with a small bonus.

She'd talked it over with Blythe and gotten full Carson approval on the idea. So he had no idea his family was coming, and everyone was forbidden to tell him.

The new house did look wonderful with all the decorations. The tree was from the north end of the property and at least twelve feet high, but a ladder and three Carson men squabbling over who was ascending it took care of the top part and Daisy and Ryder had fun decorating the rest. Ryder was getting to the age where that sort of thing was no longer his idea of fun… He'd rather be taking cute girls to the movies, and—she wasn't a fool—maybe thinking about stealing a beer or two here or there by his age, but he obligingly hung up a snowman on a branch that Daisy wasn't tall enough to reach, asking if it was where she wanted it. She imperiously made him move it over three inches.

He really was the nicest kid and humored Daisy without protest.

The Bransons were the first to arrive. Raine had met them on a swift trip to California that combined personal affairs with business, since she also met with the director of the pixel movie. Mick's mother was cool and poised, but still warmer than expected. Not haughty, just assessing. His brother was very businesslike but equally likeable, and his sister-in-law was unexpectedly a kindred spirit with her keen eye for art. They'd met for dinner at some trendy restaurant so conversation hadn't been very personal, but Raine had started exchanging emails with Mick's mother, which he found quite amusing. She'd sent pictures of the house construction, of the sun rising over the mountains, of Mustang Creek's fall festival, of Mick and Daisy absorbed in a game of chess, all designed to give her mother-in-law a glimpse into their lives.

To her surprise, it worked. She got back not just replies, but photos of vineyards, theater signs, and even a Halloween photo of Mick's mother dressed up as Scarlet from *Gone with the Wind* for a fancy party. They might be many miles apart but they were finding a way to get to know each other.

Raine was convinced that while Mick shrugged it off as if his family never spending Christmas together since his father died didn't bother him, it did. She was hardly a psychologist, but she had to wonder if it didn't bother all of them and scattering to different locations was a way to avoid the emotional impact.

Time to start better memories, or so she hoped.

When Mick walked in the door, looking wiped out after a trip to Germany that took three days longer than planned, he was greeted by the sight of a houseful of people having cocktails and nibbling on artichoke dip. He stood for a minute in the doorway before he said calmly, "I saw the cars, so I guess I'm not surprised at the crowd. Raine, I talked to you last night. You failed to mention we were having a party."

She kissed him. "Surprise! It was really your mother's idea. Welcome home."

He kissed her back, taking his time about it. "My mother wanted me to have a party? Now I have two women conspiring against me—three, if we include Daisy. I feel outnumbered."

"Well, maybe we'll have a boy to help tilt the odds. I'm due in July."

"What?" He looked like he might fall over. "Can you repeat that? We're having a baby?"

"It seems like we are. We've been trying, remember? Don't look quite so incredulous."

"*I've* certainly have been doing my best." He scanned the room and froze. "Is that my *brother* pouring himself a drink? He's here? On Christmas Eve? In Wyoming?"

"Don't look now, but your mother is right there in the corner, talking to Blythe and Ingrid. I have no idea what they're saying but I'm going to bet you're the main topic of conversation."

"That's a bet I'd be crazy to take. And nice job trying to change the subject. Raine, really? We're pregnant?"

"I'm pregnant and you're the father, so the answer to that is yes."

"I'm... I don't even know what to say. Why didn't you tell me?"

"It seemed like the perfect present to surprise you with. Last year you got a haunted cabin. How is a girl going to top that one? It was a high bar."

"I think you just cleared it." He reached for her again, but laughing, she pushed him away.

"Tonight you can tell your family face-to-face. Let's go celebrate. Mace made a non-alcoholic wine drink just for me, called Bran-Son. Drake has a new foal about to drop he's going to call Brandy. You know those two. The race is on, boy or girl."

"My family isn't up for this crowd. Or for Mustang Creek. This isn't Paris or Rome."

"No." Raine hooked her arm through his, her eyes shining. "It sure isn't. But I think they'll find they prefer it here."

He certainly did.

★ ★ ★ ★ ★

From #1 New York Times *bestselling author*
Linda Lael Miller and MIRA Books
comes a sweeping new saga set against the backdrop
of the Civil War.

Read on for an exclusive sneak preview of
THE BLUE AND THE GRAY...

PART ONE

"...entreat me not to leave thee, or to return from following after thee: for whither thou goest, I will go..."

Ruth 1:16

ONE

Jacob
Chancellorsville, Virginia
May 3, 1863

The first mini-ball ripped into Corporal Jacob Hammond's left hand, the second, his right knee, each strike leaving a ragged gash in its wake; another slashed through his right thigh an instant later, and then he lost count.

A coppery crimson mist rained down upon Jacob as he bent double, then plunged, with a strange, protracted grace, toward the broken ground. On the way down, he noted the bent and broken grass, shimmering with fresh blood, the deep gouges left by boot heels and the lunging hooves of panicked horses.

A peculiar clarity overtook Jacob in those moments between life as he'd always known it and another way of being, already inevitable. The common boundaries of his mind seemed to expand beyond skull and skin, rushing outward at a dizzying speed, flying in all directions, rising past the treetops, past the sky, past the far borders of the cosmos itself.

For an instant, he understood everything, every mystery, every false thing, every truth.

He felt no emotion, no joy or sorrow.

He simply *knew.*

Then, so suddenly that it sickened his very soul, he was back inside himself, a prisoner surrounded by fractured bars of bone. The flash of extraordinary knowledge was gone, a fact that saddened Jacob more deeply than the likelihood of death, but some small portion of the experience remained, an ability to think without obstruction, to see his past as vividly as his present, to envision all that was around him, as if from a great height.

Blessedly, there was no pain, though he knew that would surely come, provided he remained alive long enough to receive it.

Something resembling bitter amusement overtook Jacob then; he realized that, unaccountably, he hadn't expected to be struck down on this savage battlefield or any other. Never mind the unspeakable carnage he'd witnessed since his enlistment in Mr. Lincoln's grand army; with the hubris of youth, he had believed himself invincible.

He had, in fact, assumed that angels fought alongside the men in blue, on the side of righteousness, committed to the task of mending a sundered nation, restoring it to its former whole. For all its faults, the United States of America was the most promising nation ever to arise from the old order of kings and despots; even now, Jacob was convinced that, whatever the cost, it must not be allowed to fail.

He had been willing to pay that price, was willing still.

Why then was he shocked, nay *affronted*, to find that the bill had come due, in full, and his own blood and breath, his very substance, were the currency required?

Because, he thought, shame washing over him, he had been willing to die only in *theory*. Out of vanity or ignorance or pure naivety, or some combination of the three, he had somehow, without being aware of it, declared himself exempt.

Well, there it was. Jacob Hammond, husband of Caroline, father of Rachel, son and grandson and great-grandson of decent men and women, present owner of a modest but fertile farm outside the pleasant but otherwise unremarkable township of Gettysburg, Pennsylvania, was no more vital to the operation of the universe than any other man.

Inwardly, Jacob sighed, for it was some comfort, however fleeting, to know that his mistake was, at least, not original.

Was the cause he was about to die for worthwhile?

Reluctant as he was to make the sacrifice, to leave Caroline and Rachel and the farm behind, Jacob still believed wholeheartedly that it was.

Surely, the hand of God Almighty Himself had guided those bold visionaries of 1776, and led the common people to an impossible victory against the greatest army on the face of the earth. In nearly a century of independence, there had never been a time without peril or strife, for the British had returned in 1812 and, once again, the nation had barely prevailed.

How, then, could he, dying or not, withdraw his faith, his last minuscule contribution, from so noble an endeavor?

So much hung in the balance, so very much; not only the hope and valor of those who had gone before, but the freedom, perhaps the very existence, of those yet to be born.

In solidarity, the United States could be a force for good in a hungry, desperate world. Torn asunder, it would be ineffectual, two bickering factions, bound to divide into still smaller and weaker fragments over time, too busy posturing and rattling sabers to meet the demands of a fragile future, to take a stand against the inevitable rise of new tyrannies.

No, Jacob decided, still clearheaded and detached from his damaged body, this war, with all its undeniable evils, had been fated from the day the first slaves had set foot upon American soil.

We hold these truths to be self-evident, that all men are created equal...

That one phrase had chafed the consciences of thinking people since it flowed from the nib of Thomas Jefferson's pen, as well it should have. Willing or unwilling, the entire nation had been living a lie.

It was time to right that particular wrong, Jacob thought, once and for all.

And if by chance there *were* warrior angels, he prayed they would not abandon the cause of liberty, but fight on until every man, woman and child on the North American continent was truly free.

With that petition made, Jacob raised another, more selfish one. *Watch over my beloved wife, our little daughter, and Enoch, our trusted friend. Keep them safe and well.*

The request was simple, one of millions like it, no doubt, rising to the ears of the Creator on wings of desperation and sorrow, and there was no Road-to-Damascus moment for Jacob, just the ground-shaking roar of battle all around. But even in the midst of thundering cannon, the sharp reports of carbines and the fiery blast of muskets, the clanking of swords and the shrill shrieks of men and horses, he found a certain consolation.

Perhaps, he had been heard.

He began to drift then, back and forth between darkness and light, fear and oblivion. When he surfaced, the pain was waiting, like a specter hovering over him, ready to descend, settle upon him, crush him beneath its weight.

Consequently, Jacob took refuge in the depths of his being, where it could not yet reach.

Hours passed, perhaps days; he had no way of knowing.

Eventually, because life is persistent even in the face of hopelessness and unrelenting agony, the hiding place within became less assessable. During those intervals, pain played with him, like a cat with a mouse. Smoke burned his eyes, which he could not close, climbed, stinging, into his nostrils, chafed his throat raw. He was thirsty, so thirsty; he felt as dry as last year's corn husks, imagining his life's blood seeping, however slowly, into the ravaged earth.

In order to bear his suffering, Jacob thought about home, conjured vivid images of Caroline, quietly pretty, more prone to laughter than to tears, courageous as any man he'd ever known. She loved him, he knew that, and his heart rested safely with her. She had always accepted his attentions in the marriage bed with good-humored acquiescence, though not with a passion equal to his own, and while he told himself this was feminine modesty, not disinterest, he sometimes suspected otherwise.

Caroline shouldered the chores of a farmwife without complaint, washing and ironing, cooking and sewing, tending the vegetable garden behind the kitchen-house and picking apples and pears, apricots and peaches in the orchards when the fruit ripened. She preserved whatever produce they did not sell in town, along with milk and eggs and butter, attended church services without fail, though she had once confided to Jacob that she feared God was profoundly deaf. Caroline was an active member of the local Ladies Aid Society, a group devoted to making quilts and blankets for soldiers and gathering donations of various foodstuffs, including such perishables as cakes and bread, all to be crated and shipped to battlefronts and hospitals all over the North. She did all this, and probably much more, while mothering little Rachel with intelligence and devotion, neither too permissive nor too stern.

In addition, Caroline endured every hardship—crops destroyed by rain or hail, the death of her beloved grandfather and several close friends, the two miscarriages she'd suffered—with her chin up and her shoulders back.

Of course she'd wept, especially for the lost babies, but she'd done so in solitude, probably hoping to spare Jacob the added sorrow of seeing her despair. Now, with death so close it seemed palpable, he wished she hadn't tried to hide her grief, wished he'd sought her out and taken her into his arms and held her fast, weeping with her.

Alas, there was no going back, and regret would only sap what little strength that remained to him.

Besides, remembrance was sweet sanctuary from the gathering storm of pain. In his mind's eye, he saw little Rachel running to meet him when he came in from the fields at the end of the day, filthy and sweat-soaked and exhausted himself, while his daughter was as fresh as the wildflowers flourishing alongside the creek in summer. Clad in one of her tiny calico dresses, face and hands scrubbed, she raced toward him, laughing, her arms open wide, her fair pigtails flying, her bright blue eyes shining with delighted welcome.

Dear God, what he wouldn't give to be back there, sweeping that precious child up into his arms, setting her on his shoulder or swinging her around and around until they were both dizzy. Caroline usually fussed over such antics—she'd just gotten Rachel clean again, she'd fret, and here that little scamp was, dirty as a street urchin—or she'd protest against "all this rough-housing," declaring that someone was bound to get hurt, or any one of a dozen other undesirable possibilities—but she never quite managed to maintain her dour demeanor. Invariably, Caroline smiled, shaking her head and wondering aloud what in the world she was going to do with the two of them, scoundrels that they were.

It was then that the longing for his wife and daughter grew too great, and Jacob turned his memory to sun-splashed fields, flourishing and green, to sparkling streams thick with fish. In his imagination, he stood beside Enoch once more, both of them gratified by the sight of a heavy crop, by the knowledge that, this year anyway, their hard work would bring a reward.

"God has blessed our efforts," Jacob would say, quietly and with awe, for he had believed the world to be an essentially good place then. War and all its brutalities merely tales told in books, or passed down the generations by old men.

In his mind's eye, he could see the hired man's broad black face, shining with sweat, his white teeth flashing as he grinned and replied, "Well, I don't see as how the Good Lord ought to get *all* the credit. He might send the sunshine and the rain, but far as I can reckon, He ain't much for plowin', nor for hoein', neither."

Jacob invariably laughed, no matter how threadbare the joke, would have laughed now, too, if he'd had the strength.

He barely noticed, as he lost consciousness for what he believed to be the final time, that the terrible din of battle had faded to the feeble moans and low cries of other men, fallen and left behind in the acrid urgency of combat.

He dreamed—or at least, he *thought* he was dreaming—of the Heaven he'd heard about all his life, for he came from a long line of church-going folk. He saw the towering gates, studded with pearls and precious gems, standing open before him.

He caught a glimpse of the fabled streets of gold, too, and though he saw no angels and no long-departed loved ones waiting to welcome him into whatever celestial realm they now occupied, he heard music, almost too beautiful to be endured. He looked up, saw a dazzling sky, not merely blue, but somehow *woven*, a shimmering tapestry of innumerable colors, each one brilliant, some familiar and some beyond his powers of description.

He hesitated, not from fear, for surely there could be no danger here, but because he knew that once he passed through this particular gateway, there would be no turning back.

Perhaps it was blasphemy, but Jacob's heart swelled with a poignant longing for a lesser heaven, another, humbler paradise, where the gates and fences were made of hand-hewn wood or plain stones gathered in fields, and the roads were winding trails of dust and dirt, rutted by wagon wheels, deep, glittering snows and heavy rain.

Had it been in his power, and he knew it wasn't, he would have traded eternity in this place of ineffable peace and beauty for a single, blessedly ordinary day at home, waking up beside Caroline in their feather bed, teasing her until she blushed, or to watch, stricken by the love of her, as she made breakfast in the kitchen-house on an ordinary morning.

Suddenly, the sweet visions were gone.

Jacob heard sounds, muffled but distinct. Men, horses, a few wagons.

Then nothing.

Perhaps he was imagining things. Suffering hallucinations.

He waited, listening, his eyes unblinking, dry and rigid in their sockets, stinging with sweat and grit and congealed blood.

Fear burned in his veins as those first minutes after he was wounded came back. He recalled the shock of his flesh tearing with visceral intensity, as though it were happening all over again, a waking nightmare of friend and foe alike streaming past, shouting, shooting, bleeding, stepping over him and upon him. He recalled the hooves of horses, churning up patches of the ground within inches of where he lay.

Jacob forced himself to concentrate. Although he couldn't see the sky, he knew by the light that the day was waning.

Was he alone?

The noises came again, but they were more distant now. Perhaps the party of men and horses had passed him by.

The prospect was a bleak one, filling Jacob with quiet despair. Even a band of rebs would have been preferable to lying helplessly in his own gore, wondering when the rats and crows would come to feast upon him.

An enemy bullet or the swift mercy of a bayonet would be infinitely better.

Hope stirred briefly when a Federal soldier appeared in his line of vision, as though emerging from a void. At first, Jacob wasn't sure the other man was real.

He tried to speak, or make the slightest move, thus indicating that he was alive and in need of help, but he could do neither.

The soldier approached, crouched beside him, and one glimpse of his filthy, beard-stubbled face, hard with cruelty, put an end to Jacob's illusions. The man rolled him roughly onto his back, with no effort to search for a pulse or any other sign of life. Instead, he began rifling through Jacob's pockets, muttering under his breath, helping himself to his watch and what little money he carried, since most of his pay went to Caroline.

Jacob felt outrage, but he was still helpless. All he could do was watch as the other man reached hurriedly for his rucksack, fumbled to lift the canvas flap and reach inside.

Finally, the bummer, as thieves and stragglers and deserters were called, gave in to frustration and dumped Jacob's belongings onto the ground, pawing through them.

Look at me, Jacob thought. *I am alive. I wear the same uniform as you do.*

The scavenger did not respond, of course. Did not allow his gaze to rest upon Jacob's face, where he might have seen awareness.

The voices, the trampling hooves, the springless wagons drew closer.

The man cursed, frantic now. He found Jacob's battered Bible and flung it aside, in disgusted haste, its thin pages fluttering as it fell, like a bird with a broken wing. The standard-issue tin cup, plate and utensils soon followed, but the thieving bastard stilled when he found the packet of letters, all from Caroline. Perhaps believing he might find something of value in one or more of them, he shoved them into his own rucksack.

Jacob grieved for those letters, but there was nothing he could do.

Except listen.

Yes, he decided. Someone was coming, a small company of riders.

The thief grew more agitated, looked back over one shoulder, and then turned back to his plundering, feverish now, but too greedy to flee.

At last, he settled upon the one object Jacob cherished as much as Caroline's letters, a small leather case with a tarnished brass hinges and a delicate clasp.

Wicked interest flashed in the man's eyes, as he fumbled open the case and saw the tin-types inside, one of Caroline and Jacob, taken on their wedding day, looking traditionally somber in their finest garb, the other of Caroline, with an infant Rachel in her arms, the child resplendent in a tiny, lace-trimmed christening gown and matching bonnet.

Caroline had sewed every stitch of the impossibly small dress and beribboned bonnet, made them sturdy, so they could be worn by all the children to follow.

No, Jacob cried inwardly, hating his helplessness.

"Well, now," the man murmured. "Ain't this a pretty little family? Maybe I'll just look them up sometime, offer my condolences."

Had he been able, Jacob would have killed the bummer in that moment, throttled the life out of him with his bare hands, and never regretted the act. Although he struggled with all his might, trying to gather the last shreds of his strength, the effort proved useless.

It was the worst kind of agony, imagining this man reading the letters, noting the return address on each and every envelope, seeking Caroline and Rachel out, offering a pretense of sympathy.

Taking advantage.

And Jacob could do nothing to stop him, nothing to protect his wife and daughter from this monster or others like him, the renegades, the enemies of decency and innocence in all their forms.

With the smile of a demon, the bummer snapped the case closed and reached for his rucksack, ready, at last, to flee.

It was then that a figure loomed behind him, a gray shadow of a man, planted the sole of one boot squarely in the center of the thief's back, and sent him sprawling across Jacob's inert frame.

The pain was instant, throbbing in every bone and muscle of Jacob's body.

"Stealing from a dead man," the shadow said, standing tall, his buttery-smooth drawl laced with contempt. "That's low, even for a Yank."

The bummer scrambled to his feet, groped for something, probably his rifle, and paled when he came up empty. Most likely, he'd dropped the weapon in his eagerness to rob one of his own men.

"I ought to run you through with this fine steel sword of mine, Billy," the other man mused idly. He must have ridden ahead of his detachment, dismounted nearby, and moved silently through the scattered bodies. "After all, this is a *war*, now, isn't it? And you are my foe, as surely as I am yours."

Jacob's vision, unclear to begin with, blurred further, and there was a pounding in his ears, but he could make out the contours of the two men, now standing on either side of him, and he caught the faint murmur of their words, a mere wisp of sound.

"You don't want to kill me, Johnny," the thief reasoned, with a note of anxious congeniality in his voice, raising both palms as if in surrender. "It wouldn't be honorable, with us Union boys at a plain disadvantage." He drew in a strange, swift whistle of a breath. "Anyhow, I wasn't hurtin' nobody. Just makin' good use of things this poor fella has no need of, bein' dead and all."

By now, Jacob was aware of men and horses all around, though there was no cannon fire, no shouting, no sharp report of rifles.

"You want these men to see you murder an unarmed man?" wheedled the man addressed as Billy. "Where I come from, you'd be hanged for that. It's a war crime, ain't it?"

"We're not 'where you come from,'" answered Johnny coolly. The bayonet affixed to the barrel of his carbine glinted in the lingering smoke and the dust raised by the horses. "This is Virginia," he went on, with a note of fierce reverence. "And you are an intruder here, sir."

Billy—the universal name for all Union soldiers, as Johnny was for their Confederate counterparts—spat, foolhardy in his fear. "I reckon the rules are about the same, though, whether North or South," he ventured. Even Jacob, from his faulty vantage point, saw the terror behind all that bluster. "Fancy man like you—an officer, at that—must know how it is. Even if you don't hang for killin' with no cause, you'll be court-martialed for sure, once your superiors catch wind of what you done. And that's bound to leave a stain on your high-and-mighty reputation as a Southern gentleman, ain't it? Just you think, *sir*, of the shame all those well-mannered folks back home on the old plantation will have to contend with, all on your account."

A slow, untroubled grin took shape on the Confederate captain's soot-smudged face. His gray uniform was torn and soiled, the brass of his buttons and insignia dull, and his boots were scuffed, but even Jacob, nearly blind, could see that his dignity was inborn, as much a part of him as the color of his eyes.

"It might be worth hanging," he replied, almost cordially, like a man debating some minor point of military ethics at an elegant dinner party far removed from the sound and fury of war, "the pleasure of killing a latrine rat such as yourself, that is. As for these men, most of whom are under my command, as it happens, well, they've seen their friends and cousins and brothers skewered by Yankee bayonets and blown to fragments by their canon. Just today, in fact, they saw General Jackson relieved of an arm." At this, the captain paused, swallowed once. "Most likely, they'd raise a cheer as you fell."

Dimly, Jacob saw Billy Yank's Adam's apple bob along the length of his neck. Under any other circumstances, he might have been amused by the fellow's nervous bravado, but he could feel himself retreating further and further into the darkness of approaching death, and there was no room in him for frivolous emotions.

"Now, that just ain't Christian," protested Billy, conveniently overlooking his own moral lapse.

The captain gave a raspy laugh, painful to hear, and shook his head. "A fine sentiment, coming from the likes of you." In the next moment, his face hardened, aristocratic even beneath its layers of dried sweat and dirt. He turned slightly, keeping one eye on his prisoner, and

shouted a summons into the rapidly narrowing nothing-
ness surrounding the three of them.

Several men hurried over, though they were invisible
to Jacob, and the sounds they made were faint.

"Get this piece of dog dung out of my sight before I
pierce his worthless flesh with my sword for the pure
pleasure of watching him bleed," the officer ordered.
"He is a disgrace, even to *that* uniform."

There were words of reply, though Jacob could not
make them out, and Jacob sensed a scuffle as the thief
resisted capture, a modern-day Judas, bleating a traitor's
promises, willing to betray men who'd fought alongside him, confided their hopes and fears to him around
campfires or on the march.

Jacob waited, expecting the gentleman soldier to follow his men, go on about his business of overseeing the
capture of wounded blue-coats, the recovery of his own
troops, alive and dead.

Instead, the man crouched, as the thief had done earlier. He took up the rucksack Billy had been forced to
leave behind, rummaged within it, produced the packet
of letters and the leather case containing the likenesses of
Jacob's beloved wife and daughter. He opened the latter,
examined the images inside, smiled sadly.

Then he tucked the items inside Jacob's bloody coat,

paused as though startled, and looked directly into his motionless eyes.

"My God," he said, under his breath. "You're alive."

Jacob could not acknowledge the remark verbally, but he felt a tear trickle over his left temple, into his hair, and that, apparently, was confirmation enough for the Confederate captain.

Now, Jacob thought, he would be shot, put out of his misery like an injured horse. And he would welcome the release.

Instead, very quietly, the captain said. "Hold on. You'll be found soon." He paused, frowning. "And if you happen to encounter a Union quartermaster by the name of Rogan McBride, somewhere along the way, I would be obliged if you'd tell him Bridger Winslow sends his best regards."

Jacob doubted he'd get the chance to do as Winslow asked, but he marked the names carefully in his mind, just the same.

Another voice spoke then. "This somebody you know, Captain?" a man asked, with concern and a measure of sympathy. It wasn't uncommon on either side, after all, to find a friend or a relative among enemy casualties, for the battle-lines often cut across towns, churches, and supper tables.

"No," the captain replied gruffly. "Just another dead

Federal." A pause. "Get on with your business, Simms. We might have the blue-coats under our heel for the moment, but you can be sure they'll be back to bury what remains they can't gather up and haul away. Better if we don't risk a skirmish after a day of hard fighting."

"Yes, sir," Simms replied sadly. "The men are low in spirit, now that General Jackson has been struck down."

"Yes," the captain answered. Angry sorrow flashed in his eyes. "By his own troops," he added bitterly, speaking so quietly that Jacob wondered if Simms had heard them at all.

Jacob sensed the other man's departure.

The captain lingered, taking his canteen from his belt, loosening the cap a little with a deft motion of one hand, leaving the container within Jacob's reach. The gesture was most likely a futile one, since Jacob could not use his hands, but it was an act of kindness, all the same. An affirmation of the possibility, however remote, that Jacob might somehow survive.

Winslow rose to his full height, regarded Jacob solemnly, and walked away.

Jacob soon lost consciousness again, waking briefly now and then, surprised to find himself not only still among the living, but unmolested by vermin. When alert, he lay looking up the night sky, steeped in the profound silence of the dead, one more body among dozens, if not hundreds, scattered across the blood-soaked grass.

Just so many pawns in some Olympian chess match, he reflected, discarded in the heat of conflict and then forgotten.

Sometime the next morning, or perhaps the morning after that, wagons came again, and grim-faced Union soldiers stacked the bodies like cordwood, one on top of another. They were fretful, these battle-weary men, anxious to complete their dismal mission and get back behind the Union lines, where there was at least a semblance of safety.

Jacob, mute and motionless, was among the last to be taken up, grasped roughly by two men in dusty blue coats.

The pain was so sudden, so excruciating that finally, *finally*, he managed a low, guttural cry.

The soldier supporting his legs, little more than a boy, with blemished skin and not even the prospect of a beard, gasped. "This fella's still with us," he said, and he looked so startled, so horrified, and so pale that Jacob feared he would swoon, letting his burden drop.

"Well," said the other man, gruffly cheerful, "Johnny left a few breathin' this time around."

The boy recovered enough to turn his head and spit, and to Jacob's relief, he remained upright, his grasp firm.

"A few," he agreed grudgingly. "And every one of them better off dead."

The darkness returned then, enfolding Jacob like the embrace of a sea siren, pulling him under.

TWO

Caroline
Washington City,
June 15, 1863

Nothing Caroline Hammond had heard or read about the nation's capital could have prepared her for the reality of the place, the soot and smoke, the jostling crowds of soldiers and civilians, the clatter of wagon wheels, the neighing of horses and the braying of mules, the rough merriment streaming through the open doorways of plentiful saloons and pleasure houses.

She kept her gaze firmly averted as she passed one after another of these establishments, appalled by the seediness of it all, by the crude shouts, the jangle of badly tuned pianos and rollicking songs sung lustily and off-key, and, here and there, fisticuffs accompanied by the breaking of glass and even a few gunshots.

More than once, Caroline was forced to cross the road, a gauntlet of ox carts and ambulance wagons and mounted men who took no evident notice of hapless pedestrians.

A farm wife, Caroline was not a person of delicate constitution. She had dispatched, cleaned and plucked many a chicken for Sunday supper, helped her husband Jacob and Enoch Flynn, the hired man, butcher hogs come autumn, and worked ankle-deep in barn muck on a daily basis.

Here, in this city of poor manners, ceaseless din and sickening stenches, the effects were, of course, magnified, surrounding her on every side, pummeling her senses without mercy.

Runnels of foaming animal urine flowed among the broken cobblestones, and dung steamed in piles, adding to the cloying miasma. On the far edge of her vision, she saw a soldier vomit copiously into a gutter and felt her own gorge rise, scalding, to the back of her throat. The man's companions seemed amused by the spectacle, slapping their retching friend on the back and chiding him with loud, jocular admonitions of an unsavory nature.

Seeing the disreputable state of these men's uniforms, intended as symbols of a proud and noble cause, thoroughly besmirched not only by all manner of filth, but by the indecent comportment of the men who wore them, sent furious color surging into her cheeks. Only her native prudence and the urgency of her mission— locating her wounded husband, lying near death in one of Washington's City's numerous makeshift hospitals, or, if she had arrived too late, in a pine box—kept her from striding right up to the scoundrels and taking them sternly to task for bringing such shame upon their more honorable fellows.

How dare they behave like reprobates, safe in the shadow of Mr. Lincoln's White House, while their great-hearted comrades fought bravely on blood-drenched bat-tlefields all over the land?

She was mortified, as well as grieved, but anger sustained her. Kept her moving toward the rows of hospital tents just visible in the distance.

Toward Jacob.

She thought of the long-delayed telegram, tucked away in her reticule. She'd read it over and over again from the day it had been placed in her hands, read it during the long train ride from Gettysburg, the small, quiet town in the green Pennsylvania countryside she had lived in, or near, all her life.

By now, the missive was tattered and creased, an evil talisman, despised and yet somehow necessary, the only link she had to her husband.

The information it contained was maddeningly scant,

indicating only that Corporal Jacob Hammond had fallen in battle on May 3, at Chancellorsville, Virginia, and had since been transported to the capitol, where he would receive the best medical attention available.

As the granddaughter of a country doctor and sometimes undertaker, Caroline knew only too well what Jacob and others like him had yet to endure: crowding, filth, poor food and tainted water, too few trained surgeons and attendants, shortages of even the most basic supplies, such as clean bandages, laudanum and ether. Sanitation, the most effective enemy of sepsis, according to her late grandfather, was virtually nonexistent.

The stench of open latrines, private and public privies and towering heaps of manure standing on empty lots finally forced Caroline to set down her carpetbag long enough to pull her best Sunday handkerchief from the pocket of her cloak and press the soft cloth to her nose and mouth. The scent of rosewater, generously applied before she left home, had faded with time and distance, and thus provided little relief, but it was better than nothing.

Caroline picked up her carpetbag and walked purposely onward, not because she knew where she would find her husband, but because she didn't dare stand still too long, lest her knees give way beneath her.

Thus propelled by false resolution and a rising sense

of desperation, she hurried on, through the mayhem of a wartime city under constant threat of siege, doing her best to convey a confidence she did not feel. Beneath the stalwart countenance, fear gnawed at her empty, roiling stomach, throbbed in her head, sought and found the secret regions of her heart, where the bruises were, to do its worst.

She had no choice but to carry on, no matter what might be required of her, and she did not attempt to ignore the relentless dread. That would be impossible.

Instead, she walked, weaving her way through the crowds on the sidewalks, crossing to the opposite side of the street in a mostly useless effort to avoid staggering drunkards and street brawls and men who watched her too boldly. Having long since learned the futility of burying her fears, she made up her mind to face them instead, with calm fortitude—as well as she could, anyway.

As she'd often heard her grandfather remark, turning a blind eye to a problem or a troublesome situation served only to make matters worse in the long run. "Face things head-on, Caroline," the old man had lectured. "Stand up to whatever comes your way and, if you are in the right, Providence will come to your aid."

Lately, she had not seen a great deal of evidence to support the latter part of that statement, but, then again, Providence was under no discernible obligation to explain itself or its ways to questioning mortals, particularly in light of the stupidity, greed and cruelty so far displayed by the human race.

One by one, Caroline confronted the haunting possibilities, the pictures standing vivid in her thoughts, nearly tangible. In the most immediate scenario, she could not find Jacob, even after the most arduous search imaginable. There had been a mistake, and he had been taken to some other place entirely, or died in transit, and been buried in an anonymous grave, one she would never be able to locate.

In the next, she *did* find her husband, but she had not arrived quickly enough to hold his hand, stroke his forehead, bid him a tender farewell. He had already succumbed, and all that was left of him was a gray, waxen corpse lying in a ramshackle coffin. When she touched him, in this vision, his flesh was so cold that it left her fingertips numb and burning, as if frostbitten.

But there was one more tableau to face and in many ways, it was the most terrible of all. Here, Jacob was alive, horribly maimed, helpless, forced to bear the unbearable until death delivered him from his sufferings in days, weeks, months—or years.

The thought tormented Caroline.

If only she knew what to expect, she might be able to prepare somehow.

But then, how *could* one prepare for the shock of seeing a beloved husband, broken and torn? Suppose Jacob was so disfigured that she did not recognize him or, worse yet, allowed shock or dismay to show in her face, her manner, her bearing?

She swayed, not daring to draw the deep breath her body craved, lest the dreadful smells of disease and suffering and death finally overwhelm her, render her useless to Jacob just when he needed her most.

And that would not do.

YA Orlev
THE MAN FROM THE OTHER SIDE

	DATE DUE		
DEC 20 1991			
MAY 22 1992			
OCT 1 1993			
MAR 25 1994			

The Man from
the Other Side

The Man from
the Other Side

Uri Orlev

*Translated from the Hebrew
by Hillel Halkin*

Houghton Mifflin Company
Boston 1991

Library of Congress Cataloging-in-Publication Data

Orlev, Uri, 1931–
    [Ish min ha-tsad ha-aher. English]
    The man from the other side: a novel/by Uri Orlev.
        p.   cm.
    Translation of: Ish min ha-tsad ha-aher.
    Summary: Living on the outskirts of the Warsaw Ghetto during
World War II, fourteen-year-old Marek and his grandparents shelter a
Jewish man in the days before the Jewish uprising.
    ISBN 0-395-53808-4
    1. World War, 1939–1945—Poland—Juvenile fiction. 2. Holocaust,
Jewish (1939–1945)—Poland—Juvenile fiction. [1. World War,
1939–1945—Poland—Fiction. 2. Holocaust, Jewish (1939–1945)—
Poland—Fiction. 3. Jews—Poland—Fiction. 4. Poland—History—
Occupation, 1939–1945—Fiction.] I. Title.
PZ7.0633Man   1991   90-47898
                          CIP
                          AC
[Fic]—dc20

Printed in the United States of America
BP   10 9 8 7 6 5 4 3 2 1

Contents

A Word About My Friend Marek

While watching the evening news one day early last spring, I saw some shots of the smoking wreckage of a Polish airliner that had crashed near Warsaw. The passengers and crew were all killed. Only later did I find out that Marek was among them.

Marek was a Polish newspaperman I became friendly with when he visited Israel. We met by chance at the home of mutual friends. We spent the evening drinking vodka, and being about the same age, we were soon reliving memories of the Nazi-occupied Warsaw of our childhood. One reminiscence led to another, and we were hardly aware of time passing as the bottle of vodka grew empty. When we parted in the wee hours of the morning, I said to him, "I have an idea. Why don't I take you on a trip up north? I don't mind taking off a few days from work." He was happy to accept and we shook hands warmly on it.

I awoke the next day with a hangover, swearing at my rashness. I tried to think of an excuse to beg off, of some sudden illness or other calamity, but when I heard his excited voice on the telephone I knew that I couldn't back out. And so, pretending to be looking forward to it while secretly mourning the lost days that could have been put to a thousand better uses, I set out with him from Jerusalem.

By the first evening, however, I was over my regrets, and during the days of sightseeing that followed in the Galilee and Golan Heights, our talk ranged back and forth in space and time without a dull moment. I told Marek about Israel, its history and its problems, and he continued to tell me about his childhood, from which emerged a story that intrigued me more and more. In the end we spent four memorable days together, and upon returning to Jerusalem I jotted down some notes with the thought of making a book out of them. Of course, I would have asked for his permission, but he never gave me the chance. Perhaps he read my thoughts. In any case, he phoned and made me promise not to put his story in writing.

"How did you know that's what I wanted to do?" I asked. And I added, "To tell you the truth, I hate to pass up a good story, but I'm thrilled if this means you've decided to write it yourself."

"Lord, no . . ." He sounded alarmed. "It's just that in Poland . . . I mean, if anyone got wind of it . . ."

"Such as whom?" I asked.

"Anyone. My family. My friends. The government." He paused for a moment. "Even my wife. Nobody knows my background. That's still a very sensitive subject there."

2

"But if I wrote about it in Hebrew," I ventured, "no one in Poland could read it."

"Sooner or later it would reach us," he said. "I want you to promise me."

I had no choice but to give him my word.

A week later he called to say goodbye. He told me about his last days in Israel and reminded me of my vow.

"I can't say I'm happy about it," I said, "but you can count on me to keep my promise. Although only," I joked, "as long as you're alive."

"Agreed!" he laughed. "Now you have a reason to outlive me."

We parted with the resolution to meet again in Warsaw.

But the last laugh was fate's. Barely two months have passed since then and here I am sitting down to write his story.

Jerusalem, 1987

1

Down in the Sewers

I clearly remember the day my mother was convinced to let me go down into the sewers. After work my stepfather, who was a superintendent in the department of sanitation, made extra money by smuggling food into the Jewish ghetto. The Jews penned up there were literally dying of hunger and were ready to pay almost anything for something to eat.

There were just three of us in the family: my mother, my stepfather, and me.

I heard them discussing it one night until their conversation turned into one of their rare arguments. My stepfather wanted me to help him with the smuggling, since he was already carrying as much food as he could. It was high time, he told my mother, that I did something to help out.

"He's not a boy anymore," I heard him say. "He may be only fourteen, but he's got the strength of a twenty-year-old."

My mother was dead set against it, because she thought it was too dangerous. With my ear pressed to a hollow in the wall through which I could hear them better, I felt a twinge of fear. I had always pictured the sewers as a ghastly underground world beneath the streets and houses of the city, the closest thing to hell I could imagine. And I didn't like my stepfather, either. Just the thought of him made me smell sewage.

Once I was over my first fright, however, it seemed an adventure. Not a single one of my friends in school or on the block had ever dreamed of such an adventure.

I listened tensely to the argument. The more my mother was against it, the more I was for it. My stepfather explained to her that he couldn't ask anyone else: not her brother, because he would want to cut the doorman (with whom he had shady dealings of his own) in on it, and not any of his friends, because there wasn't a single one of them who wouldn't blab for a price. "Only the boy can be trusted," he said.

So I was still a "boy" after all!

Little by little, though, my mother's resistance crumbled. Finally she agreed, provided my stepfather didn't involve me in any "shenanigans."

At breakfast the next morning she said she had something important to tell me. I acted surprised.

"It's time you helped Antony carry food to the ghetto through the sewers."

"Is that all?" I asked.

Even if it wasn't news to me, I felt excited.

"We'll discuss the details tonight with Antony," said my mother, sending me off to school.

Over supper my mother asked my stepfather to explain what I would have to do. Antony shrugged

5

and said there was nothing to explain. "He'll see for himself soon enough," he said while continuing to eat. My stepfather was the silent type.

The next evening he took me down into the sewers.

I put on a pair of his old boots, which my mother carefully greased and padded with old rags to make them fit better, since they were a bit big on me. Then my stepfather put on the miner's helmet that he always wore, my mother checked the stairway to see that the coast was clear, and the two of us descended to the basement, where sacks of food were waiting.

I hadn't known until then how Antony entered the city sewer system. I had always wondered how he could smuggle anything under the noses of his fellow workers. Though it did not seem particularly logical, I had thought that perhaps there were special manholes known only to maintenance men and superintendents like himself. That is, there were ordinary manholes on every street corner — in the winter I had often seen the street cleaners dump piles of snow down them — but there was obviously no way of smuggling food through them, neither before nor after the night curfew, without being caught. Now, however, I discovered that my stepfather had his own private entrance in our basement.

I helped him move some sacks of coal into a corner. When he swept away the coal dust left behind, a trap door emerged that led straight into the sewers.

He climbed down a metal ladder and I followed by the light of the lamp on his helmet. My mother handed me a sack for him and then another for myself. At first I didn't think it was heavy, though I could see from her look that she thought otherwise. But she didn't say anything. She just called down "Good luck!" and shut the trap door above us.

The place was wet, slippery, and smelly, and there were fumes rising in the shaft of light from Antony's lamp. To be honest, my first instinct was to turn around and climb back out. But I didn't. It would have made me look pretty bad. I was ready to put up with a lot worse before I would give my stepfather the satisfaction of laughing at me.

The first part was easy. We walked along the edge of a gutter flowing with sewage, and though the sack on my back kept getting heavier, I thought I would be all right. My biggest worry was that Antony hadn't told me how long it would take. And maybe he didn't know himself, because that night he was going to some new customers, via a different route. After a while, though, we reached a point where we had to stoop and wade through the sewage, which first came up to our ankles and then to our knees. The worst part, in which we practically had to crawl through a conduit between two main sewers, was luckily short, because I couldn't have stood it much longer. I can remember feeling my hands turn to stone, and I was sure that in another minute my fingers would open by themselves and drop the sack. My feet were shaking, perhaps because I wasn't used to walking doubled over for so long, and I was out of breath. I didn't say a word, though. I would rather have died than told my stepfather I needed to rest.

7

At last we came to a recess in the wall of the tunnel that had some boards in it. Antony took one of them, propped it up diagonally, and laid his sack on it. Then he propped up another board for my sack and the two of us sat down to take a break. After he had smoked a cigarette in silence, we got to our feet again and continued, he first and me dragging after him. It wasn't until our second break that he bothered to speak to me.

"Don't think it isn't hard for me too, Marek," he said.

"How do you do it?" I gasped.

"By trying not to think. I just empty my head and think of nothing but the next few steps, as if they're all that's left. And when I've taken them, I think of a few more steps. Or else I concentrate on lifting my feet one after another. I block out everything else."

Little by little I learned to empty my head too until I understood what he meant. I suppose my body grew stronger and more used to it also. Sometimes I said a prayer over and over to myself, like the old women who ticked off rosaries in church. I was sorry I couldn't brag to my friends about it, but my mother and stepfather had warned me that I had better keep my mouth shut if I cared for our lives.

I hated those trips through the sewers from the start, but I had to take them. My stepfather was right: it was time I helped out. In fact, each time we brought back lots of money, some in American dollars, British pounds, and even gold coins. Now and then I had attacks of claustrophobia, sudden bouts of fear in which I felt that the tunnel was about to collapse and bury me underground. Fortunately, that didn't happen often. And yet oddly enough, I'm still prone to such attacks even now — in elevators, for instance, though I never know in advance when one is coming on.

My stepfather had worked in the sewer system since he was young, but he was made a district superintendent only when the Germans captured Warsaw, because both the superintendent before him and his assistant were killed in the German air raids. Antony knew the maze of the sewer system as well as I knew my way to school and back. He even knew about sewers that were no longer in use or had been sealed off by cave-ins from the air raids, so that they didn't even appear on the department of sanitation's own maps.

Which doesn't mean that my mother was wrong to be worried.

Yet it's true that no one could have known we were down there apart from other smugglers — and we never encountered any. In theory, perhaps, some sanitation worker on an emergency repair job might have run into us too, but that never happened either. Antony was sure that no one suspected him. The only possible informers were the Jews through whose basement we entered and left the ghetto, and they needed the food and made a profit by reselling part of it. Besides, they didn't know our real names or address, although if the Gestapo ever caught us, that wouldn't have been hard to find out. Maybe my stepfather wouldn't have talked, but I'm sure I would have.

In the end, though, we were discovered by a fellow worker of Antony's, a man named Krol. That's when I first understood why Antony had told my mother that first night that he couldn't trust anyone, not even my uncle.

But that's what wartime is like: suddenly you find out that everything you've thought about your friends, or your neighbors, or your relatives, is wrong. Anyone at all can inform on you or get you into hot water, because when someone is frightened, or hungry, or desperate for money, he's no longer the same person.

My mother liked to say that Antony talked tough but would never hurt a fly. That's not what happened with Krol, though. He must have suspected Antony for quite some time. Perhaps it started with his noticing how much food Antony was buying. We were lucky that he kept it to himself and took the secret with him when he died — and to a Jewish burial at that!

It happened late one night. We were struggling along with our sacks of food when suddenly we heard an ugly laugh and someone shined a flashlight on us.

It was Pan Krol. He had waited for us to approach before switching on his light, and now he stood in a bend of the sewer and said with a snicker that from now on we could split our profits with him. Antony didn't bat an eye. As if meeting Pan Krol in a sewer were the most natural thing in the world, he said perfectly matter-of-factly, "Fair enough. But that means we split the investment and the risk, too."

It certainly seemed fair to me. But Pan Krol didn't think so. He wanted to blackmail us, for us to pay him just to keep his mouth shut.

"Go wait for me beyond that bend, Marek," Antony said to me. "I need to talk to Pan Krol in private."

He lit the way to the bend for me. As soon as I was around it — naturally, I peeked to see what was happening — he put down his sack in the sewage, since there was nowhere else for it, and stepped up to Pan Krol. I was sure he only wanted to have a quiet word with him, but suddenly Krol was face down in the sewer and only then did I see the knife in Antony's hand. He wiped it off on Krol's clothes, tucked it back into his jacket, took out a white armband with a blue Star of David like the ones worn by the Jews, and tied it around Krol's arm. We always took a few such armbands with us because we had to wear them ourselves on our way through the ghetto.

Antony started to kick Krol into the gutter, thought better of it, bent down, went through the dead man's pockets, and took what I supposed was some money from them. Then he tore up some pieces of paper, threw them into the sewage, glanced in my direction, and gave Krol a swift kick that sent him floating off on the current. Only then did he call me. I pretended not to hear him the first time and made him call again before I came and helped him shoulder his sack. I never breathed a word of what I saw to anyone, not even to my mother.

In the ghetto we would surface through a basement

11

on Leszno Street and walk from there with our sacks down Karmelicka Street. I'll never forget those few blocks, though they weren't very long. The Jews at Leszno Street would give us fresh clothes to keep us from smelling (I needn't tell you how it felt to put our stinking wet pants and shirts back on before heading home through the sewers), and we stepped out into the street looking like any Jew. Sometimes I would pretend I was a Jew, just to see what it felt like. Still, whenever we passed a vantage point from which I could glimpse the Polish side of the ghetto wall, I made sure to look.

Each time I came back from a trip to the ghetto I had bad dreams at night, most often about the children who pleaded for food, or else about the beggars who lay drooling on the sidewalks. My stepfather said they filled their mouths with soapsuds to make people feel sorry for them, but sometimes they were covered with newspapers because they were dead. Antony told me not to look at the children, since he saw how badly I wanted to give them something to eat. If anyone discovered that we were smuggling food, he said, we would be finished. True, there were big-time smugglers who worked in organized gangs and weren't afraid of anything, because they had connections with the Polish police and even with the Germans, who let them come and go through their checkpoints. But we were "free-lancers" who had to hope that the sewers would keep our secret.

Sometimes the main streets of the ghetto were so

crowded that we could hardly move. Jewish police-men directed the traffic, keeping one direction to the right and the other to the left, because otherwise there would have been a hopeless jam.

I can remember my disbelief the first time I saw a Jewish policeman hit a Jewish boy. It must have been on our second trip, because the first one was at night and we didn't venture out. Until then I had thought that only Polish policemen were mean. I never thought Jews could be like that, because my mother had told me that, although they would do anything to strangers (which meant us Poles too), they would never harm one of their own. She said that the Jews always helped one another — but now I saw that their policemen were no better than ours. And later on I learned that they had informers and traitors too, just the way we did.

Another thing I couldn't believe on that first walk down Karmelicka Street was all the stores full of deli-cacies. If I hadn't seen starving children everywhere, I might have thought that the ghetto was a wonderful place to live. Antony explained to me that the corner of Karmelicka and Nowolipie streets where the Hotel Britannia once had stood was a center for the shady dealings of all the rich Jews, money changers, Gestapo agents, smugglers, and various underworld types who hung out there. So did we, because that's where our customers were.

But I haven't finished telling you about my first trip through the sewers.

By the time we arrived, I didn't think I could take another step without collapsing. My stepfather put down his sack, climbed up a ladder, grabbed an iron rod that hung from a rusty chain, and rhythmically tapped it seven times against a metal trap door. He paused and tapped again, and this time the trap door opened.

It worked like this: we telephoned in advance and announced the day and hour we were coming in a coded message that only our customers understood. The telephone we used belonged to someone called "the doctor," a Polish official who worked in a nearby brush factory and was bribed by our customers to relay our message to them. They were three brothers, religious Jews like the ones I had seen in Jewish neighborhoods before the war began. Such people had always seemed strange and ugly to me. Maybe it was their odd clothes, or their beards and sidelocks, or the strange language they spoke, and maybe it was all of those things put together, plus the poverty and congestion they lived in even before the war broke out.

In any case, the first time we arrived in the brothers' basement and I saw them reach down to take our sacks and help us through the trap door, they scared me half to death. We sat down to rest for a minute, and then — after Antony had rubbed his fingers to restore their circulation — we opened our sacks. I took out each item and handed it to Antony to display to the three Jews, who sat muttering in their language with bright eyes. Antony arranged all the bread and

14

cheese and butter and herring and apples and sugar and homemade vodka as neatly as if he were opening a grocery store while I emptied out the sacks, still out of breath from our trip.

Although my stepfather was barely able to read a newspaper, he knew Yiddish. I remember how amazed I was to find that out, because anti-Semitic Poles like him liked to make fun of the way Yiddish sounded — and yet here he was speaking it like a native, with the same funny singsong!

In the course of time Antony mellowed toward the three brothers, but back then he was still very brusque with them. They too grew friendlier once they got to know and trust him, and sometimes served us special Jewish delicacies that were brought down to the basement because we smelled too bad to come upstairs. On our first trip, they were afraid of him and shocked by the price he started out by asking, which was twice what he expected to get (he had warned me in advance not to say a word while he bargained). But they brought us tea and candy when the haggling was over. At first I was afraid to put the candy in my mouth. I thought I might catch something from it, because the Germans had put up signs on the ghetto walls reading in German and in Polish, "Warning! The Area Beyond This Wall Is Infected with Typhus!" I had seen those signs so often that I almost believed them, but the candy was really good, the kind we used to get before the war.

As we came to know the Jews better, Antony sometimes joked as he bargained with them. He was no longer in such a hurry either, so that every item was auctioned off separately. The Jews too grew less scary with time. Perhaps their strangeness had given me the wrong impression, although I certainly didn't think so at first. And even when we were used to bantering with them, I was startled one day when one of them told us a sick joke about the ghetto. Not that it wasn't funny, but I remember thinking that someone whose friends and families had been killed and who might face the same fate any day shouldn't be talking like that.

After the basement on Leszno Street there was a time when we surfaced via the basement of a store on Grzybowska Street. Pan Korek's tavern was to stand opposite this spot later, once the Germans had shipped most of the Jews off in trains to Treblinka and let the Poles have all the empty apartments in what was called "the Little Ghetto." And after Grzybowska Street we entered through the brush factory, whose employees had not been deported because they were making brushes for the German army. Getting there through the sewers took twice as long — two hours with full sacks and an hour returning with empty ones.

Gradually, my feelings toward my stepfather began to change. Part of it had to do with Pan Krol and part with all kinds of other things, like his telling me that carrying the sack was hard for him too. I never saw him slip or fall with it, though, which happened to me a lot in the beginning. Each time we came home my mother sent me straight to the bathtub and then shaved my head, because that was the only way to get the smell of sewage out of it. I didn't want to reek in school or have children asking me questions. "I bet you have lice," they all said when they saw me. "No, I don't," I told them. "I just like the way it looks." Skinheads were the fashion in the upper grades at the time, so perhaps they believed me.

As for the incident with Krol, it may have made me more afraid of Antony, but it also made me feel safer with him, because it gave me the confidence that he could cope with any danger.

When we took the long route to the brush factory, we also took more breaks along the way. Each stop had boards hidden in the wall, and at each my stepfather ceremonially propped one of them up, laid his sack carefully on it, helped me to lay mine down too, and propped up another board for us to sit on. Sometimes he lit a cigarette while I had to pretend I didn't smoke even when he let me have a puff. He didn't know that I was already smoking on the sly, both by myself and with my friends when we went downtown. I looked older than my age and was afraid only of being caught when I was close to home or to school.

There were fourteen stops along the way to the brush factory, although Antony smoked at only three or four of them. After a while he began calling them the "Stations of the Cross," or for short, the "shit stations."

If our sacks were empty, we generally stopped to rest only once on our way back. But they weren't always empty, because that autumn, when most of the

17

ghetto was already evacuated but no Poles had moved into it yet, we often took a detour through a low tunnel that nearly forced us to walk on our knees, exiting at Grzybowska Street. There, before heading home, we ransacked the deserted houses for special items that had been ordered from us earlier or simply for things that we ourselves wanted, such as silverware, dishes, clothing, and linen.

The one time my stepfather didn't take me along with him was when he went to the ghetto to sell arms. He didn't realize that I knew and that I felt left out.

I heard him talking about it to my mother one night. He told her that he had three "pieces" that he wasn't going to sell to the Polish underground because it didn't pay a fair price.

"So who will you sell them to," asked my mother, "gangsters?"

There was a moment of silence and then Antony said, "No. I'll sell them to the Jews."

I could tell by his voice how hurt he was. My mother must have heard it too, because she said she knew he wouldn't really sell guns to gangsters. And he didn't have to, he explained to her, because the Jews would give him seventeen thousand zloty for a single pistol. Why, they would pay him one hundred for every bullet! After that there were some whispers that I couldn't make out, and then a whole lot of smooching that made me cover my head with my pillow.

There was one other kind of merchandise that my stepfather sometimes smuggled, not into the ghetto but out, although strangely enough, he never kept a cent of the money he was paid for it. That was Jewish babies.

By the autumn of 1942, when what was happening to the Jews in Treblinka was no longer a secret, some Jewish families were desperate to save their small children. They would contact us through the three brothers, and Antony would carry their children out of the ghetto in a sack. I myself saw him do it three times, although it may have happened more often, because when I asked him how many babies he had smuggled he said he couldn't remember.

He took only girls, because boys were circumcised and could be identified as Jews. I had to ask him what being circumcised meant, and I didn't believe him when he told me. I was sure it was just another one of his Jewish jokes. I realized he was telling the truth only when I overcame my embarrassment enough to ask my mother, who gave me the same answer.

The first time I saw Antony being handed a baby, I was in shock. He hadn't warned me in advance, and I almost broke into tears like its mother. He never let me know about such things beforehand, because he believed in learning by experience. The baby's mother couldn't stop crying. She undressed it for the doctor, who came to give it a shot in its little behind to make it sleep, and then wrapped it up again, kissed it, and gave it to Antony together with a bag. In the bag, I was told by someone there, were the name and address of the baby's parents and of an aunt in America, so that the child could be returned to its family after the war. "And there's also some money, all of which your father claims is for the mother superior of the convent."

Although Antony looked annoyed when he heard that, he didn't say a word.

He put the baby in his sack and we descended into the sewers. After walking a while I asked him about it, and he told me that he brought the babies to a convent where they were raised to be nuns and good Catholics.

Who kept the documents? I asked.

"Oh, those," he said, as though he had forgotten all about them. He took the papers out of their bag, tore them into little pieces, and threw them into the sewage.

"But suppose its mother lives through the war and looks for it afterwards," I said. "How will she find it?"

Antony didn't think much of the mother's chances of surviving. In the first place, he said, she wasn't young and strong enough, and besides, the Germans would kill all the Jews anyway. He must have felt I wasn't convinced, because he added that it was better for the baby to grow up a Catholic and never know it had Jewish parents. Being Jewish was nothing but trouble. It always had been and always would be — that was something I could see for myself. He was simply doing the baby a favor.

Being a nun was nothing but trouble too, I said. But Antony answered that the convent was really just an orphanage and that no one had to become a nun if she didn't want to. "And don't think I'm doing it for the money," he told me. "I really do give every cent to the mother superior."

But if he disliked Jews so much, I asked, why save their babies free of charge?

"You don't understand, Marek," said Antony. "I may not like Jews, but I have nothing against human beings."

2

The Money and the Secret

Sometimes I wonder what would have happened if my mother hadn't caught me the first time. Would I have gone on doing it with Wacek and Janek? I think that if I had gone to confession and told the priest about it, I would have stopped.

In his Sunday sermons our priest sometimes mentioned "our brothers in distress." I knew he meant the Jews. He wasn't like Wacek and Janek's priest, who talked about "kikes" and "Christ killers."

I'm sure that if my mother hadn't told me about my real father, I would sooner or later have gone to confession and told the priest what I did. I actually liked seeing him, and not just because I could say yes when my mother asked me at least once a week: "Marek, have you been to confession?"

It had nothing to do with Antony either, who went to confession like clockwork on the first Thursday of each month. Confession was a way of getting away from all my problems in school and at home and of feeling better about myself. I liked our priest and looked up to him. I never told him about the money, though, because meanwhile I found out about my real father and didn't go to confession anymore. There was no point in going when I couldn't tell the truth and talk about what was most on my mind.

I've already said that Antony didn't have much use for words. He talked a lot only when he was drunk. Once, when I was dragging him home from the tavern, he said to me that no man could keep everything inside him because it would make him sick if he did. That's why he himself told my mother everything, he said, and if he couldn't tell her something, he told it to the priest. It seemed a good time to ask about what kinds of things he couldn't tell her. I thought he might mention Pan Krol, but he surprised me by saying, "I swear to you, Marek, I never go to whores. I love only your mother. And you. Why don't you call me Papa, all right?"

He began to cry like a drunk, because I wouldn't agree to let him legally adopt me. That must have been in early December, before the first snow, three or four months after I started working in the sewers.

The ground was covered with the first white frost of the year and the puddles in the street had frozen. It was early on a Monday morning. I know it must have been a Monday because I had just returned Pan Korek's three-wheel bicycle to the yard behind the tavern.

The streets were almost empty. The children hadn't left for school yet. I chose the longest puddles, gave myself a good head start, and went sliding over them.

I wondered if my mother was right that sliding wore down the soles of your shoes. Suddenly someone called my name and I saw Wacek and Janek. I remember thinking: what the heck are they doing here at this hour? Our school was in the opposite direction. "Those two young punks," my mother used to call them. She had told me to keep away from them, but I didn't. Only, what were they doing out in the street so early? They could have asked me the same question, but I had a good answer. So did they, it turned out, although it took a few minutes to find out what it was.

They weren't exactly friends of mine. They were two grades above me, but since I was big for my age and at least as strong as they were, they occasionally invited me along on their adventures. Sometimes we crossed the Kerbedzia Bridge to the Praga, which was close enough to my grandmother's for me to tell my mother I was going there, and we picked fights with the kids hanging out there. Sometimes we went shoplifting.

I don't think the two of them ever went to confession, which may be why they stole things I didn't dare to. I stole only small things like candy, for which the priest made me say two Ave Marias while adding in a mournful voice, "Thieves come to no good end, my son."

Sometimes, when we were feeling good, Wacek, Janek, and I would teach the little kids in the street "the facts of life," stopping them on their way home from school and telling them where babies came from. Wacek and Janek were good at that kind of thing. My mother said they had no conscience.

Anyway, there I was flying across a frozen puddle on the sidewalk when Wacek and Janek appeared out of nowhere. When I asked them what they were doing out so early, they answered with a nasty grin, "How about you?"

Because they knew. They knew that every Monday I had to return Pan Korek's three-wheeler after pedaling my stepfather home on Sunday night since he regularly got so drunk that he didn't know which foot was which.

They told me that the street we were on was a common escape route for Jews from the ghetto. If they saw someone walking on it early in the morning, trying to act innocent but looking pale and Jewish with eyes that popped out of his sockets, they stepped up to him and said, "Hey, mister, come over here for a minute." If he began to shake all over, they knew for sure he was a Jew.

At first they talked to him nicely to keep from arousing the suspicions of any passers-by who might want a share of the loot. Then they took him into a doorway, shook him down, and cleared out.

Although they made it sound perfectly natural, I was afraid. They assured me that they never turned any Jews in to the Polish police or the Germans, even though they could get a reward for it. They simply "shaved" their victims, that is, took all their money and their valuables. Sometimes they left them enough money to buy food or a streetcar ticket. That meant

25

they still made off with lots of cash, enough to do all kinds of things. They began to laugh so long and so hard that someone opened a window and emptied a bucket of water on the sidewalk near us. Wacek reached for a rock, but just then the doorman appeared and shook his fist at us. We moved down the street while Wacek juggled the rock in his hand, looking for something to throw it at. The target he found was a dog that had the bad luck to pass by. With hardly a whimper it stuck its tail between its legs and ran off. They asked me if I wanted to join them.

"I'm sure it's a sin," I said.

"You can always go to that commie priest of yours and confess," Wacek said.

"Don't be a sucker," said Janek. "They've got lots of diamonds and gold besides the money. Just think what you can buy with it. What are you, a Jew lover or something?"

I certainly didn't want them to think me a sucker or a Jew lover. "But suppose my mother finds out?"

"If you don't tell her, how can she?"

"He's still just a baby," said Wacek. "Let's leave Mama's little boy alone and get going."

I was fourteen and looked like sixteen, and I didn't like being talked about like that. Many of the customers in Pan Korek's tavern talked about robbing Jews who had escaped from the ghetto. I even knew a few toughs who made a regular living from it. And if I didn't tell my mother and Antony, how, really, could they know? I began to think of all the things I could buy. What are you afraid of? I asked myself. It's just this one time. Wacek and Janek will "shave" some Jew anyway, so what difference does it make if I join them?

"All right," I said. Janek slapped me on the back and we went to look for a Jew.

Pretty soon one came along. Although he wasn't walking especially quickly, he looked as though he was in a hurry. He was carrying a briefcase and was pale indeed, although that didn't prove he was a Jew of course. But though he tried to look straight ahead, his eyes kept darting every which way. We steered him into a doorway and said straight-away, "Hand over your money, kike!"

He began to plead with us. If we took all his money, he might as well turn himself in to the Germans. How could he pay for a hide-out or for food? I felt kind of sorry for him and said we should leave him something.

"You can let him have it from your share," said Janek.

And Wacek said to the Jew, "You should be thankful we didn't tear your pockets out to look for diamonds. I'll bet you've got gold coins sewn in your underpants too."

The Jew had a big wad of money on him. Wacek and Janek gave in to me and left him a little. They didn't even take it out of my share. Then they let him go. All I could think about on my way to school was how I could now buy anything I wanted without having to ask my stepfather. Then I began wondering what the two of them did with the money that made them laugh so hard. I was sure from the way they laughed that it must be something dirty. I sat through school planning what I would buy. Each time my hand touched my pocket, I smiled to myself. Yet even then I couldn't stop thinking of the Jew's pale face and eyes. It became harder and harder to get them out of my mind.

I flunked the dictation. And I didn't dare buy a thing on my way home from school. I suddenly felt as if my pocket were on fire with the money. I was afraid to put my hand in it. By tomorrow, I tried telling myself, it won't bother me. But I knew I had done something wrong.

That night my mother read me a bedtime story. Not that I didn't know how to read. I just liked being read aloud to by my mother. If I'm not mistaken, at the time she was reading Victor Hugo's *Les Misérables* in installments.

I was thinking so much about the book when I fell asleep that I forgot to take the money out of my pants.

When I awoke the next morning, the day before already seemed a hazy memory. All that remained of it was the money. I jumped out of bed knowing it would be a great day. Just then I saw my mother pick up my pants and brush them as she did every morning to make sure I went to school looking clean. I could feel myself turn white as a sheet.

"What is all this money, Marek?"

I tried making believe it was nothing. I was good at pretending with people, although until then it was a talent I had never tried out on my mother. It was

28

something I had saved strictly for school or for my stepfather.

The fact was that I hated lying to my mother until the day she died. When she was eighty-three years old and dying I told her a lie about her health, and even though that was something else of course, it was as hard for me as when I was a boy. In the end she always saw through me. If something sounded fishy to her, she would take my face in her hands and look straight into my eyes, deep into them. She was never angry, just sad. But she always knew.

I bent down as though lacing my shoes and said as casually as I could that I had found the money in the street and had forgotten to tell her about it yesterday. I didn't know whom it belonged to. Maybe some smuggler had lost it, because a big wad like that . . .

My mother listened in silence. I thought I had talked my way out of it. At most I would have to make my peace with not buying all the things I wanted, because I would have to give most of the money to my parents. That was just the lull before the storm, though, because my mother suddenly said, "I found a note among the bills." She showed it to me. It read: "Keep the bearer of this note in the apartment until the morning. I'll come to pick him up and pay you. Krupnik."

To this day, whenever the worst is about to happen, I pretend to myself that everything is normal and do my best to find something in the situation, something interesting or funny or odd, that I can peacefully contemplate. During the Russian invasion of

Czechoslovakia in 1968, for example, there was a moment when a Russian soldier angrily aimed his gun at me. And I remember thinking: just look at how that idiot was in such a rush to get dressed when his unit was mustered that he missed a button on his shirt — I'll bet he gets a reprimand. In the end he didn't shoot. I was there as a journalist.

And so, while my mother stood there looking at me, all I could think of was the name Krupnik that had been on the note I hadn't seen. I thought it was the funniest name I had ever heard. I almost looked up from the shoe I was lacing to tell my mother that. "Well," I said, "maybe it wasn't a smuggler. It could have been someone on the run. Maybe someone from the underground."

"Maybe a Jew," said my mother.

"Maybe," I said without blinking.

"You know," said my mother, "I met Wacek's mother in the grocery store the other day. I always told you to keep away from him. And from that friend of his too — they're a pair of young punks. The minute I saw that money, even before I found the note, I thought of something she told me."

I put my school bag down on the floor and sat down. There was still some tea left in my glass. I went over to the table and drank it. It was already cold, which was perhaps why it tasted too sweet. I wanted to ask my mother if tea tasted sweeter when it was cold.

"Wacek's mother told me that for the last several

months he's been going around with too much money," she said. "He's been buying all kinds of things with it and giving her large amounts too. He says it's from working in the marketplace. She never pressed him about it, she told me, because ever since the Germans took her husband she's had trouble making ends meet. As long as it helped pay the food bill. And then one day she ran into Janek's mother. When she told her about how much money Wacek was earning in the marketplace, Janek's mother laughed at her and said that it came from shaking down Jews."

"That doesn't mean — " I began to say. My mother didn't let me finish.

Although I was taller than Mother, I was seated, and now I looked up to see her standing over me. In a voice I had never heard her use before, she said, "You robbed a Jew with them, Marek. Tell me the truth!" I realized that Janek was sure to rat on me anyway. He was the biggest squealer there was, in school too. And so I told the truth.

When I had finished, my mother looked pale. I didn't try to defend myself. What could I have said? That the two of them would have done it anyway? I simply told her everything and said the Jew should have been thankful that we didn't turn him in or tear out his pockets and underpants looking for diamonds or gold.

"Who taught you such nonsense?"

"It's not nonsense. That's where the Jews hide their

valuables when they escape from the ghetto. Wacek and Janek told me."

"How many Jews have you robbed?"

"Just one," I said.

I thought she was going to yell at me. I wasn't used to that, but I was ready for it. In fact, though I didn't think it likely that she would tell my stepfather to beat me, I was ready for anything. Except for what happened. My mother sat down on the floor and started to cry. At the time, all I remember thinking is: what is she sitting on the floor for? Today, though, telling the story to you for the first time in my life, I feel like crying myself.

She cried with great big sobs, the way you cry when something terrible has happened or when you've had a great loss, the way you cry for the death of a child.

I tried lifting her into a chair. Anything to keep her from sitting and crying on the floor! She wasn't hard to pick up, but she pushed me away with all her strength. That frightened me even more. In the end, I managed to get her onto the sofa, where she went right on crying.

And all that time I kept saying "Mama, Mama" without even knowing that I was saying it. She must have been already on the sofa and wiping her nose between gasps when I realized I had been calling her name.

All of a sudden she said, "Why, Jesus was a Jew and so was the Virgin Mary! And Joseph was a Jew too. And John the Baptist. They were all Jews. It says so in the Bible." I was flabbergasted. I had never thought of it that way. And she went on, "What do you think that Jew is going to do without his money? How is he going to save himself? You sentenced him to death. Your father gave his life for human brotherhood, and you, Marek, how could you look him in the eyes now? What will you say to him when you stand before him on Judgment Day?"

She fell silent. I wanted to say something but didn't know what. I had a bitter taste in my mouth like the taste you have when you want to apologize, to explain. But it would only have been a lot of lies and half truths, a pap I would have vomited up and that couldn't have looked very pretty. I felt so guilty that I wanted to hide where nobody could see me, the way I do in a dream I sometimes have in which I'm walking naked in the street. Just then my mother got up, took the wad of money from the table, and threw it at my feet.

"Take your money, you Judas Iscariot!"

I crossed myself automatically. I really was like Judas, who had betrayed Jesus to the Romans for thirty pieces of silver.

I remember wanting to argue that Jesus was not a Jew because he had been baptized, but then I realized that wouldn't have made any difference to the Germans. One Jewish grandparent was enough for them.

My mother handed me my school bag and pushed me toward the door. "Go," she said. "Get out of here. I can't bear the sight of you."

I began to cry. It must have been ages since my mother had last seen me cry. She came over to me and hugged me. I hugged her back hard and said I was sorry and that I would go look for another Jew who had escaped from the ghetto and give the money to him. That scared her enough to say that I should leave it to her to see that the money reached the right hands. She stepped back and gave me a long look as if seeing me for the first time. Then she murmured to herself, "Perhaps I should have told him when he was thirteen, as I promised his father I would."

She looked at me again as if taking my measure and continued, "Maybe the time has come . . . " That's when she told me.

I started out for school, but my feet took me straight to church. I had to pray. I felt as if the sky had fallen. It wasn't possible. And yet my mother would never have invented such a thing just because of the money. I had always believed everything she told me. She never lied to me. She had an honesty you couldn't help but respect, and I don't think a single one of her friends ever suspected her of not being truthful. Still, she *had* lied, or at least not told me the whole truth about my father.

I prayed, mechanically, compulsively, without being able to stop. And as I did I kept examining myself — not from the outside but from within, to see if I was still the same Marek I had been before finding out the truth. Could it be that I had already begun to change and would soon turn into someone else?

Then I stopped praying and continued to kneel, looking at Christ crucified over the altar and wondering whether Wacek, Janek, and I would have taken him for a Jew. I began to talk to my father. It was different from all my other talks with him, which weren't always in church. Sometimes they even took place when walking down the street.

I felt so cold that my teeth chattered. I tried to guess if it was time yet for the school gate to open. Finally, I rose from the floor and sat down on a pew. All this time I had thought I was alone, but now I saw that someone else had entered the church, without my noticing. Or perhaps he had been there praying, because out of the corner of my eye I saw him crossing himself. There was something odd about it that I couldn't put my finger on. Only later, when I was already out in the street, did I realize what it was. It was the way he had crossed himself. He had done it backward!

3

My Father

My mother told me that my father's parents were just like the Jews I knew from Nalewki Street. His own father went around dressed in black and had a beard and sidelocks. My mother saw him only once, when they met by chance in the street, and she never saw my father's mother while my father was alive. That, she explained to me, was because when he married a Christian they sat in mourning for him and pretended afterward that he was dead.

For weeks I tried to form a new picture of my father. It wasn't entirely new. Everything my mother had told me about him over the years was still usable. Things like his height, or the color of his eyes and hair, hadn't changed. All at once, though, I had to see all these things against a new background, you might even say a new stage set, with a different spotlight shining down on them.

Not that I thought of my father all the time. I went on thinking about all the other things that boys thought about too: football, and girls, and school, and fights in the Praga. And working the sewers with

Antony. Every now and then, though, in church or in bed at night, my thoughts returned to him and I instinctively began to talk to the face I had drawn in my imagination.

My starting point was still my mother's descriptions, which I knew by heart. But I couldn't think of my father as Broneslaw Jaworski anymore. Not when his real name was Hayyim Rozenzveig. My father was given his Polish name, as well as his Christian identity and a forged birth certificate, by the Communist party before I was born, before he even knew my mother. He was already on the wanted list then. And without changing his physiognomy, I was beginning to give him a different face. It still looked a lot like the one I had imagined before, but it was different. It wasn't exactly a Jew's face. Picturing it, I knew I still wouldn't suspect him of being Jewish any more than his friends in the party did — a party that I hated in those days and was never able to connect with the brave figure of my father. Still, his expression was no longer the same. Today, I can say that it had even changed for the better. Now there was something tender about it. The cold eyes and stern face of the dedicated Communist who had died under torture without breaking seemed to have become warmer and more human.

Until then I had thought of him the way you think of a comic-book hero, the kind who talks with bubbles around his words, strong and invincible. Whereas the secret my mother told me now made him . . . well, I wouldn't have put it that way as a boy, but today I would say that he became less abstract and more down-to-earth for me, someone who really was born and lived, although in a past that was very distant, since anything more distant than his father's childhood is hardly imaginable to an adolescent.

The more I reimagined him, the more I had to rewrite the whole story of his life, to change my whole conception of him, starting with his childhood. Even then I had the honesty to make myself see him as one of those Jewish boys from Nalewki Street with long sidelocks and skullcaps or hats on their heads who always looked so pale that I felt sorry for them. Sometimes, before the war, I went bargain hunting there with my mother. And yet I consoled myself by thinking: this boy will grow up and become the man my mother will love, and then he will become my father, and then he will sacrifice his life for his beliefs. Even though I hated the Communists back then, I understood that my father had died believing that communism was the ideal solution for the poor, the workers, and the Jews.

My mother had told me that the name Jaworski belonged to a family of petty nobility that had lost all its money in the last century, so that several of its members had taken up farming and become little more than peasants. No doubt that was true enough as far as the actual Jaworskis were concerned.

I was four when my father died in prison — that is, when he was killed there. Soon after, there was a fire in our house and nothing at all was left. The two or three photographs that we had of my father went up in flames too. My mother had grabbed me in the nick of time and pulled me outside, although not fast enough to avoid a scar on her foot where she was burned. And yet though the prison and the fire were real, I couldn't visit my father's grave or light candles for him on All Souls' Day, because according to my mother the prison had donated his body to medical science. In those days medical students had such trouble finding cadavers that they sometimes paid a lot of money for them.

It upset me a lot when I was a boy that my father didn't have a grave. As if being an orphan with a stepfather wasn't bad enough, I didn't even have a father's grave to cry at! Before the war I had all kinds of answers for the children who asked me where my father was buried. When I was little I can remember telling them that he was buried in the tomb of the Unknown Soldier, which was why I had to be there for the changing of the guard. I really did go there often to see the ceremony. Sometimes I would dream of being in an old, neglected cemetery, not like the one in our churchyard that I was familiar with. Suddenly, burning on a grave, I saw candles like those lit on All Souls' Day. I approached closer and saw that the grave had a name and a date on it, but the more I tried to read them, the blurrier they became, until at last I saw nothing except for the candles still burning in the darkness.

When my father died, my mother went to 10 Nalewki Street, where his parents lived, and met his mother, my grandmother, for the first time. His father was no longer alive by then. My mother told my grandmother that my father was dead and that the prison had not returned his body, and the two of them embraced and cried in each other's arms.

I asked my mother how she got along with my father when it came to religion, because I knew that the Communists said there was no such thing as God. She answered that they found ways to compromise. In the end, she said, the Communists would be forced to make their peace with religion.

Whenever I found corroboration for one of her old stories about my father and herself, I breathed a sigh of relief. It was as if one more thing had been salvaged from my father's life, which had been left to me to resurrect. I was grateful for every little detail that could take the place of one of my fictions, so that I could stop patching and re-patching it. Like the story of how they met, for example.

They met at a May Day demonstration, because of a brawl. There were always brawls on May Day. It was the one day my mother used to lock me in the house and forbid me to go outside. But she liked to tell me how my father had rescued her from a fracas in which men were hitting each other with sticks and iron rods. Although the police, she told me, pretended to be breaking up the crowd and arresting the guilty parties, they would actually join the fray and help beat up the Reds.

She also told me about the conversations in her Communist cell. The cell had five members, two girls and three boys. When my father was tortured, he held out and didn't give them away.

Sometimes I lie in bed at night thinking of prisoners being tortured, not by the Gestapo, but by our own Polish government. I try to imagine all kinds of torments and wonder if I could hold out under them. I rather think that I could. I would simply scream and scream until I passed out from so much screaming. I would scream myself to death. And yet when I think about torture after actually hurting myself — breaking a fingernail, for example, or banging my head against something — I doubt that I could survive it. At such times I think of my father and shiver.

My mother told me that in her underground cell there were always arguments and discussions. Sometimes these went on all night long and her parents worried about where she was. The cell members called each other not "Pan" and "Pani" but rather "Comrade." They argued about how communism would come about. Was it all right to kill in order to make it come faster? Did the end justify the means? My mother said it didn't. That's why she was expelled from the party, because she refused to go against her feelings and deny her religion. But my father went on loving her, even though this greatly angered his cell members. At about that time he traveled to Russia to see communism with his own eyes. When he came back he admitted that life was not ideal there, but he stayed in the party and went on organizing. He and my mother weren't married in church, because he said he didn't believe in it. And yet he never said he didn't

41

believe in God: that was something my mother was prepared to swear to. (I knew even then, of course, that the Jewish God was the same as the Christian one, although Jews didn't believe in Jesus and Mary.) He just didn't like churches, said my mother. He didn't like to see money made from God. It didn't matter whether it was made by priests or rabbis. He had no use for either.

I've always been moved by the fact that my father believed in making the world a better place and had the courage to get up and do something about it.

Perhaps he also believed that, if there were no more rich and no more poor and brotherhood among all people, there would be no more differences between him and my mother. It's hard for me to believe that he wasn't aware of those differences, even if he said they didn't matter.

My father's refusal to have a church wedding, my mother told me, had nothing to do with his being Jewish. No one even knew he was a Jew. It was just a matter of being against organized religion. And so they crossed the German border to Breslau and were married in a civil ceremony, which was something that Poland didn't have. They didn't tell any of my grandparents about it until I was born, when everyone found out. My father's parents disowned him and my mother's parents disowned her. They didn't know my father was Jewish, but a non-Catholic wedding was not a wedding for them, which meant that my mother was living in sin. Even after I was accepted as one of the family, my grandmother, my mother's mother, used to call me "the bastard" whenever she was mad at me.

My mother had me baptized as a Catholic without telling my father she was doing it, because she was afraid he wouldn't let her. When she told him about it later, though, he wasn't angry at all. He just laughed and said that had he known, he would have baptized me at home with tap water.

He was caught and put into prison in 1933. He was there for three months before he died. My mother kept a yellow piece of old newspaper with a story about some Communist who was shot to death during an attempted jailbreak.

4

Antony

Did Antony know I was half Jewish? And if he did, how could he still have wanted to adopt me? Perhaps, I thought hopefully, my mother had never told him. Otherwise it was beyond my powers of comprehension, because after the Germans, Antony hated Jews and Communists in that order. And even if the order was sometimes reversed, so that he hated Communists more than Jews, he was bringing up a boy whose father had been both.

Immediately after my mother told me about my father, I was so involved with myself and with figuring out who I was if my father had been a Jew that I forgot all about Antony. I was already in school when I began to consider his side of it. That gave me another jolt. All I could think about until the last bell was whether he knew or not. I tried to remember if my mother had ever dropped any clue. It seemed likely that she hadn't told him after all. Wasn't it enough for him to know that my father was a Communist? After a while I began to think that Antony couldn't possibly know. He would never have married the ex-wife of a man who was both a Communist *and* a Jew. Antony knowing Father was Jewish seemed out of the question, and I desperately wanted to believe that there was some logic involved. Gradually, though, the thought of my mother's honesty began to make me more and more anxious. Suppose she decided to tell Antony the truth now? I tried thinking of some magic formula that could convince her not to. And then I had an idea: even if Antony knew, as long as he didn't know that I knew, everything would stay the same, as if nothing at all had happened.

I hurried home and waited impatiently for my mother to arrive. I kept praying that she would get there before Antony, and I put the question right to her when she did.

He did know! And so I asked my mother, I begged her, not to tell him about my taking the Jew's money. I wasn't worried about the money itself, which didn't matter that much to me anyway. And I was sure that if Antony found out about it, he would never let my mother give it away, even if he punished me for taking it. Antony hated blackmailers like Pan Krol but he wasn't about to part with good money. I tried convincing my mother to leave things as they were, because as long as Antony didn't know that I knew, he could go on feeling the same toward me. It was bad enough that I would have to feel differently toward him.

I talked on and on. My mother listened and said nothing. At last, though, she agreed.

But I still had a problem with Antony. I couldn't hate him anymore the way I used to. Worse yet, I couldn't look down on him and feel superior.

Mostly, I hated Antony because of my mother. And I began to hate him more than ever when I found out what they did at night.

The son of some neighbors, a boy older than myself, took it upon himself to tell me. He explained it in great detail. I can remember us standing in the darkness of the stairwell and breaking off our conversation each time someone passed by. Finally his mother came out, because the neighbors had told her that we were up to something or perhaps smoking on the sly.

To this day I can see the glee in his eyes at the sight of my shock, hurt, and disbelief. I was just a small boy and he was a big one, and he kept laying it on me over and over: "Your father, he sticks it into —" Well, you know the rest. I thought he must be the biggest sinner in the world, and I was sure he would be struck down by lightning any minute.

But he wasn't. And so I started to argue with him. First of all, I said, it couldn't be true because it was a sin. He agreed with that. It was not only a sin, he told me, it was the original sin for which Christ had died to save the world. But it was the only way to make babies. You did it and then you went to the priest and were given a penance. I swore up and down that he was wrong about my mother. She and Antony would never do such a thing. The proof was that they had never had any babies. But all my logic didn't do any good.

Before the neighbors' son explained all this, I hadn't paid it any attention. Maybe it was because I played so much football and ran around so much in the street that I fell asleep as soon as my head hit the pillow. From that day on, though, I began to listen. After I heard them doing it once, I began to cover my ears with the pillows each time they started.

Later on, I went into the sex education business myself along with Wacek and Janek. The lessons I gave were just like the one I received.

But I didn't stop hating Antony.

Once I saw him shaving my mother's legs with his big razor. He was doing it for her because the razor scared her to death. To tell the truth, it scared me too. I think razor blades must have been invented by then, but Antony had no use for such children's toys. I stepped into the bathroom one night when they thought I was asleep and saw him doing it. And now, suddenly, I couldn't hate him as much as I liked anymore because he knew all about me. I was in a real dilemma. I think it was a turning point in my life, because for once it made me think and use my brain.

Until then I had enjoyed thinking of Antony as a kind of caveman, the last of a long line of garbage men, which was what his family had been for generations. Not to say that wasn't work that somebody had to do, but I never missed a chance to look down on him, even for his name.

I liked my mother's maiden name: Aniela Barbara Rejmont. Her father, my grandfather, was a relative of the famous Polish author Wladislaw Stanislaw Rejmont. But I couldn't stand Antony's family name, which she took as her own. It absolutely killed me each time I heard a neighbor or shopkeeper call her "Pani Skorupa" and I always blamed her for not keeping my father's name. She could have called herself Pani Jaworski-Skorupa had she wanted, or even Pani Rejmont-Jaworski-Skorupa.

My mother called Antony by his first name, although when she wanted to put him in his place she called him "Skorupa" or "Pan Skorupa." That would make him lose his temper and call her "Pani Rejmont," which was his way of saying, "Just get a load of the fine lady!"

He was a simple, uneducated man who had barely finished fourth grade and never read a book in his life. And yet my mother had married him, which was something I couldn't understand. I was five years old at the time and I remember going to church for the wedding.

It took a long time before I agreed to call him "Antony." Instead I called him "Pan Antony." I often eavesdropped on what he and my mother were saying in their room and once or twice I heard him trying to convince her to make me change. At first he insisted that I call him "Papa." Later he dropped this demand and began to talk about adoption instead. By then, though, I was much bigger, and when my mother broached the subject I ran away from home for three days to my grandparents'. I was sure my father would turn over in his grave if I agreed. Eventually Antony gave up, although now and then I heard him say to my mother that it was a disgrace for me to address him like a stranger when he had raised me from the age of five. It embarrassed him in front of the neighbors and in front of my teachers in school. What had he done to deserve it? But I went on calling him "Pan Antony," although whenever I could I avoided addressing him by name at all.

When I was smaller, before the war, I was sometimes fresh to him and called him names like "Stinker" because he smelled of sewage. Finally, I'm sorry to say, he spanked me so hard one day that my behind was red for a week. My mother was furious at him. She had never spanked me in my life. I remember him saying that if he were my natural father he would have taken his belt and whipped some sense into me, the same way it was whipped into him when he was a boy. Had he turned out any the worse because of it? But my mother forbade him to hit me again and made me promise never again to be fresh to him. Then she had a long talk with me.

She took me for a walk by the banks of the Wisla River. It was one of my favorite things to do with her, to walk by the river on a moonlit night. We would stroll slowly while I held her arm, and if it was winter she would wear her old fur coat that I loved to touch while, surrounded by silvery magic, we listened to the crunch of snow under our feet.

As we talked my mother explained to me how she had come to marry Antony.

She had gotten to know him while my father was in prison. In the summer he used to make the rounds outside the prison building, selling ice cream from a big box strapped to his shoulder to supplement his paycheck from the municipality. Whenever my mother left the prison and sat down on the sidewalk to cry, he came over to comfort her with a free ice cream. I may not be an objective judge, but you can see from the photographs I have of her how beautiful she was. It wasn't just a matter of beauty either, because there was something about her that made people feel warm and trusting. Even when Antony found out that her husband was a Communist, and later yet, that he was a Jew on whose account she was raising a child born out of wedlock, he didn't abandon her like everyone else. Of course, no one but Antony knew that my father was Jewish. Most people were very religious and couldn't forgive my mother for living in sin.

She was forgiven only when she married Antony. That's when I first met my mother's parents, my grandfather and my grandmother, as well as the rest of the family that came to the wedding. I was very excited, because all the children I knew had at least one grandparent and several uncles and aunts, and now I would have some too.

Walking along the Wisla that night I promised my mother that I would never be fresh to Antony again, and it was a promise that I kept. In my bed at night, though, I would think of all the swear words I wanted to curse him with, and sometimes I would even whisper them to myself. Afterward I would tell the priest about it in confession. That way at least one person knew what I thought of my stepfather. The priest made me say some Paternosters for a penance, but I didn't mind. I liked praying before going to sleep anyway. It kept the ghosts away.

Nevertheless, there were times when I had to call Antony by name in order to get what I wanted. Whenever I wanted money or something like that, for instance, I had to swallow my pride and call him "Antony." I hated the way he smiled to himself then, but I had no choice, because he was in charge of the money. I couldn't even buy candy or the smallest thing without asking him, because my mother refused to do it for me.

There was one other time when I used to call him "Antony": when he was drunk. He didn't know what was going on then anyway.

Antony had an agreement with my mother that he could get drunk in the tavern once a week, every Sunday evening. That is, he could go to the tavern on other nights too and come back stinking of vodka, but he couldn't get drunk. And I must say that he kept his word.

Like all proper Poles, we went to mass every Sunday morning. Antony would put on the good suit he had bought from Jews in the ghetto for a song, I would wear my Sunday best, also bought from Jews, and my mother would have on one of the pretty new dresses that Antony had bought her. He swore they weren't from Jews, but he was lying of course, and I think my mother must have known it. She herself refused to wear Jewish clothes — out of sympathy, I imagine. Maybe she couldn't help thinking of the woman who had worn the dress before and now was dead. And so Skorupa gave her his word of honor that he had bought the dresses at a discount store. She looked so lovely in them that she made herself believe him.

After church we went for dinner to my grandfather and grandmother's on Bridge Street. When we returned home, the caveman — that's how I thought of him in those days — changed out of his good suit to spare it too much wear and went off to Pan Korek's tavern. If he didn't return in time for the curfew, my mother sent me to bring him. After the Germans instituted a nightly curfew in Warsaw, that became my regular job.

Every Sunday evening my mother would wander nervously around the house, looking constantly at her watch. I wasn't allowed out in case she should need me, and if Antony didn't come back in time, I was sent off to the tavern. I actually liked going there on Sunday evenings. It was different from the other days of the week. I knew what those were like because I worked for Pan Korek as a waiter and a dishwasher — sometimes one and sometimes the other. I never worked in his tavern on Sundays, though. My mother didn't allow it, not just because of all the drunks there, but also because of the Sabbath.

52

Sometimes when I came to get Antony he was in a conscious state and let me drag him outside with the help of Pan Korek. Pan Korek knew my mother from before the war, when she wasn't yet married to Antony, and he always lent a hand. It was all a question of whether I could manage to hold Antony up in the street and keep him pointed toward home, because he kept trying to wander off into other streets and all kinds of houses and doorways that he saw or imagined were there. I had to make sure he didn't fall headfirst through an open door he didn't see or bang his head into a wall because he was sure there was a door there.

Worst of all were the nights when he was already under the table when I came for him. That's when Pan Korek had to give me the three-wheeler he kept in the back of the tavern in return for my solemn pledge to bring it back the next morning as soon as the curfew was over. That meant at 5 A.M. (Pan Korek needed the three-wheeler that early because he used it to transport merchandise.) He would cover it with a blanket and I would promise to keep Antony from puking on it and to return it in clean condition. That meant that I had to get up on Monday mornings long before school began. Wacek and Janek knew the reason for it, which was what made them laugh when they ran into me that day.

To tell you the truth, I never knew if I should pray to find Antony under the table or still on his two feet. If he was totally potted, Pan Korek could help me seat him on the three-wheeler and I usually had no trouble afterward. It was much worse if he started home under his own power, and then, just when it looked as if he were going to make it, collapsed in the street. Sometimes I managed to catch him in time and force him to stagger on. But sometimes I didn't and he would simply fall down and flounder around on the ground.

Pan Korek's tavern wasn't far from where we lived. Still, it was a bit of a walk, and if Antony fell halfway home I had to go back for the three-wheeler, pedal as fast as I could to where I had left him, and get him onto it by myself, not to mention the times I returned to find him in the gutter or with his pockets picked by some street gang. Once or twice the police were already dragging him off to the station house when I arrived.

The first time that happened I showed up at the last minute and it was all I could do to talk them out of arresting him. The second time the police already knew me and were waiting for me to come back. "What a father you have," said one of them pityingly. I had enough brains not to correct him. I think the story must have made the rounds of the police force, because when it happened again all but one of the policemen were different and yet they sized up the situation at once and even helped me load Antony onto the three-wheeler and gave me a friendly slap on the back.

Even though the police worked for the Germans, Antony defended them. He said they had no choice and that it was just their job. Nevertheless, the word *police* became so hated in Poland that today we call it the militia instead.

When I finally got Antony home, I would whistle for my mother to come downstairs and help me drag him up. She refused to ask Valenty the doorman to help because she thought it undignified. She was after all a Rejmont, even if that meant she had to haul some sozzled caveman up the stairs. But she was happier when I brought Antony back on his own feet, despite the off-color songs he would sing at the top of his voice. I myself kind of liked them. I didn't understand all of them, but they had lots of dirty words and funny parts, and something about them rang true. If he sang a song that I liked especially, I would turn to him and say, "Sing us another, Antony." Or else I would applaud and say, "Encore, Antony, encore!"

I don't think I was ever as embarrassed by him as my mother was. After all, I hadn't married him. He wasn't my father and all the neighbors knew it. And the drunker he was, the nicer he became. He would suddenly begin to laugh, whereas usually he had a gloomy look except when he was with my mother. That was the only time he would talk to me like a friend. Once, I remember, he made some remark about my mother's behind. We had already reached our building and she heard. She came downstairs, clapped her hands, and exclaimed, "Why, you ought to be ashamed!"

5

Pan Jozek

Ever since the day my mother found the money and told me the truth about my father, my Monday mornings were different. If I had to return the three-wheeler, I didn't roam the streets when I was finished but went to church instead. It became a regular custom. Usually I would pray to the Virgin Mary. Since the unheated church was icy cold, I would go back outside as soon as my bones began to freeze to look for some sausage or roasted-chestnut vendor over whose stove I could warm my hands while waiting for school to start.

On at least three such Monday mornings I saw the man who crossed himself backward. The second time I noticed that he entered the church not through the main door but via a side entrance, creeping in silently and sitting down. When I had watched him enough to be sure that he was really making the sign of the cross wrong, I decided to move to a seat from which I could see him come in without being seen myself. The proof that he was a Jew, I decided, would be that he wouldn't bother to cross himself if he thought he was alone. And indeed, he didn't. I began to suspect that he was being hidden by the priest. This wasn't our priest, of course. I may have forgotten to tell you, but the church in question was one near my school, not the one near our house.

Finally, when he came in one day and sat down, I rose and walked by him on my way out in order to get a good look at him.

He wasn't especially frightened-looking or pale. He looked like someone who is in a strange city and has taken time out to enter a church. He wore a light gray coat and held a gray hat in one hand, and despite his youthful appearance he could have been an engineer or a doctor. Before the war he would have been taken for a student. At first glance he could even have been one of those German-speaking Poles who called themselves *Volksdeutsch*. He certainly didn't look Jewish, although there was something about him that my mother would have called "gentle" and that might have made Wacek and Janek follow him a bit to see what he was up to.

I left the church. I was already out in the street when I realized that was how I would have wanted my father to look: the light, unusual eyes, the straight nose and high cheekbones that gave him that Slavic look, the sensitive lips, the friendly, reliable expression. Today I would call it the expression of a remarkably successful impersonator. And yet as perfect a mask as it was, it left a shadow of sadness on his face.

The next time, I decided, I would wait to see if he went out into the street when he left the church or into the priest's quarters. I knew my following him might frighten him off, but I was curious and by now he knew me anyway, having seen me in church three or four times. I thought I should tell him he was crossing himself wrong and maybe even give him the money, which was still in safekeeping with my mother. Of course, we could always have given it to the Jews who were hiding at my Uncle Wladislaw's, but they were so rich they didn't need it. Sometimes when I was walking in the street I was sure that a man or a woman coming toward me was a Jew. I had no idea how to approach them, though, or what to say to them if I did. Besides, I couldn't take the money to school every day on the chance that I might meet a Jew to give it to. And yet I was beginning to worry that Antony might find it and worm the story out of my mother. If that happened, it certainly wouldn't end up in Jewish hands.

The next time I saw him, however, the man simply vanished from the church. He must have felt I was watching him and slipped away or hid. I couldn't start looking for him, because that would have been overdoing it.

And then one day, he rose and went out into the street. He was carrying a leather briefcase. Until then the only thing he had held was his hat.

I remember that day well, because it had been snowing for a week. The snow came early that year, and it was a beautiful, clear winter morning with a blue sky and no wind. It must have been about three weeks before Christmas.

58

I ran after him. He noticed me and tried to disappear around a corner. I slowed down and pretended that I just happened to be heading in the same direction. Although I made sure to keep him in sight, I had no idea what to do. I hadn't the foggiest notion of how to offer him the money. Who in Warsaw, in December 1942, was going to admit that he was Jewish? And yet if he didn't learn to cross himself right, it might cost him his life. I thought of handing him a note and leaving him, but I couldn't stop to write one now. I kept tailing him. The streets were full of people, all hurrying about their business. Lots of children were on their way to school. Suddenly everyone began to run in our direction. From far up the street a human wave was frantically billowing toward us.

"It's a German dragnet!" someone shouted.

I took a few more steps, until he turned to run too, and then I turned and ran by his side. When we reached a back alley that was a private short cut of mine, I pulled at his sleeve and shouted, "This way, mister! We can cut through here."

He hesitated for a moment. I didn't blame him. No one but the neighbors who lived there knew that it was a passageway to a parallel street. To anyone else it looked like the dead-end entrance to a house that had been leveled in the German air raids. I knew about it only because I sometimes took it on my way to school.

We ducked into the alleyway and clambered over the ruins of the building. Then we crossed a hole in a fence made by the neighbors and climbed some steps. Beyond them the ground sloped sharply downhill. We jumped over a low wall and were in the street. The shouts of "Dragnet! Dragnet!" sounded far away now.

The man set out in a direction opposite that of my school. I walked alongside him. We didn't speak until finally he said, "Thank you."

"You cross yourself backwards, Pan," I told him. "I saw you in church. If you don't cross yourself right, you'll be caught."

He pretended not to understand me. He looked at me, thought for a second, and said, "That must be because I'm a leftie." He laughed. So did I.

We ducked into a doorway and made sure no one was looking, and I taught him the sign of the cross. That is, he knew it already, he just started it from the wrong side. Maybe it really had to do with his being left-handed. I remember that when I was little and couldn't tell left from right, I always had to cross myself to remember which hand was my right one.

"If I walk with you," I told him, "you can be sure no one will suspect you." I was proud of myself for saying it so naturally, without having to think twice about it.

"I was so sure no one could tell me apart," he said disappointedly.

"No one could. Not from the looks of you. Although there is something about you that I can't put my finger on. Still, I don't think I would follow

60

you if I . . . if I were . . . out to shake you down, for example."

"And you aren't?"

"No."

"You mean you don't want to know where I'm going?"

"No."

We walked in silence for a while. I wanted to say goodbye and be off, because I had stuck to him long enough. But I still had to tell him about the money. I had thought a lot about how I would offer the money to a Jew once I had started a conversation with him. What I had decided in the end was to say that my father owed a debt of honor to some Jew who had been taken away by the Germans and that he had asked me to give the money to some other Jew who needed it. Of course, my Jew would probably ask why my father didn't give the money away himself, but I could always say it was because he had died in the meantime. It was just that I couldn't get the words out of my mouth now. I was trying to make myself say them when he said, "The problem is that I don't know where to go now."

I racked my brain thinking what to do. Should I suggest somewhere to him? But where? Perhaps this was the time to bring up the money. But the faster I tried to think, the slower my mind worked. Meanwhile he continued: "It's not that I don't have an emergency address. I was there this morning. But the people who lived there have gone away and the door-man started asking questions. He gave me a funny look, and my answers just made it worse. In any case, it's clear that they won't be back soon. I know them, and I'm sure they would have left me a message if they could have. Something must have gone wrong. If there had been a death in the family, the doorman would have told me. It must be something else. Jews aren't the only ones who disappear these days. And today I have to move out of the apartment where I've been staying."

"You mean the priest's place?"

He didn't answer.

"I've seen you in that church every Monday."

"Yes," he said. "Every Monday his sister comes from the village with a package of food for him. And she insists on arranging it for him in the pantry by herself . . . "

I didn't get it.

"That's where he's been hiding me during the day."

"And now he doesn't want to anymore? You've run out of money?"

"No, it isn't that. He hurt himself yesterday falling off a streetcar. His sister has come to stay with him until he's better. That means that in the meantime . . . but just who exactly are you that you want to know everything about me?"

"I'm just someone who thought you needed help," I answered. It was the truth.

We walked on without speaking until he said abruptly, "I don't know many people in this city who go around helping Jews. Certainly not boys your age." I had to think of something quickly, so I said the first thing that came to mind: "My best friend was a Jewish boy. He was our neighbor. My mother and my stepfather were friends of his family." (Antony would have had a heart attack if he heard me saying that!) "Until they had to move to the ghetto. I'll bet they were killed there."

"What was his name?"

"Bolek," I said racking my brain for a Jewish last name. "Bolek Rosentsveig." I sighed.

Suddenly it dawned on me what we had done, what *I* had done, to the Jew whose money we took. He had been in the same kind of fix. I felt a twinge in my heart. What kind of person was I? I wondered. I had been so eager to get my hands on the money that I never stopped to think what I was doing. Was I really no different from my Uncle Wladislaw, who cared only about money? Or some gangster in America like the ones we saw in the movies? And apart from giving away the money, I couldn't think of any penance to make up for it. Everything else was either too harsh or too lenient — like not going to the movies, for instance. I wasn't supposed to go to them anyway, because my mother didn't allow me to watch the German propaganda that was shown there, but I wanted so badly to see some action on the screen that I didn't care what it was, as long as it was a film with things happening in it. Still, it was ridiculous to think you could make up for a human life by not going to the movies.

"Don't you have any other addresses?" I asked.

He did. Two others. The first, he said, belonged to

people who were undependable and he preferred not to risk it unless there was no choice. The second he was saving for a real emergency. The people who lived there, he explained, had neighbors who were informers. He loved them too much to endanger their whole family unless he absolutely had to.

We walked on in silence again until I asked, "So you need a place to stay in, is that it?"

"Yes," he said. "I have the money to pay for it. Although," he quickly added, "I don't have it with me right now."

"I have an uncle who hides Jews," I said. "If you'd like, I can ask him if he has room."

I hoped he would say yes.

"When can you do it?"

"Right now."

"How come you have a school bag but aren't in school?"

I was about to tell him that I had been sent home for one reason or another when I remembered that we had been together since early that morning, before school even began.

"I decided to play hooky," I said. "I hate school."

"And that's where you go to play hooky, to church?"

"I had lots of time, so I thought I'd go to confession."

"Are you such a big sinner?" he asked in an amused tone.

"Everyone's always got a sin or two," I said. "And sometimes I just feel like confessing."

"You know what? Go talk to your uncle. I don't have much to lose."

"Should we arrange to meet somewhere?" I asked.

"Why don't you suggest a place."

The only place I could think of was our church. I gave him the address and told him there was a little park there by the graveyard with some benches in it. He could make believe he was visiting the grave of a friend or something.

"All right," he said. "And if I'm ever in church again, I'll cross myself properly."

He grinned and so did I.

He was a really nice man. I had never thought that a Jew could be so like a Pole. That is, I had never thought about it until I found out about my father. My mother always said that all people looked alike when they smiled. When I was a little boy I used to think that might be true of everyone except the Jews, the ones with the beards on Nalewki Street, I mean. But when I started working with Antony and met the three brothers who bought food from him, I saw that they also smiled the same as everyone even though they were religious Jews with beards and sidelocks.

We said goodbye. He turned and walked back toward the church, and I went to my uncle's house on Zelazna Street. I took the streetcar to save time. I hoped that after hearing my story my mother would give me a note for school saying I was sick or something. Anything to keep my stepfather from finding out.

No one was in at my uncle's. That is, the Jews were

there all right, but they had to pretend that they weren't. They couldn't even flush the toilet in the bathroom. If they had to go somewhere in the apartment, they did it with their shoes off, and my uncle had marked the squeaky floorboards to keep them from stepping on them. They didn't open doors either, because they might creak, or turn faucets, because the pipes might rumble. My stepfather said that happened when there was air in them, but I never understood what air he was talking about. I only knocked once, so as not to frighten them.

I decided to bring the Jew to my grandparents' house in the meantime. My aunt and uncle were sure to return by the afternoon, so that I could get him out of there again before my grandmother came home from Theater Square.

My grandparents lived on Bridge Street, in the same building they had occupied before the war. We also still lived in the same building, but theirs had been leveled by the 1939 air raids and all that was left of it was a part of their apartment that had been beneath street level. Even that had not escaped damage: the plaster had fallen off the walls and there were cracks in them and in the ceiling. The one ground-floor room had been thoroughly demolished along with nearly all of their furniture, because it had served as the living room. I still remember everything that was in it, because I liked visiting my grandparents. It was an experience that never lost its newness after all the years in which my grandparents had broken off all contact with my mother.

Now, however, Grandfather was no longer the man he once was. A year after the war broke out he had gone "off his rocker" and begun to lose touch with reality. Sometimes he didn't know his own name or thought that I was his youngest son, my Uncle Romek. "Romek," he would ask me, "why didn't you buy me the newspaper?" I never knew whether to pretend that I really was my Uncle Romek or not. Or else he might say, "Romek, how come you're back from school in the middle of the week?" That annoyed him, because Romek had been sent to a military school.

Sometimes he had no idea who I was or what I was doing in his house. That rarely happened, though. Generally he realized I was a member of the family, even if he wasn't sure just which or from when. And he almost always recognized my mother, and of course, my grandmother too. He died about half a year after these events. He just went to sleep one night and never woke up.

Before the war my grandfather was a highly respected businessman who owned a print shop and was the father of four children who were raised by Grandmother: my mother, my Uncle Romek, my Uncle Wladislaw, and a little girl who died of pneumonia in childhood. My Uncle Romek was dead too. He was killed at the beginning of the war in the famous Polish cavalry charge against a German tank division.

Now, because of his condition, my grandfather was always at home, while my grandmother sold cigarettes and things in Theater Square. I could never have told her that I was bringing a Jew to her house, not even for only a few hours. Grandmother thought that all Jews were Devil worshipers, or at least, the Devil's assistants. I wonder what she would have said had she known the truth about my father, because she was actually very fond of me.

She was a country girl, not a city lady. My grandfather's family was furious at him for marrying an "uncouth peasant." But Grandmother was far from uncouth. She may never have read Shakespeare or learned to play the piano, but she had a good head on her shoulders. I've already said that Grandfather was a Rejmont, which is something I'm proud of to this day.

Every morning Grandmother dressed Grandfather and sat him down by the glass-paneled door, which also doubled as the window. If it wasn't winter and the weather was good, she would leave the door open, and if it was hot, she would seat him outside on a metal chair that was chained and padlocked to a water pipe to keep it from being stolen. Fortunately, Grandfather was still able to go to the bathroom by himself. Grandmother had sworn never to put him in a hospital ward or in an old-age home run by the church. They had been wed, she said, for good and for bad, and if now was the bad part, there had been many good years before that, when the world had still been a sane place. Which it had stopped being, Grandmother was convinced, because of all the Jewish inventions, like automobiles that flew through the air and dropped bombs.

68

One thing my grandfather could do to his dying day was roll cigarettes. He would make them at home and Grandmother would sell them in the square. She did something else there too that I wasn't supposed to know about: as innocent as she looked, she transmitted messages for the Polish Home Army. Someone would come along and tell her something, or hand her a note wrapped in a bill he had bought his cigarettes with, and she in turn would hand it to another customer with his change.

I often helped them roll the cigarettes. They used a copper tube slightly longer than two cigarettes which opened lengthwise on a hinge in such a way that it resembled two little drainpipes, which were filled with tobacco. You had to have a sense for how much to pack the tube, because if you crammed it with too much tobacco the cigarette paper tore, and if you used too little all the tobacco spilled out.

I think the underground chose my grandmother for several reasons. One was that she was already a street peddler anyway. Another was that she lived alone with her husband in a ruined building that had no doorman. Both were good reasons for me to think that I could safely leave the Jew in her house for several hours.

Afterward I found out that his first name was Jozek. He never told me his family name.

As soon as I reached Theater Square I spotted my grandmother in the distance. She was reaching for something in one of her skirt pockets — no doubt her twenty-zloty German cigarettes. She sold different brands and kept each one in a different place, wrapped in rags that she stuffed in the many pockets of her skirts and in my grandfather's old jacket that she wore. She wore one skirt over another, just like the peasants in the countryside.

"Good morning, Grandma," I said to her.

The customer departed.

"What's this, no school today?"

I told her I was sent home for not doing my homework. It wasn't such a big lie, because I really hadn't done it.

She believed me. "Come, sit down with your old Grandma for a while," she said.

"I can't," I said. "I was just passing by and decided to say hello to you."

She believed that less. "Would you take something to Grandpa for me?"

I said I would. She took a flat can from one of her pockets and told me I could have some of it too.

"What is it?"

"Can't you read? Read it!"

I read it. Sardines. She shook a finger at me.

"I said you could have *some,* not all of it. Don't forget. Grandpa may not remember if he ate sardines or not, but I'll find out the truth."

She was just like my mother that way: she always knew when I was lying. The difference was that she would slap me for doing it.

My mother told me that Grandfather used to whip his sons with a belt. He would lay them across his knees and let them have it. The older the son, the harder the whipping. Grandmother educated my mother with slaps, but it was the-older-the-harder with her too, until one day my mother said that she was a woman already, and the slapping stopped. I wasn't sure what she meant by that. She always said she would explain it to me some day, but she never did.

"Bye, Grandma," I said, giving her a kiss.

That was a mistake. She knew right away that I was up to something because of the kiss. I really shouldn't have given it to her. I was just so happy to have found her there and to have a place to put Pan Jozek.

"I have no money to waste on you," she said. "Get along with you, you young scamp!"

"It was just a kiss," I said. "I didn't mean anything by it."

When she got home, I thought, we would already be gone. And my grandfather would be in his usual fog. You know, I believe in God. Even then I believed that God arranges things so that we can choose between good and evil. The whole point is to choose.

6

Marek Wins Over Pan Jozek

It was a very old graveyard. Many of the graves had dates centuries old. As a little boy before the war, I remember, I sometimes used to run out to it when I grew tired of sitting quietly in church on Sunday morning. I know that most children are afraid of cemeteries. I never was, though. More than anything I wanted my father to have a grave we could visit. Maybe that's why I invented a game. Since I thought that people who died could get together afterward like children during recess in school, I would walk between the rows looking for a grave with a name on it I liked, which I would decide must belong to a friend of my father's in the next world.

Pan Jozek wasn't in the park. I thought that maybe he had entered the church, but he wasn't there either. That meant, I supposed, that he hadn't trusted me enough to keep our rendezvous. Agreeing to meet me was just a way to throw me off his trail. Although I didn't blame him, I really did feel sorry. I walked through the park again, checking all the corner benches by the fence, and went back out to the street. Could he have waited for me and given up? Or maybe something had happened to him . . . Well, it wasn't my fault that my aunt and uncle weren't home. I debated whether to take a streetcar back to my grandmother's or to walk. Though I no longer hitched rides on the back of streetcars, I had a little money with me. My mother had caught me hitching a ride once and had made me promise to stop.

I fingered the can of sardines in my pockets. I felt like having something to eat. I was trying to think of the nearest streetcar I could take when I saw Pan Jozek step out of a bookstore with two books under his arm. And a newspaper. When I came closer, I saw that it was a German one. I noticed that one of the books was in German too. It hadn't been a bad place to stay out of sight while waiting for me. He knew he would see me, because he had a clear view of the street through the store window.

"Hello there," I said, as if we were old friends.

He went along with it, even though the street was nearly empty. "Why, hello there! How are you?"

I hadn't told him my name yet.

We could have passed for an elder and a younger brother, or for neighbors. Or else, he could have been my teacher. But no, he couldn't have been, not at that hour of the morning.

"Did you give up on me?"

He nodded. "It took you a long time."

73

"No one was home at my uncle's," I said. "But we can go wait at my grandfather's. They must have gone out shopping or on some business. They always come back before noon."

I told him that from my uncle's I had gone to Theater Square to make sure that my grandmother was there and hadn't stayed home with my grandfather. I told him about Grandfather and explained that the building had no doorman because it wasn't a building anymore. Then I showed him the can of sardines.

Right away someone came up to me and asked if I was selling. I said I wasn't. He insisted on knowing how much I wanted for the sardines. I repeated that they weren't for sale. He looked suspiciously at Pan Jozek and said, "I'll top any offer he makes you."

I thought it over, but I still didn't sell. When he was gone I asked Pan Jozek if he would come and wait with me in my grandparents' apartment until noon. He agreed.

"Now you look like a student, or even like Volksdeutsch," I said to him.

That pleased him so that he stretched out his arms as though giving the world a hug and said, "My, what a beautiful day!"

I too loved those winter days with a suddenly blue sky and snow glittering all around. There wasn't a breath of wind. The air was so fresh and pure that you felt you had never been so alive. I had known all morning that it would turn out to be a beautiful day, but Pan Jozek said it so feelingly that I thought he might dance in the street.

I thought of all the months he had been holed up in the priest's pantry. "Where's your family?" I asked.

"They've all been killed except for my mother. She managed to escape the Germans' clutches."

"How?" I asked.

"By dying first."

As I walked by his side I kept looking all around me, not the way I usually did but through Pan Jozek's eyes. I tried seeing everything for the first time: the snow-covered park, the newspaper vendors, the peasant women peddling food from baskets, the mothers out for a stroll in the sun with their baby carriages.

"Suppose your mother were still alive," I said. "What would you have done?"

"Are you asking me if I would have left the ghetto without her? No, I wouldn't have. As a matter of fact, we could have left long ago, before the deportations began. The Germans call them 'resettlement' — that means they resettle us in the world to come. There was a village family that was willing to hide both of us. But my mother refused to go because she couldn't keep kosher there. Do you know what that is?"

I didn't. He explained it to me.

I remember thinking: the poor Jews, as if being Jewish weren't hard enough, they have all these laws to make it even harder! The only Jewish law I had known before was the one about not eating pork. Some boys in school told everyone how the Germans caught Jews and forced them to eat it. There was one little boy there who said, "Then I'll make believe I'm a Jew and they'll make me eat it too." He had to have it explained to him that he didn't wear a hat or grow a beard like a Jew and that once he ate the pork he'd be killed.

"You can't even see the Wisla from the ghetto," Pan Jozek said.

That was something I had never thought of when picturing the ghetto. I couldn't imagine life without the Wisla. What would I do in the summer if I couldn't sit by its banks and watch the ships passing by? I'd go out of my mind, that's what. During summer vacations I used to work in Pan Mueller's boat-rental house. Sometimes, when business was slow, he would let me go for a row and dive off the boat as much as I pleased. And he would even pay me for it! Of course, he sometimes hit me too.

"How old are you?"

"Fourteen. I keep my birth certificate in my pocket so that the Germans won't draft me into a work gang. I've carried it around ever since they almost did that because they thought I was older."

"I also thought you were at least sixteen. How come they let you go?"

"There was a policeman who recognized me from Pan Korek's tavern. I work there sometimes too."

I told him about the tavern on Grzybowska Street and what I had to do there.

"I really was a student before the war," he told me. "Of medicine."

"Then you know what a doctor does?"

"Not quite. Why do you ask?"

"Because of my grandfather," I said.

But that wasn't really it. I had always wanted to know a doctor, not the way you know one when you see him in his office with a lot of people waiting outside, including your mother, but the way you know a friend. I could have asked him about all kinds of things that my parents and the priest said were a sin. Like masturbation. But of course, I didn't tell Pan Jozek all that.

He stopped to buy cigarettes and matches from the lame lady I always passed on my way to my grandparents'. Suddenly he pointed to a house and said, "That's where we lived in the ghetto."

I had completely forgotten that as recently as the previous summer the area we were walking in had been the Little Ghetto. My aunt and uncle lived in an apartment at 62 Zelazna Street, near the old Akron Movie Theater, which had belonged to Jews. They even gave me some toys they found when they moved in. They took me into a room that had two big light-blue shelves full of books and playthings and told me to take what I wanted. Some of them were broken. There were two beds that must have belonged to two brothers, because I didn't see any girls' toys, except maybe the three teddy bears and a monkey that I didn't take. But they could have belonged to a small

77

boy too. I was surprised that the books were regular Polish ones, and that the toys were just like the ones that Polish children played with. There wasn't anything in Jewish letters or particularly Jewish looking.

That, by the way, was where I found *Les Misérables*.

Children's rooms with two beds in them always made me jealous. I always wanted a little brother or sister. I just didn't want one who was Antony's child.

On the way to Bridge Street Pan Jozek decided to turn right and walk through Old Warsaw. That was a part of the city I liked to walk in too. When I visited my grandparents, I sometimes went out of my way to pass through it.

We crossed the Wisla on the Kerbedzia Bridge and stood in the middle of it looking down on the river. Here and there you could already see ice against the banks. The tour boats, rowboats, and kayaks were gone, but it was such a nice day that despite the snow and bare trees you expected a boat to come sailing beneath the bridge any minute.

What did come by as we stood there were two barges loaded with lumber. I liked looking down at the flowing water. Pan Jozek put it well when he said that it was just as hypnotic as fire. He asked me, "Have you ever been to the seashore?"

I never had. It was a long way from Warsaw, although my mother had promised we would go there after the war. I tried to imagine the Wisla without its opposite bank, the way it was on a foggy day. Was that what the ocean looked like?

I asked Pan Jozek. He said that it wasn't. I remember him saying, "A river is a river and an ocean is an ocean. Each has its own beauty, its own sound, its own smell. I love the ocean and I love the Wisla too."

I was struck by what he said because until then I had never thought that a Jew could love the Wisla the way I did.

As we came off the bridge, he asked me what my name was. I told him and explained about my mother's family name and about Antony's. He said that his first name was Jozek, and that I should call him "Pan Jozek." To this day I don't know why he never told me his last name.

My grandfather was sitting behind the closed door as he always did in cold weather, looking out the glass pane that my grandmother had scraped the frost off before leaving. I never could tell what he saw. Sometimes, when I approached from the street, it seemed to me that he wasn't seeing anything even though his eyes were wide open. He always sat with his walking stick, which he tapped so often on the wooden floor that there was a hollow in the floorboard. Sometimes he drew on the glass door with his finger. His lower jaw hung open and made him look a hundred years old, because Grandmother kept his false teeth locked in the closet.

He didn't notice us come in because he was talking to someone in low tones.

Grandfather generally liked to talk to either his older sister or one of his parents. If he was arguing, that meant it was his sister. His tone with his mother was more conversational. I tried to make out what he was saying to her, but it was impossible. Now and then a sentence would make sense, followed by many that didn't. For instance, I once heard him say, "Mama, those cigarettes could be sold for good money, but that bastard of a German didn't flush the toilet." Different stories or memories must have combined with each other in some part of his brain.

When he spoke to his father, he always called him sir. Some Polish children "sir" their father to this day.

"Good morning, Grandpa!" I shouted, because he was a little deaf in the bargain. He stood up at once, though, when I showed him the can of sardines.

"They're from Grandma," I said.

We helped him hobble to the table and sat him down there. I was afraid the house would be cold, because my grandmother usually saved the wood for the evening, but some embers were still burning in the oven and the apartment was cozy. My grandfather didn't pay Pan Jozek any attention. He seemed to take it for granted that he was my guest. Pan Jozek took off his coat and I hung it with his hat on a hanger. When Antony was being nasty about Jews, one of the things he said was that they never took their hats off in their houses. I didn't believe him, though. It was true that the three brothers kept their hats on, but that was down in the basement. I couldn't imagine anyone coming into his own home, or entering someone else's, and not taking off his hat. I was sure it was one of Antony's anti-Semitic inventions.

I took half a loaf of bread and a wedge of cheese

from the pantry and put out three mugs and some clabber that my grandmother had made by warming milk near the oven till it soured. Then I set the table with plates and silverware. We didn't have guests or sardines every day! I filled the kettle and put it up to boil, adding some wood to the fire. My grandparents had neither gas nor electricity. At night they sat by candlelight or lamplight. My grandmother said she didn't want any inspectors reading meters or collecting bills. Looking back on it today, I think it was less a matter of her being stingy than of her being in the underground.

Grandfather wanted to slice the bread himself, but his hands shook too hard. And so he just crossed himself and said the Lord's blessing while I took the key to the little closet from its hiding place and brought him his false teeth. Then we sat down to eat.

It was only then that I realized how hungry Pan Jozek was. Between one bite and the next he wanted to know why the teeth were kept under lock and key. I told him that Grandfather sometimes lay down and fell asleep, and that if he swallowed the teeth he could choke. Or else, if he took them out of his mouth to play with while sitting in his chair by the door, they might fall and break.

Suddenly Grandfather stopped eating and froze with his fork halfway to his mouth. I had hoped he wouldn't do that and embarrass me, because he sometimes forgot that he was eating and would just sit there holding his spoon or fork until his food spilled on the floor. I took the fork from his hand and fed him.

"You take good care of your grandfather," said Pan Jozek.

"I guess I'm used to it," I said. Maybe I shouldn't have added what I did, but I couldn't resist. I laughed and said, "If my grandmother knew that a Jew sat here at her table, she'd scrub it down with disinfectant."

"Does she hate Jews that much?"

"Yes," I said.

"Does your whole family?"

"Not all of it. I don't know about my uncle who was killed. My Uncle Wladislaw doesn't love Jews, but he doesn't hate them either. He just makes money off of them. Not from blackmail or informing." I swallowed hard. "From hiding them. That's the uncle I went to see this morning."

"And your mother?"

"My mother believes that everyone is equal before God. It doesn't matter what you believe, or what you wear or eat. Whatever my grandmother says, she always says the opposite."

"And your stepfather?"

I told him.

"It's just that he hates the Germans even more. And maybe the Communists too. He says that if it weren't for the Germans, we'd have to get rid of the Jews by ourselves. He thinks we should send them all to Palestine. He's even willing to pay for it. He thinks that Poland has room for only one people."

"But what about the Byelorussians and Ukrainians who live in Poland too?"

I shrugged. The subject had never come up. "Anyway you look at it, they're Christians and not Jews," I said.

"They still don't consider themselves Poles," said Pan Jozek. He asked me what Grandfather thought.

"Grandpa!" I shouted. "What do you think of the Jews?"

I didn't think he'd understand me. After reflecting for a minute, though, he declared solemnly, "The Jews — lice — typhoid fever!"

I was amazed that he remembered the German notices he had read. Sometimes he surprised me by being more together than I thought.

"Are you still hungry, Pan Jozek?" I asked.

"What else is there to eat?"

There were eggs. While the water boiled in the kettle, I fried some up. I even ate one myself. By now I was full, but watching Pan Jozek eat gave me a new appetite. Then I made Grandfather a scrambled egg and fed him. He liked scrambled eggs. He could eat them even without his teeth. I thought it a good time to take them out of his mouth, but he wouldn't let me have them. All right, I thought, I'll do it when we're finished.

Afterward we drank tea like Grandfather and Grandmother. Actually, my mother and Antony drank it that way too. You bite off a piece of a sugar cube, put it under your tongue, and sip your tea through it, which makes it very sweet. It wasn't a

83

question of saving sugar, though maybe that's how it started. It was simply the way my family drank tea. Now I saw that it was Pan Jozek's way too.

That was when Grandfather began to make a scene. He didn't want to give me his teeth back. I tried to convince him, and so did Pan Jozek. But Grandfather just shut his mouth tight and turned his back on us. He even shut his eyes and pretended not to hear.

Pan Jozek thought that as long as someone was with him, we could let him keep his teeth. And so I told him to stay put and wait for me while I went to talk to my mother. It had suddenly occurred to me that it would be better for her to speak to my aunt and uncle.

My mother was the only person who knew what I had done, and I was sure she would understand and help me to persuade my uncle. Pan Jozek, however, I now discovered, put no stock in my plans.

"It's been a pleasure, Marek," he said. "Maybe it was because we were both running from the Germans when we met, or because I saw that you weren't trying to blackmail me, or because I already knew you from the church, but for a while I really thought that going to your uncle's was a good idea. It was such a beautiful day that I couldn't resist running the risk of putting my faith in you. The more I think about it now away from the pressure of the street, though, the less logical it seems. I wanted to tell you that before, but I put it off because it seemed harmless to sit for a while in your grandfather's house while I thought of what to do next."

"What will you do?"

"First, I'll try the worse of the two addresses."

"But why? Why not try me? I'll go talk to my mother and everything will be all right. There's no problem about my uncle taking Jews."

"Suppose I agreed: what would you tell your mother? That you met a Jew in the street and want your uncle to take him in?"

I shook my head.

"Then what? Do you expect her to take the responsibility on herself? Usually, anyone hiding Jews gets them from a reliable source. Your uncle might think I was a blackmailer myself, or a double agent working for the Germans. And forgive me for saying so, but I can't help thinking that there's something strange about this whole business. Why on earth are you going to so much trouble to help me?"

I didn't know how to answer.

"Suppose your mother talks it over with your step-father, and he goes and calls the police? Or your grandmother comes home while you're not here and takes me for a burglar? It's all much too risky for me." He rose to go.

"My grandmother never comes home before late afternoon," I said on the verge of despair.

But he had stopped taking me seriously. "Anyway, Marek, thanks an awful lot. At least I ate well. That priest who hid me begrudged me every slice of bread." He smiled.

Holy Mother of God, I wanted him to stay in the worst way! That's when I decided to tell him the truth. At least some of it. I asked him to sit down again for a minute, because I had something to say to him. He sat down and looked at me curiously. I told him how I had been walking up Grzybowska Street early one morning when I ran into Wacek and Janek, and how, although I sometimes went along with them, I had never gone Jew hunting before, and how I did it this time because I was sure that they would do it anyway without me, and how I couldn't resist having all that money to throw around, and how my mother had caught me red-handed. Finally, I told him that my mother still had the money, and that I wanted to give it to him, or at least to pay for his expenses while it lasted.

I don't think I ever talked so much in my life. I went on and on until I had nothing left to say while he sat there thinking and Grandfather tapped his finger on the table: tak tak stop and tak tak stop again.

"And you really think your mother will be willing to take the responsibility for your uncle taking me in?"

I shrugged.

"All right," he said. "Let's give it a try."

7

Grandfather's Teeth
and Pan Korek

I was just in time to catch the number fifteen streetcar to Wilson Square. From there I walked to the sewing shop where my mother worked as a seamstress. I told her I had been bad in school and was sent home to bring her to the principal. Her Volksdeutsch boss laughed and wagged a finger at me when she asked him for permission to leave work, but he let her off. As soon as we had left I told her everything, starting with my noticing Pan Jozek in church and our slipping through the German dragnet, which made her ask if I had my birth certificate in my pocket. "You were lucky," she said when I told her we had gone to my grandparents' because my uncle and aunt weren't home. She wanted to hear everything Pan Jozek and I had talked about, and she hugged and kissed me when I was finished. That made me feel better already. "The first thing to do," said my mother, "is to go see that priest."

We took a bus to the church and knocked on the door of the priest's quarters. An old hag opened the door and told us we couldn't come in. "My brother has had a bad accident and isn't seeing anyone," she said sharply while slamming the door in our face.

We didn't give up. We knocked and knocked until we heard the priest's voice telling his sister to let the good Catholics in. She opened the door again, but only for my mother. I was told to wait outside.

It took a while for my mother to come back out, because at first the priest denied everything, even though she whispered her questions in his ear to keep his sister from hearing. In the end he had to send her out to buy him cigarettes and a newspaper. She understood of course that he was trying to get rid of her and stormed out the door muttering about her brother's ingratitude and something else that I couldn't make out. A few minutes later my mother emerged and told me that everything was all right. The priest had given Pan Jozek a clean bill of health.

From there we went to my uncle and aunt's on Zelazna Street. You had to enter a courtyard to reach their apartment, but the gatekeeper knew us. They were both home. Once again I had to wait in a hallway. Then I was called inside, where my uncle gave me a look that frightened me a bit. All he said, though, was that he had no room. If the back room became available, he would keep it for my Jew — provided, of course, that he was still alive and hadn't found another place. Meanwhile, he advised us to try Pan Korek, who was sure to take the Jew for less money. Pan Jozek wouldn't be as safe there as he would be at my uncle's, but my uncle was simply full up. In any case, Uncle Wladislaw said, we should keep all the money so that we could give him a big advance if we brought the Jew.

My mother answered that she wasn't going to pay a penny more than she had said she would. A month's advance was the maximum. And no deposit, either. She had never heard of a brother asking his sister for such a thing!

I realized at once that it was a mistake for her to have told my uncle about the money. The problem was that otherwise she couldn't have told him the truth — and my mother, as I've said, hated to lie, especially to the members of her family. Besides which, she was no doubt right in thinking that nothing but the truth could convince Uncle Wladislaw to take Pan Jozek at all. Still, she couldn't restrain herself from saying with a hard look at my uncle, "Pan Korek gives all the money he gets for hiding Jews to the underground."

"To each his own," said my uncle.

We left. My mother was furious. She started to say that my uncle was as money-mad as a J — but felt too uncomfortable to say the word. And she really wasn't anti-Semitic. It was just an expression people used.

It astounded me to find out that Pan Korek hid Jews. I would never have guessed it, though I worked several days a week in his tavern. True, I had never been up to the apartment above it, but you would have thought that I'd notice something. He must have gone up there to tend to things only after hours. I was sure he would take in Pan Jozek if we asked him.

We went to his tavern. It wasn't far away. I asked

my mother not to tell Pan Korek the whole truth. She should just say that she knew Pan Jozek, or better yet, his father. Something of the sort.

She promised to think of something and told me not to worry.

I was worried anyway about what we would do if Pan Korek wasn't there. And my mother would be so late in getting back to work that her boss might begin to suspect something.

I liked coming to the tavern at an hour when it was empty but already spick-and-span for opening time. It was quiet and cozy inside, and didn't stink of cigarette smoke, cheap cigars, and the homemade potato liquor everyone called *bimber*.

Pan Korek was in his office. He was an incredibly big man. My mother said that he reminded her of my father. She told me that the two of them were friends before my father became a Communist. Later, when my father came back from Russia, their relationship cooled a bit. Pan Korek was never against religion and never thought that it was the opium of the people.

Sometimes I asked my mother if she thought that I too would have fought with my father because of his views. She was sure that I would have. Back then, during the war, I had unthinkingly absorbed Antony's opinions. My father would never have stood for them, although my mother was sure he would have lost all his pro-Russian illusions after the pact between Hitler and Stalin that divided up Poland between them. My mother thought that Hitler's attacking Russia was the Russians' punishment for having betrayed us. It was like betraying your own brother, she said. But she thought the Russians would save us in the end and pay back their debt to us. If Antony were around at that point, he would be sure to add, "Sure thing! The old Russian bear hug. Good for a hundred years!"

My mother closeted herself with Pan Korek for ten long minutes while I wondered if she would keep her promise and not involve me.

When they stepped out of his office, Pan Korek said, "Your mother vouches for a young Jew whose father was a friend of Broneslaw's. She's ready to pay an advance for him. That's good, because we need the money." Pan Korek knew that I knew he was in the underground.

At this point I should explain: the People's Army and the Polish Home Army were the two main anti-German resistance movements. The first were "reds" and Communists; the second were "greens" and Catholics. Antony thought that the Home Army were patriots and that the People's Army were Bolshevik traitors. Even though it fought the Germans, the Home Army had a reputation for hating Jews. It refused to give them shelter or accept them as partisans, and was even said to turn them over to the Germans. I don't mean to say that every member of the Home Army was anti-Semitic, but there were plenty who were. And of course, not everyone in the People's Army loved Jews either. On the whole, though, they treated Jews well.

The two armies were a subject that Antony and my mother were no more able to agree on than they were able to agree about the Jews. My mother and Pan Korek were for the People's Army, whereas Antony, my grandmother, and I were for the Home Army. That wasn't what made me take the Jew's money, though. When it came to Jews as people, my views were like my mother's. All I agreed with Antony and my grandmother about was that there were too many Jews in Poland and that they should go to Palestine.

My mother and I left the tavern. She had kept my secret. I should be sure to tell Pan Jozek, she instructed me, of the "friendship" between his father and my grandfather. She had told Pan Korek that the two of them were both interested in old books, and that my grandfather had bought rare items for his library from Pan Jozek's father. After a moment's hesitation she told me where the money was hidden and how much I should pay Pan Korek, because she herself had to hurry back to work. I felt proud to be trusted with it.

"How much should we put aside for Uncle Wladislaw?" I asked her.

That made her angry all over again. "Don't worry," she said, "there's enough. But Pan Jozek can stay with Pan Korek. We won't have to bring him to my brother's."

My mother gave me change to take the streetcar home and get some money for Pan Korek. At first I thought I'd leave my school bag at home, but then I changed my mind. I had started thinking like a member of the underground — and a boy with a school bag would look less suspicious if he were accompanying Pan Jozek all the way from my grand-parents' to the tavern.

By the time I reached Bridge Street I was beginning to worry that Pan Jozek might not be there anymore. But he was. He was sitting by the table, reading Grandfather the newspaper, or rather, translating for him from the German. I told him about Pan Korek and said that my uncle might have a place for him at a later date if he was still interested. I didn't tell him that my uncle was money-mad. Whatever I thought of him, he was my mother's brother and I had to protect the family honor.

Pan Jozek said that my mother's story wasn't that far from the truth, because his father had actually been a used-book dealer back before the First World War. He had already put on his coat and taken his hat when we suddenly remembered Grandfather's teeth. We couldn't leave them in his mouth, and Grandfather, for some odd reason, refused to let us have them. Perhaps he just didn't want to be left by himself. Usually he could be coaxed into it, even if it took a while. It was harder at night, when he didn't want to be put to sleep.

One way or another, we couldn't go without Grandfather's teeth.

We tried talking to him. Nothing worked. I told Pan Jozek that we had to do something to startle Grandfather so much that he would open his mouth like a shocked child. Then we could grab his teeth. We didn't have to worry about being bitten, I explained, because Grandfather took a long time to react. He took a long time to do anything, whether it was walking, talking, or thinking. You could say three whole Paternosters between the time he had a thought and the time he put it into words.

"What do you do to startle him?" asked Pan Jozek.

"We suddenly jump on him," I said. "Or I stand on my head and kick my feet. It depends on who's here. Antony just picks him up and lifts him in the air."

I debated whether to tell him about Grandmother. I couldn't resist. "And my grandmother," I said, "does something really vulgar."

As soon as he asked me to tell him what that was I felt sorry I had said it, because what Grandmother did was to lift all her skirts at once and turn around to show Grandfather her bare bottom while I snatched the teeth from his mouth. It was easy as pie.

Pan Jozek took a look around the room and said, "Marek, I've got it!"

He took Grandfather's umbrella, which was standing in a corner by the door, told me to be ready, and went over to Grandfather. I had no idea what he was about to do. Suddenly he opened the umbrella right in Grandfather's face. Grandfather was so flabbergasted that his mouth dropped open long enough for me to grab his teeth.

That kind of trick worked well enough as long as Grandfather stayed in his fog. Sometimes, though, he snapped out of it and became his old self again. If we tried fooling him then, or treating him like a child by spoon-feeding or undressing him for bed, he would give us a shrewd look as if to ask how we could be so shameless. At times like that I felt like crawling into the ground.

Sometimes he would become lucid again for only a few minutes, other times for hours at a time. It might even last a few days, as if there were nothing wrong with him. When that happened he was shocked by how much time he had lost, because he couldn't remember a thing since he had last lost track of himself. Everything in between was wiped out, whether it was a few days, a week, or several weeks. He would sit up and wonder what had happened to all that time and ask how the war was getting on.

I remember one time when Grandmother and I used Grandmother's method to get his teeth. All at once he snapped out of his trance, looked at us both, and said to her, "What do you think you're doing? Aren't you ashamed of yourself? Why, Marek is standing right here! And you, Marek, what are you trying to do to me? How dare you? Give me my teeth. Go home this minute and don't come back until I've had a talk with your mother!"

I brought Pan Jozek to Pan Korek's. Pan Korek took an instant liking to him. He promised to bring down an old crate of books from the attic so that he could have something to read.

I gave Pan Korek the money and went home.

8

Moving Pan Jozek

For two months everything went smoothly. Until the beginning of April you might have thought I had forgotten all about Pan Jozek, because I wasn't allowed to see him even when I was working in the tavern. Once or twice I took some of the remaining money from its hiding place and brought it to Pan Korek.

And then one day I found my mother waiting for me at the school gate after class. Although I could see right away that she was all right, I was frightened nonetheless. When we had walked away from all the children, she told me what was the matter. Pan Korek had had a bad quarrel, complete with curses and blows, with Pan Szczupak. Pan Szczupak was a known informer. He had worked for the police even before the war, and now he worked for the Germans too. He was high up on Antony's black list.

Although Pan Szczupak was a regular customer in the tavern and had never informed on anyone who drank there, perhaps because he was given all his drinks at half price, Pan Korek was frightened. He was, after all, hiding Jews — and not just Pan Jozek.

Of course, Pan Szczupak knew nothing about this, but if he were to pin some rap on Pan Korek and Pan Korek's apartment were searched, the Jews would be found. Even if Jews were a good source of income and Pan Korek turned his over to the underground, no one was ready to get killed because of them. And so Pan Korek phoned my mother at her sewing shop and asked her to come at once to pick up her "merchandise." My mother went first to my Uncle Wladislaw's, but there was still no room there. Even the emergency place that my uncle kept for a "temporary," someone who was willing to pay extra for a short stay, would not be available for another week to ten days. That was when my mother told me to go speak to my grandmother. She began to instruct me how to talk to her, but I told her that I didn't need any lessons.

My grandparents' apartment was of course an ideal place to hide Pan Jozek in. Even if someone saw him enter it with us, he would be taken for a doctor visiting Grandfather.

After thinking it over, we decided on a story to tell Grandmother. Since it wasn't easy to put one over on her, we decided to tell her the truth, or rather a slightly improved version of it. We would say that Pan Jozek was an ex-teacher of mine whom I had run into in the street, and that although we knew he was Jewish, we felt we had to help him. All he needed was somewhere to stay for a week to ten days until a place being prepared for him by some friends was ready, and he was quite willing to pay for it. We couldn't take him home with us because of Antony, who mustn't know about it, quite apart from the fact that our doorman, Valenty, might suspect something.

I took a streetcar to Theater Square. Grandmother was sitting in her usual chair. I gave her a kiss, though I knew it would warn her that I wanted something. I did want something, and anyway, she liked to be kissed even if it put her guard up. She shook her finger at me and said, "I'm all out of money, and all out of sardines, and all out of everything, Marek. What is it that you want from me, my darling?" That kind of talk meant she was in a good mood.

"Grandma," I said, "this time it's serious. But first I have to ask you something."

She looked at me without a word. So I started in on Jesus and Mary. I asked her if she knew that they were Jews just like the Jews in the ghetto.

She would have slapped my face then and there if she could have done it sitting down.

"Like the Jews in the ghetto? Our Lord Jesus and the Virgin Mary? What kind of blasphemy is that, Marek? How can you kiss me and then make me so upset? I have a headache from you already!"

She clutched her head with both hands but went on looking at me curiously. So I told her the "story," and she fell for it. I was very proud of myself.

"It's only for a few days, Grandma," I said. "We'll have to get him out of here by Saturday at the latest, because on Sunday we'll come as usual with Antony, and he mustn't suspect anything."

"Why did your mother send you instead of talking to me herself?"

"You weren't listening, Grandma! He was my teacher, not my mother's. She's just trying to be helpful."

"I understand all that. But a body would think she could at least have come with you."

"Don't you know that she's afraid of you?" I said.

Grandmother laughed. I could see she got a kick out of that. But what would happen, she wanted to know, if Antony found out?

"He won't," I answered. "He'd better not!"

She wanted to know what the Jew looked like.

"He's not the kind of Jew you're thinking of, Grandma. He's a different kind. He looks just like us. Before the war he was a medical student."

"Suppose I should have to hide someone from the underground while he's still with me?"

"But you can't even tell he's a Jew, Grandma. If anyone asks you can always say he's a relative who needs to lay low in Warsaw for a week before moving on. You'll think of something. Or else he will."

"If Antony finds out, he'll throw you all out of the house!"

"He certainly will," I agreed. "And you wouldn't want him to do that, would you?"

"No," said Grandmother, half to herself, "I wouldn't want him to do that."

She sat there thinking. I had no patience to wait for her answer, and to make matters worse, a customer arrived just then and began bargaining for some

German cigarettes. He was followed by someone else, to whom Grandmother sold some matches and whispered something in his ear. Before anyone else could come along I asked, "Is it all right then, Grandma?"

"Tell your mother I want to talk to her."

I didn't like the thought of that. If my mother arrived there would be a big quarrel and nothing would come of it. Grandmother saw that I looked worried and told me not to be.

"Everything will be fine, Marek. I just want her to come and ask me herself. And don't go telling me it's not her business."

The fact was that I was equally afraid my mother would refuse to come. I knew perfectly well what happened when the two of them got together. All hell broke loose. If they didn't have something handy to fight over, they would manage to invent it. Before we were very far into a visit to my grandparents' my mother would lose her temper and become a different person. It never happened with anyone else. If the visit was short, it would end with them both in a huff. If it was long enough, there would be time to kiss and make up until the next visit. It didn't matter how often my mother swore beforehand that "this time" she wouldn't fight with Grandmother but would be nice and avoid any topic that might lead to an argument and insults. In fact, Antony and I thought it best for her to start arguing as soon as she walked in, since that left more time for a reconciliation. If she and Grandmother argued at the end of a visit, we might have to cancel next Sunday's dinner entirely.

Grandmother thought that my mother was a flaming radical, and my mother thought that Grandmother was a right-wing nationalist and practically a fascist. The truth of the matter was, I think, that they were still fighting over my father, over my mother's living in sin with him, and over my grandmother's cutting all ties with her — which was something, my mother insisted, that no real mother would ever do.

They fought over religion too. My grandmother considered my mother "a bad Catholic" even though she went to church on Sundays, and my mother believed that my grandmother was "a superstitious old fanatic." She also accused her of not taking good care of my grandfather, whom she left alone by himself all day long while she sat in the marketplace. My mother and even Uncle Wladislaw had offered to give Grandmother enough money each month for her to stop selling cigarettes and stay home with Grandfather. Grandmother's answer was that she was not going "to live on charity," but we all knew that she preferred to be out in the world and in the thick of things, especially since that meant a role in the underground. Sitting at home all day long with my sick grandfather would have been worse than death for her. She wouldn't even agree to my mother's suggestion that someone else be paid to stay with him. As with the electricity and gas, as I said before I think this was less a matter of pinching pennies than of her being in the underground, because she often hid people in her house. Not Jews, of course, although once she did hide an English pilot. And my mother underestimated my grandmother's earnings, which were considerable, both because she had a good head for business and because she cheated her customers. She once stopped talking to Antony for a month because he said that she "did business like a Jew." We missed a whole row of Sunday dinners until he apologized. Besides, my grandmother said, if someone had to stay with Grandfather, why didn't my mother do it herself? It would be no great loss if she quit her sewing shop with its miserable salary that that lousy Volksdeutsch paid her.

My mother agreed to talk to Grandmother. "She always has to be the boss!" Mother said.

In no time, of course, they began to quarrel. What about? About my mother's clothes! How could a "lady" like my mother walk around dressed like a rag woman? She might be married to a Skorupa, but she must never forget she was a Rejmont! "And you?" shot back my mother. "Look at yourself!" I could see her open her mouth to say something else and think better of it. I was sure it was going to be about the way Grandmother and I made Grandfather give us his teeth. It was a good thing my mother caught herself, because Grandmother would never have forgiven my telling her how we did it.

Grandmother replied that if she dressed like a peasant it was because of her work and as a disguise for the underground. The truth was that she had simply gone back to dressing the way she had dressed as a girl in the village. Grandfather's illness at least had the advantage of freeing her from the role of Pani

Rejmont, the wife of the eminent printer, who went about, as she put it, "tied in knots" with garters and girdles.

In the end, they kissed and made up. That day my mother and I went to bring Pan Jozek to my grandparents'.

Although it was raining, we went on foot because Pan Jozek wanted us to. My mother held his arm, he held the umbrella, and I tagged along behind them holding my school bag over my head. She looked young enough to pass for his wife, while I could have been his younger brother hurrying after him in the street.

He was at my grandparents' for exactly ten days. They were special days for both Grandmother and Grandfather. Grandfather changed visibly for the better. Not that he grew well again. And yet he not only didn't get worse, which we were used to his doing so slowly but surely that hardly a week went by without our noticing, he actually became better. Maybe it was because Pan Jozek spent so much time taking care of him. As an ex-medical student, he didn't mind that kind of thing. He was used to it too, because after the Germans took Warsaw and expelled all the Jewish students from the universities, he lived at home with his mother for a while.

Suddenly Grandfather was bathed and shaved each day. He even seemed to have put on weight. I don't think he could have gained much in a week, but being cleaner and less neglected made him look healthier. So perhaps did his not being so lonely anymore. Pan

Jozek fed him regular meals and Grandfather obediently returned his teeth after each of them. And whenever his mind cleared, he and Pan Jozek played chess.

It was the weirdest chess game you ever saw. They played it all week long, picking up where they had left off at the end of Grandfather's last good spell. It wasn't the game itself that was weird, because it was played according to the rules, but the fact that Grandfather couldn't remember the intervals between sessions, which were anywhere from a few hours to half a day long, so that he thought that all the moves were being made in one sitting.

I think it must be very odd to lose long episodes of time. My grandfather could lose a day or more at a time. I once asked a doctor friend of mine if the same thing happens in sleep. When you sleep you sometimes also wake up unable to tell if it is morning or evening, or how long you have been sleeping, or even where you are. Suddenly you don't recognize your own room: the door is in the wrong place, everything seems turned around, and nothing looks familiar. Was that Grandfather's normal perception?

We told Grandfather that Pan Jozek was an old teacher of mine who had to hide for a few days because of the war; that is, we told him in his first lucid period after Pan Jozek was brought to his house. Most of the time, however, he didn't ask any questions. He thought Pan Jozek was his cousin Witek, who had died long ago, and kept asking him how he was. Grandfather had loved Witek dearly.

104

When I said something to Pan Jozek about time "getting lost" in this manner, he remarked that the most extreme case was death itself. Then he looked at me and asked if I believed in reincarnation. I had no idea what that meant, though, and he never raised the subject again. Another time I was present when he had an argument with Grandmother about the Jews in Warsaw before the war.

I visited my grandparents two or three times while Pan Jozek was staying with them. Once I found him with a map, explaining to Grandfather why the Germans were losing the war. When Grandfather was "all there" he was so normal that it could break your heart.

Grandmother saw the change in him too. She wouldn't have admitted it, but she realized that my mother and Uncle Wladislaw had been right about her belonging at home. There was nothing stupid about her — it just hadn't gotten through to her until then. After Pan Jozek moved to Uncle Wladislaw's she began coming home regularly for lunch and spending the rest of the day with Grandfather.

Grandmother fell in love with Pan Jozek. He stayed up with her to all hours of the night trying to help her make cigarettes. It didn't take her long, though, to see that she was better off without his help, and so she rolled the cigarettes herself while he sat next to her telling stories.

Pan Jozek didn't just have left-wing views. He had two left hands also. He tried so hard to learn to roll cigarettes like the rest of us that I was sure he would pick it up in a day or two, but when I visited again that weekend, he had made no progress at all. If he didn't spill the tobacco, the cigarette paper tore or the cigarette came out comically limp. Or else the tobacco tube didn't close. Or the rod that pushed the tobacco into the paper jammed — something I wouldn't have believed possible if I hadn't seen him make it happen.

He was just as funny when he smoked. To begin with, he never managed to light a cigarette with one match: either the match went out or the cigarette went up in flames. And when it was finally lit he held it and flicked its ashes so strangely that Grandmother and I couldn't look at each other if we wanted to keep from laughing, which in the end we did anyway. Pan Jozek didn't seem to mind. He thought it funny that we laughed. By the end of his stay Grandmother was laughing dotingly right in front of him.

Uncle Wladislaw could take Pan Jozek only on the second Sunday of his stay at my grandparents'. That Saturday night I slept at their house to keep Antony from wondering why I was going there so early in the morning. When Antony went home from church, my mother would join us under the pretext of visiting her friend Wanda. It was all planned logically. That night around the supper table I listened to Grandmother and Pan Jozek talk about the Jews.

After we had finished eating I cleaned off the table and sat down to help Grandmother and Grandfather roll cigarettes. I was a real expert at it. Grandmother asked Pan Jozek to join us, and after he told us about his day with Grandfather she asked him about his medical studies.

"It wasn't easy for a Jew like me to get into the university," he said. "There was a ten percent quota on Jews, though in fact even less were accepted. Only the best Jewish students got in. And afterward of course the other students hated them for doing so well."

Pan Jozek told us how the right-wing students slashed the faces of Jewish students with razor blades tied to sticks. Grandmother didn't comment. Pan Jozek himself was never assaulted, because no one suspected him of being Jewish.

"Even I wouldn't have suspected you," said Grandmother, who prided herself on being a connoisseur. "A handsome young man like you!"

She waited until Pan Jozek finally managed to light his cigarette and added, "If the Jews would only have listened to us and gone to Palestine, none of this would have happened."

"The Jews have their own political movement that wants them to go to Palestine," said Pan Jozek. "It's called Zionism. I don't believe anything will come of it, though. The Jews will go on wandering the earth until no one cares anymore about things like nationality and religion. How could they possibly establish a normal country like Poland or Holland or France? Just imagine a Jewish army!" We all burst out laughing.

"But there were Jewish soldiers in the Polish army," I said, coming to the Jews' defense. "There was even one named Berek Joselewicz."

Pan Jozek was amazed that I knew the name. I had heard it in a story read to me by my mother not long after she told me the truth about my father. Perhaps she had been trying to sweeten the pill by showing me that Polish Jews had been not just doctors, lawyers, and businessmen, but fighters too.

Grandmother remained unconvinced. "I still say it's their punishment for crucifying Jesus."

"It wasn't the Jews who crucified Jesus," said Pan Jozek. "It was the Romans."

"Really?" I asked.

"Well," said Pan Jozek, "the Jewish establishment of those days considered him a rebel, something like a Communist today, and seems to have recommended to the Roman governor that he be put to death. Crucifixion was the standard method of execution back then, just like hanging is now."

Grandmother shrugged. "Then why does everyone persecute them?" she asked.

"That's the fate of minorities everywhere," answered Pan Jozek. "Whenever there are problems like unemployment, housing shortages, or even the plague, the minority is always made the scapegoat." He spoke as patiently as a teacher or a priest.

Something he had said before still bothered me and I asked, "What did you mean when you said that one day no one would care about religion or nationality, Pan Jozek?"

"That's just what the Communists say," chimed in Grandmother.

"Not exactly," said Pan Jozek.

"Don't they say 'Workers of the world, unite'?" challenged Grandmother.

"They do."

"Are you a Communist?" she asked.

"No."

"Do you believe in God?"

He thought it over and said that he did. I let out a sigh of relief. When you got right down to it, the Jewish God was the same as the Catholic God. But Pan Jozek couldn't let well enough alone.

"I don't believe in the God of the church or the synagogue. I believe in a God who's more abstract."

He looked to see if I understood. I didn't, but I didn't say so.

"A philosophical God," he said defensively. "A Being that we too are part of."

That was too much for me. I think it was for Grandmother too, even though she nodded. "Can such a God hear prayers?" she asked.

"I don't think so," he said upon reflecting. "But there's no knowing. I don't believe that God concerns Himself with all the little details. At least not the God I believe in. And yet, who knows? Who knows!"

The conversation shifted to Uncle Wladislaw, to whose apartment he was being moved in the morning. Grandmother said something about "the houses we got back from the Germans" after the Jews were deported from the Little Ghetto and Pan Jozek said, "You didn't get them back, Pani Rejmont, because most of those houses belonged to Jews in the first place."

"Yes," Grandmother said. "But where did the Jews get the money to buy them?"

She was thinking what all the anti-Semites thought when they said that the Jews "sucked the Poles' blood."

"If King Kazimierz hadn't brought the Jews to Poland back in the sixteenth century," said Pan Jozek, "it would never have developed its economy and its industry."

"He brought them because no self-respecting Christian would want to be a businessman," said Grandmother.

It was strange to hear her say that. What about herself? And Pan Jozek couldn't resist pointing that out.

"He brought them to be merchants because the Poles were total illiterates, Pani Rejmont. Things have changed since then. Marek tells me you're not a bad businesswoman yourself."

"Whatever you say, they're always ready to work for less and sell for less and take the bread from our mouths," said Grandmother.

"If the Jews hadn't developed the Polish economy, Pani Rejmont, there wouldn't be any bread here at all, as there isn't, I'm sure you know, in many countries without Jews."

Grandmother said she wanted to go to sleep. It was a good thing, I thought, that Pan Jozek was leaving in the morning. Maybe that's why he had permitted himself to talk like that and to call her "Pani Rejmont" so often. Still, it was thoughtless of him. Suppose he had to return for another few days and

110

Grandmother refused to have him because of this argument?

Pan Jozek slept on a mattress at the foot of Grand-father's bed while I slept with Grandmother in her big double bed, as I did whenever I stayed over. I lay there thinking about what Pan Jozek had said about prayers and feeling sorry for him. If that was what my father had thought too, I felt sorry for him also. If God couldn't hear your prayers, you were the loneliest person on earth.

I was sure I would never stop praying and believing in Him and that I would never stop going to church. The workers of the world could unite all they liked, I would always be a Pole and pledge allegiance to our flag and none other. Certainly not to the Communists' red one.

When I think of the flag I always think of Uncle Romek, because he was the flag bearer in the Polish cavalry charge against the German tanks. When I told Pan Jozek about him, he said it was a shame to sacrifice so much human life for national honor.

Despite my fears, Pan Jozek and Grandmother were lovey-dovey at the breakfast table the next morning. Pan Jozek paid Grandmother the compliment of saying that while she may have had no education, she knew more in her little finger than all the professors knew in their heads. She had wisdom, intuition, and a lot of horse sense, he told her, and he added, "And you're a beautiful woman too."

Grandmother was proud. They were a real mutual admiration society!

I had never thought of Grandmother as a beautiful woman. My mother was beautiful, but Grandmother was just an old grandmother. When I think about it today, though, I realize that she couldn't have been more than fifty-five at the time. She didn't have a birth certificate, but in those days women had their first child when they were twenty. Grandmother may have dressed like an old peasant, but what are fifty-five years in a woman? Today many women that age seem attractive to me, including my wife. Pan Jozek was much younger than Grandmother, perhaps by twenty-five years or more, but he might well have thought her beautiful, even if I was sure he was only trying to flatter her.

I thought that after getting to know Pan Jozek Grandmother would think differently about the Jews. She didn't. But she didn't scrub the house down with disinfectant when he left, either.

9

The Quarrel

The next day, Sunday morning, my mother arrived and the two of us left with Pan Jozek. Crowds of people were out walking by the Wisla. Although there was no need this time to bunch up under one umbrella, my mother took Pan Jozek's arm again and I took hers to make us look like a family out for a stroll on a spring morning. Everything would have gone well if we hadn't run into Antony.

Spring had broken out all over. I plucked a green leaf and put it in my pocket for safekeeping. Not that boys my age still played "Green," but I was always ready to be challenged by small children. I don't know whether Pan Jozek saw me pick the leaf or whether the spring weather reminded him of his own childhood, but suddenly he turned to my mother and said, "Green!"

They fought over who had won. The only green things my mother had in her possession were her pocketbook and Pan Jozek's coat sleeve. She began to laugh and argue that anything green counted, but Pan Jozek insisted that it had to be part of a plant. I didn't

113

butt in, although I had always played by the same rules as my mother.

In the end she gave in.

"And now," said Pan Jozek, "you have to give me one of your shoes. You'll get it back from me after we've rested a while on a bench." My mother let him have it.

When we were children, whoever lost at "Green" had to pay a consequence, like singing a song, or hopping on one foot, or kissing one of the girls. Wacek and Janek used to make me steal candy from the grocery store next to our school. That wasn't easily done, because the owners watched the children like hawks and didn't let more than three of them into their store at a time.

We sat on a bench looking at the boats on the Wisla while Pan Jozek told us how the war would end. Then he told us how all wars would end.

"One day," he said, "the planet Earth will be attacked by enemies from space. Maybe from Mars. Then all human beings will realize that they're earthlings and this planet will become their common home."

"We were so sure that the First World War would be the last one too," said my mother. "Who would have thought that it would take Martians to unite us?"

"It won't, Pani Aniela," said Pan Jozek. That's what he called her instead of "Pani Skorupa." "Wars will stop before that. They have to. The history books of the future will describe a strange, incomprehensible age of human life full of senseless slaughter and suffering."

"God help us," sighed my mother.

All at once Pan Jozek began reciting a poem about springtime and peace. My mother had tears in her eyes. Maybe she was thinking of my father. Antony didn't know any poems by heart.

Today I think that a lot of Antony's hatred for Jews, Communists, and book learning came from being jealous of my father. My father was dead, of course, but Antony must have felt that he still lived on for my mother. He loved her a lot, and I only poured oil on the fire by refusing to let him adopt me.

We rose to go. My mother slipped her arm back under Pan Jozek's and I walked on the other side of her. That was when we met Antony. I never found out what he was doing there or why he hadn't gone straight home from church. As soon as he saw us he froze in his tracks. I saw the blood drain from his face, which had his murderous look, and his big fists clench. My mother was frightened but good. Pan Jozek didn't understand what was happening. I told him in a whisper. My mother left us, ran to Antony, and said something quickly in his ear. He gave Pan Jozek the once-over but didn't say a word. My mother tucked her arm in Antony's. She wouldn't let him shake it off, and we walked like that to Zelazna Street to bring Pan Jozek to my uncle's. Pan Jozek and I entered the courtyard under the eyes of the doorman and his wife, who were Uncle Wladislaw's partners in hiding Jews and in other things, such as changing money on the black market. We climbed the old wooden stairs to my uncle's apartment, and my Aunt Irena ushered Pan Jozek into the little room that was set aside for him and sent me straight home. I was afraid to go there, though. I went to Theater Square to look for Grandmother, but she wasn't there. That gave me such a fright that I rushed to her house on Bridge Street, only to discover that it was a false alarm. Grandmother had simply begun her new regimen of going home every afternoon. She made me tea and we sat and talked, about Antony, of course. I told her we had run into him. She didn't say anything. She just nodded a few times, as if she knew exactly what would come next.

"What happens now, Grandma?"

She didn't want to venture any guesses.

"What will happen to my mother?"

She didn't know. Or else she knew and didn't want to tell me.

I went home with a heavy feeling. For the first time since Antony came to live with us I was afraid that he would beat my mother. That must have been what Grandmother almost told me but didn't. I wasn't worried about myself. It was all my fault anyway. But if Antony laid a hand on my mother, I thought, I would kill him. I would take a knife and stick it into him at night. I even began to think of how to dispose of the corpse. I had all kinds of ideas, most of them utterly absurd. I just couldn't stand the thought of Antony beating up my mother. Even today I think that if he had done it, I really might have killed him.

Already on the stairs I could hear them shouting, although they had been home for two hours already.

"You women are all the same!" yelled Antony.

"You're eaten up by your own jealousy!" screamed my mother.

"Why can't you get it into your head," shouted Antony, "that there are other things in the world besides jealousy!"

"Like what?"

"Like trust, my dear lady, like trust!"

By then I had reached the door. I put my ear to it and heard my mother say quietly, "I know you like the back of my hand, and Marek had to atone for what he did."

She had told him!

They didn't see me come in. Antony grabbed hold of my mother and began shaking her hard. I didn't know if that was beating her or not or if it meant that I already had to kill him. I couldn't tell if he had hit her already, either. There was no sign of it on her face. The windows were closed to keep the neighbors from hearing. Not that it helped very much. Antony was white as a sheet and my mother was flushed and disheveled.

"Take your hands off her right now!" I shouted.

Only then did they notice me. "Stay out of this," said my mother. "It's none of your business."

Now she was taking his side against me! I had never seen her in such a state before. Antony let go of her, grabbed hold of me, and slapped me so hard that I saw stars. My mother began to scream. "Look who's talking about trust! You talk about trust and then you hit my son!"

"He's already a man," said Antony, "and I'll thank you to let me educate him." He turned to me. "You're not going to put this whole family in danger, do you understand me? If I ever see you having anything to do with Jews again, you're going to get it."

"You're not my father," I said.

He gave me a scathing look and said, "You're lucky your father isn't here now." And with that he stalked out of the room.

Holy Jesus, I thought, she's told him everything! I looked at my mother. He had had a reason for saying what he did. And in fact she confessed. "I told him that you knew about your father, Marek. I had to, because otherwise . . ."

Otherwise what? She never told me, although I kept asking her for years.

Those two things killed me: being hit by Antony and being betrayed by my mother.

"I'm leaving home," I said.

"Where are you going?"

"I'll move in with Grandpa and Grandma. And don't you come looking for me there until he apologizes."

I went to my room and packed a few things in my old school bag. My mother followed me, trying to talk me out of it. Antony, she sought to explain, had good reason to feel furious. We should have told him.

"He would never have agreed to help Pan Jozek," I said. "He would have said it was too risky."

My mother didn't answer. She knew I was right.

"Don't leave, Marek. Don't be impulsive. You know Antony won't apologize. Certainly not soon."

"It's not just because he hit me," I said.

"I know. But I had no choice."

Now that he knew, that both of us knew, I couldn't stand his presence any longer. I walked out and slammed the door behind me.

What I really wanted to do was to cry.

10

The Uprising

It started on a Monday, exactly a week before Easter. I remember the day well, less because it was the day after I moved in with my grandparents than because of what happened in the ghetto.

When Grandmother came to wake me, my first thought was that it was time to get up for school. Right away, though, she said to me that I didn't have to hurry and could even go back to bed once I had stepped outside and told her where the shots she heard were coming from. Grandmother was hard of hearing in one ear, which was why, as Pan Jozek had explained to her, it was hard for her to locate sounds, just as it's hard to judge distances with one eye.

I opened the door and stepped outside. The shots were coming from the ghetto. We hadn't heard shooting from there for a long time — at the most a few scattered reports now and then. This time, though, it sounded more serious. Reassured, Grandmother went back to bed, while I continued to stand there and listen. There were some bursts from a machine gun. I thought of Pan Jozek. He was lucky to be out of there.

Maybe he would be one of the few Jews to survive this war.

I got back into bed and thought of what Antony had said about my father. I wondered what would have happened to him if he had still been alive. Would anyone have discovered he was Jewish? Were there people who knew and might have informed on him?

I couldn't fall asleep and got out of bed again. In any case, I had to start out earlier for school from my grandparents' than from home. Meanwhile, the shots grew louder and more frequent. I heard explosive charges too. Or perhaps they were hand grenades. I didn't know that much about such things. Then there were ambulance sirens — not just one, but a whole lot of them. I couldn't imagine why the Germans were evacuating wounded Jews from the ghetto in ambulances. Could it be something else? Had the shots perhaps been fired by the Polish underground and only seemed to come from the ghetto? I started to get dressed so fast that I put the wrong shoe on the wrong foot.

"Where are you rushing off to, Marek?" asked Grandmother.

Before I could answer she had already guessed and made me swear to stay away from the ghetto. She would have insisted on walking me to school if I hadn't promised to take the streetcar. She even gave me money for it. I didn't mind fooling Grandmother. She was always fooling everyone herself.

I walked down Freta Street as far as Swientojerska Street, hugging the wall of the ghetto until a policeman shooed me into Kraszinski Park. Even though he knew me from Pan Korek's tavern, he wouldn't let me go any farther. It was too dangerous, he said. And maybe he was extra careful because he knew me. Anyway, Kraszinski Park wasn't a bad vantage point. There was a German machine gun there with some soldiers who were firing long rounds down Wolowa Street, right into the windows of houses. I could see soldiers stationed along the ghetto wall every twenty or thirty meters. I asked some people what had happened.

"They're finishing off the Jews," an old man said to me.

"It's about time," said a young one. He laughed.

Before my mother caught me with the Jew's money and before meeting Pan Jozek, I would have felt the same way.

"What do you think," asked someone, "will they give us back the Jews' houses?"

"Why shouldn't they?" said someone else. "Didn't they do it in the Little Ghetto?"

"What's all this talk about 'giving back'?" asked a woman who seemed very brave to me. "Those houses belong to the Jews." Everyone looked at her suspiciously and a man sniggered and said, "She must be a Jew herself."

We had no way of knowing that not one of the houses behind the ghetto wall would be left standing. Nothing would remain of them but piles of ruins.

It was unbelievable. It seemed to defy the laws of nature. And yet there was no denying that a real war was being fought there. Now and then truckloads of German reinforcements and ambulances of the German Red Cross, their sirens wailing, drove past in the direction of the ghetto. And to think that all this was the work of the Jews! Jesus, I thought, I'd better run and tell Pan Jozek about it.

No power on earth could have sent me directly to school that morning. I walked on. All up and down Leszno Street stood sentries with bayonets fixed in their rifles, facing the ghetto wall. Some Ukrainian auxiliaries were trying to come on to several Polish girls who were on their way to the grocery store to buy bread. The explosions, shots, and sirens carried even as far as there. A girl asked a policeman across the street if the ambulances were for wounded Jews.

"Fat chance!" he said. He beckoned to her and I followed her. In a whisper he told us, "They're evacuating German dead and wounded." He looked at us for a moment and said, "You think I'm kidding, don't you?"

I didn't. The girl did.

"You don't have to believe me, young lady, but this time the Jews are fighting back."

Before the day was over some people were already calling it "the Third Front."

"Green!"

Nothing could have been further from my mind. Had it been anyone else, I would have ignored him or socked him. But it was our neighbor's little son Wlodek, and so I pretended to search my pockets before telling him he had won. That made him happy, because whenever I lost I owed him a piece of candy. I promised not to forget and he ran away laughing.

I told everyone in school what I had seen. Other boys already knew too. The only things we talked about all morning were the Jews shooting at the Germans and the ambulances full of German casualties. I couldn't remember when I had last been so eager to go to work at Pan Korek's, because I was hoping to hear more news there. And indeed, in the tavern too that night the talk was all about the Jewish uprising. New customers kept drifting in with fresh reports, and the need to outdo one another at astounding us drove them to all kinds of wild stories.

Or maybe it was not so much the need to astound as to believe that it really was possible, that it really was happening, because if the Jews could rise up against the Germans, we Poles could go them one better. Someone claimed to have seen a tank enter the ghetto. Someone else said that it was accompanied by two armored vehicles. A third person spoke of three tanks. Others had seen artillery pieces on the move, an airplane circling overhead. It even flew over the tavern. Each time it made a pass I ran out to look at it until Pan Korek barked at me to clean the tables.

And yet even on the first day of the revolt voices were raised against the Jews too. Someone said they had stockpiled arms airlifted from Russia in order to set up a Bolshevik enclave that would attack the Poles.

"Why should they attack us?" asked a customer. "Their fight is with the Germans, just like ours."

"You must be a Bolshevik yourself!" replied the first man.

The tavern-goers didn't know whether to laugh, because no one knew who the man was. He could have been a Volksdeutsch, or an agent provocateur. He had never been in the tavern before, and so everyone sat quietly while he continued: "Did you hear what happened over on Nowojerska Street? They put a whole block of people to death because they found some kikes in some house. The same thing happened on Freta Street."

That wasn't so, and I said, "You're wrong. They just arrested them for three days and let most of them go."

"Most of them? Not even half of them! And you know why they were arrested? Because the Jews went and squealed on the Poles who hid them. We risk the lives of our wives and children to save those vermin, and that's the thanks we get. Mark my words. Oh, I know them, I do!"

No one said a thing. Pan Korek sent me off to the kitchen to keep me from opening my mouth again. After the stranger had left, perhaps to spread his poison elsewhere, more regulars dropped in and the conversation picked up again. There was more news. One man reported that the Jews had burned German tanks with Molotov cocktails, and not just the tanks, but the soldiers inside them too. Someone else confirmed the story. Through binoculars, he said, he had seen German soldiers on fire running and screaming through the streets.

125

"Don't ask me what they were screaming. 'Mama!' I suppose, or '*Mein Gott!*' "

Those words affected me strangely. It had never occurred to me that a German might scream for his mother or for God. I thought that if one screamed, it would be only to say Heil Hitler! or something like that.

Pan Korek must have read my thoughts, because he said, "It's horrible to think that they pray too. That's more than I can understand. Or accept. At least they do it in German."

He looked around to see who was listening. Pan Szczupak wasn't there.

Before I left the tavern, two more men arrived with the news that the Jews had run up two flags in Muranowski Square, the Polish flag and another, blue and white one of their own.

I felt goose pimples all over me. There was a long silence. Then Pan Korek declared, "Well, that's the first Polish flag in Warsaw in nearly four years. We'll see lots more of them one day when we run them up ourselves, but meanwhile, hats off to the Jews!"

His glance traveled over us. He said, "The Jews will all die, but they'll have died with honor. Here's to the Jews who raised the flag in Muranowski Square! It's on the house, boys."

I ran from one customer to the next, pouring out glasses of bimber. I didn't drink any myself, of course. Pan Korek had promised my mother that he wouldn't let me drink. But I did join in the toast.

I had promised my grandmother to come home well

before the curfew so that she needn't worry, but I wanted to stop off at my uncle's on the way to tell Pan Jozek about the uprising. I told Pan Korek that I had to be home early and he let me go, even though the tavern was more crowded than usual.

My uncle opened the door and brought me straight into the kitchen. That's where he always took me when he wanted to have a private talk. He told me that he had visited my parents and that he wanted to know what had happened between my mother and Antony. He wasn't in the habit of dropping in on us and he must have noticed my surprise, because he added, "Your Jew wants to go back to the ghetto to join the uprising and is willing to pay anything to get there. I thought that maybe Antony . . ." He left the sentence unfinished. He wasn't supposed to know about Antony's smuggling business. Was that my mother blabbing again?

"He wants to go back *now?*" I had never heard of a Jew voluntarily leaving his hiding place to return to the ghetto — and at a time like this! I couldn't believe it.

"You may not realize it, but young Jews have been going back there to fight. The doorman downstairs told me about another case. But I wanted to talk to you about your mother. She didn't go to work today. I found her at home crying and Antony wasn't there. Was he at the tavern tonight?"

"No," I said. "He wasn't."

I suddenly felt both worried and sorry for my mother. I had already forgiven her everything. I wasn't even sure I felt happy that Antony had left her. I decided to go home.

"They had a fight," I said. "It was over Pan Jozek, because Antony saw us with him on our way here." I thought for a minute and added, "They were walking arm in arm. You know, to look like a family."

My uncle laughed. "What made you move in with your grandmother?"

I told him that Antony had hit me.

"How come?" he asked.

"To make me mind my own business."

"I told that ninny to tell Antony. Your grandmother also thought it would end badly." He looked at me and said, "You certainly have gotten your mother into hot water!"

I said hello to Aunt Irena and went to look for Pan Jozek in his little room. He was pacing back and forth in his stockinged feet and smoking one cigarette after another. My aunt and uncle had already told him what was happening. He was delighted to see me and wanted to hear about everything I had seen and heard in the tavern. All day long he had been standing by the window, listening to the shots and the sirens. I told him everything, even the things I would rather have skipped over.

Pan Jozek began to talk nonstop. I didn't have time to listen, because I had to run to my grandparents', take my things, and go home. I was worried about my mother. He talked on and on about the rebels and Jewish honor, how they were saving it for posterity and all that.

"But no less important, and perhaps even more so, is their having saved Jewish honor for the Jews! The Jewish people," he declared fervently, "have begun to fight back against the Germans."

I was infected by his enthusiasm. "My uncle says you're thinking of going back to the ghetto."

"I'm not thinking of it. I'm going. Tonight."

His mind sounded made up. He had decided to join the uprising. I didn't know whether to feel pity or pride. I was sure he would never get out of there alive. In fact, he didn't stand much of a chance of getting in there alive either. All at once I realized that it was my duty to bring him there safely. That was the least I could do.

"When are you going?" I asked.

"Your uncle promised to talk to your stepfather. I told him I would pay anything. As much money as I have. And I should think that your stepfather would be glad to get rid of me after yesterday. Not to mention your uncle, who's already gotten a three-month advance for me. I've been waiting to hear from them all day. Your uncle says your stepfather wasn't home."

Oh, yes, by the way, my mother had given Uncle Wladislaw all the money I had taken from the Jew!

"They had a fight and Antony walked out on her," I said.

"Your parents fought because of me?"

My parents! I said yes. He shrugged and remarked, "Well, none of that matters anymore." For a moment he seemed lost in thought. "You won't find many

129

women like your mother," he said at last, and then returned to the subject of the ghetto. "If your uncle can't think of something by tomorrow morning, I'll go myself. I'll walk along the wall like any Pole who's curious to know what's happening and I'll find some way of slipping through. The Germans have thought a lot more about keeping Jews in the ghetto than about keeping them out. I'm sure I can outwit them."

"You don't stand a chance, Pan Jozek," I said. That's when I told him about our smuggling route.

At first he was skeptical. He thought it was too risky for me. I told him that I was used to traveling in the sewers once or twice a week, and that if Antony had left home, he had probably gone to his sister's and wouldn't be back so soon. I just couldn't take him at night, because I would never find my way in the dark. Of course, it was dark down there in the day-time too, but Antony had taught me to navigate by the manholes overhead, through which a bit of sunshine filtered. "I'll bring you there in the morning and come right back. Even if Antony comes home in the meantime, he'll never know I was gone."

"You'll have to let me pay you in full."

"I wanted it to be my present," I said.

"No," said Pan Jozek. "I want to pay you for it."

He wouldn't yield. In the end I said I would hold the money in trust until he returned.

We agreed on that and shook hands. The plan was for me to leave home as usual in the morning as though I were going to school and to take extra food and water in my school bag. I would loiter on the street opposite my uncle's until I saw him leave the apartment with my aunt and then I would go up and get Pan Jozek.

"How do we get into the sewer?" he asked.

"I'll show you tomorrow," I promised.

I haven't mentioned this, but one of the first things that Antony asked me and my mother after finding out about Pan Jozek was whether Pan Jozek knew our address. He didn't. I might have told him if he had asked, but he never had. Antony breathed a sigh of relief. He would kill me if he found out that Pan Jozek had been in our house on his way to the ghetto!

The only problem was that there would be no one to close the trap door behind us. That was a risk I had to take, though. If my mother went down to the basement before I got back, I would be discovered, but by then Pan Jozek would be in the ghetto.

I took the streetcar to my grandparents' and caught the last car home before the curfew began. That is, it wasn't exactly the last car home, because it stopped quite far from our house. I ran all the way and got there right after the curfew had started. My mother wasn't worried, because she thought I was sleeping at Grandmother's. She had been crying all night over Antony.

Over the years I've often wondered how she could have loved two such different people: my father, who was perhaps a bit like Pan Jozek, and my stepfather. And yet it was Antony himself who had told me on the nights I brought him home drunk from the tavern that "a woman's heart knows no reasons."

My mother hugged me. She asked me if I was still angry. I said I wasn't. Whatever had happened was over and done with.

"But I did leave work early without eating and I'm hungry," I said.

She made me something to eat and sat down with me. While I ate, she apologized for what had happened. She had to tell Antony the whole truth, she said, because it was the only way for him to understand why she had agreed behind his back to let me take responsibility for Pan Jozek.

"But why has he left you?"

"Were you at your Uncle Wladislaw's?"

"Yes. I went there to tell Pan Jozek about the uprising. He already knew about it."

"Wladislaw was here. He was looking for Antony. Antony wouldn't allow me to tell him that he was called away on some business of the underground. I was crying because I was frightened, but I told Wladislaw it was because we had a fight. And we really did have one yesterday."

"I thought Antony had walked out on you."

"How could you ever think such a thing, Marek? You're just not used to seeing us fight. That's something you don't understand yet."

"What did Uncle Wladislaw say to you?"

"That Pan Jozek wants to join the uprising." She nodded and paused before adding: "God help him!"

"So Antony's off on some job for the underground?"

"Yes."

"Having to do with the Jewish uprising?"

"No," sighed my mother. "It has to do with something else."

It suddenly crossed my mind that perhaps my promise to Pan Jozek had been too hasty. If anything were to happen to me . . .

I was worried about what would happen to my mother.

I went on eating while she told me how everyone in the grocery store had spoken up for the Jews that morning and how Valenty the doorman had said that if they held out for a week, he would take back everything he had ever said about them.

I told my mother what I had heard in the street and in the tavern. She sighed each time I described someone's pleasure at the thought of all the Jews being killed. All at once she exclaimed with open anxiety: "Who knows how God will punish us for all this, for having sinned against the Jews! Who knows."

Before going to sleep I kissed her and hugged her, and she kissed me and hugged me back lovingly.

"Don't worry," I told her. "Antony can take care of himself. He'll come back safe and sound."

I didn't hate him so much anymore.

I fell asleep at once, but in the middle of the night I awoke and tiptoed to my mother's bedroom to see if Antony was back. She was sleeping by herself with one hand on Antony's pillow.

I awoke several more times that night. Each time I went to the window and looked out at the dark street, thinking of the morning.

11

Stranded

I was so tired in the morning that it was all my mother could do to rouse me. But as soon as I realized the time I was out of bed without further prodding of the kind that I needed on ordinary school days.

Antony still wasn't back and my mother looked as though she hadn't slept a wink. I decided against taking Antony's miner's lamp, because he might notice it was missing. Instead I took an old flashlight I had once been given for my birthday and put it in my school bag with a bottle of water and several sandwiches.

A new problem occurred to me: how would I know if my aunt and uncle had left their apartment already? I should have thought of that in advance. My mother reluctantly prepared to go to work and left a note for Antony asking him to call her at her shop if he arrived. We were like most people in having no telephone at home, but we could always call from old Pani Korplaska's stationery store.

We left the apartment together and said goodbye in

the street. I tried to make it sound like any other goodbye so that she wouldn't suspect anything.

Since I had no way of knowing if my aunt and uncle were still home, I waited in the street for a while and walked right in the front gate, saying hello to Pan Kiszke the doorman. In the middle of the courtyard was a garbage pit that stank terribly. I ran up the stairs and gave the doorbell the ring that Pan Jozek and I had agreed on, and he came to open the door. For some reason, I still remember that doorbell. It was old and worked like a bicycle bell, the only difference being that the handle revolved instead of clicking up and down.

My uncle and aunt were gone and Pan Jozek was ready to start out. There was an eerie silence in the apartment. I asked about the Jewish family that my uncle hid in the back room, where he and the doorman had built a double wall with a hidden entrance under a bed. I often saw them in the mornings when I came on some errand from my mother, sitting in the living room and playing cards behind drawn curtains. Pan Jozek told me that he hadn't met them yet, because astonishingly enough, they had paid my uncle extra to let them return to the ghetto for the Passover holiday, which came a week before Easter that year. I later found out that many Jews hiding with Poles had done the same in order to spend the holiday with their families. Pan Jozek thought this foolish and irresponsible. He was sure the Germans had found out about it and decided the time was ideal for liquidating the ghetto.

I told Pan Jozek that Pan Korek had said liquidating the ghetto was the Nazi occupation force's present to Hitler, whose birthday was that Thursday. Most likely the Germans had thought they could finish the job in a day and had not counted on Jewish resistance. Pan Jozek thought about it for a minute and said that both explanations could be right. In any case, when the Germans moved into the ghetto, there were more Jews present than there should have been. Perhaps other Jews had informed on them. I've already said that it wasn't only we Poles who had our collaborators and informers.

At first Pan Jozek had planned to say goodbye to his friend the priest, but now he chose not to run such a last-minute risk. Instead he gave me a note and asked me to give it to the priest when I got back.

We set out on foot. We had barely reached the corner of Zelazna and Grzybowska streets, where the Germans had erected one of the loudspeakers they used for broadcasting announcements and propaganda that we Poles referred to as "woof-woofs," when we saw a large crowd of people. They were listening to a German broadcast about the Russian murder of captured Polish officers in the Katyn Forest. A list of the murdered men was being read, and we stood and listened to it with everyone to keep from standing out. Every now and then the announcer would stop reading and declare: "These are the victims of the Jewish Bolsheviks! The Jewish Bolsheviks killed our officers in cold blood! The Jewish Bolsheviks will stop at nothing to kill, to plunder, to slaughter women and children." Then he would resume the list of names.

German propaganda was so full of lies that many people refused to believe that the Russians had a hand in the Katyn massacre at all. They thought the Germans had done it and were trying to palm it off on them. According to Pan Jozek, the graves had been discovered soon after the German invasion of Russia in 1941, when the Nazis overran the Russian-occupied zone of Poland. The Russians had murdered ten thousand Polish officers, whose names were later published every day in the newspapers as their bodies were dug up. Now, however, the Germans were rebroadcasting the entire list to divert attention from the ghetto, where they were mercilessly exterminating every last Jew. They wanted the Poles to have their minds on other things, which would keep them from sympathizing with the "Jewish Bolsheviks."

As we neared our building I told Pan Jozek to walk past it, double back after a few minutes, and enter the stairway to the left of the gate while I engaged the doorman and his wife in conversation.

I knocked on their door and asked if they had by any chance seen Antony, because I had forgotten a note my parents had given me for school and had been sent home. They were used to my raising hell in school, but they hadn't seen Antony. Well, I said, I didn't have the key, but perhaps I would go ask little Wlodek's mother, because sometimes we gave her the key to our apartment. Out of the corner of my eye I saw Pan Jozek start up the stairs, and I asked them if they had heard any news about the revolt in the ghetto. I let them talk on and on, and when they had finished telling me all the things I already knew I ducked into the stairway and descended to the basement instead of up to little Wlodek's apartment.

Pan Jozek was waiting for me there. I wasn't worried about what the doorman and his wife would think when I didn't reappear. If no one asked for me they would forget all about me, and in any case, I would be back no later than when I regularly came home from school.

By the time we entered the sewer it was after nine. At once Pan Jozek began to slip and slide. He had never been in a sewer before, and I walked as slowly as I could while he got used to it. All of a sudden I was in Antony's shoes. I remembered my excitement the first time he took me down with him. I had felt like a big hero, like the Frenchmen in the catacombs of Paris in Victor Hugo's *Les Misérables*. Pan Jozek understood what I meant by that comparison, whereas Antony would have had no idea. He would have said, "All we're doing is walking through some shithole. What does that have to do with a book written by some Frenchman who died long ago?"

Today I know that Antony was far less primitive than I took him to be. And yet that was how he wanted to be thought of, perhaps in order to be as different as possible from my father, with whom he didn't want to have to compete.

We reached the first rest stop and sat down on some boards. Except for Pan Jozek saying that the

138

fumes made it hard to breathe, we didn't speak to each other. They really did make you feel you were choking, especially if it was your first time. We sat listening to the sounds from Leszno Street over our heads. We were still under the Polish part of Warsaw. Pan Jozek asked how much farther we had to go. I told him that by Antony's reckoning it was three more kilometers down Leszno Street before we entered the ghetto.

At the second or third rest stop I remarked that there was too much water in the sewer. Perhaps, said Pan Jozek, the Germans had decided to flood it to keep it from being used as an escape route.

We could tell the minute we reached the streets of the ghetto, because it suddenly grew quiet up above. We couldn't even hear shots. Pan Jozek glanced at his watch in the light from a manhole and declared that it was already ten-thirty. It would take another hour or hour and a half, I said, because we were progressing slowly. Antony and I could cover the whole distance in less than two hours with heavy packs on our backs, but of course we were used to it.

There was a strange sound overhead. It wasn't an automobile. We stood and listened to it come closer.

"Tanks!" Pan Jozek exclaimed.

I had already told him about the tanks and armored vehicles. Now he was hearing a tank move into the ghetto with his own ears, followed by another, and another. Then it was quiet again. We kept walking.

"They're not fooling around," Pan Jozek said with

an odd joy in his voice. "That means they're taking us seriously."

He was thrilled even though he knew as well as I did that the Jews could not possibly win. Their defeat was a foregone conclusion. Tanks would just make it happen faster.

We were still under Leszno Street when we heard the tramp of soldiers. They were singing as they marched, passing overhead with a single rhythmic tread. All at once there were two loud explosions. Pan Jozek was frightened for a moment, but then he began to laugh like a madman, because right away we heard the curses and the screams of the wounded. And shooting. The Germans had opened fire with machine guns and automatic rifles. Then it was quiet again and the marching resumed. This time, though, no one sang. Soon we heard the distant wails of ambulances.

After a while we stopped to rest again. Before sitting down on a board, Pan Jozek took my flashlight to read the number that Antony had written on it. It was seven.

"How many stops are there?" he asked.

"Fourteen," I said. "Antony says it's the same number as the Stations of the Cross."

Pan Jozek said something strange then. He asked me, "What do you think, Marek, if Jesus were alive in Warsaw now, would he join the revolt in the ghetto?"

I didn't know what to answer.

He went on, "Do you think he would return to the ghetto to be crucified again?"

We were sitting in darkness so as not to use up our

batteries. The sewage fumes stung our eyes. I still didn't know what to say. And so he asked me a third question, "Do you think Jesus would be able to forgive the Germans?"

This time I did answer, and I remember exactly what I said, because there was no forgiving the Germans for what they had done. I didn't think that even Jesus could do that. And now it was my turn to ask something that was often on people's lips in those days: "But where is God, and how can He permit all this to happen?"

"Marek," said Pan Jozek, "a lot of Jews wonder where God is too. But God doesn't operate the way men do. His punishments for their crimes aren't conceived in terms of human logic."

"Then the Germans won't be punished?" I asked.

"They will be," he said. "But not with the kind of punishments we're used to."

"What other kind is there?" I asked.

"Think of what it will be like for the next generation of Germans, the Nazis' children, to know that their parents were mass murderers. That could be part of the punishment."

It didn't sound like a punishment to me. Suppose their children never even found out? A punishment had to be something real, like laying all Germany waste, for example. Of course, that would mean killing still more grownups and children who weren't to blame for what was happening in Warsaw, but anything less than that, like the kind of punishment Pan Jozek had in mind, seemed ridiculous when compared with what the Germans had done to us and the Jews.

Pan Jozek was worrying me. He was losing his footing a lot and breathing heavily. I was debating whether to move on or to let him rest some more when suddenly there was a loud boom very close to us and we both went flying into the sewage. I managed to lift the flashlight clear of it just in the nick of time.

"Are you all right, Marek?"

I was. We both rose to our feet.

"That was down in this tunnel," said Pan Jozek. "Back where we came from."

"Yes," I said.

"We have to backtrack and see what happened."

I didn't say anything. The same thought had occurred to me too. If the blast had blocked the route we came by there was no way for me to get back.

Pan Jozek tried wiping some of the filth off himself while I shined the flashlight on him. He soon saw it was hopeless and said, "It doesn't matter. Let's go."

He hoped, he said, that the blast had been not directly behind us but in some more distant branch of the tunnel, because sounds carried farther underground. In fact, that seemed so likely that I was ready to assume as much and head on, but Pan Jozek insisted we double back. And it was a good thing we did, because the explosion had caved in a section we crossed and left it sealed off in darkness. Pan Jozek said that the charge must have been laid in advance and that we were lucky it didn't go off when we were closer.

"Who laid it?" I asked.

"Certainly not the Jews," he said. "Marek, how will you get back? I should never have agreed to your coming. You should just have drawn me a map. . . . What are we going to do now?"

"We'll think about that once we're out of here," I said. "There must be other ways out of the ghetto, and I'll bet they're cleaner than this one." Yet even though I tried to make him laugh, I could feel the fear creeping into my voice.

We headed on. My head whirled with thoughts, mostly about my mother, of course. I imagined the look on her face when I didn't come home and Antony found the open trap door in the basement. He would realize at once what had happened. In fact, that was my best hope. Any Poles like me found in the ghetto would be shot on sight, but if Antony noticed the open trap door he would go straight to my Uncle Wladislaw's, and once he saw that Pan Jozek was missing too he would figure out where we were. Don't worry, Ma, I thought, I'll make it back.

We reached the last rest stop about noon. We kept going without taking a break. We walked in silence, broken now and then by some comment about the low ceiling. We were under Nalewki Street and had hardly any clearance. It was from there that Antony and I had sometimes exited into the ghetto to loot the empty houses.

143

"Nalewki," I said. Pan Jozek sighed.

After crossing a low, narrow passage on all fours, we reached a part where the tunnel became higher again, though we still had to walk doubled over. I promised Pan Jozek that soon we could straighten up, and before long we did.

I don't think he could have held out another half hour. He was at the end of his strength when we arrived. It wasn't just the physical effort. It was perhaps most of all the bad air. As I climbed the iron ladder I heard him wheeze and pant behind me and say in a rasping voice, "Marek, there's something I have to tell you."

He sat down on a rung of the ladder and waited to catch his breath. Then he said, "I'm responsible to your mother for your getting back safely. I want you to do exactly what I tell you. You have to promise me now."

I promised him without thinking twice. All I wanted was to get back. The sooner, the better.

12

In the Ghetto

I handed Pan Jozek the flashlight and told him to beam it on the Jews' trap door. Then I took the metal rod that hung from the chain and rapped on the door as hard as I could. I tried beating out the same rhythm as Antony did, though I had no idea who was up there. There was no response. And so we took turns banging with all our might on the metal cover above us.

Perhaps, I said to Pan Jozek, the house had been deserted in the uprising, but I thought we could open the trap door ourselves, because I didn't remember it being covered with heavy sacks or objects the way Antony covered ours, just with a smelly pile of dirty rags. No sooner did we begin to push than we heard excited voices above us. There were sounds of running and of someone shouting, first in Polish and then in Yiddish: "Who's there?"

The door was opened. The pile of rags was as I remembered it.

Pan Jozek introduced himself and told them that I had guided him through the sewers and was stranded, because the Germans had blown up the tunnel. The Jews nodded now and then and whispered among themselves while throwing suspicious glances our way. They went to call someone and we sat down uninvited on the rags, which were cleaner than we were. At last one of the three brothers appeared and recognized me at once.

"Why, it's Marek, Pan Antony's son," he said, pointing at me.

"But they haven't brought anything," someone else said disappointedly.

It seemed that Antony had promised to bring them some "candy" that day. That filled me with hope, because even if the tunnel was sealed, he was sure to find some other route and take me back out with him.

"Candy," by the way, was our code word for bullets. "Food parcels" were guns, "eggs" were hand grenades, and "sausages" were pistols. As for rifles, they were called "Auntie's favorites."

The Jews whispered among themselves some more.

"Where is Antony, Marek?" asked the brother who knew me.

I told him the truth.

"Pan Prostak!" he called out. "Pan Prostak!"

"Pan Prostak?" murmured Pan Jozek to himself in a startled tone.

The man called Pan Prostak appeared. He didn't recognize Pan Jozek at first, perhaps because of the filth, but Pan Jozek recognized him and exclaimed: "Edek, I hoped it would be you!"

Now Pan Prostak recognized him too. He reached

out gladly to shake his hand but quickly backed away.

"Come," he said. "The first thing is to get you to a shower."

"Wait a minute," said the other Jews, taking him aside to consult. There was some more whispering and constant looks in my direction while Pan Prostak nodded in agreement. Perhaps they were thinking of some way I could help them obtain the bullets.

Pan Jozek introduced me to Pan Prostak. He did it as formally as if I were at a dinner party. By now, though, I knew better than to shake hands.

"This is Edek," said Pan Jozek to me. "He's an old school friend. I know him from the good old days. What do you say, Prostak?"

Pan Prostak led us and we followed him. Although it was the same basement Antony and I had been in many times, it didn't look the same. It looked more like the air-raid shelter we had sat in back in 1939 when the Germans had bombed Warsaw. The Jews called it "the bunker." They were planning to seal off the entrance from above so that no one would know it was there. Shelves and mattresses were everywhere. There was even a well they had dug and pipes for air. Some men and women were busy with last-minute construction, and as filthy as we were, Pan Jozek wanted Pan Prostak to show and explain everything to us. Pan Prostak said that there was no time, however, and that we had to be brought to a friend's house at once. When some workers came over to ask who we were and where we had come from, he asked them to step aside and let us out.

"Excuse me," he said, "but I have to bring these two gentlemen to a friend's house so that they can wash."

My eyes met those of a woman standing next to us. We both looked at my and Pan Jozek's filthy clothes and at our wild mats of hair and smiled at each other, because "gentlemen" was hardly the word to describe us just then.

On our way Pan Prostak explained to us that the bunker had been built by 20 families that numbered 80 souls and had been successfully kept a secret so far. Because of the Passover holiday, though, many Jews who had crossed over from the Polish side or come from elsewhere in the ghetto to be with their families were now trapped here, so that 120 people had to be crammed into the available space. They could manage all right for a day or two, but it would be a disaster if they had to spend weeks there.

"Weeks?" I said to Pan Jozek. "Why, they'll choke to death in two hours."

He looked at me but said nothing.

Of course, there were air pipes; I had seen them myself. But there was no way they could supply enough oxygen for more than a few dozen people. I tried to imagine the bunker packed past capacity. I wouldn't have been caught in it for all the money in the world. Pan Jozek must have guessed my thoughts, because he suddenly said, "What would you do, Marek, if you were here in the ghetto with a child or two of your own?"

What would I do? I could feel my hands ball into fists.

"I would fight," I said.

We crossed several courtyards and reached Swientojerska Street. All of a sudden we saw a strange sight. Someone was standing on a ladder propped up against the ghetto wall and talking to the Polish side. I couldn't see his audience, of course. Perhaps it was down below in the street, or perhaps in Kraszinski Park opposite the wall. The man was delivering a speech. He could easily have been shot by a German soldier, but apparently there were none around. He was saying that it was up to the Poles to come to the aid of the Jews. "Come join us!" he cried from the wall. "Let us fight together, shoulder to shoulder! The time has come to do battle! The time has come for all of us, Poles and Jews, to unite! The Day of Wrath has arrived! Let us rise up against the German conqueror who has ravaged our homeland!"

And it really was *our* homeland, I thought. They might have been Jews, but they were born and raised in Poland the same as Poles. And so were their parents and their parents' parents before them. The speaker warned his Polish listeners to watch out, because soon the shooting would begin again, and finished by crying out: "Long live Poland!"

There was applause from the other side of the wall while he climbed down the ladder. I was glad Pan

149

Jozek had heard it. I didn't want him to think that all Poles were like Janek and Wacek.

"You see!" I said to him.

But Pan Jozek just shrugged. He asked his friend Edek what he did in the Jewish underground, and Edek answered that he was just an ordinary soldier, if you could call the resistance fighters soldiers at all. He was also in charge of the bunker. Had the passage through the sewers been difficult? he asked. He too was worried about the blast down there. I didn't know it at the time, but apart from bullets, Antony had promised to bring some Jews back out of the ghetto in return for a large sum of money. If anything happened to him . . .

Pan Prostak said goodbye and went back to oversee the work in the bunker. He was sorry, he said, that he couldn't look after us himself, but he was leaving us in the hands of his friend Pan Rappaport, who would take us to an apartment where we could wash, change clothes, and have something to eat. And that's what we did. I was even offered a fresh pair of shoes, but Pan Jozek made me clean my dirty ones and put them back on, because if I had to walk through more tunnels or make a run for it, I wouldn't want someone else's shoes on my feet. He took two big wads of money from his wet clothes and handed them to me.

"As per our agreement," he said.

I took the money and sniffed it. It was slightly damp and it stank. Who was it who said that money has no smell?

Pan Rappaport and his friends invited us to sit down and eat with them. Pan Jozek saw how amazed I was by all the food and explained that it was because we were eating the leftovers of the Passover seder. If those were the leftovers, it must have been some meal! It was hard to believe that at a time when the Germans had begun killing off the last Jews in the ghetto, these people had gone to such trouble and expense to prepare a banquet.

The first thing I noticed — so Antony hadn't made it up after all! — was several men sitting around with hats on their heads. They were the oldest men there, but there were also several younger ones whose conversation I tried listening in on. Pan Rappaport took part in it too. I couldn't make it all out, but it had to do with the story of a man who had escaped from a place called Treblinka. It was a real horror story, because Treblinka sounded worse than hell. The man said it was where the Germans murdered all the Jews whom they deported in trains from Warsaw. Pan Jozek put down his fork. He couldn't eat anymore. I told him he had to eat if he wanted to have strength, and after a while he began again, though you could see his heart wasn't in it.

Pan Jozek wanted to know how the resistance fighters were organized. Pan Rappaport explained to him that our sector, which included the brush factory, was divided into five teams of fifteen or twenty young men and women. I shouldn't dismiss the women lightly, he said, noticing the look on my face. He wasn't annoyed. He simply explained to me that they were pioneers preparing for a hard life in Palestine and that they carried weapons like the men. Everyone had a pistol, but there was not enough ammunition to go around, and no more than a rifle or two per team. There were plenty of hand grenades, though, and homemade bombs and Molotov cocktails produced by the cottage industry of Pan Michael Klapfisz and Partners.

After we had finished eating, a young man showed Pan Jozek how to use a rifle and a pistol. The whole lesson took ten minutes. I had my doubts whether anyone could use a gun after that kind of cram course. Certainly not Pan Jozek. Mostly he was shown how to aim. If a Jewish fighter was killed or wounded, or if any weapons were captured from the Germans, there might be a gun for Pan Jozek too. Meanwhile, he could fight without one. I myself didn't seem to count.

Pan Prostak called us back to the table, which had been cleaned and covered with a fresh cloth. Pan Jozek spoke first, although it was obvious that Pan Prostak had something important to say to us. Pan Jozek tried to convince Pan Prostak that a way had to be found to get me out of the ghetto. Pan Prostak listened, but in the end he just shrugged and said, "We're all in God's hands now."

We both got the hint. When the fate of so many Jews was hanging in the balance, no one was going to go out of his way to save a Polish boy. Not many people, if any, were going to survive in any case. The person Pan Prostak really wanted to talk about, however, was Antony. He looked at me and said, "Your father

152

hasn't come. Our people who do business with him say that isn't like him. What do you say, young man?"

"He's off on some job for the underground," I said. "If he gets back, he'll come. He'll come because of me."

"How will he know you're here?"

I explained to Pan Prostak that if Antony returned some time during the day, he would do his best to keep his promise, no matter how tired he was. That meant he would go down to the basement, and once down there, he would realize where I was. Pan Prostak asked how I could be so sure, and I said, "Pan Prostak, only Antony and I know about that trap door, and I left it open so that I could return. No one but he would notice that it's open, but he couldn't possibly miss it."

I didn't want to say anything more and he didn't ask me. If Antony found the trap door open, I explained, he wouldn't start out for the ghetto right away. First he would look for me in school, then at Pan Korek's, and then at my grandmother's and my uncle's. All that would take a long time. Besides which, he couldn't take the direct route through the sewers because of the explosion. But he was sure to find some other route and in the end he would arrive.

"It's not just the ammunition that worries us," said Pan Prostak. "It's his other promise too. He gave us his word and was even given an advance in British gold coins. I was assured he could be trusted."

Now that I was here, Pan Prostak said, I might as well know: a group of Jews that had crossed into the ghetto for the holiday had paid Antony an advance to make sure he would take them back. He had promised them that a truck from a building-supplies warehouse would be waiting for them by a manhole on Grzybowska Street at exactly 7:30 P.M., that is, half an hour before the start of the curfew. He also had arranged with some villagers to bring the Jews to a cabin in the woods where they could stay for up to a week, so that they wouldn't all return to Warsaw at once; they would have to make their way back there by themselves, which they could do because they already had forged papers and places to live. Some even had steady jobs. Such Jews were very wealthy, since it cost a fortune to arrange things of this sort. If German soldiers or Polish police did not happen to pass by the manhole as they were exiting, the operation had a good chance of going smoothly.

I knew that manhole well. We sometimes exited from it at night, back in the days when it was in the Little Ghetto. I knew the owner of the truck too, because he was a friend of Antony's who was given the warehouse at the same time that Pan Korek was allowed to move his tavern to an ex-Jewish storefront on Grzybowska Street.

As we were talking a young man approached and handed Pan Prostak a note. He read it quickly, glanced at me, and said, "Antony has gotten in touch via the usual channels. The deal is on, though he'll be a little late. There's a postscript, however." He read aloud from the note: "The deal will be called off if you don't take good care of my merchandise." That meant that Antony had guessed my whereabouts. I felt a wave of relief.

"Marek," said Pan Jozek, perking up, "you're going to make it out of here. Am I glad to hear that!"

"I don't know whether you'll make it out of here or not, young man," said Pan Prostak, "but we have to take good care of you until your father comes. We'll keep you in the bunker."

I almost jumped up and shouted no! I caught myself at the last minute, because I knew that my chances of getting away at the first opportunity were better if I behaved myself quietly. I simply couldn't imagine surviving with all those people and children beneath a ceiling that was barely two meters high. I was racking my brain to think of something when he added, "Which means, young man, that you're coming with me right now."

Pan Jozek shook my hand warmly. I wished him luck and promised him that if he got out of the ghetto alive, he would always have a place with us. Just let him come to my grandmother's and he would be taken in with no questions asked. Not that I believed I wouldn't see him again before Antony came for me, because there was no way they could keep me in that bunker.

Pan Prostak gripped my arm and steered me out of the apartment. "We're in a hurry," he said to me. "We've ordered everyone into the bunker by two o'clock, and I want to be there a few minutes before then."

He brought me back down to the bunker and

handed me over to one of the three brothers. It was the same man who had recognized me when I emerged from the sewer with Pan Jozek. Meanwhile, Pan Prostak checked the last-minute preparations. Before long we heard footsteps running down the stairs and loud, excited voices drawing nearer. A crowd of people burst through the narrow entrance all at once, sending us reeling backward. Before I could grasp what was happening, they were fighting for room on the shelves for their belongings. Wives screamed at their husbands, while the husbands shoved one another to the sound of wailing infants and frightened children. It was an awful sight. You would have thought that death itself was driving them from behind, although in fact each family was simply frantic that there wouldn't be enough room for them.

The quickest and strongest soon found themselves places and fortified themselves on their cots, while the others crowded together in the middle of the bunker by the tables and cooking areas. One of the three brothers shouted in Yiddish and waved his arms, but no one listened to his exhortations until finally Pan Prostak took out a pistol and waved it in the air. That made a great impression. Pan Prostak climbed on a table, and when the last family had pushed its way inside he asked for quiet and announced that everyone would be admitted whether they were paying shareholders in the bunker or not. But he was the boss. He alone could lock the bunker from outside, and he would do so only when all his instructions were carried out. The first of these was that nothing was allowed in except for food and blankets. The second was that the space would be divided up equally. (This set off a good deal of grumbling among the shareholders, but Pan Prostak took no notice of either the complaints or the cheers and declared that there would be no privileged classes as long as he was in charge.) The third was that everyone would get half a cot. "Half a cot per person!" he repeated. As for the food, it would be decided later whether to pool it or have everyone eat his own. It depended on how many days or weeks or months they would have to stay down there. When Pan Prostak finished speaking there was silence. It finally dawned on me how grim the situation was.

Just then Pan Jozek looked in to see how I was. We shook hands again amid all the shouting around us before he elbowed his way back out.

I looked around me. There were old men and women, families with babies, mothers with children of all ages, even people who looked educated and distinguished. For the first time I grasped concretely what the liquidation of the ghetto, which was something my mother, Antony, and I had often argued about, actually meant.

Pan Prostak was a shrewd, untiring man who knew how to get what he wanted. According to Pan Jozek he had been the manager of a large factory before the war. But as the bunker dwellers began collecting their excess belongings and carrying them back outside, he forgot all about me and I slipped out with the crowd and made my getaway.

Holy Jesus, if I had been shut up in that bunker any longer, beneath a ceiling I could reach up and touch, among all those people who were sure to start gasping in two hours, I would quite simply have gone out of my mind! I knew that no one would look for me. They had more important things to worry about just then. And once Pan Prostak had locked the bunker and departed, there wouldn't be anyone to look.

My mother was right, I thought. God help all those Jews, because who else could help them? God help them and have mercy on them, amen.

13

The Jews' Finest Hour

The Germans marched down the middle of the street as if they were in a parade. We counted them. There were nearly three hundred men. We were crouched behind a little window on Walowa Street, from where we could see clearly the main entrance to the brush factory. I was in an observation post with Pan Jozek and some other unarmed fighters. No one had told us what was going to happen.

It hadn't been hard to find out where Pan Jozek's team was positioned, because he was already known to everyone as "the sewer rat." As I climbed the stairs to him I saw different spotters at different windows and on different floors. Pan Jozek was shocked to see me and gave me a dressing down. When he was through talking, I said, "Pan Jozek, I couldn't stay down there. It was like crawling into my own grave. I felt that I was choking. Maybe if I had had little children like all those people did, I would have felt that I had no choice."

He looked at me and nodded sympathetically. "You'll stick with me now, Marek, and no monkey business. I just hope that Antony gets here soon. If I die, I want to do it with a clear conscience."

All in all, I think he was glad we were together again.

The Germans had reached a little square before the front gate of the factory. They were about to storm inside when suddenly there was a huge boom and everything went flying through the air. The fighters I was with were beside themselves. They laughed and shouted and hugged each other, crying for joy and unable to believe their own eyes. Everyone was trying to get to a window to see the scene for himself. The unbelievable was taking place.

It wasn't the first time that Jews had killed Germans. That had happened in Warsaw before, although not very often. Until the first day of the uprising such incidents were few and far between, however, whereas now a real war was being fought. The invincible, world-conquering German army was being driven back by the Jews! Of course, we all knew it couldn't last. No one had any illusions. But no one was thinking that far ahead. We had eyes only for the Germans crawling on the ground and hugging the walls of the buildings, hysterically firing in all directions while their dead and wounded lay scattered about, bleeding and screaming. I couldn't believe it. Pan Jozek put an arm around me and said, "If I have to die, Marek, seeing this will make it easier."

The Germans began to withdraw, dragging their wounded after them. They hugged the walls and beat a retreat, routed by an electronically detonated mine.

One of the spotters in our observation post had set it off. You could see how proud he was.

We received an order to pull out and crossed the street on the run under feeble German fire. Seeing me lag behind, Pan Jozek came back for me shouting angrily. I told him I had seen a German soldier knocked by the blast down some steps leading to a basement and that I wanted to take his rifle. Without a word Pan Jozek joined me. The rifle was still there. I was so excited that I almost forgot to take the bullet belt too.

I gripped the rifle while everyone regarded it jealously. Although Pan Jozek said nothing, the way he stared at it was so unbearable that in the end I let him have it. After all, I thought, he deserved it more than I did.

We were sent to a fourth-floor apartment under the command of a Pan Diamant, where I was given two hand grenades and a bomb as a token of appreciation. All three were homemade and had fuses that had to be lit with matches. The bomb was made out of a half-liter metal container filled with TNT.

I had a good throwing arm. I couldn't wait for the Nazis to come back.

I sat next to Pan Jozek while Pan Diamant put him through a rifle drill. He told Pan Jozek to fire only at clusters of Germans, never at single soldiers. That way he was sure not to miss. Two other fighters were stationed alongside us, so that if Pan Jozek was put out of action one of them could take his weapon.

Some girls came along with food and drinks to

hand out. I made myself take some, even though I wasn't hungry.

I'm not sure how much time passed before the Germans renewed their attack. It could have been an hour or even more. This time they didn't march down the middle of the street but rather hugged the walls in pairs. After managing to blow up the gate of the factory, they burst inside and a pitched battle began. The Jewish fighters fired on them from the windows and hurled bombs at them. For a while I stayed by Pan Jozek's side to see how he handled his rifle. He himself stuck close to Pan Diamant, who had been a soldier in the Polish army before the war and knew what to do. He took his time, too. The others kept urging him, "Come on, Diamant, shoot already, what are you waiting for," but he paid them no attention. He aimed carefully and every shot he fired was on target.

Pan Jozek was so excited that he shook all over. He got in his own way and kept using the wrong hand to cock and aim his rifle because he was a lefty. He had trouble with the sights too, which he complained made everything blurry, and after firing a single shot he handed the rifle to someone else. In its place he was given two genuine hand grenades and two homemade ones like mine, and we went down to the first floor to throw them from close range.

Those young Jewish men and women were not trained soldiers and did all kinds of things that no soldier would have done. Still, you could see they were ready to die and wanted only to take as many Germans as they could along with them. Some of the girls

162

were only a few years older than me. One of them, I remember, was named Dvora. She stood on the terrace of a second-floor apartment and blasted away at the Germans without even hunkering down. She seemed protected by a magic charm, because no matter how much they shot back at her, they kept missing. Someone else bounced a Molotov cocktail off a German soldier's helmet, which shot up in flames and sent the man running on fire down the street like a maniac. He should have thrown himself down and rolled on the pavement, but his brains were too fried to work. I had just thrown the second of my two hand grenades when a German grenade flew through the window. A young man standing next to me picked it up and flung it back at once. His name was Luszek, and I never forgot it because he saved my life.

In the excitement Pan Jozek forgot all about keeping an eye on me. There was too much going on all around us and no one's life seemed that important anymore. I too got into the spirit of things and forgot all about Antony. I even forgot about myself. It didn't matter to me whether I lived or died. My own private fate no longer mattered and I was ready to be killed alongside the Jewish fighters. I don't think that was recklessness. I think it was self-transcendence.

The Germans began pulling back. Once more the Jews had to rub their eyes. To tell you the truth, so did I. The Germans were gone. We whooped with joy and hugged one another again.

What happened next was even more incredible. Three German officers stepped forward and asked to parley. They had white ribbons tied around their arms and kept their weapons pointed at the ground.

Afterward I found out that they had asked for fifteen minutes to collect their dead and wounded. They also announced that whoever surrendered would be sent to a work camp in Poniatow or Trawniki along with all his possessions. Suddenly several dozen people, most of them women, children, and old folks, stepped out into the street and gave themselves up. There were even a few young men among them. The poor devils! I don't know whether they had left that asphyxiating bunker or come from somewhere else. No one tried to stop them. We figured that none of us would live to tell about it anyway.

Even today I don't understand why the Jewish fighters didn't kill those German officers. It was hardly a time for gallantry. They should have let them speak and shot them dead. And in fact, a runner soon arrived ordering us to send five men on the double to a house on Franciszkanska Street, because the Germans had used the truce talks to break through our defenses via the roofs and attics there.

The Germans were shooting from all directions. So were we. But our firing was sporadic and we were running out of ammunition. So far we had taken few casualties, although only one of the men sent to Franciszkanska Street came back. Proudly he told us how the Germans had been fought from rooftop to rooftop and stairway to stairway until their advance was stopped. Once again they had retreated. But this time there was less joy than before. A lot of youngsters had been killed in the hand-to-hand combat, including Pan Michael Klapfisz, the news of whose death traveled from house to house. It was he who had set up a home-bomb factory. The young man who came back from Franciszkanska Street had seen him killed. He was cut down by a German machine gun firing from behind a chimney. So were many others before the gun was finally silenced.

Today, when I try to remember how much time all this took, I don't seem able to. The actual minutes spent shooting and throwing grenades couldn't have been that many, but each one passed so slowly that I can remember exactly what everyone around me was doing, whereas the long hours of waiting between one burst of action and the next have contracted to almost nothing in my memory.

I also remember the airplane that started circling overhead. Someone remarked that it was a bad sign, and in fact, it turned out to have been spotting for the German artillery that began to shell us toward evening. The Germans also sent small squads of sappers who started blowing up buildings. The fire spread to the adjacent houses, and we could see Polish firemen stationed beyond the ghetto wall to keep it from spreading still farther.

An order came to pull back to a bunker on Swientojerska Street. As there was a lull in the bombardment, our commander decided to withdraw via the rooftops. We climbed up some stairs and began to cross a roof. I myself was unarmed, while Pan Jozek had the pistol of someone who was killed but no bullets. He was hoping to find some. We were the last ones up on the roof and were starting across it on a chimney sweep's plank when a German soldier popped up in front of us. To this day I don't know how he got there.

"A German!" shouted Pan Jozek.

Someone with a rifle doubled back from the top floor of the next building, but he was too far away for a good shot. The German fired at Pan Jozek. Everything happened with lightning speed, although each time I picture it I see it lasting forever. Each one of the German's and Pan Jozek's movements drifts through my memory in slow motion. The German shot at Pan Jozek with a pistol. He must have been an officer or an artillery spotter, because he wasn't carrying a rifle. He kept firing again and again, standing on the chimney sweep's plank. And Pan Jozek ran straight toward him on the plank! It wasn't a long distance. He ran it with his arms held out in front of him, as though he had just seen a long-lost friend and were running to embrace him. The German grimaced. His face grew more and more contorted. He kept firing at Pan Jozek and Pan Jozek kept running toward him until he reached him. He threw his arms around the German, and the two of them lost their balance and began to tumble down the sloping tin roof. Each time they turned over and the German came up on top, he fought with all his might to free himself. He had lost his grip on his pistol, which slid down the roof by itself. He screamed. At the very last second Pan Jozek turned his head and our eyes met. I opened my mouth to shout something. I don't know what it was. Today I can't even imagine what it might have been. And then they were gone.

For a moment I stood there with my mouth open, listening to the German's scream grow more distant. Then there was a thud from the courtyard. The young man who had tried to come to the rescue reached me and pulled me back after him. I shook myself free. I didn't want to go with him. I had to get to Pan Jozek, at once. He was still trying to talk me out of it when a new bombardment began and we heard a shell shriek nearby. He let go of me and ran back toward the next roof while I ducked back into the building and ran down the stairs. Down below everything was in flames. The Germans had set the whole ground floor on fire. There was no way to get through. I ran into an apartment, looking for a blanket I could wet and wrap myself in. There was no water. I threw a blanket over my head, ran back to the stairs, slid down the banister through the flames the way children do at home for fun, tossed the burning blanket away, and ran out into the courtyard. It was empty except for Pan Jozek and the German. I ran to them. They were covered with blood. I tried to pull them apart, using every ounce of my strength. I can remember shouting: "Pan Jozek! Pan Jozek!"

His eyes opened wide for a moment as if with surprise, and I thought I saw the trace of an understanding smile. Then it was over.

I got to my feet and tried to pull the bodies apart again. It was impossible. Pan Jozek was still gripping the German as hard as he could, as if he hadn't let go even in death.

Suddenly there was a huge crash and a part of the house collapsed. I heard terrible cries from under the ground. They came from a bunker whose ceiling had caved in beneath the debris. Men and women began crawling out, dragging their children after them. The wounded had to drag themselves. I remember sitting there next to Pan Jozek and the German and thinking: What now? Where will everyone go? What will they do? I let go of the dead body and tried to help them, although I knew they didn't stand a chance.

I tried to pull a woman with a baby in her arms from the ruins, but the baby was already dead. For all I know it had choked beforehand. Then I lent a hand to an old woman. After that I remember only endless hands and faces, and voices, a jumble of them that I sometimes still hear in my dreams.

We pulled out everyone we could. The survivors told me to come with them. Someone said there was another bunker nearby. Someone said its occupants wouldn't let us in. Someone said he'd like to see them keep us out. His voice was full of menace.

"That's the rich folks' bunker," he said.

I asked a young man to help me separate Pan Jozek's and the German's bodies. The two of us couldn't do it either. Finally, a third man came along and we managed. No one even asked who the German was. Someone looked for his pistol, but his holster was empty. Once again the survivors invited me to come with them, but instead I started to drag Pan Jozek away from the burning building.

They trooped off. I could still hear muffled groans from within the caved-in bunker, but there was no way of reaching anyone through the debris.

The bombardment continued. And yet I felt that it had nothing to do with me. The sounds of the shells seemed to come from far away. I tried to wipe the blood from Pan Jozek's face. I shut his eyes and thought that I should bury him. I couldn't possibly leave him as he was.

He wasn't the first person I was close to whom I saw die. I had an old aunt who died when I was little. I remember how scared I was. And what I thought about then was the same thing I thought about now: was the soul still here, lingering by its master, or had it already gone to heaven? Long afterward I sometimes used to wake at night in a cold sweat and stare into the darkness of my room to see if anything was moving. I thought that perhaps my aunt's ghost was in the room with me.

I began to pray and stopped. What good were Catholic prayers for a Jew? But I couldn't not pray and I didn't know any Jewish prayers, so I began again. That was the least I could do for the man.

When I had prayed I hoisted Pan Jozek on my back and began to walk with him. I didn't stop to think what I was doing. I could feel his blood soaking slowly through my clothes and dripping down my shoulders and back.

I crossed a courtyard in which lay several half-burned bodies. The buildings around it were untouched and showed no signs of fire. Perhaps these people had caught fire in some hideout and been killed by the Germans when they ran out into the yard. I had seen things like that happen when Warsaw was in flames from the German air raids in 1939.

I have no idea how I managed to walk, or where I went. No memory at all. I just kept walking. Pan Jozek was getting heavier and heavier. Above me the sky was full of smoke, but down below at street level all was quiet. I don't even remember whether the bombardment continued or not. I don't know whether five minutes passed or only one. In the end I stepped out through some gate and ran into a frantic-looking man. At first he dodged me and ran through the gate. Then he came back and asked, "Aren't you Marek, Antony's son?"

I must have said that I was. Once he realized that Pan Jozek was dead, he tried to convince me to leave him behind.

"Where?"

He pointed to a corner behind us. I refused. "I'm taking him with me," I said. I wasn't going to abandon him.

"Antony won't keep his promise to get us out of here until he finds you," said the man. "Everyone who knows what you look like is out searching for you. There's no time to lose because the truck will come for us exactly half an hour before the curfew. Do you understand what I'm telling you? He won't take anyone until you're brought to him dead or alive. He wanted to look for you himself, but Pan Prostak wouldn't let him. He was afraid he wouldn't come back."

Suddenly it penetrated: Antony had come! There was hope after all. I might see my mother again. He had come to save me from this hell.

"Come on," said the man, losing his temper. "What are you standing there for? Let's go!"

He took me back to the three brothers' bunker. The door was open and its occupants had come out for a breath of fresh air. They looked awful, although to judge from how they stared at me, I must have looked even worse. I suppose that's because I was full of blood, even if it wasn't mine. Two men lowered Pan Jozek from my shoulders. They laid him on the ground and I sat down beside him. Pan Prostak and Antony appeared a minute later. I said to them, "We have to bury Pan Jozek."

"Marek," said Antony, "you don't know what you're saying. We have over twenty people to cross back with, and if we don't start out in ten minutes we won't make it in time. Do you hear me?"

I must not have responded, because he put his face close to mine and said, "It's me, Antony, your father."

"Pa," I said, "we have to bury Pan Jozek. I can't come with you if we don't."

That got through to him. He straightened up and said, "Pan Prostak, we have to bury Pan Jozek."

Pan Prostak thought for a minute. "Marek," he

said, "it's been decided to bury Michael Klapfisz tomorrow morning with full military honors. If we manage to do that, I promise you to bury our friend Pan Jozek along with him. You have my word of honor."

I believed him.

Michael Klapfisz was buried the next day, at 4 A.M., in the garden of the courtyard of 34 Swientojerska Street. A single shot was fired in salute. A year later he was awarded the Cross of Military Honor by General Sikorski on behalf of the Polish government-in-exile. There were fierce protests at the time by right-wing Poles in Poland and London over this "profanation of the highest Polish decoration." I was never able to discover if a second man was buried alongside Klapfisz.

Someone asked Pan Prostak if it was safe for the bunker occupants to return to their apartments for a while. He advised waiting another hour and then told all the people going with Antony to line up and get ready to move out.

I was given something to drink. I was offered food too, but I couldn't have gotten it down. I began taking off my blood-soaked clothes. As Pan Prostak handed me a fresh jacket I remembered something.

"Pan Prostak, there's a whole lot of money that Pan Jozek gave me in my pants' pockets."

"All right," he said. "I'll take care of it."

Antony reappeared with a package wrapped in wax paper. He took me aside and asked if I had managed to pull myself together. I told him I had. He asked whether anyone apart from Pan Jozek knew of the entrance to the sewer system in our house. At first I didn't understand. Then I said no.

"Why didn't you tell me, goddam it? I would have brought him myself. I had to come anyway."

"The hell you would have! And anyhow, I never meant to stay here. It's just that an explosion blocked the way back . . ."

I was shaking all over despite the dry jacket I was wearing. My teeth chattered. Antony went to bring me a blanket. He wrapped me in it and told me to lie down. I did as he said.

"You're still in shock," he said. "You'll come out of it."

"And besides," I continued, "you wouldn't have gone to get him from Uncle Wladislaw's. You would have said it was too risky to take him through the streets to our house."

"Marek, don't be a fool. The sewers can be entered in all kinds of other ways. Don't you realize you should never have taken him through our house?"

He pointed to the package wrapped in wax paper and told me to listen carefully. "There are some clean clothes in here for you to put on when we reach Grzybowska Street. Hold this package tightly all the way and make sure it's over your head when we wade through water."

I nodded.

Antony briefed me on what would happen when we got there. "As soon as we hear the truck pull up, I'll open the manhole and you'll jump out with me and two armed men. The others will follow and get on the truck. By then there'll be lots of curious onlookers. You, Marek, will pretend to be one of them who just happened to be walking down the street. You'll keep your distance from us. Above all, you have to look clean. You won't change your clothes until we're standing on the ladder beneath the manhole."

"What about you, Antony?"

"I'll do the same." He pointed to a second package lying against the wall. He looked at me for a moment and said, "You're still not yourself, son."

"How can you tell?"

"If you were, you'd want to know what kind of clothes I'm dressing you in."

He was right. I made an effort to smile, but my face wouldn't obey me. Soon everyone was ready. Our escort consisted of two young men with pistols and a young woman with a flashlight. She was the same person who had smiled at me earlier that day when Pan Prostak called Pan Jozek and me "gentlemen." Her job was to sketch the route we took so that the three of them could find their way back. Like Pan Jozek, they didn't want to leave the ghetto. They wanted to stay and fight.

We entered the bunker. Antony went over to one of the three brothers and was handed a baby. It was still business as usual! A cloth bag with the baby's documents was pinned to her blanket.

Antony hesitated for a moment before taking her.

"If the baby cries it will give us away," said a

woman member of the group. "This isn't what I paid my money for."

"Dr. Maier will give the baby a shot to make it sleep," said Pan Prostak to reassure her.

The scene that followed was familiar except that there was no tearful mother saying goodbye. The doctor bared the little behind and gave it a shot. The baby cried only for a minute. Someone said we should hurry up. As I helped Antony wrap the baby I detached the document bag and hid it in my clothing.

Someone opened the trap door and we began to descend one by one, Antony first and I next. Then came the young woman with the flashlight and one of the young men with a pistol. The other armed young man brought up the rear.

None of the group had ever been in a sewer before. There was one woman who began to scream and begged to be let out. Someone said that she was claustrophobic. It was only then that I realized I was too, but in a much milder form. The woman's husband tried to reason with her. Then he began to shout and to threaten that he would leave her and go by himself, followed by more pleas. Nothing helped. Everyone standing on the ladder had to back up and let the two of them climb out again. When the last man was in the tunnel I heard Pan Prostak shout something, first in Yiddish and then in Polish.

"Bon voyage!" was what it was.

Then I heard the metal trap door clank into place behind us.

14

Back Home

Antony was nervous and kept swearing at everybody, because he was afraid we would be late. It wasn't easy for them, though. To tell you the truth, it wasn't easy for me either, because I was exhausted. The worst part was where we had to wade through water up to our necks, although *water* wasn't really the word for it. Antony held the baby, his package tied to her bundle, over his head. His miner's lamp was strapped to an elastic band around his head instead of to his helmet, and his pistol and holster were tied to the clothes on his head too. It was the first time I had ever seen him take it with him.

We weren't alone in having a package of clothes. Everyone else had one too. They too would have to get back to their lodgings looking like normal human beings. Except, that is, for the two young men and for the young woman with the flashlight, who walked behind us sketching a map. When the water deepened she held her sketchbook and pencil above her head and several more pencils in her mouth. She too had her flashlight strapped to her head, where it looked like a doctor's viewer. The three of them had no need for fresh clothes because they were returning to the ghetto.

As hard as our route was, however, the people with us made it only harder. One woman fainted and would have drowned had she not been caught from behind. Almost everyone had matches and a candle, but the candles kept going out, either from the air currents people made or from the fumes of the sewage. They also had trouble keeping both arms above their heads in deep water. Some threw away their candles and kept shifting their clothes from arm to arm. But no one swore and no one complained. Everyone knew it was a matter of life and death.

In spite of everything, we made it in time.

Antony and I reached the narrow ledge that supported the ladder more than ten minutes before our rendezvous. Antony sent a message back down the line for the second pistol bearer to come forward and told me to change my clothes. He was annoyed when I asked him to turn off his flashlight. In the end he turned his head away so that the light didn't shine on me.

"This is a fine time for your nonsense," he said.

"Suppose the truck doesn't come?"

"We'll cross that bridge when we come to it. Whatever happens, you go first."

My package had only four articles of clothing in it. That made sense considering how little time I had to put them on, quite apart from the difficulty of dressing in the darkness, in a narrow space I had to keep to if I was to avoid getting smeared with grime. I didn't have a second to spare. There were actually five articles of clothing, the fifth being a neckerchief to conceal my having nothing on under my jacket. It was stuffed into the jacket pocket and Antony had to point it out to me. In addition, there was a pair of pants, a pair of shoes, and a cap. Antony kept telling me to hurry up, because he couldn't change clothes himself while holding the baby. When I was done, I held her for him. He had the same four items as I did, except that instead of shoes he had boots. We threw our dirty clothes into the sewage and I thought of Pan Krol as I watched them float away.

Antony had also brought something else with him. From one of his boots he took out a jar of glue and a large mustache, which he pasted over his upper lip. Suddenly I no longer recognized him.

He kept looking nervously at his watch. The two of us might get away with it, but if the truck didn't come and left everyone stranded in the street, at least half the group was sure to get caught at once, if not by the Germans or the Polish police, then by blackmailers. And the others would never make it to their hiding places unless they found somewhere to change clothes, which they couldn't do in the tunnel because there was room for only Antony and me. I wondered whether Antony would suggest the back yard of the tavern, but at once I ruled that out. There would be too many people around.

Antony told me to take the baby. He showed me how to carry the bundle while I pretended to be an innocent passer-by. I should hold the baby face down, he said, so as to leave her a breathing hole without her being seen.

Just as Antony was slipping his pistol off his belt we heard the truck drive up. There was a general sigh of relief.

"Is this it?" someone asked.

Antony didn't answer. He simply crossed himself. So did I. Then he pushed open the cover of the manhole.

Everything seemed to happen all at once. It didn't take a minute for someone in the street to notice what was happening, and before long a crowd had formed all around me. I think that some of the people must have come from Pan Korek's tavern and were already on their way home. Fortunately, Pan Szczupak was not among them. I doubt that anyone saw Antony come out of the sewer, and certainly no one saw me, because I went first. That is, it later turned out that someone did see Antony, but the mustache made him look like someone unknown who had come to open the manhole for the Jews. The waning light of the cloudy spring day must have worked to our advantage as well.

The two young Jews stood covering us with their pistols while the girl stayed down below. "Jews! Kikes!" someone shouted all of a sudden. And yet I don't think that had anything to do with the two German soldiers who drove by just then on a motorcycle. It was just our bad luck. As the motorcycle stopped, the Jews opened fire. The last people out of the sewer scrambled onto the truck, which was already in motion, assisted by the outstretched hands of those above. Two of them had lost their clothes packages. The onlookers dived for safety.

I ran with my bundle toward Pan Korek's tavern with Antony on my heels. Suddenly I sensed that he wasn't there anymore. I spun around, saw him running back, found something to hide behind, and watched what was happening.

One of the Jewish fighters was lying in the middle of the street. Antony ducked behind a billboard and drew his pistol. He and the other Jew fired away and wounded the two Germans, or perhaps they killed one of them, because he made no sound. The second moaned and cursed in German while the engine of his motorcycle kept running until the Jew stepped up and silenced him with another bullet. Then he and Antony ran to his wounded friend. They bent over him and turned him face up. Later Antony told me that he had been shot in the head. The Jew took the dead man's pistol and disappeared into the sewer. Antony shut the manhole after him and started running toward me. It was only then that I noticed he was limping badly. I tried to support him, but he said he could make it on his own. We both knew without saying that we were heading for Pan Korek's back yard. I gave Antony my arm to lean on again.

Pan Korek must have seen us through the window, because he was out the back door and waiting for us before we arrived. Antony told me to give him my bundle and explained to him where to bring it before

180

the baby woke and caused problems. He had been hit, he told Pan Korek, by a bullet in his leg. Pan Korek took the baby from me and held her awkwardly, like a man who has never held a baby before. "Does it have a name, or any papers?" he asked.

"There was something pinned to it, but it must have fallen off on the way," said Antony. "Tell the mother superior that I'll bring her the money myself."

Just to be on the safe side, I had decided to give the baby's papers to my mother. I wanted the Jews to be able to find her after the war. But how would I know which child the papers belonged to? I thought fast and said to Pan Korek, "Her name is Julia Theresa."

Pan Korek smiled and said, "All right, Mr. Godfather, I'll pass that on to them."

I felt proud of myself.

I helped Antony onto the wooden seat of the three-wheeler. He told me to go fetch a blanket and some vodka. I ran inside through the storeroom and the kitchen.

Antony wrapped himself in the blanket, grunting from the pain in his leg. He took a slug from the bottle I brought and poured some of it over himself.

"What are you doing?" asked Pan Korek.

"Leave it to me," said Antony, pulling off his mustache. "I'll bet they'll have roadblocks up before we get home."

We set out. Although it wasn't a Sunday, as soon as I realized why Antony had doused himself with the vodka I knew that everything depended on our being stopped by local policemen who knew us.

Antony was right. Someone must have tipped off the police, because right away we heard a siren in the distance and soon we ran into four policemen who arrived to cordon off the street. Without a moment's hesitation I pedaled right toward them and prayed. No sooner had they stopped us than one of them exclaimed, "Why, it's Marek!"

A second policeman, who was standing back, said with a chuckle, "I can smell Antony all the way back here. What's the matter, son, has your old man taken to getting potted on Tuesdays too?"

"Hello, officer," I said. "It's really no joke. I hope it's just this once. He'll catch it from my ma, my pa will!"

They laughed and let us through.

When my mother heard my usual Sunday-night whistle she was so confused at first that she didn't know what to do. I heard her frightened steps as she ran down the stairs, but as soon as I told her in a whisper to go along with the act, she fell right into the role. I don't think the neighbors suspected a thing. And as usual, their respect for my mother kept them from mentioning the scene afterward. As we dragged Antony up the stairs I prodded him to sing something, but that was more than he cared to do.

When the door was safely locked behind us, my mother threw her arms tearfully around me and began to ask how I could have done such a terrible thing. As soon as she saw that Antony was unable to get off the floor and lay there as if he were really drunk, however, she left me and ran to him. She glanced at the pistol and worriedly ran her hands over him.

"It's nothing," he said, "just my leg. All that matters is that the boy is back."

She fell into his arms and Antony groaned with pain. It was only then that we saw that both of his pants legs were soaked with blood.

My mother didn't stop berating me for a whole day, in the course of which I told her what had happened and explained that I had meant to bring Pan Jozek to the ghetto and come right back. Early the next morning I went to ask Grandmother to send us the doctor who worked for the underground. I had to tell the whole story all over again, from start to finish. She was very sad to hear about Pan Jozek and said she would light a candle for his soul even if he was a Jew.

After Antony had two bullets removed from one leg and some ricocheted slivers from the other, he felt much better. Within a few days he was ready to travel, because meanwhile we had decided to visit his sister in the country for Easter and perhaps even to stay with her for a while. It wasn't just a matter of being afraid that some informer might have seen us climbing out of the sewer. It was also on account of my mother, who couldn't stand the sight of the smoke hanging over the ghetto and the way it was talked about all over Warsaw.

I took a walk to the ghetto wall to try to see what was happening inside. There's nothing more horrible than seeing burning people jumping out of windows, but I felt it was something I had to witness from the Polish side of the wall. I think the reason must have been that part of me was still in there, with the Jews. And then too, I wanted to see what I had been saved from.

All the houses in the ghetto were on fire. Their tenants were trapped inside them, and whoever tried to save himself was shot by the Germans and their helpers. There were Jews who jumped to certain deaths simply to get it over with. From where I stood with a crowd of Poles, firemen, and Germans, we saw a man step out on a balcony with two children. Everything around him was in flames. He blindfolded the children, threw them down one after the other — the balcony was on the fifth floor — and leaped after them.

Even before this, while I was still in the ghetto, the terrible doubt had entered my mind whether there really was a God. I remember how frightening it was, because I had to stay on good terms with God in order to get out of the ghetto alive. And yet the logic of it was elementary: there was no God. There just wasn't. All humanity, all life, was alone in this world, and whatever we did concerned only us and no one else.

When I think of it today, I know that isn't so, because pure logic cannot refute the feelings that I have. Not only when I pray, but when I search my soul as well, I find something there that did not originate with me. I don't mean to say that I feel God *in* myself. It isn't that. It's more being able to feel the vastness of Him *through* myself.

After I came home and my mother wept on my shoulder as if I had returned from the underworld (which in a manner of speaking I had), she kept asking me over and over to tell her what I had seen. In the end, she decided she had to go and see for herself.

The Germans allowed the Poles to stand outside the ghetto and look. They even permitted Polish children to stand next to their artillery and machine guns as they fired into the ghetto. My mother came back sick at heart, not only because of what she had seen, but because of what she had heard. Even those Poles who felt sorry for the Jewish children would often add: "Still, it's good we're finally rid of them." In Kraszinski Square, my mother told us, an Easter carousel had been erected directly opposite the ghetto wall, and Poles rode on it to loud music while the smoke of the ghetto swirled overhead.

At first the average Polish man in the street was so taken by surprise that the Jewish uprising filled him with enthusiasm. Even people like our doorman couldn't get over the Jews' courage. But the longer the fighting dragged on and the Jews who were left inside the walls kept it up, the more the citizens of Warsaw began to grumble about the smoke and the disruptions in streetcar service. They grew used to what was happening in the ghetto. The shots and explosions were no longer a cause for excitement. They were just something that kept you up at night.

My mother said that she couldn't go on living as if nothing at all were happening when men, women, and children were perishing in flames not far away.

185

Antony had reasons of his own for leaving Warsaw. He obtained medical papers testifying that he and my mother had pneumonia and that I had chicken pox and couldn't go to school, and the three of us departed from Warsaw.

One morning in the village Antony called me to his bed and asked me to sit down for a minute.

I sat.

"I have a question for you."

"All right, shoot," I said, because he had been unnaturally quiet for too long.

"Do you know what I'm going to ask you?"

I honestly had no idea.

"Will you let me adopt you?"

I pretended to think it over for a minute and agreed. I don't think it was because I had no choice.

"You can go on calling me Antony afterwards too," he said. "And bring me a glass of water."

I went to get it. I had had no intention of calling him "Papa" anyway.

It must have been the only time in my life that I saw him get emotional without being drunk.